11 MINUTES

A Crime Novel of Melbourne's 1976
Great Bookie Robbery

Gregory M Carroll

gregorymcarroll.com

ISBN: 978-1-7642226-0-0

Cover design by: Gregory M Carroll

Printed in Australia

Australia National Library Reference is available on request.

gregorymcarroll.com

This is a work of fiction. Although most events actually occurred, some timelines and people involved have been altered for dramatic effect. Characters and organisations in the novel are the product of the author's imagination, or if real, are used fictitiously without any attempt to describe their actual conduct. However, references to real people and organisations documented in footnotes at the end are accurate. Footnotes are real.

Dedicated to Ian Revell Carroll

Gone but not forgotten.

PROLOGUE

It happened just after midday, the Wednesday following the Easter long weekend. Six masked men appeared out of nowhere, bursting into the Settling Room of Melbourne's Victoria Club. Dressed identically in overalls, faces hidden behind balaclavas, they moved like a military unit, armed with heavy weapons: machine guns, Tommy guns, automatic assault rifles.

Who am I to tell this story?

I was there, but not in the way that mattered. A passenger. At the edge of something bigger, something dangerous. I watched. Listened. Learned. Not a player, but close enough to feel the heat, to smell the blood, to hear those unspoken things. Ian Carroll was my brother, my best man, and the body I had to identify at the morgue. He lived it. Owned it. And I, too young, too eager, saw him not for what he was, but for what I wanted him to be. Hero worship, nostalgia, call it what you want. That is why I need to tell this story. Not to justify, not to redeem. Just to remember. The way things really were.

This is a story about the lives and deaths of the Great Bookie Robbers. The Great Bookie Robbery, as it came to be known, remains Australia's biggest armed robbery. The Victoria Club was where Melbourne's bookmakers gathered after the weekend's races to settle accounts with their big punters. That Easter weekend had been particularly busy, with races at four different courses over the Saturday, Monday, and Tuesday. This was before the internet and telephone betting. It was all cash. The kind of cash no one talked about. Rumour had it that the haul could have been as much as $15 million. The equivalent of $80 million in today's money. No one was ever convicted. The money never recovered. But within a decade, all would be dead. And the fortune? Gone.

In the Melbourne underworld, a gang is called a crew. And the crew that carried out this robbery was a who's who of Melbourne's armed robbers:

- Raymond "Chuck" Bennett, the General. The leader and mastermind;
- Ian "Fingers" Carroll, Bennett's right-hand man and confidant;
- Normie Lee, the Accountant, whose family ran a dim sim and spring roll factory;
- Vinnie Mikkelsen, the hardest man in town, and Carroll's long-time protector;
- Laurie Prendergast, a young, likeable larrikin and Bennett's protégé;
- And Tony McNamara; the weak link.

Yes, the culprits were known to the police. They just could not prove it. In fact, the Victorian Police Commissioner later referred to them as *the greatest team of armed robbers ever assembled.* They were all tied to the Painters and Dockers Union, which controlled Melbourne's waterfront and most of its crime.

Melbourne in the 1970s was built for this kind of crime. It was Australia's second-largest city. The younger, grubbier sibling of Sydney. Like all second-born, it had a chip on its shoulder. A harder edge. Once the national capital, now the industrial heart. Auto and heavy industries. Oil and gas from Bass Strait. As with all large industrial cities, it was a dichotomy of the indecent wealth of old money and the desperate poverty of the working class. A place of wealth and struggle.

Old money, built on the 1850s gold rush, belonged to industrialists and pastoralists. They lived well. The poor did not. Immigrants and working-class locals crammed into the city's inner suburbs. Cramped. Dirty. A time before safety nets. Before workplace health and safety. Unskilled work was dangerous, poorly paid, and erratic.

The rich spent their spare cash on racehorses and gambling. The poor spent theirs on food—and gambling. Everyone loved a punt. They still do. Even today, Victorians take a public holiday for a horse race. But I digress.

All this is the God's honest truth. But never one to let fact get in the way of a good story, let me tell you a tale of how all this came to pass…

PART I

THE CRIME OF THE CENTURY

CHAPTER 1

The Arrival

A white Transit van rolled to a stop on Queen Street. The engine hummed. The morning was crisp, a Melbourne autumn wind swept dry leaves across the street. That autumn was the driest since 1923. Little rain had fallen in the months leading up to Wednesday, April 21. The sky hung low, grey and indifferent. The Bureau predicted showers and a high of 18. It didn't rain, and the top was 14. A workday in the business district. People busy.

Frankie killed the engine. His fingers drummed on the steering wheel, then stopped. He checked the mirrors. Old habits. The plates were swapped at dawn. *The Australian Financial Review* signage fixed to the sides. The van stolen the night before and wiped down. Clean, or as clean as a stolen vehicle could be. Frankie's boyish charm and easy grin masked a sharp, calculated criminal mind.

Ray sat silent in the passenger seat. Knee bouncing, face stone-carved. He had mapped every second of this day in his head. Over and over. He glanced at his watch. Early. Good.

"All right, boys," Ray said, his voice a rough whisper against the van's silence. "Stick to the plan. Frankie, eyes sharp. You see the consorting arseholes; you know what to do." Frankie gave a curt nod. No words. Words felt too loud.

Queen Street, a tree-lined boulevard in Melbourne's central financial district. Down from the Victoria Club on the other side of the road, two men were working on a broken-down sedan. Serendipity. Not their doing. Too cliché. But that's what would be remembered. Not a newspaper van around the corner from its publisher, John Fairfax & Sons; made it invisible.

Laurie moved first, dressed in the same overalls as the others, but with the flap of a refrigeration repair company. He adjusted his cap, wiped his hands on his thighs. Then he was out. The door clicked shut. He waited, watching traffic slide by in slow waves, then crossed the street with the easy gait of a man on an honest job. Disappeared through the doors of the Victoria Club.

The Victoria Club loomed as a relic of old money. A pre-war neo-classical façade carved in granite. Three stately entrances opened onto a world where every step matters. The main grand hall bathed in light from five towering floor-to-ceiling stained-glass windows. Deep, sculpted stucco columns marked its era of refinement. Above, an Italianate mezzanine overlooked the heart of the club. The bar, an enclave of polished mahogany and velvet.

Inside the van, the air was still. No one spoke. The only sounds: the faint tick of the dashboard clock and the distant hum of Queen Street.

Ian sat in the back, head against the cold metal wall. Beside him, Vinnie, Tony, and Normie. Three oversized duffle bags at their feet. One contained masks, overcoats, and empty mailbags. The other two bags heavy with guns. Thompson and Owen machine guns, a pump-action shotgun, and an M16. Overwhelming force.

Minutes passed. Five. Ten. Fifteen.

No truck.

Ian shifted in his seat, rolling his shoulders. His years in the ring had never left him. Fit, coiled and ready. He broke the silence. "They're late."

Vinnie grunted, his fingers tapping against the stock of the M16 sticking out of the bag. A no-nonsense man. Broad shoulders cutting through space, heavy and deliberate. "Money's always in by 11:40. Like clockwork," he added.

Ray didn't turn around. "Shut it. Focus."

Ray's jaw clenched. Sitting here, it felt like the plan was already slipping through his fingers. His mind raced through contingencies, each one darker than the last. A busted plan was one thing. A busted plan in motion was a death sentence.

A passer-by glanced back through the front windscreen. Ray's hand slid inside his jacket onto the butt of his .38. The passer-by turned and kept walking. Ray's eyes stayed on him until he was out of sight.

Frankie shifted in his seat, clearing his throat like he was about to speak, but Ray cut him off with a glance sharp enough to draw blood.

Then, finally, the Mayne Nickless truck lumbered into Frankie's rear-view mirror. Late. Too late for comfort.[1]

"Showtime," Frankie announced to the cabin.

Ray let out a long, slow breath. Not relief. Just breath. He stepped out first. The others followed.

They turned left, not toward the club but into the building next door. A hollow, empty shell overlooking the street through dust-caked windows. Up the stairs, one by one. The rhythm of footfalls against old concrete, five hearts syncing to the same grim beat.

The Mayne Nickless armoured van rolled past the newspaper van, did a U-turn at Little Collins Street, and pulled back outside 141 Queen Street. Two men up front, two locked in the back with the cash. Two unmarked support cars shadowed it. One man per car. Not from the Consorting Squad, they were security company. They pulled up on either side of the broken-down car. Frankie smiled to himself. Mayne Nickless called the footpath the danger zone, pick-up or drop-off. So the two support men loitered outside nearby. Relaxed. Watching.

The town hall clock in the distance chimed twelve times.

Ray reached the third floor first, which aligned with the second floor of the Victoria Club. He opened the door to the empty office they had prepared earlier. Walked over to the side wall and dropped to one knee. A peephole had been carved into the side of a makeshift doorway. His eye locked onto the Settling Room. [2]

Ian and Vinnie followed Ray in. Heaved the two heavy duffle bags onto a steel table. No chairs. No distractions. Zippers rasped open. Metal spilled out under the weak light. Normie dropped the third bag on the floor.

From the third bag, they pulled balaclavas and dustcoats. Slipped them on. No words. Just the shuffle of fabric. Then, the weapons. Ian grabbed the pump-action and an M16. Vinnie took a Thompson. Tony an Owen for himself and another for Laurie. Normie slid the silver .45 into a spare dustcoat, then reached for the other Thompson (Tommy) gun.

No words. Just the faint, distant murmur of the club next door, laughter mingling with the rustle of money.

Meanwhile, down on the street, the guards unloaded the truck. Strongboxes. Large. Four on the first trip. Four more after. Heavy enough to break your back, wheeled up on hand trolleys. [3]

Ray kept his eye on the hole, muscles coiled tight. Bookies crowded the tables, voices low, counting, settling. Smoke hung in the air as a never-ending haze. Forty-six bookies plus another thirty punters in the bar and billiard room.

Ian crossed to Ray, nudging the M16 into his side.

Ray took possession without breaking concentration. His fingers flexed around the grip of his weapon. No second chances.

Downstairs, in the club's foyer, Laurie waited. Once the delivery was fully unloaded and inside, the support cars left. Laurie's cue. He strolled through the ground-floor members' bar. The rich smell of fine tobacco and aged whisky filled the air. Every detail exuded an understated elegance. Past the receptionist, nodding like he belonged. Because he did. That was the trick.

The club opened four years shy of a century earlier. It took up the first three floors. The bar filled on the ground floor and the dining room the first. Dim, not used much by members. They preferred the lounge upstairs for drinks, sandwiches, or hot snacks. The second floor stretched nearly one thousand square metres, ten thousand square feet in old money. Thirty-five by twenty-eight, split in two. The main area: a long, elegant mahogany bar with an adjacent billiard room. The other: the Settling Room with a teller's cage. This is where bookies settled their bets and layoffs after race meetings. Two interconnecting doors joined them.

Laurie rode the lift to the second floor. Stepped out. Grabbed a chair. Jammed it in the lift door. Smooth and quick. No interruptions.

From the lift foyer, Laurie walked through the lounge, past the bar. Thirty men at tables eating, drinking, discussing horse form. He circled around to the hidden door next to the Settling Room. Leaned against the wall to the side. Two sharp knocks.[4]

Ray lifted his head from the peephole. Eight strongboxes. Twice the usual haul.

Time to go to work.

CHAPTER 2

11 Minutes

12:07 PM. The Victoria Club buzzed with its usual energy. The clatter of glasses, the low murmur of deals being made, the sharp scratch of pens tallying debts and winnings. Men in expensive suits and polished shoes milled around, oblivious to the impending storm about to hit.

Ray took a step back. He hit the door with his full weight through the flat of his foot.

The wall exploded open. A deafening crash. In they stormed. Like a perfectly choreographed ballet in slow motion. Laurie's cap flew off. His balaclava slipped. He caught the dustcoat Normie tossed him, and slid into it as he grabbed the Owen from Tony.

Six men. Identical. Balaclavas. Overalls. Knee-length dustcoats flowing as they moved. They spread wide, weapons raised.

Vinnie was second into the Settling Room. He wanted it that way. If there was going to be trouble, he wanted to be on top of it. That's how you do it. How you handle fear. Take control. Scan the room. Faces, body language, movement. Who to scare, who to handle. It was all in the eyes.

Only two guards were expected. But Easter weekend meant more cash. It meant an extra guard. The young guard had the eyes. Vulture eyes. Cold. Dangerous. Not fear, indecision. But that was Ian and Ray's problem.

Silence fell. Then it began.

"Nobody fucking move!" Ray's voice thundered over the stunned silence. It cut through the cigarette haze. His gun was up, his stance solid. His presence commanded the room.

"You lot against the wall!" pointing at the younger bookies' clerks. "Everyone else, on the floor."

Chaos. Chairs scraped. Papers scattered. Men stumbled.

First, they secured the three armed guards. Ray and Ian moved fast. All were hard against the wall. Heavy weapons pinning two of them.

* * *

At the same time, Normie took the bar and billiard room. The crash from the Settling Room already had everyone's attention. But the appearance of a man in black holding a 1920s style Thompson (Tommy) gun stopped club members' laughter mid-breath. Normie stepped forward. Slow. Deliberate. His gun commanded the room. Large, black, and heavy. No one argued with it.

"Everyone down. Now!" His voice shattered the silence.

Someone gasped. A chair tipped over. Glass broke on the floor. Bodies hit the floor.

Normie swept the barrel across the room. "Face down. Move and you're dead."

Surprise had their attention. Fear kept them down.

* * *

In the Settling Room, Vinnie moved fast, shoving the bookies' clerks hard against the wall. Watched their hands, jackets, and pockets like a hawk. Any movement would not be completed. Tony followed, patting them down. Quick hands frisking for weapons. Brutal, efficient. Some clerks carried a weapon for self-protection. They often carried large amounts of cash. In this situation, it made them unpredictable. No one wanted a shootout with someone trying to be a hero. A twitchy finger could spark a bloodbath.

Ray and Ian stripped the first two guards of their weapons, tossing them behind. Then a quick pat-down. Nothing else concealed.

Then the young third guard, on Ian's blind side, twitched. Ian did not see it. The guard reached for his .38.

Vinnie caught the movement before it finished. He swung the butt of his Thompson with bone-cracking force. The guard hit the ground, dazed. Vinnie planted a boot on his chest, muzzle pressed to his eye.

"You try that again and I'll blow your fucking head off."

Ian nodded a silent "Thanks."

"Becoming a habit," Vinnie returned off-handed.

Tony slung his Owen gun over his back. Grabbed the guards' pistols and hurled them into the teller's cage. No time for trophies. He headed for the lounge. Time for the phone run.

First, the grey wall phone outside the Settling Room. Yanked it. Snapped the cord. Flung it across the room. It sailed, cracking against the floor. He grabbed the table it sat on and hurled it toward a nearby pillar. A thirty-foot throw. Wood splintered on tile.

He vaulted the bar one-handed, left hand gripping the gun, right hand planted low on the counter. Clean over. Landed upright. Ripped out the first phone behind the bar.

He spun. Ran. Hit the next phone. Ripped it. Then the next. Cords trailed behind like cut veins.

One more turn. Into the admin office. Two more phones. Gone.

Down the hall. The barber's room. Locked. He didn't stop. Slam, he smashed the glass door with the butt of his Owen. Shattered glass flew. He stepped through, reached inside, and tore the last phone from the wall. Wires dangled. Silence. No calls. No alarms.

Two minutes. That's all it took.

"Phones are dead!" he shouted, already running back for the lounge.

* * *

Laurie was already gone. His Owen slung over his back. He slipped back downstairs. The last guard stood at the foot of the stairs, watching the street. Laurie crept behind. The man never heard him coming. The hard, cold steel of a Colt .45 barrel pressed into the back of his neck.

"Easy, sport."

Laurie disarmed him in a swift, practised motion and then marched him back upstairs. A silent trophy of control.

* * *

In the lounge, Normie herded five staff from behind the bar. Three women, two men. Pale and shaking in disbelief.

Vinnie corralled the bookies, clerks, guards, and bankers from the Settling Room into the lounge near the billiard tables. "Everyone face down! Nose to the carpet." His yell almost manic.

Seventy-odd men and women. No heroes.

Tony returned from his phone run. Laurie brought in the last guard to join his mates. With everyone contained, Normie went to help Ian and Ray.

The lounge smelled of beer, stale cigars, and fear. Everyone on the floor, faces pressed against the faded carpet, hearts pounding.

One bookie, Wally, a mountain of a man, hesitated. Too long. Vinnie shoved him down. Hard. "Down. Now." The floor groaned under the impact.

A young bookie's clerk edged up behind Wally. If bullets started flying, he wanted cover.

Vinnie locked eyes with the older barmaid who had been seated behind Wally. Not fear. Resentment. Years of running the lounge had taught her how to stay composed.

"If anyone tries anything, the women go first," Vinnie announced, looking directly into her eyes. His voice low but carrying. Without breaking eye contact, she raised her arms slowly, steadying the two younger girls on either side of her. Both were crying.

Frank Murray, the club secretary, came out from the alcove behind the bar with his hands up. Found himself behind a man with a machine gun. A bad place. If he moved wrong, things might get worse. He edged back behind the large couches. Got down. Slow. Careful.

Silence. Only the buzz of the lights overhead and whimpering from the floor. Room contained.

Then the tell-tale ding of a lift. Vinnie looked at Laurie. The rear, disused lift Ian had rigged. No one should know it was in use.

Vinnie shook his head. Best laid plans.

Laurie raced to the rear lift lobby, confronting two new punters. A man in a white barber's jacket and an old bookmaker named Stewart, affectionately referred to as "The Guv'nor". Stewart grinned. He then saw the gun.

"Gentlemen," Laurie said, waving them into the lounge. Stepping behind them, he quickly grabbed another chair and jammed it into the second lift's door. He then courteously ushered them to join their friends. He helped The Guv'nor to the floor and whispered in his ear, "If you lay down flat, nothing will happen." But once down, the old man felt like he was drowning. He reached for his heart pills.

"Don't move!" Vinnie snapped.

The Guv'nor did the math. Die from a heart attack or a bullet? He decided to risk his heart. Eyes darted. A few heads lifted.

Vinnie snapped. "Down. If you lift your head, I'll blow it off."

A pause …

"That means you, Ambrose." Tony's words cut the air. A sharp knife through the silence.

Ambrose Palmer, prize-fighter. A local legend, but now a man in his 60s, and a victim of a couple of heart attacks. He turned his head. Recognition flickered in his eyes.[5]

Tony knew he had fucked up. Hadn't thought. He had known Palmer since he was four.

Vinnie shot Tony a glare that could kill. The tension spiked. For a second, Vinnie imagined putting a bullet through the middle of Tony's forehead.

He didn't. But the die was cast.

* * *

Ian reached the teller's cage. He pulled a set of bolt cutters from under his dustcoat, ready to cut his way in. The gate was not locked. He swung it open. His balaclava hid his grin. He passed the bolt cutters to Ray. Inside, eight big green metal strongboxes and one small wooden box. All padlocked.

Ray started cracking open each cashbox with the heavy bolt cutters. Steel bolts pinged as the locks snapped. Ian upended each box in turn. Calico cash bags spilled out like blood from an open wound. Over one hundred cash bags, all filled with untraceable bank notes.

Ian moved fast. He emptied the cash from the calico bags into large mail sacks. As a mail sack was filled, Ian dropped it at the entrance to the Settling Room.

Last, Ray cracked open the small wooden box. One hundred and fifty thousand dollars in crisp, brand-new notes. They had been delivered earlier that day by the bank. The float. "Keep this separate," Ray said. They were traceable. He stuffed them into a separate mail sack.

When Normie joined, he started work on the cash from the bookies' race bags. Half was already unpacked onto tables, ready for settling.

The money collected by Mayne Nickless and delivered that morning was the excess. When bookies take bets, the money goes into their race bag. When the bag is full, they transfer the cash to a calico bag and deposit it in an on-course armoured van. This is held by the security company and delivered back to the bookie on settling day. At the end of a meeting, bookies still carry considerable cash in their race bag.

Normie scooped cash with both hands, filling a mail sack on his own. He then proceeded to put his excess on top of the new notes. That could be sorted later. The air was sour. The kind of smell that clung to counting rooms and cash long touched by dirty hands.

When done, Ian went to wipe his forehead before remembering the balaclava. *More than expected*, he thought. A lot more.

The last mailbag sealed and dropped at the door. Ray nodded.

"Time," he called.

Normie looked over at the last bundle of bookie's cash on the far table. He looked at Ray.

"Time!" Ray repeated.

Normie picked up his mail sack and left.[6]

* * *

Back in the bar's lounge, Vinnie looked at his watch. Time.

The hostages lay silent. Too scared to move.

A slight flick of his head indicated to Tony that it was time to leave. Laurie slipped out behind him. Vinnie eased back toward the lift.

"I'll be waiting outside for ten minutes. Anyone who shows their head gets it blown off."

* * *

The two weapon duffle bags now sat on a bookies' table at the entrance to the Settling Room. Before each man grabbed a mail sack of cash, he dropped his weapon in a duffle bag. All were foreign, unmarked and untraceable. A present for the dogs. It would give them a rabbit hole to go down.

"What a waste," Vinnie muttered to himself, looking down at the pile of weapons left behind. He pushed the access door closed and headed for the stairs.

In eleven minutes, the raid was over, and they were gone.[7]

CHAPTER 3

The Crime Scene

The Settling Room was silent. Just minutes ago, it had been chaos; men shouting, bodies hitting the floor, the mechanical clatter of bolt cutters tearing through padlocks. Now, only the hum of the fluorescent lights and the faint rattle of a jammed elevator clicking filled the space.

A low murmur started. Someone coughed. Then Wally, still flat on his stomach, muttered, "Has it been ten minutes?"

Slowly, heads lifted. The bookmakers, punters, and staff stirred, some dusting off their coats, others sitting up as if waking from a bad dream. One of the girls started crying uncontrollably.

Frank Murray was the first to move with purpose. He shoved himself up, brushing his hands on his trousers. Behind the bar, a shaken waitress picked up the phone. Nothing. The line was dead.

Murray reached the barbershop, breathless. "Call the police!"

The barber, standing amongst the shattered glass, gave him a look. "With what?"

He ran to the lift. Seeing it jammed, he considered it for a moment, then decided to take the stairs. "Jesus Christ," he muttered, taking them two at a time.

By the time he reached the ground floor, he only had enough breath to call out, "We've been robbed. Call the police." A few men straightened their ties, finished their drinks in one gulp, and slipped out the door without a backward glance.

"Where the hell are you going?" Murray called after one well-dressed punter heading out the door.

The man barely slowed. "Don't need the cops asking me questions."

Another punter nodded in agreement, heading for the exit. "I wasn't here."

Murray turned, scanning the thinning crowd. He could already hear sirens in the distance. Too late for some. Not soon enough for others.

* * *

The first police to arrive at the Victoria Club were uniformed officers. They had run down from the law courts, further up Queen Street.

Uniformed and out of breath, they entered the Victoria Club running. Hands on holsters, eyes scanning. Chaos met them at the door. People shouting. Some faces pale, stunned. Others already gone. Those who stayed looked like ghosts.

"Nobody leaves!" one officer barked, throwing an arm across the entrance to block a patron trying to slip out unnoticed.

The officer's partner said, "I'll check upstairs." He pushed through the crowd.

More uniforms arrived, adding to the chaos. They called out to those behind the bar, "Where's the manager? Who's in charge?" It was like they were speaking Swahili. No one responded, no one was listening.

"Can everyone sit down," another called out, to little avail.

More uniforms headed upstairs. Upstairs, the Settling Room was a mess; papers scattered, chairs overturned. The lounge, however, was the antithesis of downstairs. The patrons sat at tables, silent, stunned. The manager sat comforting one of the female staff, still lightly sobbing.

A guard sat on the floor, a bloodied towel pressed against his head. His hands shook. One of the uniformed officers crouched beside him. "You all right, mate?"

The guard blinked, unfocused. "Didn't see 'em coming ... They were ghosts ... Then guns, everywhere."

The officer grabbed his radio. "We need an ambo at the Victoria Club. Head wound, possible concussion."

More sirens screamed from outside. Then came the boots. Dozens of them. Doors flung open, heavy footfalls pounding up the stairs. Radios crackled, orders flying. The club filled with the sound of leather and disarray.

For a moment, bedlam downstairs reached a crescendo. Then—silence.

Two Detective Inspectors strode in, suits creased, faces hard. They did not need to shout. The uniforms snapped to attention at their presence.

"Lock it down," the first one ordered. "Names, addresses. Anyone who left, track 'em down."

"Get statements," the second added. "And don't give me 'nobody saw a damn thing'. Someone always sees something."

A young constable approached. "Check entry points. Forced doors," the first DI ordered.

"Nothing, sir. They came in clean."

The Inspector frowned.

They turned toward the lift. One jabbed at the button. Nothing.

"Broken," the constable said. "They jammed it."

The detective swore under his breath. "Stairs, then."

Both stood at the bottom of the stairs, looking up. Resigned, they started up the seven flights of stairs.[8]

By the time they reached the Settling Room, both were winded, lungs burning. They were not young anymore. The first detective wiped his forehead with his sleeve.

First thing they noticed was a chair jammed in the lift door. "Basic but effective," one said to the other.

The second one surveyed the scene. He let out a slow breath. "Christ."

Cage open, cashboxes upside down. Empty. Furniture scattered. Calico money bags spread everywhere.

A crime scene. But no crime. Just the echo of one.

* * *

Front and centre sat two duffle bags on the table. Big, heavy. Left behind on purpose.

D.I. Alan, head of the Armed Robbery Squad, opened the first bag. His breath hitched. Tommy guns and Owen machine guns. An M16 and 12-gauge pump-action shotgun with cut-down stocks. Not a single handgun in sight. Military-grade firepower. This wasn't some back-alley stickup crew. This was serious.[9]

Forensics arrived, cameras flashing, dusting for prints. A tech crouched near the jammed lift, brushing powder across the doors. DI Alan barely looked up. He pointed to the table.

"Start with these." His voice tight. He knew they would not find anything. This crew would not be that sloppy. But why leave them at all? It didn't make sense.

He turned toward the teller's cage. The teller had settled back into his chair, wire-rimmed glasses perched low on his nose. He was staring at a tally sheet, muttering as he recounted figures. DI Alan leaned in.

"How much did they take?"

The teller squinted, pushed his glasses higher. "One million, three hundred, eighty-seven thousand," he said.

Alan blinked. "Say again?"

"$1.387 million," the teller repeated. He nodded toward the bookies milling around in the background. "Plus whatever they lost out of their bags."

Alan shook his head. "You can't be serious." He swept his gaze over the Settling Room; eight strongboxes cracked open, empty cash bags littered the floor.

"How many cash bags?" he asked one of the armoured van guards, leaning against the wall.

"118," the guard replied.

He turned back to the teller. "$1.387 million?"

"That's what the receipts say," the teller said.

Alan grabbed the sheet from his hands, scanning the numbers. He frowned. "This covers all forty-six bookies?"

The teller shook his head. "No. That's for all one hundred and sixteen bookies settling today. They share clerks."

Alan felt his jaw tighten. "One-point-four million across one hundred and sixteen bookies?" He let out a dry chuckle. "That works out at only twelve grand a piece. Half these bastards wouldn't get out of bed for twelve grand, let alone work three race meetings."

His gaze turned to the floor again. He stared at the scattered cash bags. He did the math in his head.

"One hundred and eighteen cash bags off the armoured car, each holding thirty, forty grand? That's over four million. Add in what the forty-six bookies here had in their own race bags, that's another two, easy. We're talking six plus million. And they're claiming one-point-four?"

Alan shook his head, disbelief settling in. [10]

Footsteps behind him. Heavy, measured. Detective Inspector Paul from the Consorting Squad. Alan didn't turn.

"They reckon it was only 1.4," he said, his voice flat.

DI Paul had extensive experience providing "private" security to these guys. Anyone looking to place less than a monkey ($500) would be courteously redirected to the tote. It was not unknown for these guys to carry a hundred grand in their bookie bags, or run two bags. That meant the need for protection. Consorting squad officers were always around, looking for a handout, so they were the easy choice. Plus, they knew the experienced crims. However, experienced crims would not be stupid enough to try anything. Most bookies were well-connected. But young, inexperienced crims and druggies might think of it as an easy mark. [11]

DI Paul snorted. "Yeah. And I'm the Queen of England." He folded his arms, scanning the scene. "They've always underquoted their turnover. If they suddenly reported holding five times their usual take, it wouldn't just be the racing commission and insurance guys crawling up their arse. The taxman would crucify them."

Alan nodded. "They pay tax on turnover. Win or lose."

"Or stolen," Paul smirked. They've been lying about it for years."

"What about the alarm?" Paul asked the teller. Alan glared at him; it was his investigation. Paul was there to advise.

The teller hesitated. "Not working," he said.

Alan's head snapped up. "Since when?"

The teller licked his lips. "Since today."

Silence. Alan and Paul locked eyes.

Automatic weapons. Alarm disabled. A professional crew. There must have been inside knowledge. Six million plus in cash gone without a trace. And not a damn thing they could do about it.

"Sir, this is where they entered," one of Alan's detectives interrupted. He opened the hidden door and pointed to the sawn-off slide bolt. "It leads to the building next door. It's empty for renovations."

"Damn. They left through there." Alan paused. "Right, I want every uniform combing Queen Street in both directions. Someone must have seen something. It was goddamn lunchtime after all. Ask in every office." Alan dismissed the young detective.

* * *

Meanwhile, in the lounge, Detective Sergeant Lauder continued interviewing witnesses.

It did not help that the room still carried the smell of fear and Scotch poured too fast. Neither did the uniforms crowding the room like seagulls on a bin.

DS Lauder stood with his hands in his coat pockets as he listened to the men and women coil and uncoil their stories.

"Start again," he said. "You saw how many?"

"Four," said the barman, rubbing the back of his neck. "Or maybe five. Hard to say, it all happened quick. One came through the bar, I think. Small bloke, moved like he was late for something. Real fast. Like a gymnast, yeah."

"Face?"

"Covered. Red and black ski mask. You know the kind."

Lauder turned to the waitress. She looked young, too young for guns and vaulting men.

"I thought it was some Kung Fu thing," she said, shaking her head. "He just jumped the bar like he'd done it a hundred times. Like it was nothing."

"Voice?"

"Hard to say. Fast. Angry. But polite too. He told Ambrose to get down. Called him by name."

"Ambrose?"

"Palmer. The old boxer. He's in the lounge. Might have known him."

Lauder grunted. "Might have?" He made a note in his pad.

Next, he spoke to the old-timer, Stewart.

"Nice young fella. Most considerate."

All Lauder got was that a man with a machine gun had paced by the red couches. They all said that. Said he was calm. Said he watched them. Some said ten minutes. Some said two. No one agreed on what he looked like, only that he was big and quiet. Didn't raise his voice.

Lauder turned to Vivian, the senior barmaid, if he had to guess. She was the only one not falling apart, leaning against the bar, arms folded like she'd seen worse drunks on a Friday. Not drinking, not crying. She had been behind the bar when it happened.

"The first guy forced us out and made us sit at a front table."

"Us?"

"Joan, Mary, and me."

"Did you get a good look at any of them?"

"Only the big guy. Seemed older. In charge."

"You saw him up close?"

She nodded. "Close enough."

"Describe him."

She looked past him. "Not much taller than me."

Lauder looked down at her six-inch heels. That doesn't help.

"Stocky. Dark eyes. Cold eyes," she continued. "Didn't yell. Didn't flinch. Moved like he wasn't worried about time. In control."

"You saw his face?"

"A glimpse. Enough."

Lauder let that sit. Waited.

"Could've been anyone," she said finally.

Lauder left her with that. He crossed to Frank Murray and pulled out the chair across from him.

"You're the manager?"

"Club Secretary!" Murray responded indignantly.

"You were here the whole time?"

Murray nodded. "Had my lunch early. Roast beef. Was coming back through the bar when the little one jumped it."

Lauder opened his book. "Walk me through it."

Murray's voice was quiet. Matter-of-fact. "Lunchroom's through the back. I came out. Saw Josh, the barman. He looked pale. Eyes like saucers."

"Then what?"

"I tapped him on the shoulder. Told him he could go eat. He didn't say anything. Just stood there like someone had pulled the plug."

Lauder didn't interrupt. Just let the man talk.

"Then I saw him, the little bastard. Red and black ski cap. Eyes like pins. Gun out. Long thing. Might've been a silencer."

"What did you do?"

"Stepped back. Figured I didn't need to be a hero."

"And then?"

"He vaulted the bar. Light on his feet. Like he'd done it before. Grabbed the house phone. Ripped it clean. Threw it. Picked up a whole table and flung it across the floor. Kept going. Every phone, one after the other. Admin office.

Barber's room. Broke the glass. Tore through the place like a Tassie devil."

Lauder nodded once. "What'd you do?"

"Retreated. Alcove behind the bar. No phone in there. Waited it out. Then I came out. Just in time to see the bigger one, the calm one, ushering the bookmakers toward the billiard tables."

"He say anything?"

"Said it was serious. Said if everyone followed instructions, no one would get hurt."

"Did you believe him?"

Murray looked directly at him for the first time. Like he was from another planet. "What do you think?"

"What'd you do next?"

"I helped. Told the others to lie down. Tried to keep people calm. Young Joan, the waitress, she was shaking. I told her to do what they said. That helped her, I think."

Lauder glanced over at Vivian. He knew who he believed.

"You saw the man with the machine gun again?" he continued.

"Only his feet. He was pacing. Back and forth. Could see his shoes below the couches."

"When did he leave?"

"12:18 by my watch. He said he'd be watching for ten more minutes. Then nothing. Silence."

Lauder scribbled something.

"Then?"

"I called down to the kitchen through the old two-way speaker behind the bar. Told Alf to get Mrs Casey to ring the police. He did."

"You've seen this kind of thing before?"

"No," Murray said. "But I know discipline when I see it."

Lauder let that sit. "What can you tell me about a repairman seen wandering around?"

"One of the bar fridges carked it yesterday. I left a message for Mrs Casey to call a refrigeration mechanic this morning."

"Oh," Lauder sighed. Another line of inquiry shot. Anything else?"

"Old Mr. Gorman came out from the reading room. Thought they were filming an episode of *Homicide*."

That drew a smile from Lauder. First of the day.

"I told Josh to pour drinks," Murray said. "On the house. Some of the old boys looked like they needed it."

Lauder closed his notebook. "You handled yourself then."

"I handled the club," Murray said.

Lauder nodded. Left Murray to his work. The fingerprint team had already called it. Everything clean. Nothing useful. Gloves or ghost hands, it didn't matter.

Out on Queen Street, a van had been seen. White. Fast. Or maybe blue. Two men, or one. Someone said balaclavas. Someone said dustcoats. One said there was no van at all.

It was always the same. When things happen too fast, people see little; make up the rest. Fill in the blanks with whatever scares them the most.

"You've all been very helpful," he lied. Detective Sergeant Lauder left.

The Club held the echo of a moment that had moved too quick, too clean. No trace.

CHAPTER 4

The Getaway

Ray and his crew did not run down. They went up. Like smoke, they disappeared into the floors above.

Normie had rented an office two floors above, the month before the robbery. The cops would tear the building next door apart once they realised it had been the point of entry. But no one ever thinks to look up!

The mailbags were stuffed to the limit, heavier than they'd planned. They trained for this, but the extra weight, ten kilos more in each sack, made the climb brutal. No bounding up the stairs this time. Just a slow, punishing slog up two floors. Normie grunted under the weight, muttering something about needing a chiropractor after this job. The haul was bigger, sure, but it felt like it was dragging their arms from the sockets.

One by one, they reached the office. Dropped their sacks in front of the safe. Then, almost on cue, collapsed against the wall. Chests heaving. Limbs shaking. No chairs. Just cold floorboards under them.

Normie moved through them, pulling a small bundle of used notes from each sack. He handed it over without a word. Walking-around money. Enough to blend in. Nothing more.

As they caught their breath, he packed the sacks into the safe. One in, one up. A rhythm.

Vinnie was the last to leave, and therefore the last to arrive. He dropped his mail sack at Normie's feet. Without stopping, he turned, walked up to Tony, and in a single movement, hit him with a full-on right hook. It lifted Tony's body off the floor and landed two feet further on.

"What the ..." Ray exclaimed. The job had gone to plan.

"This fuckwit called Ambrose by name!" Vinnie yelled.

Ray's attention immediately swung to Tony. He knew that was going to be a problem.

"And Ambrose recognised it," Vinnie continued.

"He couldn't have," Laurie interjected.

"Of course he fucking did." Vinnie was fuming. "This fucker can sink us all."

Tony was still curled up on the floor where he had landed from Vinnie's blow. Whimpering, "I'm sorry. I'm sorry."

Last thing Ray needed was a confrontation two floors above a crime scene. He looked at Ian. Ian picked up his lead.

"My problem, Vinnie," said Ian, asserting his authority over Vinnie. Ian was the only one who could. "Leave it, I'll handle it."

Ray came back in. "Focus," he commanded. "The job isn't finished."

As if woken from a nightmare, they all started moving again. As one man stood, he stripped off his dustcoat, overalls, balaclava. Dropped them into the last duffle bag by the door. Then left. Another man took his place.

They slipped out one by one. Down the back stairs. Gloves off as they took the side exit. Just men in street clothes, walking into the city. Queen Street moved like it always did. Men in suits. Women in heels. Taxis. Trams. Life carrying on.[12]

Frankie sat behind the wheel, engine idling, fingers drumming. His eyes flicked between the rear-vision mirrors and the street ahead. A white Transit van parked in a city 'Loading Zone' should not draw attention. Even so, Frankie felt exposed. The late arrival of the armoured van had extended his time there. He was thankful when the others started returning. One by one, they climbed in.

Normie was the last out, taking a final look around before shutting the safe. He scooped up the last duffle bag of clothes, gave the empty room a nod and slipped down the back stairs. Outside, he crossed to the van. Opened the back door, tossed the bag in, and climbed in after it.

As Frankie pulled away, the faint wail of sirens rose in the distance.

The van disappeared into the traffic.

Gone.

* * *

The Transit van's first stop after leaving the Victoria Club was only a few blocks down the road. It rolled to a stop near the Waterside Hotel. Frankie kept the engine running.

"You're up," Ray said.

Laurie swiped everyone's hands as he and Tony passed down the van. "Good luck!" They slipped out of the van, crossing the street like they belonged.

"This is the part I hate," Tony said, as they entered the public bar of the Painter and Dockers' favourite watering hole.

Laurie grinned. "Relax. If asked, these blokes will swear blind we've been here since breakfast." Painters and Dockers were always being hit up by the cops. Everyone always responded, "Been here all day," when asked by police.

Inside, the air was thick with cigarette smoke and the smell of stale beer. Familiar faces lined the bar.

"Laurie! Tony!" A voice boomed from the corner. "What's this? Early finish?"

Tony clapped the nearest bloke on the back. "Something like that. Long morning. Been here since midday," he announced to the room.

Laurie waved to the bartender. "Couple of pots, mate." He checked the wall clock. Perfect. By the time the cops came asking, the whole pub would swear they had been there for hours.

* * *

Next stop, North Melbourne. On the way out to the Dim Sim factory, Normie casually commented, "Lucky the dogs didn't show today."

"Maybe they had a tip-off of a major job going down on the peninsula," Frankie called from the front seat.

Ray and Normie looked at one another and smiled.

Frankie pulled up short of Normie's. Ray and Normie got out and stretched their legs. The van did a U-turn and left.

"Clock's twenty minutes slow?" Ray asked as they walked towards the factory.

Normie smirked. "Changed it myself this morning before work."

"Fix it tonight," Ray added.

Inside, the workers bustled over steaming baskets. Normie clapped a few on the shoulder, joking about orders being late.

"Boss," one of the workers called, "you bring the big fella in for quality control?" Nodding at Ray.

Ray grinned. "Best dumplings in Melbourne, mate. Thought I'd stop in and check up on Normie. Make sure he's not running this joint into the ground."

Laughter.

The factory clock read **12:10 PM**. By the time anyone checked, the confusion would be enough to throw off any timeline.

* * *

Ian and Vinnie stepped onto the pavement outside the Windsor Hotel. The van pulled away.

"Business lunch?" Vinnie muttered. "I don't even own a tie."

"Just be yourself," Ian said. "You're here as my friend."

Inside, a round table of men in pressed shirts and loosened ties were already entrenched. Ian led Vinnie over. "Everyone, this is Vinnie. An old mate of mine."

Walking around the table, Ian continued, "Vinnie, you know my little brother Greg," shaking his brother's shoulder as he passed. Although a successful businessman in his own right, and a half inch taller, Greg was always Ian's little brother.

Vinnie grinned. "Yeah, g'day, squirt." Cuffed him lightly on the back of the head. "Still growing into your shoes, I see."

Greg smiled, tight. Said nothing.

Vinnie dropped into a seat. "Hope you blokes aren't on mineral water. Wouldn't want this to turn into a Rotary Club meeting. What's a business lunch without a few drinks? Waiter!" he called. "More beers."

They laughed. The tension melted. Vinnie was in his natural habitat. A group of men with beers in their hands. He regaled them with his shady side of life stories, true and not-so-true. He was a hit.

He launched into a yarn. "Don't ever try robbing a TAB in Footscray with a Greek getaway driver. Jesus. We're sprinting out the back, right, me, Ray, and this bloke, Costa. He stalls the bloody Cortina. We're shouting, he's crossing himself, and I swear he starts reversing into traffic like he's looking for a parking spot. I yell, 'Drive like you're late to church or we're all gonna meet God!'"

The table cracked up. Even Greg let a smile slip.

Vinnie continued: "Later he says, 'I don't panic under pressure, but I thought I saw my cousin working the counter.' I said, 'Mate, you lot got more cousins than an Athens phone book.'"

More laughter.

Someone asked how he and Ian had met.

"Turana," Vinnie said. "I was there for pinching a bike. Someone had to protect him from the paedo warders."

Ian shook his head. "He's not wrong."

Vinnie leaned toward Greg. "Your brother was a quick learner. Taught me to pick locks. I taught him how to fight with more than his fists. Good trade."

Greg raised his glass. "To my brother Ian."

Vinnie followed suit. "*My* brother."

When it was time to settle the bill, Vinnie, already bigger than life, said, "I'll pick up the drinks tab." He grabbed the bill wallet and extracted the itemised drink bill. As he expected, each individual drink was listed along with the time it was rung up. They started at 12:01 PM. He smiled.

"Waiter, put these on my card, and add 10% for yourself," he announced to the room.

Laughter.

Ian kicked him under the table. This would be the first time Vinnie did not use cash, let alone leave a tip.

Vinnie just winked, neatly folded both receipts and slid them into his wallet. Alibi done.

* * *

36

Late afternoon, the Waterside was humming. Laurie and Tony leaned against the bar, laughing at a joke, when the pub doors swung open.

Two cops. They scanned the room. The chatter did not stop, but eyes followed. The taller one stepped up. "Laurie Prendergast. Tony McNamara."

Tony sipped his beer. "Something on your mind, officer?"

"Victoria Club got hit today. Midday."

Laurie turned to the bartender. "Hey, what time did we get here?"

The bartender scratched his chin. "They've been sitting there since before noon. Same as every bloody day."

"See," Laurie grinned at the officer.

The cop stared a beat longer. Then they turned and left.

Laurie smiled. "We're good."

* * *

Frankie parked the van behind the Union office and killed the motor. Still work to do.

He stepped out, stretched, and picked up the remaining duffle bag of job clothing. Walked to the dumpster with the red lid labelled DANGEROUS WASTE. Lifted the lid and threw the bag in. By the morning, it would be incinerated.

Inside the office, the usual crowd lounged around, reading papers and drinking coffee. "Frankie," a voice called. "Long morning?"

"Something like that," he said.

He slumped into a chair. No need to push it. The whole building would swear blind he had been there since sunrise.

Tomorrow, he would take the van and have it crushed. Tonight, he would drink.

PART II

WHERE IT BEGAN

The Painters and Dockers

The Melbourne docks: a beast that never sleeps. Sixteen miles of waterfront, sprawling across 1,200 acres, fed by a ceaseless tide of steel and cargo. More than 1,000 ships pass through each year, their bellies fat with goods from across the world. It was the best-connected port in Australia, pumping AU$7.5 billion into the economy a year. Beneath, another world thrived. One built on greed, muscle, and silence.

Men worked the docks by day, unloading crates, shifting cargo, filling the pockets of the city's wealthiest. By night, a different crew took over. Smugglers, thieves, men with knives tucked into their belts. A few grand here, a missing crate there; no one asked questions if they knew what was good for them. The union controlled who worked and who did not, and stepping out of line meant more than losing a pay cheque. A whisper in the wrong ear could see a man beaten, tossed into the Yarra, or worse. To disappear, never to be seen again.

It also meant the city's underworld had a direct line to anywhere in the world. Drugs, guns, stolen cars; 900 new vehicles rolled in every day. Not all of them made it to their rightful owners.

Beyond the floodlights and the hum of cranes, West Melbourne crouched in the shadows. A working-class slum on the edge of the CBD, where men drank hard, fought harder, and learned young that the docks were not just a place to make a living. They were a place to make a killing.

Like elite sportsmen, criminals are not born. They're made. And for the bookie robbers, it all started with the Federated Ship Painters and Dockers Union...

CHAPTER 5

Raymond 'Chuck' Bennett

Welcome to the Docks

A young Raymond Patrick Chuck, as Bennett was known before his UK sabbatical, stood at the wharf gates, his boots skimming the line between boyhood and something uglier. Born into a poor working-class family, they moved regularly, normally the night before the rent man was due. When old enough, it was expected he would contribute to the household expenses.

Standing outside the dockyards, the sting of salt air on his tongue, the stench of diesel and rusting steel, and the deafening clang of metal on metal as cranes shifted cargo, both excited and overwhelmed the young Ray. At fourteen, wiry and tall for his age with a softness still in his cheeks that marked him as green, he stood waiting. Around him in the pre-dawn glow, men smoked and spat, their faces weathered and eyes wary. He was one of them, part of the hopeful crowd waiting. Waiting for a chance for work. The foreman appeared.

"You, you and you," he said, handing out yellow day work chits. The others would come back tomorrow and try again. Ray was one of the lucky ones.

"You'll need to see the Union Rep first," the gateman announced, nodding to the third building on the left. "Federated Ship Painters & Dockers' Union of Australia. Victorian Branch", read the sign on the tin shed. Ray paused, squeezing the work chit in his hand. He entered.[13]

Freddy "The Frog" Harrison sat behind a small desk, his sharp eyes studying Ray like a butcher sizing up meat. Freddy was not a big man, but he did not need to be. His name carried enough weight to crush anyone who doubted him.[14]

"You the kid?" Freddy asked, voice rough and clipped.

"Yes, sir," Ray said. His hands fidgeted in his pockets, but he kept his chin up.

Freddy looked him up and down, then smirked. "You'll do."

The job was simple, Freddy said. Fabricate pay records. Registering ghosts, men who did not exist. Ray listened, nodding at the right times, but the words felt foreign, unreal. "Ghosting," Freddy called it. A harmless word for something darker.

"You do this right, you make yourself useful," Freddy said. "You make yourself useful, you stay safe."

Ray hesitated, but only for a second. The docks did not leave room for doubt. He took the clipboard, a pen, and names from a phonebook that belonged to no one. Each stroke of the pen felt like a step into something deeper, uneasy.[15]

When it was done, Freddy slapped him on the back. "Good lad," he said. "You'll go far if you keep your mouth shut."

Just as he thought his day was ending, Freddy came over. "Now go see Brody over at Dock 4. He's got a job for you."

Ray headed out, searching for Brody.

* * *

"You listening, kid?" said Brody, a thick-necked man with a voice like gravel. He loomed over Ray, his shadow long against the dock's concrete. In his hand, a crowbar hung loose, but its weight was implied. Ray nodded. He had learned early that talking too much only got you noticed in ways you did not want.

Brody grunted approval. "Good. First thing, you don't talk about what you see. Ever. Second thing, loyalty. You're either with us or you're against us. And third…" He paused, leaning in close enough so that Ray was staring at his yellow tobacco-stained teeth. "You don't hesitate. You hesitate, you're done. Understand?"

Ray nodded again. His hands were shoved deep in his pockets, hiding the way they trembled. Brody's eyes searched his face, looking for cracks. Ray forced himself to meet the gaze. It was a small victory, but it felt like passing some invisible test.

The initiation was not formal; not the way a kid might imagine a secret society. No blood oaths or ceremonial knives. Just a job. A small one, they said. A test. That was how it started. Slipping into a docked ship's cargo hold at night, removing something, usually small, sometimes valuable, often both. No one noticed. Or, if they did, they didn't say. The first time, Ray's role was simple: hold the bag, stay quiet, and follow Brody's lead. He moved like a shadow, swift and sure, while Ray's heart pounded in his ears loud enough to drown out the creak of the ship's hull. When it was over, Brody slapped him on the back and called him a natural.

The second time was not as smooth. Ray slipped on a patch of oil and landed hard. It rang like a bell in the hollow belly of the ship. Brody's hand was on him in an instant, not to help but to pin him to the ground. They froze, listening. When the silence held, Brody lifted Ray up to his full height. His fist smashed into Ray's face. They did not waste time bullying on the docks. Violence was the currency of education. Brody's grip loosened, and he leaned in close.

"You screw up again, you're not walking out. Got it?"

Ray got it. Blood running down his chin. The lesson etched itself into his bones that night: mistakes were not just costly, they were fatal. And Brody was not the type to bluff.

* * *

Over the weeks and months, the jobs grew riskier. What started as quiet thievery evolved into something harder to define. Moving contraband, roughing up rivals, sending messages the way only fists and broken ribs could deliver. Each task came with its own brand of danger, but none shook Ray as much as the duplicity. The smiling faces that turned cold the moment your back was turned. The men who laughed and drank with you, only to disappear when things went sideways.

Loyalty was a word they threw around like confetti, but Ray learned quickly that it had tiers. You were loyal to the union, sure, but within the union, there were lines. Brody was a line, thick and dark. Cross him, and you were out: out of work, out of favour, out of luck. Ray watched how the older men manoeuvred, their alliances fluid and their smiles tight-lipped. It was not friendship. It was survival.

One night, Ray found himself standing in the glow of a bare bulb in a warehouse off the docks. The room was empty except for a metal chair in the centre where a man sat tied and bleeding. Ray did not know his name, but he knew what he had done: talked to the wrong people about the wrong things. Brody's voice was calm as he handed Ray a baseball bat.

"Your turn, kid."

Ray's stomach turned. He had seen beatings before, had even held a man down while Brody worked him over. But this was different. This was active, deliberate. His fingers wrapped around the bat's handle. He looked down at the man in the chair, blood at his feet.

"I…"

"Don't hesitate," Brody said. His voice was steel, and his eyes dared Ray to falter.

Ray raised the bat. The first blow felt like striking a wall; jarring, sickening. The man groaned, and Ray's vision tunnelled. He swung again. By the third hit, something inside him broke, or maybe just shut down. When it was over, his hands ached, but he had Brody's approval. Silent but palpable.

Alone in his room, Ray stared at his hands. They were clean, but he could still feel the phantom stickiness of blood. He didn't sleep that night. Nor the next.

* * *

The jobs did not stop. One after another, like waves breaking against the shore. Each one taught Ray something new, even as it chipped away at something inside him. He did not show it. That was not the way. You buried those feelings deep, where even you could not find them.

Brody was the kind of man who did not just survive in their world; he thrived. He moved like he owned every room he stepped into. His voice, his laugh; it was all part of the act. Ray studied him, watched how he carried himself. Confidence was not about being the loudest. It was about being the most certain.

"Always walk in like you've already won," Brody told him one night after a job. They sat in the back of a bar, the room filled with smoke and the clink of glasses. Age was never an issue in Painter and Docker pubs. Brody leaned back, his arm slung over a chair, the picture of ease. "People sense doubt, kid. Show them none, and they'll follow you anywhere."

Ray nodded, filing it away. Brody talked like that a lot; little lessons disguised as offhand remarks. Most of the crew did not pay attention. Ray did.

* * *

The next job was a warehouse on the outskirts of the city. It was supposed to be easy. In and out. Grab the cash from the office safe and disappear before anyone notices. But things rarely went to plan.

They were halfway through when the night watchman showed up. He was older, heavyset, with a flashlight in one hand and an old-fashioned cosh in the other. He froze when he saw them, his face pale under the flickering bulb reflected from the loading dock.

"Shit," muttered Tommo, who was supposed to be keeping a lookout. His hand twitched toward his pocket. Ray stopped him with a glance.

"Hold up," Ray said, stepping forward. His voice was calm, steady. "Evening, mate. We're just here for a quick look around. No need to make this a big deal."

The man's eyes darted between Ray and the others. His grip on the cosh tightened.

"What the hell are you doing here?" the watchman demanded, his voice trembling just enough for Ray to hear it.

Ray kept his hands at his sides, open, non-threatening. He stepped closer, slow and deliberate, like he had all the time in the world.

"Same thing you're doing," Ray said. "Trying to make it through the night in one piece." He smiled, just enough to take the edge off his words.

46

The watchman blinked, uncertain. Brody's words echoed in Ray's mind: *people believe what you make them believe.*

"Look," Ray continued, his tone dropping into something softer. "We're not here to hurt anyone. You go back to your rounds, and we're gone in ten minutes. No one's the wiser."

The man hesitated. Ray could see the fear in his eyes, the calculation. He did not want a fight. Neither did Ray.

"Ten minutes," the watchman said finally, stepping back. He turned and walked away, his footsteps fading into the night.

Ray released a long breath, the tension in his shoulders easing.

"You had it covered," Brody said later, back at the safe house. "Didn't even flinch."

Ray shrugged. "He just needed to hear the right thing."

Brody grinned. "You're learning, kid."

Ray did not answer. He was learning, all right. The kind of lessons that did not come from books. How to read a room, how to talk someone down, how to hide the unease that never quite left him.

Strength was not about muscles or guns. It was about control. Control of the situation, control of the people around you, control of yourself. Ray was getting better at it. And that scared him more than he wanted to admit.

* * *

Sending a Message

By seventeen, Ray was not a boy anymore. The docks had carved him into something harder, sharper. He carried a gun now, though he rarely had to use it. His name was known, not loud but quietly whispered like the tide pulling at the edges of the pier. He had learned to move with the currents, to see power in the spaces where others only saw men.

"Ray, we got a fucking problem," Freddy snarled, his eyes darting nervously.

"What kind of problem?" Ray responded.

"Fucking Tommo's been talking to the dogs," Freddy explained.

Ray shook his head. "Never trust a weak prick!" His expression hardened, his jaw clenching with barely contained fury. Betrayal was a sin punishable by death in their world, and Tommo had sealed his fate with his loose lips.

"No. Just needs to be given a warning," Freddy said, picking up Ray's anger.

"Where is he?" Ray's voice was calm, belying the storm that raged within him.

"Down by the pier, meeting some arsehole suit," Freddy replied, his voice barely above a whisper.

Ray nodded and turned.

"Wait. The boss has someone he wants you to take along. A kid from Leo's gym, 'Fingers' Carroll. He's done a bit of Golden Gloves, can really handle himself."

"I can handle Tommo," Ray objected, resenting the implication.

"It's not about handling, it's about sending a message. Not just to Tommo. Overwhelming force sends a message. Someone steps out of line: you hurt them. They pull a knife: you pull a gun. They pull a gun: you take five guys with artillery."

Ray got the point. Tonight, there would be no mercy, no second chances. For in the world of the docks, loyalty was the only currency worth its weight in gold.

Without another word, Ray turned on his heels and went to find "Fingers" Carroll.

CHAPTER 6

Ian 'Fingers' Carroll

Turana Boys Home

Ian Revell Carroll also grew up on the streets. At 14, convicted of larceny, he was sentenced to 18 months in juvenile detention. It was euphemistically named the Turana Boys Home. [16]

Only it was not a home, and when you came out, you were no longer a boy. It was an old-school facility aimed at breaking the rebellious, not rehabilitating them. A sprawling two-story brown brick complex, it looked like a cross between a convent and an aircraft factory. All windows were small wire-reinforced panes. Light came in, but not much of a view out. The lawns outside were for appearance, not for play.

Run by sadistic paedophiles whose first resort was to a severe beating. At night, screams could be heard through the dorms, as warders made their night visits to the younger, fresh-faced ones. Fortunately, an older boy, Vinnie Mikkelsen, took Ian under his wing. Vinnie taught him how to hide, how to scrounge, and how to survive the hellhole. [17]

Vinnie and Ian were released the same day. Outside, Ian felt like he guessed normal kids felt on the last day of school.

They laughed, slapping each other's backs. Vinnie took off, crossing the main road, splitting traffic. Ian followed. Cars swerved, horns sounded. A big white yank tank missed Ian by inches, blaring its horn.

Vinnie turned. "Fuck off!" he yelled, giving the car the finger.

Ian stood staring after it. Big tail fins. Whitewall tyres. "One day I'll have one of those," he said to no one, as if putting it out into the ether would somehow make it come true.

"What, a Caddy? You're dream'n," Vinnie laughed. Throwing his arm around Ian as they walked across Royal Park, he said, "Stick with me and I'll show you how to make real money."

"Where we going?" Ian asked after a while.

"Leo's boxing gym. Good place to pick up loose change, running for the older guys. Contacts and ideas. Never think of your own if you can pinch someone else's," he joked.

That was Vinnie. Not a big thinker.

* * *

Leo's Boxing Gym

Ian did not smoke. Most street kids did. They lounged outside the gym, cigarettes dangling, talking big and doing nothing. Ian was not like them. He went straight to Leo and offered to clean up in exchange for gym time.

He swept floors, emptied spit buckets, and picked up towels. All the while keeping his ears open. Leo coached fighters like a general leading troops. Ian watched, listened, and learned. He mimicked their moves, their training routines. Every spare minute, he was in the gym, punching, skipping, sweating.

Vinnie shook his head, leaning against the ropes, smirking. "You're wasting your time, Ian. A street fighter beats a boxer any day. No rules out there. No ref, no bell." Vinnie knew no one could touch him in a street fight. His punches were fast, his kicks faster, and he had no qualms about playing dirty.

Ian didn't argue. He just kept training. Harder. Longer. The punches came cleaner, the footwork sharper. Leo noticed. At first, he just gave Ian a few tips in passing. A correction here, a nod there. Then one day, Leo called him over.

"You've got something, kid," Leo said, sizing him up. "Because you're younger than the others, you're lighter. And I've got a gap at Lightweight. Let's see what you can do."

Ian did not say much. He never did. But he worked even harder after that. Leo brought him into the stable. Soon, Ian was sparring, taking punches, and giving them back. It was not just about the boxing. It was about being noticed.

The fights got him respect in the boxing world, but that was not all. People outside the gym started noticing too; people who needed debts collected, bets enforced, and problems solved. Having a known boxer at your side made things easier. Ian did not have to raise his fist. His reputation spoke for him.

But Ian wasn't content with small-time collections. He figured out who the real players were—the ones running the gambling rings, the money men. He started going to them directly, cutting out the middlemen. The payouts were bigger that way.

That did not mean he and Vinnie stopped working together. They still ran jobs on the side, lifting goods where they could. Vinnie was the muscle, Ian the brains. Together, they made a solid team, one punching through the streets, the other keeping an eye on the prize.

Ian did not waste time talking about his future. He was too busy building it. [18]

         * * *

Ray found Ian at Leo's gym. He was easy to spot. Younger than the other fighters in the gym, but respected. Not like the street kids that hang around boxing gyms looking to pick up gofer jobs.

Ian was different. Ian did not drift; he drove. Older by just a year, Ian was already an enforcer, his reputation built on blood and resolve. He did not care for whispers; he wanted results. When a debt needed collecting or a problem needed fixing, it was Ian they sent.

Ian was sitting on a bench against the back wall, unwrapping the strappings from around his hands.

"Fingers?" Ray asked, eyebrow raised.

"Ian," Ian shot back, not bothering to look up, his hands still working the wraps off his knuckles. He disliked that moniker intensely, but in their world, you have no control over the nickname you were given.

"Ray Chuck," Ray replied, looking at 'LOVE' and 'HATE' tattooed on Ian's knuckles. "Professional?"

"No, Golden Gloves. Fifteen wins, two losses, five KOs."

"Five knockouts," Ray repeated, nodding his head impressed. "Interested in making some real money?" Ray asked, voice casual but eyes sharp.

Ian paused, then looked up, meeting his gaze. "Always," he said, and meant it.

"The Frog sent me. Got a job." Ray said. "Do good and you'll earn what matters."

What mattered, Ian knew, was loyalty. Not the kind you chose but the kind you owed, like a debt stamped into your bones. Betrayal was not forgiven. It was hunted, broken, and left as a warning.

As they left the gym, they passed another young boxer entering.

"Fingers," grunted Kane.

"Brian." Replied Ian flatly, respect but not friendly.

"Chuck." Said Kane as they passed. Ray did not reply. He vaguely knew Kane from the docks. However, the union had factions that did not get on. Sharing spoils was not a big thing in their circle.

They found Tommo by the pier, where he had met the Consorting detective. Ian moved like a storm, fists and boots, the sound of bones breaking lost to the clanging of cranes.

When it was done, Ian returned to Ray. "That's loyalty," he said.

Ray did not flinch. He was savvy enough to know that Ian was not seeking approval. He was demonstrating his value. And Ray was paying attention.

* * *

Ian made the most of his introduction to the Painters and Dockers.[19] He made himself available for any dirty job, gaining the notice and respect of those who mattered. However, he still kept up his extracurricular activities that had earned him the taunting moniker 'Fingers'. Although it had been the reason for his 18-month holiday at Turana Boys Home, they taught him well.

Combined with the opportunities and contacts on the docks, thieving was working much better now. Now it was to order. From consumables, legal and not-so-legal, to cars fresh off a ship. No need for middlemen. No worries about disposal. Disposing of stolen goods is where most thieves get unstuck.

Ray introduced Ian to how the knowledge of shipments from docks could be sourced to make thieving more profitable. Dockland warehouses are located close to the docks for easy access, but outside the restricted area. Distribution lorries did not need dock clearance. It also made them soft targets at night when the streets around the docks were deserted and poorly lit. Dock consignment manifests were perfect shopping lists. Buyers could be found in advance, thereby minimising the dangers of holding stolen goods.

Their first independent job together was meant to be simple. It wasn't ...

* * *

The warehouse was silent. A cold wind blew in through the broken window, carrying the sharp tang of salt and oil. Ray stood by the open door, his breath visible in the dim light of the streetlight outside. He checked his watch. Two minutes to go.

"Cold tonight," Ian muttered, pulling his collar up against the wind. He was leaning against a stack of crates, a crowbar resting on his shoulder. His face was calm, almost bored, but his eyes darted to the shadows every few seconds.

"Stay focused," Ray said without looking at him.

Ian smirked. "Always. I'm not the one checking my watch every thirty seconds."

Ray didn't reply. He listened instead to the creak of the metal door in the wind, the faint rumble of a passing truck. Everything felt sharp tonight, but he still had a feeling that told him this could go wrong fast. A low whistle came from outside. Frankie's signal. The truck was here.

"Let's go," Ray said.

Ian pushed off the crates, rolling his shoulders. "Showtime."

They moved quickly. Ray threw up the roller door, stepping out into the night. The truck's headlights were off, its engine idling as it backed toward the warehouse. Frankie was in the driver's seat, a cigarette dangling from his lips.

"You're late," Ray said as Frankie climbed out.

"Had to take the long way. Saw a paddy wagon up on Dock Road," Frankie replied, shrugging.

"Everything clear now?" Ian asked.

54

"Yeah, it's clear. Let's make this quick," Frankie said, tossing a pair of bolt cutters to Ray.

Ray caught them and motioned toward the padlocked gate separating the truck from the loading dock. He went to work on the lock while Ian kept watch, the crowbar loose in his hand.

"You ever done this before?" Ian asked, his voice low.

Ray did not look up. "Plenty of times. You?"

"Not something this big," Ian admitted.

Ray snorted. "Could've fooled me."

The lock snapped, and the gate creaked open. Ray gestured to the truck. "Back it in. Let's load up."

Frankie climbed back into the cab, reversing the truck into the warehouse. Ian moved to the crates, prying the lid off one with practised ease. Inside were rows of sealed boxes, the markings on the side identifying them as imported electronics.

"Nice haul," Ian said, tossing the lid aside.

"Don't admire it, load it," Ray replied.

They worked quickly, stacking the boxes into the truck bed. Ray kept an eye on the warehouse entrance, his hand never far from the revolver tucked into his waistband.

"You always this tense?" Ian asked, throwing another box into the truck.

"You always this chatty?" Ray shot back.

Ian grinned. "Just saying, you could loosen up a bit. It's not like anyone's gonna show."

As if on cue, the sound of tyres screeching echoed through the night. Ray froze, his head snapping toward the entrance. A car's headlights flooded the street outside the warehouse, and a voice shouted, "Police! Stay where you are!"

"Shit," Frankie muttered, diving into the truck cab.

Ray pulled his revolver, motioning for Ian to move. "Out the back, now!"

Ian did not need to be told twice. He grabbed the crowbar and bolted toward the rear of the building, Ray close behind. The sound of boots hitting the pavement grew louder as the cops entered the warehouse.

"This way," Ray hissed, pushing open a side door.

Ian slipped through, finding himself in a narrow alleyway. The wind was colder here, biting at his face as he scanned the dark for an escape route.

"Up there," Ray said, pointing to a fire escape.

Ian nodded, leaping for the ladder and pulling himself up. Ray followed, his boots clanging against the metal rungs. They climbed to the roof, the sounds of the cops shouting below fading as they disappeared into the night. Over one roof to the next. On the final roof, Ian leaned against the edge, catching his breath. "That was close."

"Too close," Ray muttered, looking out over the docks. His gun holstered, his jaw tight.

"Will Frankie be alright?" Ian asked as he sat against the wall.

"He's a docker. Staunch. Won't talk to the dogs."

Ian chuckled. "Admit it. You liked it."

Ray turned to him, his expression unreadable. "Liked what?"

"The rush. The chase. The fact that we pulled it off."

"We didn't pull it off. We left the truck behind," Ray said.

"Yeah, but we're alive," Ian replied, taking out a packet of gum. He held the pack out to Ray, who hesitated before taking a piece. They sat in silence for a moment, the tension easing as the night stretched on.

"You did good in there," Ray said finally.

Ian raised an eyebrow. "Didn't you think I would?"

Ray shrugged. "Had to see for myself."

Ian grinned, watching his breath fog in the cold air. "Told you I always stay focused."

Ray did not respond, but a faint smile tugged at the corner of his mouth. For the first time, he felt like he was not doing this alone. So started the 'lifelong' partnership between Ray 'Chuck' Bennett and Ian 'Fingers' Carroll.

CHAPTER 7

On the Waterfront

Union Factions

The docks have always been dirty. Not just the grease and grime. They were the lifeblood of cities, bringing in goods and sending them out. That made them a target. Smugglers, thieves, and killers all found their way to the waterfront.

In the USA, the Longshoreman's Union has always been a target for organised crime. In Australia, the union was the organised crime. The Federated Painters and Dockers Union was less about honest work and more about power and profit. Members called themselves Painters and Dockers, but few painted or docked. They joked that a wharfie's wages were eighty quid plus half the cargo. The Victorian Police Commissioner once said 70 per cent of the state's top criminals were tied to the union.

The union had factions, but alliances did not last forever. Melbourne docks were split into two factions, run by Billy Longley and Pat Shannon. Longley's nickname, 'The Texan', fit. He wore a Stetson and carried a Colt .45. An old-fashion criminal, hard and uncompromising. He held on firmly to his working-class roots.[20]

Pat Shannon was a square-jawed man with the easy confidence of someone who knew his worth. His grey suit fit sharp. A green opal ring flashed as he rolled cigarettes from a tin of rum-cured Capstans. Said he made a hundred a week, plus twenty for expenses, but ordered expensive red wine by region and year.

Both were union executives. An uneasy truce existed, but a lot of animosity brewed just under the surface.

"What the fuck was the Ferret doing at Dock 21 yesterday," Tex yelled at Shannon.

"Why, you don't own Dock 21," Pat retaliated just as aggressively.

"It's our turf! Keep your hands off it or I'll chop them off."

Shannon weighed his options. Both of them knew war was bad for business.

"You know Ferret's a fucking dickhead," Shannon finally replied offering an olive branch. "I'll have a word to him. Fair enough?"

"Fair enough," Tex repeated grudgingly. Longley knew the Ferret would not have acted without Shannon's authorisation. Shannon's backpedalling showed he was back in line. Longley didn't need Shannon to admit it. The warning had landed. That was what mattered. [21]

* * *

On the docks, dock workers started early, before sunrise, and finished early. That was so ships could get out through the heads while still daylight. One afternoon, Ray had just picked up his pay and was heading home. Ahead, he saw Freddy "The Frog" loading some boxes onto a trailer behind his car. He had obviously come in to collect his unearned pay and decided to collect some souvenirs as well.

Ray headed over to say hi. The man who taught him ghosting and the way of the docks. His first mentor held a special place in his heart. Before he could talk to him, another guy walked up behind him and called out, "Hey Freddy." Freddy turned to be greeted by a shotgun pointed at his face. "This is yours, Fred!" He pulled the trigger and blew Freddy's face off. Ray stood dumbfounded. Next thing, Ray felt a strong hand grab him on the arm, pulling him back into the shed.

"You weren't there; you didn't see a thing. Got it?" It was Brody. His face almost touching Ray's.

"Freddy?" Ray stammered.

"On the wharves, you hear a gun, you duck first, and then forget everything. Never, never, talk about it. Not to friends, family, and definitely never to the dogs. Do that and you'll stay healthy."

Brody shoved Ray away. "Now beat it."

Ray didn't say a word. He just nodded and walked.[22]

* * *

Ray stood outside the Rising Sun Hotel. He had been sent to help a newbie, Laurie, who was meeting a union man who had not paid his dues. Laurie had been working the man for a week, but nothing had come of it.

"Let me handle this," Ray said.

Laurie hesitated. "This one's slippery. Talks a big game but never delivers."

Ray nodded. "I know his type."

Inside, the union man sat at a corner table, nursing a beer. Ray walked straight to him, pulling out the chair across from him.

"Morning," Ray said staring straight at him.

The man did not look up. "Who the fuck are you supposed to be?"

"I'm the man who makes sure people like you don't forget their obligations," Ray replied.

The man looked up and smirked. "And if I do?"

Ray leaned in. "Then I make sure you never have to worry about obligations ever again."

The man laughed, but it was a nervous laugh. Ray's eyes did not waver.

"Fine," the man said, pulling out a wad of cash. "Here's your bloody dues."

Ray took what was owed and a bit extra for his time. He stood and dropped the rest back on the table. "Pleasure doing business."

Outside, Laurie grinned. "You didn't even touch him."

"Break an arm or leg and he can't work for six weeks. Six weeks, we don't get dues." Ray smirked. "Hurt a man and he'll remember. Promise to hurt him, and he'll remember longer."

* * *

The following morning, after handing in his collections, Ray went for a walk. He was not one to sit around the office getting fat and lazy. He leaned against a stack of crates that day, watching the kid from the night before. The kid was unloading cargo, joking with the men around him. One of them, a big bastard named Steele, was not laughing.

"You talk too fucking much, kid," Steele growled, stepping closer to Laurie.

Laurie did not back down. "Maybe you don't talk enough. Want me to teach you?"

Steele's face darkened, and he hit Laurie hard, sending him stumbling back against a crate. The men around them stopped working, watching to see what the new kid would do.

Ray figured Laurie would fold. Most did. Steele was twice his size and mean as hell.

But, regaining his balance, Laurie stepped forward. He wiped the blood from the corner of his mouth with the back of his hand. "That all you got?" he asked, grinning through his split lip.

The men laughed nervously. Steele didn't. He swung a fist, but Laurie ducked it, quick as a cat, and drove his shoulder into Steele's gut. The big man staggered, and Laurie followed up with a big left hook that cracked against his jaw. Steele hit the ground, stunned. He hadn't been prepared. Underestimated the kid.

Ray remembered standing there, mouth open, watching the kid wipe his bloody hands on his pants. Laurie wasn't just scrappy. He had something in him: a fire, an edge that set him apart.

Tex walked up beside Ray, shaking his head. "Damn kid's gonna get himself killed," he muttered.

"Maybe," Ray said, watching Laurie. "But not today."

* * *

Ian's official job on the docks was Ship's Rigger. The work was brutal and unforgiving. They loaded and unloaded cargo from a ship's hold. No containers, just sweat and muscle. Men risked their lives for their pay.

One afternoon, smoko time coming, Ian decided to take the fast way down. The crane groaned, raising a pallet load out of the ship's hold. Ian grinned and leapt onto the load, balancing on top like it was a carnival ride.

"Careful there, kiddo," called Paddy, the dogman, his voice sharp with an Irish lilt. Paddy stood in the centre of the load, one hand gripping the sling. An old-timer, steady as they came, Paddy shook his head.

Ian didn't care. The wind hit his face as the load rose high above the ship's superstructure. He looked out over the dock and the cityscape beyond. For a second, he forgot the noise, the rules, the danger. Felt free.

Then the load jerked, as it was swung back over the docks.

Ian's footing went out from under him. Before he could react, he was sliding off the edge. His hands flailed in an attempt to grab anything. His legs went over the edge, then nothing. His stomach dropped as he fell towards the hard concrete dock thirty metres below.

Suddenly, he felt a strong hand clamp onto his arm like a vice. Ian's other hand shot out instinctively, grabbing back. His heart slammed in his chest.

"Not a smart move," Paddy muttered. His grip was firm, his face calm. He hauled Ian back onto the load with a strength that came from years on the docks. Paddy had kept an eye on Ian, knowing of the pending change in direction. At the jerk, he knew Ian was a goner. In a single movement, he wrapped his foot around the sling and threw himself, not at Ian, but where he anticipated Ian would go off. He landed at the same time Ian's head disappeared.

"Thanks, Paddy," Ian managed, his voice barely more than a whisper.

Paddy didn't reply, just steadied the load as they continued down onto the dock. Ian shifted to the centre, closer to Paddy, his heart still pounding.

When they reached the dock, Ian jumped off, feet hitting solid ground with a thud.

"Fucking dickhead," Brody's voice rang out from behind.

Ian didn't turn around. Just kept walking, his legs unsteady beneath him. He was alive. That, he owed to Paddy.

* * *

Ray and Ian's "union work" established them well on the docks. Both commanded respect and authority over the general workforce. However, by nineteen, Ray and Ian's paths started to diverge. Ian gravitated to Shannon. Ray chose Longley.

Although Longley had Brian Kane, another boxer from Leo's stable, Kane was a very blunt instrument. Longley preferred to use Ray for more delicate matters. Ray thought on his feet and got results without resorting to bloodshed. Normally, that worked out better financially. Blood was expensive.

* * *

Ian, on the other hand, was now working directly for Pat Shannon. This opened more doors, more opportunities, more respect. Tasks ran from riding shotgun on Shannon's out-and-abouts, to 'debt' collection. He had proven himself on both accounts. He liked Shannon because he was a man with a plan. Ian was happy to ride the whirlwind and enjoy the spoils. Shannon liked Ian because there was no moral ambiguity there. To Ian, you owe, you pay. Simple. He lived by the code. The man could be trusted. A loyal knight.

But even the best knights sometimes stumble. For Ian, it was the time he had to collect 'contributions' from one of the few old-timers still working on the docks. The rule was a percentage of any job done on the docks went to the house. Everyone knew it. It was the tax for doing business. If not, Ian would visit. But sometimes …

* * *

Ian leaned forward in the wooden chair, the weight of his .38 heavy against his ribs. The room smelled of stale beer and sweat, the remnants of a long night at the Rising Sun. Across the table sat a man, vaguely familiar, but whose name Ian had not bothered to learn. Slumped over, his face a bloodied mess.

"Tell me again," Ian said, his voice low, measured.

The man groaned, spitting a tooth onto the table. "I don't know… I swear… I don't know…"

Ian glanced at Frankie, standing by the door. Frankie shrugged, a smirk playing at the corner of his lips.

"He's lying," Frankie said. "Always the same story. 'I don't know.'"

Ian nodded. He knew the man was lying. The missing money did not just disappear, and the boss did not send Ian after ghosts. This man had it, or he knew who did.

Ian reached for the beer bottle on the table, swirling the dregs before downing them in one gulp. Then he leaned close enough that the man could read the faded tattoos on his knuckles.

"You've got one more chance," Ian said. "After that, it's not my problem anymore."

The man dropped his eyes. His mouth moved, but no words came. Then, "I… I needed it… My wife, she—"

Ian slammed the bottle down, and the man flinched.

"I don't care about your wife," Ian snapped. "Where's the fucking money?"

Tears streamed down the man's face, mixing with the blood. "It's gone… Spent it… Hospital bills…"

The words hit Ian harder than he had expected. Hospital bills. He thought of his wife Raelene, the nights she had spent crying over him, over the risks he took. He thought of the promises he had made, to her, to himself, that he would make something of this life.

Then suddenly it hit him like a brick in the back of the head. Paddy. The moment replayed in his head. An arm reaching out to save him from a 30-metre fall, and Paddy's face looking down at him.

Ian stood, shoving the chair back with a scrape that echoed in the room. Frankie raised an eyebrow.

"Let him go," Ian said.

"What?" Frankie stepped forward. "The boss won't like it."

"Let him go," Ian repeated.

The man looked up, his face a mix of relief and confusion.

"You don't get off free," Ian said, glaring at him. "You'll pay it back. Every cent. And if you don't, I'll find you. Understand?"

The man nodded quickly, too quickly, scrambling to his feet and stumbling toward the door. Frankie stepped aside, shaking his head.

When the room was empty, Frankie turned to Ian. "You going soft, Fingers?"

Ian did not answer right away. He walked to the window, looking out at the faint glow of the docks in the distance.

"Maybe," Ian said finally.

Frankie laughed, lighting a cigarette. "Good luck explaining that to Shannon."

Ian didn't respond. He watched the lights flicker in the distance, the shadows stretching longer as dawn approached. He didn't know if he'd regret it. But the tightness in his shoulders had eased.

He rolled his neck side to side, swung on his coat, and walked out, his gait a little longer.

CHAPTER 8

A Criminal Life

A Calling for Armed Robbery

In addition to his extracurricular income, Ian focused on union activities. Climbing higher, carving his place with steel and resolve. Ray, though, wanted more. Armed robbery called to him; the thrill of it, the precision, the money. He had a knack for the preparation, for seeing the whole picture before the first step was taken.

'Tex' Longley saw it too. A senior figure in the union, Tex, took Ray under his wing. Ray worked as security for Tex, enforcing union deals with steady hands and a hard gaze. In return, Tex brought him into the bigger jobs. Robberies that required more than muscle, that demanded planning, patience, and the ability to walk away clean.

Tex's approach was simple: *Overwhelming Force*. "Come in hard and loud, with big weapons. Make sure they're looking at the gun, not you. And like poker, a fast game's a good game. Get in and out fast, less room for error."

"Always know the exits," Tex told Ray. "And never trust a man who smiles too much."

Ray listened. He learned. Unfortunately, Tex did not practise what he preached.

The van stopped hard behind the post office. Tex cut the engine and turned to the crew. His eyes were sharp, but his face was loose, cocky. Ray sat in the back with the others. He did not like them. They were not ready. Scar had been drinking. Lenny could not stop sweating.

"This one's easy," Tex said. "Five minutes. In and out. Don't make it harder than it is."

Scar laughed, loud and grating. "Five minutes?" he mimicked. "Whatever," dismissing Tex's instruction under his breath.

Ray did not say anything. He had spent a week watching this place. The money did not come in until later. He had told Tex, but Tex waved him off. "I know what I'm doing, kid," he had said. Ray kept his mouth shut after that.

"Everyone clear?" Tex said. His hand rested on the wheel, calm like he was not about to pull a job. "Scar, Lenny, you handle the front. Me and Ray will take the office. Let's move."

Scar pulled a pump-action shotgun from under his coat. "Don't worry, boss. I'll make sure they remember me," as he cocked the pump action. "chk-chk". An unexpended round flew out of the chamber and rattled onto the van floor.

"Fucking clown," Ray said, shaking his head. "You've been watching too many movies." These men were loud, sloppy. He looked at Tex. Tex grinned, then opened his door.

Ray pulled down his balaclava. Lenny laughed, "What's that for? You checked it out, there's no cameras!" Lenny and Scar jumped out of the van.

Ray followed. They moved fast, cutting through the side door. The place had the musty odour of old paper and ink, and the hum and clattering of an office going about its business. A clerk behind the counter looked up, confused.

Scar shoved the shotgun in her face. "On the fucking ground!" The clerk dropped, hands over her head.

Ray swept his eyes over the room. No cameras on this side. Two more clerks were behind the counter, staring at them. One was a kid, maybe twenty, pale as a ghost. Scar had his attention now. He waved the shotgun like it was part of the show.

Tex leaned toward Ray. "You, with me," he whispered. They moved toward the back office. The door was locked. Tex did not hesitate. He kicked it open and stormed inside. The manager, a balding man with round glasses, stumbled back, his hands in the air.

"Open the safe," Tex growled.

The manager fumbled with a set of keys, his hands trembling. Ray glanced at the safe. It was not big enough. He knew the timing here. The real haul didn't come in until later. This was a waste.

Tex noticed him staring. "What's the problem?"

"The money's not here," Ray said, low. "It comes later. This is nothing."

Tex narrowed his eyes. "You think I don't know what I'm doing?"

Ray didn't answer. He turned toward the front. Scar was still mouthing off as Lenny stuffed the teller's cash into a duffle bag. The kid clerk was crying now, his face pressed to the floor. This was getting messy.

The open safe contained bundles of low-denomination notes.

"What did I tell you?" scoffed Tex. He grabbed Ray's arm. "Stick to the plan."

Ray pulled free. He did not say anything, but his stomach turned. He heard the sound of money being pulled out. It was not enough. Not for this risk.

Tex came out with the bag. "Let's move."

Scar fired a shot into the ceiling. BOOM. "Nobody fucking move!" he screamed.

"Jesus Christ," Ray muttered. He grabbed Scar by the arm and yanked him toward the door. "What the hell are you doing?"

"Just keeping things lively," Scar said, grinning like an idiot.

Ray shoved him out the door. "It's come in loud, not go out loud!" Ray said to the back of his head as they piled into the van. Tex floored it, tyres screeching as they hit the street. The sound of sirens followed.

"You told me this would be clean," Ray said, his voice cold.

Tex glanced at him in the rear-view mirror. "It is."

"No, it's not," Ray snapped. "We weren't ready. The money wasn't there. Scar nearly blew the whole thing."

Scar laughed again, leaning back in his seat. "Relax, kid. We got what we came for."

Ray turned to him, his eyes hard. "You think this is funny? You're a liability."

"All right, enough," Tex barked. He pulled the van into an alley and killed the engine. He turned in his seat, his face inches from Ray's. "Listen here, kid. You're smart, I'll give you that. But you don't know shit from clay about how things work."

"I know you're running a clown show," Ray said. His voice did not rise, but the words cut. "You don't plan. No recon. You don't know when the money comes in. You think you just walk in and grab it."

Tex's jaw tightened. "You don't like it? Fine. Go do it your way. See how far you get. Otherwise, shut the fuck up!"

Ray stared back, unflinching.

Tex didn't say another word. Just lit a cigarette and stared through the windscreen. "Get out," he said. "All of you."

Lenny and Scar dispersed, disappearing into the alleyways of the city. Ray stayed behind. He watched Tex for a moment, the older man sitting in the driver's seat, smoking like he didn't have a care in the world.

Ray turned, lifted the collar on his coat, and walked away. Tex's way was not his way. He had learned enough that day. Enough to know what not to do.

* * *

MSS Robbery

Ray took Tex's advice, even if it had not been meant that way. He could do it better. Job ideas were always abundant on the waterfront. Lots of guys had lots of ideas, but either no guts or not the brains to pull them off. Ray had both, and everyone could see that. So when Creasy approached him about a job he had, Ray knew this was his opportunity. The job was the robbery of the armoured car company, MSS.

First, he needed a crew he could trust. Ian was his first thought. The new young kid Laurie, could be worth blooding as well. He liked him. His humour masked an inner strength. Creasy was the weak link, but that could be managed.

He found Ian after work, propped at the bar in the Waterside Hotel.

"Interested in a step up?" he put to Ian.

"Always" came the standard reply. Ian left his beer on the bar, and they adjourned to Ray's car.

"Creasy's got an in at an MSS depot. Their cars are tight, but their weak link is the depot the night before deliveries."

Unlike Tex, this would be all in the planning. Tight and clean.

"He has someone on the inside. Been learning every detail for six weeks."

"But Creasy, for fuck's sake" Ian replied. "He won't hold his bottle when the dogs start sniffing. He's a major liability."

"Don't you worry about that. Every problem has a solution. Are you in?" Ray countered.

"Always," Ian replied. After all, it was Ray.

The following week, Ray and Ian broke into an empty MSS van in Camberwell, loaded with about 100 keys. Two nights later, they hit the East Melbourne Police Station. They stole a uniform cap and coat, no fuss.

At 2 AM, Thursday morning, the standard payday of factories, they made their move. The security guard at MSS buzzed the intercom. "Who's there?"

"Police," said the man in uniform. "Returning your stolen keys."

The guard buzzed them in, none the wiser. He opened the internal door and headed back to his desk as the two policemen let themselves in. All he noticed was that one was a young constable, the other in a cheap suit, a detective, with his hands in his pockets. Both wore side arms. "Here's the lot," the constable said, dropping the keys onto the counter so they slipped to the floor.

The guard bent to pick them up. That's when the gun came out. It pressed hard into the back of his head. "Down," the detective snarled. With that, another two men entered through the door left unlatched. Wearing overalls and balaclavas, one carried bolt cutters and the other a duffle bag.

They zip-tied the guard's hands and feet and shoved a pillowcase over his head. "Cooperate, and you get to go home tonight," the fake detective continued, calm as the night outside. The heavy-duty bolt cutters snapped open the wire cage lock and subsequent cashboxes. They emptied it clean. The final count: $289,233. By the time the guard worked the pillowcase off, they were gone. [23]

In the car, Ray drove. Laurie sat next to him, removing the police jacket and cap. Ian sat in the back in a crumpled suit, eyes on Creasy who was sweating profusely. Ian shook his head. Suddenly, Ray pulled up outside a dim sim factory.

"What are we doing here?" asked Creasy, confused.

"We have to give Normie his cut," Ray said.

"Why, what's he done?"

"My job, my rules. Grab one of the sacks and bring it with you." With that, Ray got out of the car and strode into the factory. Creasy grabbed one sack and chased after him. Inside, he found Ray standing at the side of a big mincing machine and Normie at the other end. Normie seemed out of place in white overalls, rubber gloves, and knee-high rubber boots.

"Give Normie the bag," Ray commanded.

"I still don't understand what he did for it," Creasy complained as he crossed the floor and handed Normie the sack. Normie turned and put it on a shelf behind him. Creasy was so confused that he had not noticed Ian following them into the factory. Nor did he notice him raising his gun. Ian fired point-blank. One shot. Creasy's body crumpled. The second shot was not needed, but rules are rules. With that, Ian and Ray turned and left the building.

"Told you," Ray mused as they walked to the car. "Every problem has a solution."

"I certainly won't be eating dim sims for a while!" Ian added.[24]

CHAPTER 9

Painter and Docker Wives

The second rule of the Painters and Dockers was simple: work was work, and home was home. Never mix the two. No plans, no job discussions, no contraband under the floorboards. Home was a sanctuary. At home, men like Ray Bennett and Ian Carroll were gentle and attentive. Loving, even. Jekyll and Hyde. On the docks, they were hard bastards, but they also developed the sense of humour and bravado necessary to survive in a hostile world. Women found it irresistible.

It took strong women to marry men like them. Even legitimate dock work came with odd hours and dangerous days. These women, often upper-class and professional, were drawn to the charm and confidence their men exuded. They rarely knew what they were getting into. If they did, they never spoke of it. That was the unspoken pact: *don't ask, don't know*.

* * *

Ian met Raelene at her work. He was there to organise the purchase of a warehouse factory he had just bought near the docks.

Raelene was a legal secretary, her desk piled with contracts and conveyancing papers. She barely noticed the young man who emerged from the conference room. His blue and white striped bell-bottom trousers and pale silk shirt made him look more ready for a disco than a law office.

He had noticed her on his way into the conference room. It was his first major property purchase. She was a stunning brunette with green eyes. Athletic and well-proportioned. She had made his heart beat a little faster. Not something he had experienced before. Maybe a year or two older than his chronological age, but the docks made a man look and feel older. He had asked Joe, his lawyer, if she was attached. He didn't believe so. Once he concluded his business with Joe, he decided to take a detour past her desk.

"Hi, beautiful," he said. "What's your name?"

Rae looked up, startled. His smile disarming, his eyes warm and mischievous. "Raelene, …, Rae," she replied.

"Where can I get a decent coffee around here?"

"Mancini's, around the corner," she stammered, her voice betraying her nerves.

"Hi, I'm Ian," he said, holding out his hand. "Can you show me?"

"I can't—" she began.

"You get a coffee break, don't you?" he interrupted.

"Joe, mind if Rae takes a break?" Ian called back toward the conference room. Before she could argue, Ian took her hand and led her out the door.

At Mancini's, the coffee break turned into an hour. They talked. About Rae's work, her family, her horses. Ian listened, joked, and asked questions. He didn't talk about himself much, just enough to say he was seeing her boss as he was buying a factory near the docks, for his distribution business.

That weekend, Ian took Rae to the beach. She wore a new polka-dot bikini, bought just for the occasion. Ian could not take his eyes off her. He opened doors, held her chair. Over dinner, she summoned the courage to ask about the tattoos on his knuckles.

"LOVE" and "HATE" stared back at her.

"Grew up in a boys' home," Ian said casually. "Didn't get along with my mother's new fella. Fell in with a bad crowd; got drunk one night and woke up with these; a bad joke."

Rae's face fell.

"Boxing straightened me out," he added quickly. "Met a guy starting an import business, changed my life. Now I'm doing the same. Used car parts from the States. Cheap there, good margins here."

Rae relaxed. Ian smiled. She was hooked.

* * *

Ray met Gail more traditionally, or as traditionally as a Painter and Docker could.

Ian and Ray had just finished a job. Pulling off his balaclava, Ray grinned. "Easy as pie. What did I tell you?"

Ian, Vinnie, and Laurie laughed as they transferred duffle bags from the job car to their own vehicles.

"Nice place, Ian," Laurie said, gesturing to the empty warehouse. "Quiet, no eyes, perfect."

Ray ignored him. "Vinnie, take care of the car," he ordered. Then to Ian: "Normie and I are hitting the Underground tonight. Coming?"

Ian shook his head. "Got a date."

Ray just rolled his eyes.

* * *

The Underground was crowded that night. Music pounded through the upmarket nightclub as Ray approached two women. One was striking, a bobbed blonde with sharp eyes and an easy smile. The other brunette, younger, looked like she was trying too hard to fit in.

"Hi, girls," Ray said, stepping between them and the sleaze they were talking to.

"Oy!" the man grunted.

Ray did not bother turning around. "Beat it. You're not wanted."

The man hesitated, then disappeared into the crowd.

"Thank you," mouthed the bobbed blonde. "I'm Gail, and this is my sister, Helen."

Helen looked barely old enough to be in the club, but no one checked IDs at the Underground. Especially if you were cute.

"This is Normie," Ray said, nodding to his wingman. Normie took the cue, moving to Helen's side.

Gail said she was a teacher and Helen a trainee nurse. Ray did not catch much else over the thumping music, except for her number. They danced, drank, and laughed until Gail called it a night.

The next evening, Ray took her to Vlado's, Melbourne's famous steakhouse. Vlado was the arrogant chef and owner. Open at five, closed at nine; throwing out any diners who thought they could linger. The menu was steak or steak; maybe a sausage for an appetiser. A man cave.

"Ray!" Vlado greeted him at the door. "My best table for my favourite customer!"

Gail arched an eyebrow as they were led to a corner table.

"Come here often?" she teased.

"Everyone's his favourite customer," Ray said with a grin.

Gail ordered steak, medium rare, and drank red wine. She flirted with Vlado, and Ray found himself captivated. She was sharp, witty, and completely at ease. Ray's line of business involved a lot of time waiting. Waiting for the boss, for a ship, or in a cell. He filled it with reading. Ray had become an avid reader, for which, until now, he had no outlet. With Gail, he found that outlet; they talked. Books, history, places he had never seen. For the first time in years, Ray felt more than a man with a gun and a plan.

At nine, Vlado came by their table. "Mind if we close up? The wife and kids are waiting."

Gail laughed. Ray was stunned. Vlado had never been civil before.

So began their whirlwind romance.

* * *

Marriage changed things for the boys. But not too much. Ray and Gail, and Ian and Rae started spending weekends together. Dinners, theatre, footy games. Gail and Rae fit seamlessly into Ray and Ian's world, unaware of the real world in which they dwelt.

For a while, life felt normal. Gail and Rae introduced Ray and Ian to the finer things: gallery openings and classical music. Ray and Ian brought them into their world: barbecues, races, and occasional poker nights.

By the time Ray was twenty-one, he and Gail had a son, Danny. Ian and Rae had a daughter, and plans for another.

For a time, Ray dreamed of leaving the docks behind. Of starting afresh. But he knew better. The docks never let go.

* * *

The knock on the door came late one night. Gail answered, her heart sinking at the sight of the two men in cheap suits on the step.

"Mrs. Chuck?"

"Yes," she said, her voice shaking.

"We need to speak with your husband," one said, holding his warrant card out at head height.

Ray appeared behind her. "Evening, officers."

They didn't bother with pleasantries.

"Just a few questions, Chuck," one of them said. "Can we come in?"

"No," came Ray's firm reply. He stepped outside, closing the door behind him.

* * *

Gail poured two cups of tea, visibly shaken. Raelene sat across from her, composed. Her eyes betrayed the concern she felt. The house was quiet, the men had already left for the day, and the children were playing in the living room.

"I didn't sleep," Gail admitted, stirring her tea without purpose.

Rae nodded. "I wouldn't expect you to, after that visit."

"They didn't even explain why they were here," Gail continued. "Just questioned Ray outside for half an hour and left. No arrest, no charges. But it's clear they know him. Rae, I feel like I'm drowning. What's going on?"

Rae took a sip of her tea. "You're not alone, Gail. You know that, right? We've both married men with secrets. After a while, you stop trying to understand it. You just ... decide what you're willing to live with."

"How?" Gail asked, her voice breaking. "How can you just...accept it? Don't you ever wonder what Ian's really involved in? What he's doing?"

Rae placed her cup down gently. "Of course, I wonder. But what good would it do? Ian's not the type to explain himself, and I'm not going to waste my breath asking questions he won't answer."

"But we have children, Rae. What if something happens? What if one day they don't come home?" Gail's eyes filled with tears.

Rae reached across the table and placed her hand on Gail's. "I'm not saying it's easy. I've thought about walking away. But Ian isn't just my husband; he's my life. He's a good father, and he keeps us safe. That's what I focus on. The rest...I let it stay outside. You'll drive yourself mad trying to figure out everything they don't tell us."

Gail looked at Rae, searching for strength in her calmness. "I don't know how to smile at Danny when everything in me's screaming. I can't live like that?"

Grabbing both Gail's hands, Rae said, "You're stronger than you think, Gail. We'll figure it out. Together."

* * *

That night, Ray walked through the door, his jacket slung over his shoulder, looking tired but unbothered. Gail stood in the kitchen, arms crossed, waiting.

"Evening, love," Ray greeted her, but the tension in the room stopped him.

"Sit down," Gail said, her voice firm.

Ray raised an eyebrow but complied, pulling out a chair at the kitchen table, hanging his jacket over the back. "What's this about?"

Gail placed her hands on the table, leaning toward him. "The police. Last night, Ray— they're not just asking you questions; they're watching us! I can't keep pretending that I don't know why."

Ray sighed, stood, and took a step towards her. "They're fishing, Gail. They've got nothing."

"Don't do that," she snapped, pushing him away. "Don't brush me off like I'm some idiot. I've pretended. I've looked the other way. I'm not stupid. I deserve to know what's going on."

Ray rubbed his face, silent for a moment. "It's better you don't know."

"No, Ray. It's not better. Not anymore. We have a son. You need to tell me what kind of life you're dragging us into."

Ray pushed his chair back under the table, scraping against the floor. "You think I want this life? You think I enjoy looking over my shoulder? I do what I do to keep us afloat, Gail. To keep you and Danny safe."

"Safe?" Gail's voice rose. "How is this safe? How is having the police at our door safe? How is Danny growing up without knowing who his father really is, safe?"

Ray's voice dropped, cold and sharp. "This is who I am. I am still the same man you married. Now, you can either trust me to handle it, or you can leave. But I won't have this discussion again."

* * *

Ian sat in the living room, bouncing their daughter on his knee, making silly baby noises. Raelene walked in and stopped in front of him, waiting.

"We need to talk," she said.

He saw her face and paused. "Hang on."

He stood, carried their daughter to her room, laid her in the crib, and kissed her forehead. Then he closed the door, came back, and sat down.

"What's up?" he said.

"It's about what you're involved in," Rae said, her voice steady. "The police are coming around, Ian. I haven't said anything, but I'm not silly. I need to know."

Ian sat back. "No, you don't."

"Don't dismiss me like that," Rae snapped.

Ian leaned forward, his elbows on his knees. "What do you want me to say? That I'm a saint? That the dogs are wasting their time? You want the truth? Fine. The truth is, you don't want to know the truth."

Rae crossed her arms. "I deserve to know what risks you're taking with our family."

Ian stood, looking coldly into her eyes. "I'm taking the risks so you don't have to. That's the deal. You don't get to question it."

"Maybe I do," Rae countered, her voice rising.

Ian's tone turned icy. "If you want out, say it. Otherwise, drop it."

Rae glared at him, her jaw tight, her eyes flashing. In the end, she turned and walked out of the room, slamming the door behind her.

* * *

As the midday sun beat down, Gail and Raelene sat on the porch swing in Gail's backyard. Danny and Raelene's daughter playing in the sandpit. The children's laughter masked their conversation.

"I tried talking to Ray," Gail said, her voice quiet.

Raelene nodded. "I talked to Ian. Didn't get far."

Gail let out a bitter laugh. "Ray told me it's the docks. Said they don't let go."

"That's the truth," Raelene said. "They're in too deep. I've known that for a while."

Gail looked at Raelene. "How do you live with it?"

"I focus on what I can control," Raelene said. "My daughter. The house. Making sure Ian has something to come home to. It's not perfect, but it works."

Gail shook her head. "I don't know if that's enough for me."

Raelene placed her hand on Gail's. "It doesn't have to be perfect, Gail. It just has to work. And you're not alone in this. We have each other."

Gail gave a small, tired smile, touching heads; a silent, *thank you, Rae.*

The two women sat in silence, watching their children play. For the first time in weeks, Gail felt a sliver of hope.

They would figure it out. Together.

* * *

From then on, everything changed. Gail and Raelene learned the truth in bits and pieces: the police visits, the whispers, the late nights. The illusion of separation between work and home no longer existed.

CHAPTER 10

The Dirty Blue Line

It was said that Victoria had the best police force money could buy. The most lucrative branches were the Armed Robbery and Consorting squads. They were closed shops, heavily guarded by their respective senior management. Newbies needed references from existing or previous members to get in. Although lucrative, it was dangerous work. They did have to handle the toughest nuts in the underworld, meaning they had to be as hard, if not harder. Some in the underworld had no qualms about taking out a cop. Consorting dealt with known underworld figures, tracking and assisting the Armed Robbery squad when dealing with known criminals, which was most of the time.

The Consorting Squad "dogs" were dirty. More bent than the run-of-the-mill coppers, these dogs were a law unto themselves. Best avoided if possible. They did not ask questions; they took bribes and threw punches. All Painters and Dockers were fair game to them. [25]

* * *

Brian "Skull" Murphy

It didn't take long for the cops to start looking at Ray for the MSS job. The Consorting Squad and the Armed Robbery boys were sniffing around. Dirty as they came, "Skull" Murphy led the charge. The usual game: tear up the place, terrorise the family, squeeze out a cut of the take. It was never about evidence; they knew professional crims never kept incriminating evidence in their house. It was about intimidation.

They hit Ray's house when he was out. Murphy and his crew smashed drawers, flipped furniture, leaving chaos in their wake. Gail stood frozen. Murphy sauntered into the bedroom and scooped up Ray and Gail's twelve-month-old son.

"Catch," he barked, throwing the boy to Gail.

She caught him. Clutching the boy, eyes wide, she screamed, "Get out!" Her voice cracked as she backed against the wall. "You don't touch my son!"

The yelling spilled into the street. Neighbours stepped onto porches, watching. Murphy smirked, satisfied. "Message delivered," he muttered to his crew. They left the house torn apart, Gail shaking with rage and fear.

* * *

That night, when Ray came home, Gail told him everything. Her words tumbled out, broken by sobs. When she got to the part about Murphy throwing Danny, Ray's face went dark. He stood without a word, picked up the phone and called Laurie.

"I'm finding Murphy," Ray said, voice like stone.

He tracked Murphy to a pizza joint in West Melbourne. Murphy was leaning against a car outside, chewing on a slice. Ray's car screeched to a stop. He got out, slamming the door hard enough to get Murphy's attention.

"You came to my house," Ray growled, closing the distance between them. "You crossed the line. You touched my family."

Murphy put on a smirk, but his eyes darted, searching for an escape. "You've got it wrong, Chuck. I did no such thing."

Ray turned, went back, popped the boot of his car, and pulled out a shotgun. "You're nothing but a cunt," he said.

Murphy froze.

"You think this is a game?" Ray shouted, raising the barrel.

Before he could do it, a group of young workers came around the corner, laughing, oblivious. Ray paused, the fury in him boiling over. He cursed under his breath, lowered the gun and tossed it back into the boot.

"This isn't over," he said, "You're a fucking dead man. Mark my words."

"Yeah, well, start it now," was Murphy's blunt reply, secure that he now had an audience.

"No. When I'm ready, Murphy. Not before." Ray stepped close enough for Murphy to feel the heat of his breath. "At the time of my making, at a place I choose, I'm going to blow your fucking head off."

Ray got in his car and drove off. Murphy stood there, sweating, the slice of pizza forgotten in his hand. [26]

* * *

Ray pulled up outside Laurie's house. Laurie opened the door and stepped out. He turned back to look at Ray. "Thanks for the ride."

Ray nodded. "Get some rest."

Laurie hesitated, then grinned. "You ever think Murphy's got a death wish?"

Ray smirked. "If he doesn't, he's doing a good impression."

Laurie laughed, then shut the door. Ray watched him go in and waited till the light went out. Laurie had done good tonight, hadn't flinched when he pulled the shotgun on Murphy.

He thought back to when he first noticed Laurie wasn't just another loudmouth kid on the docks. Fresh-faced, quick with a joke, and quicker with a comeback. Too quick, Ray thought at the time. Thought a kid like that wouldn't last long in their world. He'd been wrong.

Ray pulled out into the street. It was quiet, but not the quiet that gives any solace.

The kid had something in him. Ray saw it that first week on the docks. And he'd seen it tonight.

His stomach unclenched.

In their world, that was enough.

* * *

Death of Neil Collingburn

Ian Carroll also learned how far these cops would go. He and Neil Collingburn, a fellow Docker, were pulled over by the Consorting Squad late one afternoon.

"Out of the car," said the bald detective. The blue light from the unmarked car flashed against the street. "You too, Fingers."

Ian stepped out of the passenger side. Stillman grabbed his arm, spun him and slammed him against the car.

"What the—" Ian started, but Stillman cuffed him and pressed him down on the bonnet. Neil was already pinned, facing him on the other side.

"Possession of stolen goods," Murphy said, nodding at Neil's golf clubs on the back seat.

"They're mine!" Neil shouted.

Ian gave a small shake of his head. *The code. Don't talk. Don't give them anything.* He knew it wasn't about stolen goods. It was a shakedown. Neil didn't know any better. He wasn't built for this life. Quieter. Softer. Ian had taken him under his wing, trying to toughen him up or push him to quit.

"You're coming to Russell Street," Murphy said, ignoring Neil.

They were bundled into the back of a divvy van. Neither spoke. The cops had orders to rattle Neil, to squeeze him for information about his older brother Keith. Keith would become one of Australia's biggest drug dealers, but that was well into the future.

At Russell Street Police Headquarters, they were processed and separated. Ian knew what was coming. Neil did not.

Murphy took Ian, Stillman took Neil.

"These pricks don't talk," Murphy informed the younger Stillman before separating. "They wouldn't tell you the time if they had a watch on every finger."

"I'll get him to talk," said Stillman, tapping the truncheon hanging from his hip. "Me and my trusty 'billy club'."

"Yellow Pages works better, and doesn't leave marks," Murphy advised. Stillman was not listening.

* * *

Ian sat cuffed to a chair in the 'interview' room, back to the door. Bare, except for a small table and another chair. Concrete floor. Green walls. No one-way mirrors. Just emptiness.

The door opened behind him. Footsteps. No warning.

Whack.

The chair tipped, and Ian flew across the room and hit the wall, hard. He saw stars. The chair followed, crashing into him.

Murphy stood over him, holding a thick phone book, smiling. "Oops," he said.

Ian pulled himself up. He repositioned the chair against the wall and sat down, facing Murphy.

"Guess you don't know where Keith is?" Murphy asked, stepping closer, grinning.

Ian stayed quiet.

Murphy kicked the chair from under him as he brought the phone book down in a full swing. Whack. Ian hit the side wall.

Murphy moved in, landing a kick to Ian's ribs. Ian stayed down, coughing, waiting. He got up slowly, dragging the chair with him. Sitting. Taking his time, pacing himself. This was going to take a while.

And it did. Question. Whack. Wall. Kick. Repeat. Murphy took his time. Ian didn't break. By the time the chair was upright again, he'd stopped hoping it would be over soon.

When Murphy finally tired and left the room, Ian was slumped on the floor, unconscious.

Sometime later, Murphy returned. Ian was back in the chair, face bloody and swollen, his eyes barely open. He looked like he had gone fifteen rounds with Mohammed Ali. Ian braced himself for the next round as Murphy approached. However, Murphy unlocked the cuffs and dragged Ian to his feet. He led him into the next room.

Neil was on the floor, not moving. Stillman grabbed Neil and threw him into a chair. He smiled at Murphy, then swung his truncheon down on Neil's head. Neil crumpled back onto the floor.

"What was that?" Stillman mockingly asked. Nothing. He kicked Neil's head like a football.

Ian snapped. He broke free of Murphy, charging across the room. His shoulder slammed into Stillman, driving him into the wall. Ian grabbed Stillman's head and smashed it against the concrete.

Then came the crack at the back of Ian's skull. Murphy. Ian's knees folded. Murphy's arm slid around Ian's neck into a chokehold.

Everything went black.

* * *

By 10 PM, they were both in St. Vincent's Hospital. Ian was alive. Cracked ribs and a fractured skull. Neil was not that lucky.

"What happened to him?" asked the physician attending Neil. The patient was bloodied and bruised all over. Both eyes swollen, one totally closed. His main concern was the swelling in his abdomen.

"Fell off a chair," came the smug reply. The doctor noted the name on the accompanying constable's name tag: C. Stillman. He also noted the lack of visible injuries to the officer.

"Where?" enquired the doctor in disbelief.

"Russell Street," came the reply. "He attacked me while being questioned," said Stillman, finally realising this would be on the record.

"You should've brought him in hours ago!" the doctor snapped, waving the orderly over. "He's septic. He can't even walk."

"Said he was fine," Stillman replied, not looking up.

The orderly wheeled Collingburn off to theatre.

* * *

The next day, Murphy got the call. Collingburn was dead. He called Stillman to come in.

When Stillman arrived, Murphy met him out in the hall.

90

"How do you think we'll go on this one?" Stillman asked.

"Don't worry," Murphy replied. "We'll get out of this for sure."

"How?"

"We just need to get some photos of your injuries."

"What injuries?"

WHACK. Murphy hit Stillman with a straight right. Cracked a tooth, cut the lip.

"I'm not doing my pension for you."

* * *

A coroner's jury of seven found that Stillman and Murphy had "feloniously and unlawfully killed" Collingburn. However, the subsequent manslaughter trial acquitted both of them on the grounds of self-defence. The morgue photos had somehow disappeared. Other police testified to having witnessed Collingburn and Carroll attack Stillman; from outside the 'interview' room. Go figure. Murphy and Stillman walked free.

Ian carried the scars; the ones you saw, and the ones you didn't. [27]

* * *

Ray's animosity towards Murphy didn't abate. It only grew over time. First Danny, now Ian. The dog had to go. It was now just a matter of time and place.

He sat at the Rising Sun nursing a beer, making his plans. The bar hummed with low chatter and clinking glasses. A nudge in his back broke his concentration.

"Chuck," a thin voice said. "Longley wants to see you."

Ray turned, slow and deliberate, to find a wiry kid behind him. He did not like the look of him. Without a word, he swung backhanded, catching the kid clean on the chin.

91

The kid hit the floor with a thud.

"Who the fuck are you?" Ray asked, his voice low and sharp.

The kid wiped blood from the corner of his mouth. "I'm Les Kane. Brian's brother," he said, like it should mean something.

Ray stared down at him, unimpressed.

"Mr. Longley sent me," Les continued, his voice steadier now. "Wants to see you at the Rose and Crown."

Ray snorted. "Get up, kid. You look pathetic."

* * *

At the Rose and Crown Hotel, Ray spotted Longley in the corner, hunched over a table with a guy in a cheap suit. Longley didn't look up, just raised a hand, signalling Ray to wait. Ray leaned on the bar and ordered a whiskey.[28]

A minute later, the guy in the suit stood, Longley handed him a small paper bag, and he walked out. Longley waved Ray over.

"Ray," Longley said, leaning back in his chair. "We've got a problem."

Ray slid into the seat across from him. "We do?"

"Yeah, we do. I heard about Murphy. You've gotta let it go."

Ray's jaw clenched. "He threw my kid across the room. He's only one," he spat.

Longley's gaze hardened. "Watch your tone," he said, the warning clear.

Ray bit back his anger, but it was there, simmering under the surface.

"Murphy says it didn't happen that way," Longley continued, his voice calm but cold. "Gail got upset. She misread it. The boy's fine. I've talked to them, and it's done."

"What about Neil?"

"Murphy's not to be touched. And you're to leave Murphy's family and his home alone." [29]

Ray stared at him. Longley did not blink. There was no debating Longley. Not if you wanted to keep breathing.

Ray nodded once, sharp. He stood, turned, and walked to the door.

Halfway there, Brian Kane stepped in front of him, his face a mask of menace.

"You touch my brother again," Brian growled, "and you'll answer to me."

Ray didn't stop. Didn't flinch. He stepped around Kane like he wasn't even there and kept walking. Out into the night.

He'd had enough of this mob. Enough of their rules, their lies, their bullshit.

CHAPTER 11

Waterfront Wars

Over the next few weeks, Ray's thoughts returned to Ian. Someone he knew he could rely on. His gut told him it was becoming increasingly important, so he gave him a call.

Waiting for Ian at Dock 4 reminded him of his start on the docks…

His mind wandered back: the young Ray wipes the sweat from his brow, the salt air thick and sticky. The morning sun glared down on the docks, catching on the rusted hulls of freighters and the shifting cranes overhead. He was fourteen again, scrawny but wiry, with a mop of dark hair that never stayed flat no matter how hard he tried.

"Come on, kid, keep up," Freddy Harrison growled, leading Ray into the shadows of the shipping warehouse. Freddy's nickname, 'The Frog', suited him. Wide face, unblinking eyes, and a smile that meant trouble.

Ray kept close, his boots clunking on the concrete floor. Freddy stopped at a table cluttered with papers and nodded to a clock-punching machine.

"You know what this is?" Freddy asked, his voice gravelly.

"A clock?" Ray replied, frowning.

Freddy grinned. "Smart kid. It's a magic trick too. Watch."

He grabbed a stack of timecards and started punching them in quick succession. Names Ray didn't recognise were scrawled across each one.

"What's that for?" Ray asked.

"For the boys who aren't here," Freddy said. "Ghosts, kid. You clock in for 'em, punch out for 'em. They get their pay, no questions asked."

Ray hesitated. "Isn't that… stealing?"

Freddy leaned in, close enough for Ray to reel from the sour rank of his tobacco breath. "Listen, kid. Stealing is when you take from someone who can't afford to lose it. This? This is keeping the system honest. You want to eat, don't you?"

Now standing at Dock 4, Ray still had Freddy in his head. Not words, just that look. That grin. The rules hadn't changed; they'd gotten clearer. It had seemed simple then, but now he knew better. Ghosting was not just about money; it was about control. Freddy had not been teaching him how to work. He had been teaching him the rules of survival.

"Thinking again?" Ian's voice broke through the memory.

Ray turned, watching his old friend approach.

"Yeah," Ray said. "Thinking how it all started."

Ian smirked. "Let me guess, Freddy and his magic clock?"

Ray chuckled despite himself. "Bastard knew exactly what he was doing."

Ian leaned against the railing. "You ever wonder what we'd be without guys like Freddy?"

Ray did not answer. The ghosts Freddy, Brody, Jimmy— were always there, whispering reminders of what it took to survive.

Ray changed the subject. "How are you recovering?"

Ian's face twitched, quickly replaced with a grin. "Tender, but had worse."

"Sorry mate. Longley's put a ring fence around Murphy."

Ian gave a slight nod. He knew the lay of the land.

"There's room for you with Shannon," Ian said, changing the subject.

Ray looked up surprised at how Ian could read him.

"We need good men," he continued.

Ray continued the stare.

Ian turned the knife. "But I guess that would piss off Tex and Kane."

"Fuck'em." And that was it. Ray and Ian were back together. Loyalty was relative, alliances fluid.

* * *

By his early twenties, Ray had extracted himself from Longley's circle and was back with his old friend Ian Carroll, working for union boss Pat Shannon. Not as dock workers. They were both acting as enforcers and minders for the Union Secretary.

Ray had graduated to running his own armed robbery crew. Banks, payroll deliveries, anything that promised a decent amount of cash. His reputation grew. Even commanding respect from the police. Murphy, though one of the toughest cops, now kept his distance. Ray was the only man he ever feared.

Ian was a fast learner. He followed Ray's lead, picking up how to make money at the end of a gun. Together, they had Shannon's back as he fought for control of the union. Pat Shannon, had become Union Secretary after the death of Jimmy Donegan. This set the stage for a power struggle with Longley, the unofficial President. He wanted Shannon gone, replaced with his own man.

* * *

The Eve of War

As union elections loomed, Shannon called a union committee meeting.

"All guns in the safe," he said. Eight men nodded. Even Ray and Ian complied and then took seats at the back of the room.

The room was tense. Before much could be discussed, the door slammed open. Longley walked in, flanked by his minders, Jim Bazley and Brian Kane. He stood silent, making a mental note of all in the room. Pat knew it was for effect.

"What can I do you for, Tex?" Shannon asked without turning.

"A word," Longley replied. He walked out. Shannon followed.

Ray and Ian were on their feet in seconds, retrieving their guns from the safe. Then followed their boss. Shannon made his way down the hall to Longley's office. Bazley and Kane stood aside. Shannon strode past them into Longley's office without slowing a beat. Kane and Bazley moved back and blocked the door.

"You wait here," Kane growled.

"Really?" Ray said, cold and sharp.

"Jim." Ian acknowledged Bazley with respect.

"Fingers," Bazley replied, smirking. He liked to poke at Ian's tattoos.

All four stood there, face-to-face, not a word, not breaking eye contact.

Inside, Shannon stood in front of Longley's desk. Longley leaned back in his chair.

"Who was behind Crotty's bashing?" Longley asked.

Shannon shrugged. "He's got a smart mouth. Got himself into trouble."

"I heard it was that prick Ferret. He's one of yours, isn't he?" Longley continued.

"No. It was a fight in a pub. Who cares."

"A brick in the back of the head is more than a fucking pub fight," Longley said. "This could quickly get out of hand unless we both step in and take control." [30]

"My people are all under control," Shannon retorted.

"Just keep Chuck and his pit bull on a short leash," Longley said, terminating the discussion.

"Don't worry, they won't do anything without my approval." Shannon quipped. He turned and left the room. Bazley and Kane stepped aside as the door opened. Ray and Ian followed, falling in behind their boss.

"It's on," Shannon said to no one, as they strode back.

* * *

The next day, Longley made the first move. Shannon was in his office. Ian and Frankie waiting in the outer office.

The first shot shattered the office window. Ian ducked instinctively, pulling Frankie down with him. Several more shots followed. Glass rained onto the desk. At least two shooters, Ian estimated.

"Stay down!" Ian barked, his hand already on his .38.

Another shot hit the wall just above their heads, sending plaster dust cascading to the floor.

"Longley's boys," Frankie muttered, his voice tight with fear.

Ian did not reply. He crawled toward the window, peering out just in time to see the black sedan speeding away. The roar of its engine echoed down the street.

"They missed," Frankie said, his laugh shaky.

Ian stood slowly, brushing the dust from his jacket. "Not for lack of trying."

He walked to the door, stepping over shattered glass and papers strewn across the floor.

"Where are you going?" Frankie asked.

Ian turned, his expression hard. "To remind Tex why he shouldn't miss."

* * *

Open Warfare

The union elections added grease to the fire. A week before the election, Longley's house got hit. Shotgun blasts shattered the night, ripping through the windows. His wife and daughter had left minutes earlier, but the message was clear. No one was safe.

Two days later, fire gutted the union office. Flames ate thirty years of files. The building crumbled under the weight of heat and ash. But the ballot papers were safe, locked in a vault downtown.

That same night, a bomb tore through Longley's veranda. Gelignite and lead. Glass sprayed the street. Longley was not home, but everyone heard the explosion. The war was in his house now.

Election day started quiet, but not for long; South Dock felt ready to burst. At 8:05 AM, the first shots cracked the morning. A car by the ballot box was riddled with fifty bullets. Automatic fire. Glass shattered. Metal screamed. No one saw a thing when the cops came. On the docks, you did not talk.

Inside, Bazley stood gun in hand, boot planted firmly on the lid of the ballot box. Men cast their votes, eyes on the gun, not the paper. Bazley said nothing; his presence a silent message.

At ten, seven bullets poured into the union office in South Melbourne. The wood splintered, glass shattered. Retaliation by Longley's crew, but again, no one saw a thing, no one said a thing.

That night, union executive Doug Sproule's car burned. A 1957 Holden reduced to a blackened shell. Flames lit the street, but no one saw who lit the match. Sproule grinned the next day: "Spontaneous combustion," he joked, but it was a false smile. No one laughed.

Jim Bazley was shot outside his home. Narrowly missed by the shotgun blast, two .38 bullets hit him in the shoulder and leg. Undeterred, Jim drove himself to the Royal Melbourne Hospital, plucking the bullet out of his shoulder on the way. At the hospital, he refused to be questioned by police.

On New Year's Eve, the war turned sharper. At 1:05 AM, Chamings drove down Gertrude Street. A car pulled alongside, windows down. Shots came ripping through his shoulder before he could react. Blood poured. His car hit a lamp post. The other car vanished. Chamings staggered out, alive but marked. He had fifteen months to live.

For those fifteen months, the docks became a battlefield. Bombs went off in homes. Bars shattered. Bodies vanished, never to be found. Shannon and Bazley were both wounded. But that did not stop them. It did not even slow them down.

The Homicide squad tried to keep a lid on it. Unlike the Armed Robbery and Consorting boys, they actually wanted to serve and protect. They patrolled, made their presence felt, confiscated guns. Ian was arrested while minding Shannon. Charged with carrying a concealed weapon. The .38 in his shoulder holster. He paid the $150 fine. "A stitch-up," he said, smirking. No one believed him, but no one pressed. He didn't talk. The code held.

Others were not so lucky. Frankie Bayliss got caught with gelignite and a sawn-off shotgun. Questioned, he said he needed them for his own protection, adding. "You're not silly. You know what's going on."

Brian Sulley wasn't so lucky. Took two bullets to the head outside the union office. Johnny "The Face" Morrison didn't walk away either. They found him buried in a paddock, shotgunned.

The war raged on, each act of violence feeding the next. It was not a struggle for power anymore. It was about who walked the docks tomorrow, and who didn't. The docks were no longer a workplace. They were a battleground, and the bodies kept piling up. [31]

* * *

As Pat Shannon's minders, Ray and Ian had been in the thick of it. They had survived, but it was taking a toll.

Ray leaned against the rusted railing of the dockyard, waves slapping against the pylons below. The night was cold, the kind of cold that cut deep into you. He watched the water churn, its black surface reflecting the dock lights in restless patterns.

He came here after jobs. Always had. The quiet helped let the adrenaline settle. But this time felt different. It had been a clean job. Payback for the attack on Shannon. A hit on the two shooters outside a hotel after closing. No witnesses, no police chase. But one of them was just a kid. Ray had not hesitated. His revolver was out, and the shot fired before the kid even knew what was happening.

The look in the kid's eyes had been brief but unforgettable: shock, confusion, then nothing. Ray had dragged the body into the van himself, dumping it in the long grass off the highway. Standard protocol. You didn't leave loose ends.

Now, standing on the dock, that look clawed at the edges of his mind.

"Couldn't have been older than eighteen," he muttered.

He ran a hand over his face, the rough stubble on his jaw reminding him how long the day had been. He had killed before; plenty of times. It was part of the life. You did not make it this far by hesitating or showing weakness. On the docks, a soft man did not last a week.

But this felt different. The kid had not been a threat. How could he have been the shooter? He was just scared, heading home, trying to stay invisible. How could Shannon be sure it was him?

Ray clenched his jaw and stared at the water. He'd just done his job. Faster, colder, and more prepared, but now the silence of the night pressed on him like the weight of the ocean.

"What else could I have done?" he asked aloud, his words swallowed by the waves.

Ray shook his head. No, that was not right. The kid had a gun. He'd made a choice. And Ray made his. That is how it worked. That is how it had to work.

For the first time, the logic felt hollow. It was not just about survival anymore. It was about what survival had made him. A man who did not hesitate, who killed a boy, because that was the job.

The wind picked up, sharp and biting. "Don't think about it," he muttered, pushing himself off the railing and walking back toward the street. "It's just the way things are."

But the waves did not stop, and neither did the memory.

CHAPTER 12

London Calling

The following night, Ian asked Ray, "Shannon's off to the Druids. You coming?"

"No," Ray said. "I need an early night. You're OK by yourself, Frankie and the others will be there."

Ian nodded. Ray sounded tired. This life demanded sharp instincts. A break was rare.

"Okay, see you tomorrow," Ian said as he grabbed his jacket and swung it on to cover his shoulder holster.

The last 18 months were starting to take their toll on Ray. Even if it did not show. Constant vigilance and Shannon's irrational retributions and reprisals were draining. What had started as clear was now confused, spiteful, and petty.

The house was still when Ray walked through the door. Too still. No hum of the radio, no clatter of Gail in the kitchen. Just the soft ticking of the clock on the mantel. He threw his coat onto a chair and stepped into the kitchen.

Gail sat at the table, her shoulders hunched, her head bent low. A half-empty glass of wine rested near her trembling hands.

"Gail?" Ray said, his voice low. He never liked raising it at home. It was not the place for loud voices.

She didn't look up. Her fingers traced the edge of the glass, over and over.

"Darl, what's wrong?" he asked, stepping closer. He crouched beside her, resting a hand on her arm.

Her breath hitched, then the tears came. "I can't do it, Ray. I just… I can't."

Ray stayed quiet, waiting. Words were not his strength, and he knew better than to rush her.

"I don't know when, or if, you're coming home," she said, her voice breaking.

Ray tightened his grip on her arm, but she pulled away, standing suddenly. She paced the small kitchen, her hands running through her hair.

"You disappear at all hours of the night, and I'm sitting here, waiting. Every phone call, every knock at the door, I think it's someone coming to tell me you're dead."

Her words landed harder than any punch. Ray had no reply.

"It's just work," he said. Even he didn't believe it.

"Work?" she snapped, spinning to face him. "Bombs going off in people's homes, Ray! Men shot in the street like animals. That's not work."

"It's how things are," he said, standing. He reached for her. She stepped back.

"It doesn't have to be. You don't have to be part of it," she said. Her voice softened, but the tears still came. "You could leave it all, Ray. We could leave."

The room fell silent, save for the ticking clock. Ray looked at her, really looked at her. The woman he'd married, strong and sharp, now stood in front of him, broken.

He thought of the docks, the union, the violence that had become routine. He thought of Ian, who would understand if he told him to run, but never forgive him for doing it.

"I'll talk to Shannon," he said finally. "We'll leave."

Her eyes widened, and for a moment, he saw the woman he married again. "What?"

"We'll leave Australia," he said. "Go to England. Start over. They can have it all. It's not worth this."

She stepped closer, searching his face. "You mean it?"

Ray nodded. "But we don't tell anyone until we're ready to go. Not Raelene, not Ian. No one."

She threw her arms around him, clutching him tight. "Thank you," she whispered into his chest.

Ray held her, his hand resting on the back of her head. He did not tell her what he was really thinking. That he didn't know if it was even possible. That leaving meant running, and running meant weakness, and weakness on the docks was a death sentence.

He kissed the top of her head. "Start packing. We'll leave soon."

* * *

Later that night, Ray sat alone in the darkened living room, a glass of whisky in his hand. Gail was upstairs, probably already asleep. He hadn't been able to follow her.

The weight of the decision pressed on his chest like a block of cement. Leaving was not just about walking away from Shannon or the docks. It was about walking away from everything he'd built. The name he'd made for himself. The respect he had earned, even if it came with fear.

He thought of Ian. They had come up together, shoulder to shoulder in fights, fists bloodied from the same battles. Ian, who had his own demons, but never wavered. Could he leave Ian behind?

The glass felt heavy in his hand. He stared at it, then set it down on the table.

He thought of Gail again, sobbing into his chest. The fear in her voice. The way her hands had gripped him like she was drowning. Her words lingered in the quiet. *I just want to get away from it all.*

He lifted the glass and threw it back in one swallow. Looked at the calendar pinned to the wall. October 1972. Another name, another face, another body buried under the weight of this life. Shannon was demanding more. Longley would not stop until there was nothing left. And Ian, loyal, unflinching Ian; he was in deeper than he realised.

Ray poured another swig. The whisky was warm to the swallow, but it didn't matter. He had told Gail they could leave. It slipped out; quick, final, like the pull of a trigger. But now, alone in the dark, the reality of it pressed down on him. He had spent years building this life, earning his name, clawing his way out of Longley's shadow. On the docks, respect was not given. You took it, one broken jaw at a time. And now, Gail wanted to leave it behind.

The phone rang, cutting through the stillness. Ray did not move. It was late. Calls this time of night were never good.

I don't know when, or if, you're coming home. Gail's voice echoed in his head.

He let the phone ring.

* * *

The next morning, Ray stood by the pier, staring at the water. The sun was low, the air thick with salt and diesel. Sunrise. Men shouted, cranes clanged, and trucks rumbled across the docks. It was a soundscape he had known since he was fourteen. The docks had made him, shaped him. They had turned a scrawny kid into a man other men feared, but they had taken their toll.

"Morning, Ray."

Ray turned. Ian walked toward him, finishing a croissant as he walked. His jacket hung open, revealing the butt of the .38.

"Morning," Ray said, his voice even.

Ian leaned against the railing and flicked the remains of the croissant into the water. "Shannon wants to see us tonight. He's got something lined up."

Ray nodded, but didn't speak.

Ian squinted at him. "You all right?"

Ray shrugged. "Thinking."

"Dangerous habit," Ian smirked, but his eyes stayed sharp.

"I've been at this a long time, mate," Ray said, his voice low. "Long enough to know it doesn't end well. Not for us."

Ian didn't respond right away. He inhaled deeply, holding his breath before speaking, unsure where this was going. "You're talking like an old man."

"Maybe I am." Ray turned to face him. "But you've seen the same things I have. Shannon won't back down. Longley won't back down. Sooner or later, one of us gets caught in the middle."

Ian turned towards the water. "You're worried about Gail."

Ray did not answer. He did not have to.

"Look," Ian said, turning back, "it's not forever. This thing with Longley, it'll sort itself out. It always does. And Shannon, he's not stupid. He knows how to keep us out of the crossfire."

"Does he?" Ray asked. "Because I've been dodging bullets for months, Ian. I've buried too many blokes, and I'm not keen on being next."

Ian studied him for a long moment. "You're thinking about walking away."

Ray nodded slowly.

Ian's jaw tightened. "And you think they'll let you?"

"They don't have to let me," Ray said. "I'm not asking permission."

* * *

That evening, Ray sat in Shannon's office. Ian was to his right, Shannon behind the desk. Papers were strewn across the surface: ledgers, rosters, lists of debts collected and favours owed.

"Longley's pushing again," Shannon said, lighting a cigarette. "I need you two to keep an eye on things. Make sure the lads know who's in charge."

Ian nodded. "Consider it done."

Ray did not respond.

Shannon cocked his head. "Something on your mind, Ray?"

Ray leaned forward, resting his forearms on the desk. "I'm out, Pat."

The room went quiet.

"What do you mean, *out*?" Shannon's voice was calm, but his eyes were sharp.

"I mean, I'm done. Gail and I are leaving. Tonight."

Shannon blew out a long plume of smoke, tapping ash into the tray. "You think Longley won't hear about this? You think he won't send Kane or Bazley to make it permanent?"

"I'm not worried about Longley," Ray said.

Shannon leaned back, studying him. "You've been with me a long time, Ray. You've made good money, built a name for yourself. You walk now, you lose all of it."

Ray met his gaze. "Better to lose it than end up like Crotty. Or Sulley. Or Morrison."

Shannon did not answer right away. He looked at Ian. "What about you?"

108

Ian shook his head. "I'm staying."

Ray stood. "Then that's that."

As he walked to the door, Shannon called after him. "You leave, Ray, and you're on your own. Don't come back."

"I won't," Ray said, not turning.

* * *

By the following night, Ray and Gail were on a plane, champagne in hand. Gail smiled, her hand resting on his arm.

"I don't believe it," she said. "We're really doing this."

Ray nodded, but his mind was elsewhere. He thought about the docks, about Ian, about Shannon. He thought about the life he was leaving behind and the life waiting ahead.

"To a new start," Gail said, raising her glass.

"To a new start," Ray echoed, clinking his glass against hers.

The champagne was cold, but it did not ease the bitter taste in his mouth.

CHAPTER 13

Ian's Ascendancy

Ian walked around the Channel 9 van parked in front of the Union office. A reporter, a cameraman, and a pretty girl stepped out as he opened the door. He watched her as she passed, admiring her shape.

"What was that about?" he asked inside.

"Boss just gave an interview," Frankie said, grinning. "You should have heard him, 'No stray bullet or bomb has harmed a non-unionist,'" he mimicked with a laugh. "That'll be on the news tonight."

Before Ian could take off his jacket, Pat Shannon's office door flew open. Shannon filled the doorway, glaring.

"Where the fuck have you been?" he barked, his voice booming.

"Private business," Ian said, steady.

"Private fucking business," Shannon repeated, stepping closer.

"You work for me!" he roared, his arm shaking as he pointed at Ian.

Ian stood firm, unreadable. He made no move to argue.

"Union first."

"Always," Ian replied, his voice calm.

Shannon snorted, his anger cooling. "They got Johnny last night," he said, his tone even now. "Take care of it." He turned and added, "And go see Doug. You're on the committee," before slamming his door shut.

With that, Ian became a union executive.

He turned to Frankie. "Give Laurie three large for Johnny's family." Then he headed down the hall to see the Vigilance officer, Doug Sproule, to finalise the paperwork.

* * *

The next morning, Ian was in early. He needed the time to think. Shannon was losing his grip. Ray's words played in his head: *Sooner or later, one of us gets caught in the middle.* Ian decided it wouldn't be him.

"Morning, boss," Frankie said, stepping into Ian's new office with two coffees. He set one on the desk.

Ian took a sip. "Frankie, find Vinnie Mikklesen. Tell him I need to see him. Check Leo's Gym."

Frankie nodded and left, closing the door behind him.

* * *

Frankie called in at Leo's gym. A trainer on the door pointed to a large guy leaning against the ring. Not in boxing kit. Just talking to Leo.

"Hey Vinnie," Frankie opened, walking up behind him. No reaction.

"Fingers asked if you'd mind calling into the Union Hall to see him," he continued, backpedalling at Vinnie's glare. Obviously, not someone to get on the wrong side of.

Vinnie gave the slightest nod.

That was enough for Frankie. He left.

* * *

That afternoon, a heavy-set man walked into the Union office. No jacket, no gun, but an air of authority that no one questioned.

"Where's Ian?" he asked.

Ian's door opened.

"Vinnie, come in," Ian beckoned. "Coffee?" Vinnie nodded. Ian looked at Frankie, who got the message.

Vinnie sat across from Ian, looking around the room as he sipped his coffee. "You've done all right," he said.

"Interested in joining the Union? I could use your help." Ian said.

"No thanks. I like living," Vinnie replied with a smile.

"I'm exposed here," Ian said. "With Ray gone, I need someone to watch my back."

Vinnie shook his head. "I looked after you in Turana. Wasn't meant to be a lifetime gig."

They talked about old times. Turana. Boxing. Jobs they pulled.

"Remember that first tyre factory job?" Ian said, finally playing his ace.

In the early days out of Turana, Vinnie's 'jobs' had consisted of lifting goods from shops, or breaking in after hours to steal smokes. He would then sell them to older fellas at the gym or in a pub. A hundred dollars had been a good earn for Vinnie. Ian changed that.

One other skill Ian had learned at Turana was how to pick a lock. Not just doors, but padlocks and old-fashion safes. Smaller offices still used keyed safes to store cash overnight.

"Look, Vinnie," Ian explained, standing outside an old tyre factory. "Saturday's their biggest day. People work during the week, so they have to get their new tyres on Saturday."

Vinnie nodded. He liked Ian. He was always thinking.

"And guess what?" Ian continued. "The banks are closed till Monday. All their takings are sitting in there until they can take them to the bank."

"Waiting for us," Vinnie smiled. "How do we get in?"

"Through the roof. Remove a sheet of tin, and come down through the ceiling." Ian led Vinnie to the corner and looked up at the downpipe that ran to the roof. Every few feet, a bracket stuck out, fastening the pipe securely to the building. "Give us a hand."

With that, Vinnie boosted Ian up onto a ledge. He then pulled Vinnie up. From there, they climbed the waterspout to the roof. Ian found an edge, pulled out a pair of tin snips, and cut it loose. He bent it up, and they slid into the ceiling cavity. Then they helped each other down into the office.

"Jesus, a safe," Vinnie muttered.

"Not a problem," Ian replied, pulling two thin steel picks from his shirt pocket. He set about working on the safe's key lock. It took a few minutes. Vinnie was hearing every sound outside, willing Ian to hurry.

"Wal'lah," Ian announced, using an expression he had heard somewhere before, as he swung the safe door open. "You got that shopping bag I asked you to bring?"

"Wow. How much you reckon?" Vinnie asked, pulling the canvas bag from under his shirt.

"Not now. We'll count it where it's safe." Ian was already stuffing the cash into the bag.

When the safe was clean, Vinnie threw the bag over his back and said, "Ok, give us a hand up," looking up at the manhole they had come in through. Ian just looked at him. Shook his head. He turned, walked out the front, unbolted the workshop door to the street and left. Vinnie followed.

Back at Ian's bedsit, both sat on the bed, the cash spread out before them.

"That makes it two thousand, four hundred and fifty quid," Ian announced. "Twelve hundred each."

Vinnie's mouth was still open. More money than he had ever seen.

As Ian divided the cash between them, he said to Vinnie, "Now look. The first thing the cops will be looking for is someone with loads of cash. Stash it. Don't talk about it to no one. Only keep twenty quid in your pocket at a time."

Vinnie nodded. Ian knew he was not listening, but that was Vinnie.

* * *

"Wish I'd listened to you more back then," Vinnie countered, back in the present.

"That's what mates do," Ian said letting it sit.

When Vinnie finished his coffee, he stood and said, "All right. I'll protect you. You. Not the bloody Union. No bullshit."

Ian nodded. "Good enough."

Vinnie took to his new role like a duck to water. No one wanted a visit from Vinnie. Fear turned into loyalty, but not to Shannon.

When Shannon asked about him, Ian shrugged. "Just a friend," he said. A timecard with Vinnie's name showed otherwise, but Shannon did not push.

With Vinnie enforcing, the crew ran smoother. Morale improved. Day-to-day operations fell under Ian's control. His extracurricular activities expanded too, this time with Vinnie at his side. Ray's motto of overwhelming force became their creed.

* * *

Then the worst thing happened.

A ten-year-old boy was killed by a stray bullet in the Moonee Valley Hotel. Shannon had sent 'The Bear' to hit one of Longley's crew. No one remembers why. The Bear was not the sharpest tool. He chased Longley's man into the toilets, where gunfire was exchanged. A father and son were in the wrong place, wrong time. The boy was hit by a ricochet. Shannon tempted fate with his 'no non-unionist harmed' speech, and fate had bitten back. [32]

The Bear was arrested but, as usual, acquitted. No witnesses. Regardless, all hell broke loose. The opposition demanded that the Government do something. The press printed stories of all the deaths on the waterfront and the links to organised crime. The police were forced to start doing their job. Dozens were arrested, and it became difficult to do business.

* * *

Ian arrived home late. Again. Rae was still up in the kitchen. He took off his jacket and swung it over a chair. The butt of his .38 stuck out of the shoulder holster.

"Get rid of that," was the only greeting he got from Rae. She was tired. "I'm going to bed."

He slipped the holster off, walked to the study and placed the gun and holster into the safe. Locked it. He headed back to the kitchen. As he opened the fridge, there was a knock at the front door. Not the bell. Considerate, he thought. He went back up to the front and opened the door. No one there. He looked again, focusing out further. A shape. He went to open the screen door.

A flash. Bang.

A second Bang. The door frame splintered.

Ian clutched his abdomen. Blood oozed out between his fingers. He fell to the floor.

"Ian!" Rae screamed, running up the hall. She looked down at him, not sure what to do. Panic welled inside her.

Then, "Mummy, what happened?" came the little voice from down the hall. She immediately turned and raced back to her. Scooping her daughter up onto her hip, she turned so her daughter had her back to the front door. She picked up the phone on the hall table and called emergency services.

"Ambulance, my husband's been shot," she blurted out. The operator had her focus, got their details, and talked her down. "Thank you," she finished and hung up. She held her daughter tight. She carried her back to her room, pushing her own emotions back down. Put her daughter into bed, tucking her in. As she gave her another hug, she wiped her residual tears, hands free, onto the pillow.

"What happened, Mummy?" her daughter asked again.

"Daddy fell over and hurt himself," she lied.

"Is he OK?"

"Yes, I called the doctor who will take him to hospital and fix him," she added. "You need to sleep now, so we can go visit him tomorrow." Her daughter nodded and closed her eyes.

Rae left the room and closed the door. She grabbed a towel from the bathroom and went back to Ian, pressing the towel into his wound. His hands closed around hers. *He's still alive*, she thought.

With that, flashing lights appeared outside. She held the door open as the paramedics attended to Ian. They put him on the gurney and wheeled him off. Coming, they had asked. No, she had a child asleep inside. They left. She closed the door and looked down at the pool of blood.

Rae felt the tears welling up inside again. She pushed them down. No time for that. She went out back, collected a bucket of sand from her daughter's play box, and took it back inside. Pouring it out over the pool of blood, she buried her own feelings. It would be a long night. Her daughter would never see the effects of her father bringing his work home.

* * *

Two weeks later, Ian was back home, recuperating in bed. He had been lucky. Their front wire screen was security mesh, not flywire. It had taken a lot of power out of the shot. It had also caused other medical issues, but the hospital staff had been quick and effective.

The house was quiet.

For the first time that night, Rae sat still. A gin and tonic in front of her untouched. She traced the rim with one finger, slow circles, fighting the sadness she was coming to know.

Ian had survived. A miracle, they called it. A shot fired from directly in front, and he was still breathing. He was home now, sleeping.

The stain was gone. The scent of it had not.

She sighed. Closed her eyes.

The gunmen could have missed. Could have made a mistake. They didn't. They came to kill. And next time, they might not fail.

Her fingers tightened around the glass.

She thought of her daughter asleep down the hall. The weight of her small body that night, curled into her side, asking if Daddy was going to be okay.

She had lied.

A slow, dull rage burned inside her. The kind that did not scream or break things. The kind that sat in silence.

Ian had promised her once, long ago, that they would never be like the others. That he would know when to walk away.

Now she knew. He never would.

117

The clock on the wall ticked.

She drank.[33]

…

The next morning, Rae walked in and sat on the bed. She placed her hand on Ian's arm. His eyes opened. He wanted to hold her. Thank her. She placed her finger on his lips.

"You told me you would never bring your work home." Her voice was low but steady. "Our daughter was down the hall, and a bullet could have easily hit her." No emotion, just fact.

"Never again." Firmer. It was not a demand. It was an absolute condition for them to continue.

Ian nodded and closed his eyes.

Never again, he promised himself.

Ian had had enough.

CHAPTER 14

Change of Management

Peace Negotiations

By now, the war was choking the docks. Men whispered of it in bars, in alleyways, and in the quiet moments before the day's work began. Too many were gone. Too many were left waiting for bullets in the dark or bombs under their cars. Ian decided to try a feeler.

In a small, smoke-filled bar at a neutral pub, Ian sat in a back booth across from Jim Bazley. Bazley's face was worn, but his eyes sharp. They spoke in low voices, the room heavy with unspoken truths.

"The war's bad for business," Ian said.

Jim nodded, lighting a cigarette. "Bad for everyone."

Ian leaned forward, elbows on the table. "Tex and Shannon won't stop. They're too deep in it. This war's all they know."

Jim took a drag, studying Ian. "What are you suggesting?"

"Management needs to retire," Ian said flatly.

Jim exhaled slowly, the smoke curling between them. He understood the words.

"So," Jim said, his voice steady, "you'd be fine if Shannon retired?"

Ian's gaze did not waver. "I believe you and I could work together if Tex and Shannon both retired."

Jim nodded again, this time slower. "Let's keep in touch." He stood and left without another word.

* * *

Ian's plan took shape in the weeks that followed. He moved quietly, carefully. Shannon, drunk on his own bluster, did not see the cracks forming. Tex Longley didn't either. The old guard had grown careless. Ian saw it and exploited it.

Shannon had been unpredictable lately; angrier, more reckless. Ian had been on the receiving end of too many outbursts, too many accusations. The man was unravelling.

It was a call from Jim Bazley that set the final piece in motion.

"It's time," Jim said. "I think your mum needs a visit."

"How soon?" Ian asked.

"Tomorrow would be good."

Ian nodded, though Bazley couldn't see him. "I'll tell Shannon."

The next day, Ian approached Shannon in the Union office. The boss was in his usual place, a whiskey glass in hand, barking orders to Frankie.

"Where the hell have you been?" Shannon snapped the moment Ian entered.

"Family business," Ian said, calm as ever.

Shannon grunted, waving him off. Ian stood silently, waiting. Finally, Shannon sighed. "What do you want?"

"I need to go to Sydney. My mother's sick," Ian said.

Shannon snorted. "Fine. Go. But be back in two days. I don't need you running off while I'm cleaning up your messes."

Ian nodded. "Of course."

That afternoon, Ian boarded a plane to Sydney. He was not going to visit his mother.

As the lights of Melbourne disappeared beneath him, Ian's decision weighed heavily on him. He closed his eyes willing the thought away. Now there's no turning back. It was a done deal.

* * *

Taylor slipped into the public bar of the Druids Hotel just before closing. He stood to the side, a firm grip on the .22 running down under his coat. It was Tex's gun he had been given. Told to wait until Frankie went to take a leak before leaving. The clock above the bar struck ten, closing time. Frankie disappeared. Taylor stood, took three steps towards Shannon, who was standing in the centre of the room.

He raised the gun and fired. Bang.

Everyone hit the ground. Shannon harder than the rest. The noise of gunfire was well known in this circle. It created automatic blindness and amnesia to all within earshot.

Bang ... Bang.

Taylor turned and left the building. He drove to Dock 21, threw the gun into the water where he had been instructed, then left. Job done.

The next day, the police received an anonymous tip implicating Longley and stating where to find the gun. The news hit the docks hard.

Ian returned from Sydney the next day, expression grim but composed. He offered condolences to the men in the office, shaking hands and speaking in hushed tones.

"We'll get through this," he said to Frankie.

"You think Tex had something to do with it?" Frankie asked.

Ian shrugged. "Doesn't matter. The police will pin it on him anyway." [34]

* * *

Ian was right. A week later, an arrest warrant was issued for Tex Longley. Tex made himself scarce, having received a heads-up that he was about to be arrested for Shannon's murder. Sometime later, he handed himself in to face trial. His trial became a public spectacle, dragging the union's dirty laundry into the open.

Longley, defiant to the end, denied everything. But the evidence piled up, as did the witnesses against him, likely bought or coerced, his fate sealed. He was sentenced to life in Pentridge Prison.

The morning after, there was a knock at Ian's office door. Doug Sproule, the union Vigilance Officer, entered. "You're up," was all he said, turned and left.

Ian picked up his papers and moved into the office next door. [35]

* * *

It was 1974. Ian Carroll had risen to Union Secretary. He had survived the bloodshed and emerged stronger. On the docks, they respected him. To the police, he was just another thug.

In his new office, Ian sat behind a polished desk. The room was tidy, the air clean. Raelene had insisted on the changes, saying they made him look more professional.

Frankie knocked and entered with two cups of coffee.

"Morning, boss," Frankie said, setting one on the desk.

Ian nodded. "Morning." He sipped his coffee, savouring the quiet.

"Shannon's gone, Tex is locked up. Guess that makes you the man now," Frankie said with a grin.

Ian gave a small smile. "Guess it does."

Frankie hesitated, then asked, "You had nothing to do with Shannon, right?"

Ian looked up, his expression unreadable. "You ever see me use a rabbit shooter?" he asked, referring to the small-calibre .22 with which Shannon was shot. "Do I look like a girl to you, Frankie?"

Frankie laughed nervously. "No, boss. Course not."

Ian leaned back in his chair, watching Frankie squirm. Then he dismissed him with a nod.

* * *

That afternoon, Ian met with Bazley in a quiet bar near the docks. They sat in a booth at the back, away from prying eyes and ears.

"Cheers," Ian said.

Bazley nodded, raising his glass. "Peace is good for business."

"Good for everyone," Ian agreed.

They shook hands, sealing their unspoken agreement. The war was over, but Ian knew the peace would be fragile. He had plans to make, alliances to strengthen.

As he walked back to the Union office, Ian felt the weight of the last three years lift slightly. The docks were quieter now, the air less charged. But he knew better than to relax.

Sooner or later, one of us gets caught in the middle, Ray had told him once. His eyes scanned the horizon. It was not going to be him. He got into his white '59 Cadillac De Ville and drove out through the dock gates.

123

PART III

THE MAKING OF A LEGEND

CHAPTER 15

At Her Majesty's Pleasure

The Kangaroo Gang

Ray stood in Bond Street arguing in hushed tones with an older man in a bowler hat. Behind them stood a pretty young girl in her early 20s, bored and disinterested. Red double-decker buses and black cabs curved up past the Regency buildings. Men in bowler hats hurried by, heads down, umbrellas tucked under their arms. The rain had finally paused. A typical day in London town.

"Enough with the shock and awe, Ray," Brian said, the man in the bowler hat. Brian was a member of the Kangaroo Gang, a group of older Aussies who worked in England and Europe in the '60s and '70s. "We've got a system here. Tried and true. We lift high-end pieces and ship them back to Oz. They claim the insurance; we take a cut of the resale. Clean, simple. If we get caught, we're looking at eighteen months in minimum security. Your way? It's ten years."

"You're in there too long. Everyone gets a good look at your face," Ray replied, showing his frustration. "My way, we're in and out in under a minute, faces covered, no one looks at you. They're shit scared on the floor trying not to wet themselves."

"Not here. Not in London," Brian shook his head. "This isn't Australia. We do it my way." Brian terminated the argument. "Come on Veronica, do your thing."

Veronica took the chewing gum out of her mouth and put it in her handbag. She was wearing a tight V-neck sweater, cut low, a white miniskirt, and high leather boots. Her long blond hair was cut in a straight fringe, flowing halfway down her back. "Cum on luv' let's do it," she said, looping her arm through Ray's. Her South London accent cut through his anger.

The jewellery store smelled of polish and new carpet. Money. They entered; Ray showing her disinterest; playing his part. The two male attendants both moved to serve her. The older man asserted his seniority, taking the lead. "How can I help you, miss?"

"Rings. Diamond ones," Veronica giggled, leaning close to the display case and pointing to a tray. The attendant's eyes fixed on her cleavage.

Brian entered separately. "How can I help you?" the younger one asked Brian, still glancing at Veronica.

"Just looking," Brian said flatly.

Satisfied, the younger clerk turned back to Veronica, drawn to her like a moth to a flame. She danced between the cases, trying on rings, laughing, and pouting as she handed each one back.

Brian moved quickly. His hands were steady, his movements fluid. In a few precise lifts, he scooped gold and emerald necklaces into his case. No wasted motion, no hesitation. He gave Ray a quick nod as he slipped out of the store unnoticed.

"I'm not sure," Veronica said, pulling off another ring. "Maybe we'll keep looking."

Ray placed a hand on her back, guiding her toward the door

They barely made it a few steps outside when Ray felt a firm hand on his shoulder.

"You're nicked, Sonny Jim," said a bobby, Sergeant stripes on his arm, his grip like a vice.

Ray turned. Two constables stood behind him. Further down the street, Brian was flanked by two more. His face was calm, but his eyes burned with frustration.

Ray did not fight. There was no point. The Kangaroo Gang had always said you took the fall with grace. [36]

* * *

HMP Parkhurst

Brian was right about one thing. They only got eighteen months apiece. But instead of minimum security, Ray found himself in Her Majesty's Prison Parkhurst, Isle of Wight. England's Alcatraz.

The prison was cold and damp, but alive with tension. The walls were high, the cells narrow. Guards patrolled like vultures, always watching. It was not the time for small talk or friendly alliances. Survival was about knowing when to speak and when to stay silent.

Ray kept to himself at first. Observing. Learning. The prison had its own hierarchy; its own rules. And among the inmates, one name stood out: Reggie Kray. The Kray brothers ruled the London underworld. He and his brother Ronnie. Al Capone was a choir boy compared to them. They had been done for murder, and the powers that be thought best to split them. Ronnie to Broadmoor, Reggie to Parkhurst. [37]

* * *

They crossed paths in the yard one morning. Ray recognised him immediately. The infamous gangster from the East End. Kray's reputation was as sharp as the knife he was rumoured to keep tucked away.

"You're the Aussie," Kray said, lighting a cigarette.

"Ray Chuck."

Kray nodded, sizing him up. "What's your game?"

"Blagging," Ray replied using the English vernacular for armed robbery.

"Proper jobs or that smash-and-grab rubbish?"

"Proper. Go in heavy, come out clean."

Reggie smiled, a hard, knowing smile. "We'll get on just fine."

* * *

Ray learned more in Parkhurst than he had on the streets of Melbourne. The Krays did not just rob banks. They built empires. Their methods were ruthless, but their discipline was unmatched.

"You don't just plan a job," Reggie told him one rainy day in the exercise yard. The smoke from his cigarette curling in the dim light, "You train for it. Drill your crew like soldiers. Have every move down pat. Every man knows his role."

Ray listened. He absorbed it all. The importance of timing. The necessity of adaptability.

"All plans turn to shit when the first shot's fired," Reggie added. "Your men have to be able to think on their feet. Smart as well as hard." [38]

* * *

One day, an argument in the yard turned violent. Ray did not see the knife until it was too late. The blade caught him in the side, shallow but enough to send him to the infirmary.

The prison medical officer cleaned the wound, his hands steady and efficient.

Ray looked up. He saw the name tag on the medical officer's white coat: J Bennett. Ray thought for a moment,

130

Ray Bennett. The name rolled off his tongue easily. It felt right.

The officer didn't look up. "You'll live."

Ray left the infirmary with more than a stitched-up side. He left with a new name and a new approach.

* * *

Genesis of the Plan

Prison gave a man time to think. Too much time. They said it was meant to make you rethink your ways; to step off the path of crime. Ray was not so sure about that. What it gave him was a long, hard look at himself. He had made Gail a promise once. He had told her he would leave it all behind. He had not kept that promise. That was worse than the bars, hurt more than doing the time. He would not let her down again.

Next time, he would make it right. He would make enough. Enough to buy their freedom, for good. No more piss-ant jobs with second-rate crews. No more botched chances. Next time, he would find the big one. Something that made all the risks worth it. Something to set them up for life. The details he had yet to figure out.

One night, after lights out, he lay on his cot staring up at the ceiling. The cell was dark, but his mind was awake. It drifted back to another time, another cell. Remand in Pentridge. He remembered sitting in the holding cell, the cold stone under him, the smell of damp walls. That time, he was not alone.

Jockey Smith had been there too. Not much of a jockey, Ray thought. Probably was not much of a criminal either. There were too many Smiths around, so they all got nicknames. Greedy, Neddy, and Jockey. He had even known another "Jockey" Smith up in Sydney. Go figure. This one was small, wiry, with a mouth too big for his frame.

Jockey had big ideas. Always talking. Always scheming. Ray had heard it all before. His type never had the brains or the guts to back it up. But there was one thing Jockey had said, just in passing, that stuck in Ray's head now. He didn't know why it floated up, but it did.

"Races are where the money's at," Jockey had said, pacing the cell. "Cash flows like water. You hit the right spot, you're set for life."

Jockey probably did not have the nerve to hit anything harder than a pub till. But the words had stayed. Cash flows like water. Set for life. Ray turned the idea over in his mind. Racing. Cash. A lot of cash. Enough to make a man forget the life he had lived before.

He sat up, his feet flat on the cold floor. It wasn't a plan yet. It was just a thought. But it was the kind of thought that made a man's blood move again, that gave him a reason to look past the bars and see the horizon.

That night back in Pentridge, Jockey rambled on, his voice bouncing off the cold stone walls. He talked about what could be the biggest job of all time. "The Victoria Club," he said, his eyes darting around like he was already planning his escape. "It's where the big punters go. The whales. Try to lay less than a monkey and they'll send you to the tote with a smile. These bookies handle millions, mate. And they don't declare half of it; dud the taxman, keep it all in cash. Untraceable. A million bucks or more on a good day, easy."

Ray had leaned against the wall, arms crossed, listening. "If it's so good, why hasn't anyone done it?" he asked, taking in Jockey's rambling with a grain of salt.

Jockey grinned, a flash of teeth. "No one's got the balls. Most bookies are tied up with top-level crims. You get past the Consorting Squad acting as security on settling days, and every man and his dog would come for you. Toecutters from

Sydney. The Kanes in Melbourne. It's suicide." He paused, his grin fading. "It just can't be done. Pity."

Jockey moved on to his next grand idea, but Ray was not listening anymore. He had tuned out, writing Jockey off as just another wanker full of big talk and no action. Back then, Ray had written him off. But now, in Parkhurst, the words lingered.

Ray and Ian had done plenty of work for bookies over the years. Debt collection, mostly. Gamblers always ran out of money sooner or later, and someone had to collect. They had learned a thing or two along the way. First, most bookies were full of shit. They weren't as connected as they liked to pretend. If they were, they would not need the likes of Ray and Ian to sort out their problems.

Sure, the Toecutters or the Kanes might come after you if you crossed the wrong bookie. But Ray knew one thing: every problem had a solution. As for the Consorting Squad? That would take a new level of overwhelming force, but force was something Ray knew how to manage. He let the thought simmer, turning it over in his mind. The corners of his mouth curved into a small smile. He closed his eyes and let the darkness take him.

* * *

In the weeks that followed, the plan began to take shape. Ray had always been a thinker, a planner. Now he had the time to refine every detail. During a family visit, he asked Gail to pass a message to Ian. "Tell him to get in touch with 'The Architect,'" he said quietly. He rattled off a phone number from memory. "Use my name."

A week later, a warder approached him. "You've got a call," the man said, his tone suspicious, as if he could not believe it himself. "Three minutes."

Ray walked to the population pay phone and picked it up.

"Chuck," came the voice on the other end. Calm, precise. "'Fingers' said you have a commission."

Ray nodded, though no one could see him. "That's right. You interested?"

"I only deal with the principal," The Architect replied. "Your record speaks well enough, but I don't know Carroll." Ray stressed it was his job and that he would only have to deal with him once he returned. He accepted the commission.

"I'll start developing plans for 131 Queen Street. Implementation schedules too. Expenses go through Carroll. Fees to be settled before delivery. That acceptable?"

"Fine," Ray said, his mind already moving to the next step. "Let Ian know the fee."

"And we don't use names. What do I call you?"

Ray thought for a moment. "Bennett."

"I only deal with you," The Architect reiterated.

The line went dead. Ray hung up. No reaction. Not that anyone could read him anyway. But the wheels were spinning fast now. The pieces were starting to fall into place.

This was not just a job; it was THE job. The one that could set him and Gail free for good.

CHAPTER 16

Home Leave

Unlike the Australian penal system, the UK system genuinely seeks rehabilitation. To that end, just prior to the end of their term, prisoners are given a short 'home leave'. This allows them to readjust to outside life and prepare for their future. Ray had other uses for it.

"Welcome home, Mr Bennett," greeted the immigration officer stamping Ray's new passport. Ray walked out of the Australian arrivals hall first, no bags checked, no patience for delays. Ian was waiting, steady as always. They hugged like men who'd known each other too long for formality. Ian grabbed the carry-on, said nothing, then led the way to the car.

Inside, Ian pulled a Gladstone bag from behind the seat. "Here," he said. "The money you wanted. Fifty large. I hope it's worth it."

Ray opened the bag and glanced at the cash. "Any trouble getting it?"

"No. A factory payroll out in Dandenong. Don't think they've seen a gun out that way before," Ian smiled.

"Everything quiet? Anyone know I'm here?" Ray changed the subject.

Ian looked ahead, his face calm. "No one knows. Everyone still thinks you're in Parkhurst. All's quiet."

Ray nodded. That was good. Quiet was better than luck.

* * *

The two men stood on the corner, staring up at the eleven-storey Brownstone across the street. Solid. Old. The Victoria Club was home of the AJC, the Australian Jockey Club. A name that belies its membership of horse owners, trainers, and punters.

Ian asked, "What's the security?"

Ray, authoritative and confident, replied, "Three consorting dogs. Lazy. They show up now and then."

"You sure?" Ian frowned. He trusted, but he always asked. That's why Ray liked him.

"Jockey scoped it," Ray said.

Ian swore under his breath. "Christ no, not Jockey. Ran into him inside. Small man with a big mouth!"

"He's in Sydney," said Ray, his jaw tightening at the implied judgment. "He's not a part of this."

The town hall clock rang noon. Across the street, an armoured van pulled up. The guards moved slow, routine in their steps. Three strongboxes went on trolleys and rolled inside. Ray and Ian crossed the street. They dodged cars, their pace steady, their eyes sharp.

Inside the Victoria Club, the smell of cigar smoke and whisky. Men crowded the bar. The racing crowd; trainers, punters, owners. Up early, off early. No one looked up. With a Gladstone bag in hand, Ray looked like any other bookie.

Ray and Ian climbed the back stairs, stopped at the second floor. Through the crack of the door, they could see through to the Settling Room. They watched the guards unload the boxes. Calico sacks passed into the cage. Ian knew what was inside: money. Thirty, forty grand a sack.

Ian whispered, "Five hundred easy."

"At least. That's the Settling Room. Where the bookies pay out after the weekend races," Ray said. "No small-timers, only whales. Depending on the meeting, they could be holding a million. Kerry can drop two-fifty on one race."

They went back downstairs and found a quiet booth in the bar far from prying eyes or ears. Ian changed the subject. "When are you heading back?"

"Friday. Soon as I'm out, we move. Meantime, start working on logistics. Seven should do it. Six inside, one out. But no one we don't know."

Ian frowned. "What happened? You said you'd never deal with those Kangaroo Gang wankers. You knew they'd screw you."

"I didn't work with them. It was a jewellery job with Brian. He's an old friend," Ray said, his voice quieter now.

"No difference. He is one of them, and they were being watched. Now you're paying for it," Ian said. He saw the look on Ray's face and backed off. Changed the subject. "You're really pushing your home release, though. The Poms wouldn't be happy knowing you've flown back to Oz. I don't know how you pulled it off; then flying back to England to finish your time at Parkhurst."

"Travelling under the name Bennett. This way, I'm clean when the job's done. After something like this, everyone will be under the microscope. I want no dirt on me," Ray said.

"Kudos to you. Dinner before you go? Raelene would love to see you."

"When I'm back. Tell Rae I'll bring Gail next time. We'll do a proper dinner," Ray said, cutting him off.

Ian nodded, though he knew it was a brush-off. They shook hands, and Ian crossed the road and got into his white '59 Cadillac De Ville. Ray watched him drive off, shaking his head.

"After all I've taught him," Ray muttered. "I'll have to fix that when I'm back."

* * *

The Architect

The Architect was generally not known in the Melbourne underworld and unknown to detectives. He worked hard to keep it that way. Luckily, Ray was one of a select few. Described as a "time and motion expert", he had planned some of the biggest armed robberies in Melbourne, Perth and Sydney. His access to architectural plans, security protocols, and police intelligence, meant his plans were money in the bank. He was methodical and precise. He provided timing of deliveries and transfers, identified schedules and rosters, and mapped routes, access and escape points. But only on his terms. His rules were not negotiable.

On the second day of his quick visit back to Oz, Ray hired a rental. He drove out to the address he had written on a scrap of paper. After pulling up outside, he checked the house number against what was written, twice, took a lighter out, lit the scrap of paper, and dropped it in the ashtray. Ray grabbed the Gladstone bag off the back seat and got out.

The front door was steel with reinforced hinges and door frame. In front of that was a screen door. It was for keeping out more than flies. Ray knocked three times, stood back, and waited. And waited. The Architect was obviously checking him out and the street around them. The house was well sited, with good views in both directions. It would be difficult for either police or a hit team to approach without being seen.

The door opened. "Bennett?" asked a small man in his late fifties. He wore wire-rim glasses. Weathered. Quiet. Looked a lot like Charles Bronson. [39]

"Yes," Ray answered. The outer door opened, and Ray stepped in. The Architect closed the doors and then led Ray into the front room. Probably originally a living room, it was now an office. In the centre, a large plan table, filing cabinets lined the far wall. Maps of Melbourne, Sydney, and Perth

138

cities hung on the wall. There were two telephones on a small desk under what would have been a window. Now it looked like it was permanently sealed.

Ray turned and held out his hand. "Ray."

The Architect looked at his hand, then in the eye.

"Rule 1: No Names. No real names, personal details, or identifying information will be shared. I will remain anonymous. You will only refer to me as The Architect. You gave the alias Bennett. I will use that.

Rule 2: No Contact Beyond Designated Channels. All communication will occur through pre-approved methods and intermediaries. No direct phone calls or in-person meetings unless explicitly arranged by me. Contact is only to be initiated by the client when absolutely necessary.

Rule 3: No Personal Jobs. The job must be business. Not revenge, personal disputes, or vendettas. Emotional jobs lead to mistakes, and mistakes lead to exposure. I will refuse any job I deem too risky or poorly motivated.

Rule 4. Payment Upfront. Full payment is required before the plan is delivered.

Rule 5: Follow the Plan Exactly. Deviations from the plan are not permitted. The strategy I provide is meticulously designed for precision and safety. Any changes increase the risk of exposure. For everyone.

Rule 6: No Ties to The Architect. I do not participate in the execution of the job. My role and all contact ends when the plans are delivered. You must not mention The Architect's involvement to anyone, ever. This includes crew members.

Rule 7: Clean Up After Yourself. I will advise on disposal methods for tools, disguises, vehicles, and other materials to minimise exposure. Follow them.

Rule 8: No Follow-Up Requests. Once the job is complete, the relationship ends. The Architect will not handle disputes within the crew, additional planning, or post-job complications.

Rule 9: Professionalism is Mandatory. All crew members must adhere to professional conduct. Unstable, reckless, or unreliable individuals are not permitted to participate in jobs designed by The Architect.

Any breach of these rules will result in immediate termination of this contract and any future services."

"Do you understand and accept all these rules?"

"Yes," was Ray's solitary reply.

Ray handed him the Gladstone bag. He just nodded. Did not open it to check the amount. It was always correct. The Architect turned, stepped over to the plan table, and put the bag under it. He spread out the plans sitting on top.

"The Victoria Club. Here is the Settling Room on the second floor." He rolled out a second plan. "This is the building next door. It is under renovation. Its third floor is empty and aligns to the Victoria Club's second floor. There is a sealed up access door here, between the two buildings. Probably from an older renovation." He rolled them up and handed them to Ray.

"Here are my suggested plans, plus estimates of times, in, collection, and out," handing Ray a manila folder. Six fit men, carrying a 20kg mailbag each. That's the weight of $1 million cash. That allows for double what you expect. Always err on the side of caution. When you give me the exact day, I will provide the delivery schedules, staff rosters, and related timings."

The Architect turned and led Ray to the front door, opened it and waved Ray out. As Ray stepped outside he reiterated:

"The rules are the foundation of my success. Clients who follow them to the letter stay off the radar, and everyone walks away richer and free. Ignore them, and you'll never hear from me again."

He closed the door. Ray left to return the rental.

* * *

The Third Day

The taxi pulled up outside the Dim Sim factory. Ray paid the driver and got out. The place was squat and utilitarian, the kind of building that did not ask for attention. A large roll-a-door stood open, spilling the stench of steamed cabbage and oil into the street.

Ray walked in like he belonged there. The first person he saw was an elderly Asian man who broke into a wide grin when he recognised him.

"Mr. Chuck, long time no see," the man said.

"Yes, Mr. Lee. I've been overseas," Ray replied.

That's what Lee liked about Ray: respectful, unlike most Australians. "Normie's in the office upstairs," Mr. Lee said, gesturing. "Go up. He'll be excited to see you."

Ray nodded, crossed the factory floor, and took the stairs two at a time. He opened the door without knocking. Normie looked up from his paperwork and froze.

"Ray!" he exclaimed. "Well, I'll be buggered."

Before Ray could reply, Normie was on his feet, grabbing him in a bear hug. Ray broke free, patted him on the arms, and stepped to the window overlooking the factory.

"I'm only here for a quick trip," Ray said. "But I had to say hi."

Normie pulled a bottle of Macallan from his desk drawer and two glasses. He poured, then sat at the table in the corner, shuffling a deck of cards. No small talk was needed. They had always talked over a game.

"Fucking Carroll's an asshole," Ray said after a long drink.

Normie rearranged his hand, waiting. "What's he done now?"

141

"Have you seen the monstrosity he's driving? A bloody yank tank. I don't care how much he's paying the cops; he's painting a target on his back. After all I've taught him! I'm gone a couple of years, and he's acting like a wanker." Ray shook his head. "I came to offer him the biggest payday of his life, and he's got the balls to question my actions in the UK. Then he climbs into that ugly tank. He can go to hell."

Normie played his turn. "Three out," he said, tossing cards and drawing new ones.

"Fuck him," Ray said, throwing down three cards of his own. He was settling now.

"What's the job?" Normie asked.

"The Victoria Club."

Normie froze mid-game. "You're kidding. That's impossible."

"It's not," Ray said. "And I'll do it, we'll do it."

Normie poured them both another drink. They sat in silence for a while, the game forgotten.

"I need you to straighten Ian out," Ray said finally. "Get him off his ego trip. I need him for this."

"Don't worry," Normie said. "I'll talk to him. He'll come around. I guarantee it."

Both men knew the problem was not just the car. For two hours, they played cards and talked about old times and Ray's stint in the UK. Ian was not mentioned again.

When the taxi arrived, Ray stood. "We can do this," he said. "Make a copy of these plans," he continued, handing him the manila folder. "Give the originals back to Ian. Get him to find a four-storey warehouse we can work out of."

Normie nodded.

As Ray stepped into the taxi, his eyes locked with a young police officer standing across the street. Without missing a beat, he ducked his head, climbed in, and told the driver to go. The officer stared after the car, frowning, unsure who he had just seen but knowing he should have known.

Normie arranged to meet Ian after work on Thursday. He gave him the original plans. They discussed the warehouse. Normie did not know why it had to be four storeys. But Ian did. Ray wanted to mock up the 131 Queens Street layout.

"If you need a lease, let me organise it. I can arrange a ghost lease," Normie offered.

Ian shook his head. "I think I'll be right." Ian stood ready to leave.

"A quick word," Normie added. Ian sat again.

Trying to work out how to raise the issue, Normie led: "Ray's wanted me to stress the need to be low key." Ian raised an eyebrow. Like all societies, there was a hierarchy. Although a good friend of Ray, Ian did not consider Normie a rank that could question him.

"What?" Ian returned indignantly.

"Well, the car ..."

"What about the car?"

"A 59 Caddie with tailfins and whitewall tyres is not that low key." Normie stammered.

"I'll think about it," Ian said, dismissing Normie. He grabbed the plans, got up and left.

That Friday, Ray returned to the UK and Parkhurst, no one the wiser to his sojourn. He finished his last three months and was released.

CHAPTER 17

I Still Call Australia Home

Welcome home

The steel gate clanged as it slid back open. The smell of free air was always sweeter. Ray knew that it was psychosomatic, but it was real just the same. It did not bother him that there was no one there to greet him. Gail had already returned to Oz and was setting up their home for his return.

As he walked out of the Parkhurst prison gates, "Chuck" came the matter-of-fact command from his left. He immediately turned. It showed how fast you become institutionalised in prison. He did not know the face, but knew who he was. A copper.

"You are to be deported back to Australia on release," the copper announced. "Mother England neither requires nor wants you any further. Her Majesty's Government has booked and paid for your air ticket. I am here to escort you to Heathrow and see that you get onto that flight back to Australia."

Ray smiled to himself. That saves me the cost of an airfare.

* * *

The arrivals board flickered: Landed.

Gail pulled Danny closer, feeling the sharp bones of his shoulders through his jacket. He was taller now. His grip that of a child, no longer a toddler. It had been two years since he'd seen Ray in the flesh. At an age when memories quickly faded, letters and phone calls did not count.

Her breathing quickened, shifting on her feet. The terminal was crowded, bodies pressing too close, the air thick with body odour and cheap coffee. A tinny announcement crackled over the PA.

Then she saw him.

Ray walked out, only an overnight bag slung over one shoulder, eyes scanning the crowd. Then—his gaze found hers. His mouth pulled into that familiar grin. The one that still made her chest tighten.

"Gail!"

He was in front of her before she had time to think, arms wrapping around her, solid and warm. For a second, she let herself sink into it, the smell of him, the weight. Then Danny coughed, and Ray pulled back, grinning wider.

"Jesus, mate, you've shot up." He ruffled Danny's hair.

Danny shrugged, shifting awkwardly. "S'pose."

Ray laughed. "That's all I get?"

Danny smirked, but it was small. Hesitant.

Ray's fingers squeezed his shoulder. "We'll fix that."

Then another voice. Low. Even. Unmoved.

"Long flight?"

Gail stiffened before she even turned. Ian stood off to the side, hands in his pockets, like he'd been there the whole time. Like he belonged in this moment.

Ray dropped his bag at Gail's feet. "Yeah, mate. Long enough."

She felt it then. The shift. Ray had barely been home sixty seconds, and already, the world outside them was pulling him away.

Ray's hand brushed her waist. "You get us set up, yeah? I'll come by later."

Gail's stomach tightened. "Where are you going?"

Ray grinned. "Got business to catch up on."

His grip on Danny's shoulder loosened, then released. He turned, walking toward Ian without waiting for her reply.

Danny watched his father go, his face dropped. Gail forced a breath, fingers curling into fists.

Welcome home.

* * *

Ian led the way out of the terminal doors. He turned and stood by a Jaguar in the no-standing area. Smile beaming.

"Nice wheels," Ray commented.

Ian smiled, "It's yours," he replied, throwing Ray the keys. "Don't thank me, Gail organised it," he continued.

Ray knew that wasn't true, but left it as accepted. Gail would not have had the contacts or funds for a car of this ilk, although she probably had a hand in its selection. Ray walked around and got in the driver's seat. Ian took his usual spot, riding shotgun.

They drove from the airport back into town in silence. "I never really apologised for leaving you in the shit when I left," Ray said after about 20 minutes.

"It wasn't a problem. Better than the alternative," Ian replied. They both knew that once you lose your edge, you're a danger. Not only to yourself but to those around you. "Laurie stepped up, and we got through it. It's a lot quieter now around the docks. Shannon's gone and Longley's locked up for it."

"Laurie, really? I always thought he had it in him. What about Kane and Bazley?" Ray enquired.

"Bazley's gone to ground, probably up in Sydney. The Kanes are always a problem. Brian's OK but that Les is a nutter. One day we are going to have to handle him." Ian and Brian Kane still trained at Leo's boxing gym in Richmond. They had sparred a few times, but had never met formally in the ring, so there was no ranking between them, just a healthy respect.

"Pull over here," Ian said with a smile on his face.

Ray glanced at him, then pulled up outside a pub in South Melbourne as directed. He thought he recognised it, but it had had a major refit. Gone upmarket. Posh. He looked at Ian, querying.

"Thought you might like something to eat and a cold beer after your long flight," Ian said, answering the unasked question. Ray nodded. They went in, found a table, ordered two beers, and two steaks.

Once the waiter had gone, Ray started. "I plan to hit the bookies after a long weekend with multiple meets. They could be holding three times the normal amount of cash."

"We'll need a tight crew," Ian said. "That kind of haul will draw out every cockroach in town. Any change to how many do you think we'll need?"

"Still, six plus a driver should do it," Ray replied. "We will need guys who can control their sphincters when the dogs and cockroaches come calling."

Ray did not want novices. Most of Ray's crew, if caught, would be known to the police. That was one of the pitfalls of collecting professionals. They discussed recruiting the crew. The group would be the best gang of armed robbers ever assembled in Australia.

"I'll get Laurie for legwork and Normie for handling the cash. Can you get Vinnie? We'll need real muscle."

"Easy."

"But make sure he keeps his head straight. No booze, no girls, no loose lips. We can't afford slip-ups."

"Don't worry. He's solid. You keep an eye on the others; I'll take care of Vinnie," Ian replied.

"That's five. We need two more. Think on it." Ray checked his watch. "Time I got home."

"Rae wants to have you and Gail over as soon as you are settled," Ian said as Ray dropped him at home.

"I'll let you know," was his curt reply.

Ian smiled to himself as he watched Ray drive off.

* * *

Some days later.

Raelene set the wine bottle down. Full. Unopened. "Won't last long," she muttered.

Ian leaned in the doorway, watching her. His shirt unbuttoned at the top, sleeves rolled. Relaxed. "Ray's changed."

She twisted the corkscrew. "Ray's never changed."

Ian smirked but said nothing.

The front doorbell. Ian disappeared. Footsteps. Laughter. Male voices, deep and rough. Ray loud, Gail softer, uncertain.

Raelene poured two glasses before they even reached the kitchen.

Ray hugged her first. He smelled of cheap duty-free cologne. He pulled back, grinning. "Miss me?"

"Like a toothache," she returned, passing him a glass.

148

Gail stepped into the kitchen. She looked at Raelene, then Ian. A half-second pause. Like she was measuring something.

Ray draped an arm over Ian's shoulder, laughing at something from their past. In their world, private, exclusive, untouchable.

Gail set down her purse. "Smells good in here."

"Roast lamb," Raelene said. "Thought you might need real food after that British crap."

Gail smiled. "I missed this."

Liar, Raelene thought.

Gail sat down, smoothing invisible creases on her dress. She looked at Ray, then at Ian. Something unsettled passed behind her eyes.

Raelene poured her a drink. Gail held the glass but didn't sip.

Ray's voice boomed across the table. "To old times."

Ian clinked his glass. "To the future."

Gail and Raelene locked eyes. Neither toasted.

* * *

The dishes sat in the sink. The men were outside, cognacs in hand, whispers in the dark.

Raelene leaned against the counter, arms crossed. "You all right?"

Gail sat at the kitchen table staring at her glass. "Yeah." A beat. "No."

Raelene nodded. "Figured."

Gail let out a shaky breath. "He promised things would be different."

"They never are."

Silence stretched between them.

Gail rubbed her temples. "It's like they don't even have to talk. It's just there. Under their skin."

Raelene sighed. "It always was. They go back a long way."

A flicker of laughter outside. Low murmurs. More laughter.

Raelene pushed off the counter. "They'll be away more now, planning."

Gail did not look up. "I know."

"You still gonna pretend?"

Gail finally met her eyes. "You ever stop pretending?"

Raelene tilted her head, considering. Then she reached for the wine. She poured another glass. For both of them.

* * *

The Sixth Member

As Raelene predicted, a few nights later, Ray and Ian were out again. Planning.

"The sixth," Ray started. "What about Peter?" Melville Peter Schnitzerling, better known as Russell 'The Fox' Cox. Australia's top bank robber. Articulate, cool, disarming, but utterly ruthless. A textbook sociopath. Later, the media would label him 'Mad Dog'. However, he was currently serving twelve years in Sydney's Long Bay gaol, Australia's highest security prison. Inescapable.

"But he's in Long Bay?" Ian questioned.

"Yeah, and in Maitland before that. Didn't stay there long." Ray shot back.

"But he got caught, didn't he?"

"Only because he couldn't be bothered running. He's resting between jobs. That's what prison is to him. And he won't be able to resist this job. Don't worry, he'll climb over

150

broken glass to get here," Ray smirked at throwing in that little pun.

Ian nodded, smiling. The smile dropped from his face. "How do we get a message to him in maximum security?" It was more a pondering thought than a question. "No one with a record will get within a mile of him."

"Every problem has a solution," Ray grinned. "We just have to find it."

They left it at that.

* * *

On the way home, Ray thought back to the first time he met Cox. The law of probabilities said it had to happen, but he had never heard of it happening before …

Ian pulled into the shopping centre car park. He chose a corner, mostly empty except for one other car. It was 10 AM, too early for regular shoppers. He parked well away but still in line with the bank. Good view. Easy access.

Ray glanced at the other car. Two men. Heavy coats for a spring day. Black beanies rolled up on their heads, the same as he and Ian. The other driver looked back at Ray. A sly smile crept across his face. Recognition. Not of the face, but of the intent.

Ray chuckled.

Ian turned and looked past Ray. His reaction was the same. The passenger in the other car did the same.

Four men. Two cars. Watching. Waiting.

The armoured van arrived. Unloaded. Left.

Cox shook his head. Not in anger. More like amused disbelief. Ray nodded. The other car drove off.

"Let's have a chat," Ray said.

Ian pulled out. Followed them.

They stopped at a roadside cafe. Cox knew they were behind him. Didn't seem to mind. Inside, they ordered coffee. Talked. Compared plans. Laughed. Joked.

Cox was smooth. Easy going. But all business where it counted. Ray liked him. Ian did too. Next time, they agreed, maybe they'd check schedules first. Then they went their separate ways.

* * *

At Ian and Ray's next meeting, Ian got there first. Ray could see he was thinking something.

"What?" Ray asked sitting down.

"Any chance you could get Helen to visit Peter in Long Bay? No one knows her, she's squeaky clean," Ian proposed.

Gail's younger sister Helen had no record, nor any affiliation with known criminals. She would not have a problem getting a visitor's pass into Long Bay's maximum security. However, that broke Ray's unwritten rule of separating work from family.

Ray glared at Ian. He thought for a while shaking his head. But then said, "OK, I'll ask," despondently.

"So six then?" Ian said trying to get Ray's mind back on topic.

"That's all we need. Six good men, in and out in 10 minutes."

"What will we do with Peter when he joins us?"

Ray nodded. "We will need to arrange a safe house for him to keep low."

"No worries, I've got an old rental about to become available. He can squat there for a while."

"A rental?" Ray queried, raising an eyebrow.

"Raelene's trying to make me legit. Got me investing my spare cash," Ian shrugged it off.

"Good," Ray said dismissing Ian's excuse. "We'll get the boys together as soon as he gets here." Ray ended the discussion. He now had bigger concerns.

CHAPTER 18

Russell Cox

That night, Ray closed the door gently but did not sit down. Gail stood at the kitchen sink, hands in the soapy water, staring out the window. She did not turn to look at him.

"I need to ask you something," Ray said, his voice low.

"Something about work?" Gail's hands stilled. She turned, her eyes sharp.

Ray sighed and leaned against the counter. "One last job. For us. For Danny's future."

"You promised, Ray."

"This is different," he said quickly. "It's the last one. Big enough to walk away for good. No more piss-ant jobs. No more debts to pay off. Just us."

"And you want me to do what?" Her tone was cold, clipped.

"I need you to talk to Helen."

"Helen?" She stepped back, wiping her hands on a towel. "You said we'd keep her out of this. Out of everything."

"It's a visit. That's it," Ray said, looking down at his feet. "Cox is in Long Bay. We need him for this. Helen could ..."

"Could what, Ray? Walk into a prison and charm a man she's never met? And what? Deliver your little message?"

Ray finally met her gaze. "You're right. She shouldn't be part of this. But she's the only one who can get in there without raising eyebrows."

Gail threw the towel onto the counter. "You're asking me to send my sister into a prison to meet a criminal."

"A professional," Ray corrected. "And she won't be in any danger."

"Danger?" Her voice rose. "Ray, she's a nurse, not your bloody accomplice."

"This job gets us out," Ray said, his voice firm now. "A clean slate. No more late nights, no more knocks on the door. I don't want Danny growing up around this. But we can't do it without Cox."

Gail shook her head, her eyes brimming with frustration. "You always have an excuse, don't you? Always a reason why this time is different."

"It is different," Ray insisted. "I'm doing this for us."

She looked at him for a long time, searching for something in his face. "If I ask her, and she agrees ... this is the last time, Ray. The last time I let you bring this life into our home."

Ray nodded. "The last time. I promise."

* * *

Helen sat cross-legged on Gail's couch, twirling a strand of her dark hair. "You want me to what?"

"Visit someone in Long Bay. Just ... have a conversation," Gail said, her voice careful.

Helen's dark eyes widened. "You're serious? Like, a prisoner? What for?"

"It's for Ray," Gail said, not meeting her sister's gaze.

155

Helen grinned, leaning forward. "Ray? What kind of adventure is he sending me on?"

"It's not an adventure," Gail snapped. "It's serious, Helen."

Helen's smile faded, but her curiosity did not. "What's his name?"

"Russell Cox."

Helen's eyebrows shot up. "Cox? As in 'The Fox'? I've read about him. Armed robber, isn't he? Bit of a legend."

"Helen, this isn't a joke," Gail said.

"I know, I know," Helen said quickly. "It's just ... I'm not sure why you're asking me."

"Because you're small, approachable. They won't see you as a threat," Gail said. "And because I trust you."

Helen tilted her head, studying her sister. "What does Ray need him for?"

Gail hesitated. "I don't know. I didn't ask. And neither will you."

Helen's lips curved into a sly smile. "All right. I'll do it. Might be fun."

Gail's jaw tightened. "This isn't fun, Helen. Be careful."

* * *

Helen sat on the hard plastic chair in the visitor's room, her hands clasped tightly in her lap. The door opened, and a tall, lean man walked in. His blonde hair was cropped close, his blue eyes bright and alert.

"Russell Cox," he said, sliding into the seat across from her. He gave her a smile that was equal parts charm and danger. "And you are?"

"Helen," she said, her voice steadier than she expected. "Gail's sister."

"Gail," Cox said, leaning back. "Ray's wife, right? So, what can I do for you, Helen?"

Helen cleared her throat. "Ray wanted me to ask ... if you can get out. Soon. He has something special for you. A step up."

Cox tilted his head, his smile not faltering. "Straight to business. I like that."

"Can you?" Helen pressed.

Cox chuckled softly. "Ray always did think big. Tell him I'm working on it. Shouldn't be too long."

Helen nodded. "Good. That's ... good."

He studied her for a moment, his eyes narrowing slightly. "You're nervous."

"It's my first time in a prison," she admitted.

Cox laughed. "Well, welcome to my world. It's not so bad once you get used to it."

They fell into an easy rhythm, talking about everything but the job. Helen found herself laughing more than she expected, drawn in by Cox's quick wit and easy charm.

As their time ran out, Cox leaned forward. "Tell Ray I'm in. And tell him thanks for sending you."

Helen stood quickly, knocking her chair with her knee. "I'll tell him."

As she walked out of the room, she couldn't help but glance back. Cox was watching her, that same disarming smile on his face.

* * *

Long Bay Breakout

This was the job he had to be in on. It was not about the money. He had done a number of six-figure jobs before. If

Ray said this was a step up, it was going to be big. A statement. It did not take long for Cox to make his move.

Gunfire echoed in the afternoon heat. Not a common sound at Long Bay. Inmates were up against the bars, listening, eyes sharp.

"What's that?" one muttered.

"Escape," said another.

The tower screws were shooting, but not inside the walls; outside, on the road. It had to be big.

A guy at the window shouted, "They're making for the gate!"

They watched the guards on edge, their radios crackling. There were whispers that it was "The Fox." Russell Cox. Smart. Calculating.

* * *

Down at the front gate, Cox moved fast. He and two other prisoners were trying to escape. The truck idled, its engine growling. One of the other escapees dragged prison officer Cafe toward the cab as a hostage.

"Open the weapons cabinet," Cox ordered the gate guard, his voice cold.

The guard hesitated. Cox raised the .25 Beretta to his head. Small gun. Ridiculed as a woman's piece. But deadly enough in the right hands. No one knew how he had smuggled one into the maximum security prison.

"Do it!" Cox barked.

The guard opened it. His accomplice grabbed two Smith & Wesson .38s. Cox did not waste time.

"Get him on the bonnet," Cox said, nodding at Cafe.

The guard was shoved onto the truck's hood, a gun pressed to his temple.

"Let's go." Cox climbed into the driver's seat and floored it.

The truck lurched forward. Tower guards fired, bullets pinging off the metal, but no one risked hitting Cafe.

The truck barrelled toward the boom gate, but fate had other plans. A bread van appeared, slamming into the truck. The impact jolted everyone inside.

"Shit!" yelled Cox's accomplice, clutching his pistol.

"Move!" Cox ordered. They abandoned the truck, dragging Cafe with them. Bullets ripped through the air. Tyres blew. The trio ran, their human shield stumbling in front of them.

Another shot. Cafe went down, clutching his leg. Cox felt the burn of a bullet graze his side but kept moving. Then their other accomplice staggered and collapsed. A bullet had hit his shoulder.

"Keep going!" Cox yelled.

But the screws were on them now. A final shot, and Cox dropped to his knees. Blood seeped through his shirt. He raised his hands up. It was over.

* * *

The inmates heard the commotion when they dragged Cox and the other wounded prisoner back into the Observation Section (OBS). The word spread fast. They had been dumped naked onto the concrete floor, bleeding out.

"Wounded bad," someone whispered. "Think they'll make it?" asked another. "Doubt it," said yet another.

The yard buzzed. Men paced, tension rising.

"If they let them die," a yell echoed through the cell block, "we'll riot." It was not an empty threat. By morning, the feeling inside Long Bay was electric. Ready to blow.

* * *

Finally, at 2 PM, the screws relented. A nurse and a doctor were brought in. Inmates watched through the bars as the medics were rushed toward the OBS.

At 5 PM, Cox and his partner were wheeled out on stretchers. Bloodied but alive. A riot averted, for now.

The Fox had lost this round, but a man like him would not stay down for long. [40]

* * *

The Infirmary

Cox lay still in his hospital bed, listening. All was quiet, just the occasional shuffle of someone passing and the hum of the fluorescent lights overhead. The stench of antiseptic filled the air. His side burned, but pain never bothered him much. It was just something else to ignore.

The nurse walked in. Slim. Careful in his movements. Nineteen, maybe twenty. Soft hands. A clean, scented smell. He hesitated at the doorway, adjusting the clipboard in his grip. His eyes covertly flicked to the patient. A quick glance, then away. Too quick. Too deliberate.

Cox noticed. He always noticed. The kid's eyes had lingered just a second too long on his face. Cox's blonde hair and square jaw. The kind of rugged look that some people found hard to ignore. The nurse swallowed hard. His fingers flexed against the clipboard.

Cox let the silence hang. Made the kid wait. Made him wonder if he'd been caught looking. Then, slow and easy, he turned his head on the pillow and met the boy's eyes.

The nurse's breath hitched. A faint flush on his cheeks. He recovered quickly, clearing his throat, stepping forward, focusing a bit too hard on the IV line. Professional. But not as steady as he wanted to be.

Gotcha. Cox smiled, easy, warm. The kind of smile he used when he needed something. "You got a name, mate?"

The kid hesitated. "Patrick."

Cox held the smile. Letting silence do the work.

Patrick fumbled with the IV. Cox watched his fingers move, light, precise. No calluses. No rough edges. This one had not done a hard day's work in his life.

"You're handling me awful gentle," Cox said, voice low, testing.

Patrick swallowed. "Just… making sure I don't aggravate the wound."

Cox let the pause stretch. Patrick shifted on his feet. Wet his lips.

Interesting. "Relax, mate." Cox chuckled, easy, knowing. "I won't bite."

Patrick gave a nervous smile. "You're… not like I imagined."

Cox tilted his head. "That right? And what'd you imagine?"

Patrick hesitated. "I don't know. Rougher. Angrier. More …"

"Like a monster?" Cox finished for him.

Patrick shrugged, embarrassed.

Cox sighed, slow and heavy. Regretful. "People love their stories. But I'm just a bloke who made choices. Some good. Some bad." His eyes softened. "You ever make a bad choice, Patrick?"

Patrick nodded, lips pressing together.

"Then you get it," Cox said, voice smooth as glass. He reached out, fingers deliberately grazing Patrick's wrist. Just enough. Patrick didn't pull away.

The kid liked the attention. This was going to be useful. Maybe not today. Maybe not even soon. But people always came in handy when you needed them. People like Patrick always remembered another man's kindness. And medical staff? They had access.

Cox smiled again. "You've been good to me, mate. I appreciate it."

Patrick looked down, adjusting the IV. "Just doing my job."

"Course you are." Cox let his eyes linger, just long enough to let the thought settle. "But still. You never know when a favour might come back around."

Patrick met his gaze then. Uncertain but curious.

Cox just smiled.

People were just puzzles. You find the right pieces, and they slot into place.

CHAPTER 19

The Crew

Next morning, Ray sat playing with Danny in the sandpit. Gail loved seeing the inner child in Ray when he played with Danny. The phone rang, it was Ian. Ray bounded into the house as Gail took his place. He kissed her on the cheek as he passed. Inside, he picked up the phone.

"We have a problem," Ian said, no preamble. His voice was tight.

The grin on Ray's face disappeared. "What's happened?"

"Cox's out. Shot during a break at Long Bay."

Ray let the silence hang, the weight of Ian's words sinking in.

"How bad?" Ray finally asked.

"Bad enough. Even if he pulls through, he won't be walking, let alone making another break for months. He's out of the job."

Ray sighed, pinching the bridge of his nose. "Damn it. We need six."

"I know," Ian said. "What do you think?"

Ray rubbed his temple. "We can't run it with five. The plan is the plan. We can't change it. That's the deal. Start looking for an alternative. We need someone."

"Not easy to replace someone like Cox," Ian muttered. But as Ray's Sergeant at Arms, it fell on him.

"No, it's not," Ray agreed. "But we don't have a choice. Find someone, Ian."

Ray hung up without waiting for a reply.

* * *

The next afternoon, Ian showed up at his dockside warehouse, Laurie in tow. Ray was already there, pacing, waiting, takeaway coffee in his hand.

"Laurie's got a suggestion," Ian said, nodding at the younger man.

"Tony," Laurie said, straightening up. "He's solid. I'll vouch for him."

"Tony?" Ray's brow furrowed. "Who the fuck is Tony?"

"Tony McNamara," Laurie replied. "I've worked with him a couple of times. He's sharp. Trustworthy."

Ray turned to Ian, his eyes narrowing. "You know him?"

"I've seen him around Leo's gym. The docks, too," Ian said. "Don't know him well, but Laurie's vouching for him."

Ray snorted, taking a long pause. "A couple of fights in a gym and loading crates doesn't make a man Cox."

"No, it doesn't," Laurie said, his voice steady. "But Tony's hungry. He listens. He'll do what he's told, no questions asked."

Ray stared at Laurie, weighing his words. "Hungry is good. Stupid's not."

"He's not stupid," Laurie said firmly. "He's green, sure, but he learns fast. He won't get in the way."

Ray kicked non-existent dust on the floor. "This isn't a schoolyard scrap. It's the biggest job of our lives. One mistake, one screw-up, and we're dead, not just in Pentridge."

"I know," Laurie said, meeting Ray's gaze. "And I wouldn't put my name on him if I didn't believe he could do it."

Ray looked to Ian, his expression unreadable. "What do you think?"

Ian shrugged. "We need six, Ray. I don't see anyone else knocking on the door."

Ray sighed, tossing his empty coffee cup into a bin. "Fine. Bring him in. I want to talk to him."

Laurie nodded. "You won't regret it."

Ray turned back to Ian as Laurie left to fetch Tony. "You better be right about this," he muttered.

Ian just nodded. "We'll make it work. I'll make sure."

Ray stared at the warehouse wall, the weight of the job pressing down. They were in it now. No turning back.

* * *

First Get Together

It was a lazy Saturday afternoon. The industrial precinct was deserted. Tony pulled the car to the curb. The street was lined with old, mainly disused, buildings. Felt almost post-apocalyptic. Across the road stood the address. It had probably been a warehouse in its day, given its proximity to the docks. Either late 19th or early 20th century. Faint remnants of a painted street number clung to the second story with its arched windows bricked in long ago. Four stories high, the building loomed, its top row of windows filled with wire-reinforced glass, dirty and grey.

"This is it," Tony said, checking a scrap of paper. He glanced at Laurie, who sat in the passenger seat.

"You sure?" Laurie asked, his tone doubtful as he scanned the lifeless surroundings. "This place looks dead."

"It's the address he gave me," Tony replied. He flicked his lighter, igniting the paper. Holding it until the flame reached his fingers, he dropped it into the ashtray and watched it burn to ash.

They stepped out of the car. Laurie looked up and down the deserted street. Not a car, not a soul. "Figures. This is Ray, after all," he muttered. Tony was already halfway across the road, heading for a narrow doorway on the building's right side.

Inside, the space was cavernous and empty except for steel trestle tables toward the back. Ian sat on one, legs swinging idly.

"Who picked this dump?" Laurie called out, his voice echoing in the vastness as he and Tony approached.

"It's his," came a voice from behind. Laurie and Tony turned to see Vinnie and Normie stepping inside.

"Good for storage," Vinnie added with a smirk. Ian stayed quiet, his eyes fixed on Vinnie, a flicker of annoyance crossing his face. Ian did not like people talking about his business.

"Hi 'Chops'," Tony greeted Normie with a grin.

"That's my uncle," Normie shot back, shaking his head. "Dickhead," he muttered under his breath.

"Who the fuck is he?" Normie asked Vinnie, jerking his chin toward Tony.

"Done a few jobs with Laurie. Seen him around Leo's gym," Vinnie replied casually.

Ian stayed silent, watching the group. Ragtag crew, he thought. *I hope Ray knows what he's doing.*

Laurie looked around the building. There was a steel staircase running up the right-hand side of the interior, opposite Ian. Looked more like a fire escape. At each floor there was a short landing, before turning back on themselves. A rest stop. The stairs were quite steep. At what would be the 3rd floor, they turned back on themselves again, up to a gantry that then ran across the back of the building in front of a set of half-glassed offices. Suddenly, footsteps clanged on the metal above.

Ray appeared on the gantry, leaning over the railing. "Good, you're all here," he said. "Grab a mail sack under the stairs and bring them up." He disappeared into the offices without waiting for a response.

They followed orders, each grabbing a sack. Ian slid off the table and followed the others to the stairs. Last to the pile, he picked up the last two, threw one over each shoulder and bounded up the stairs, catching the others with ease. Unlike the rest of them, Ian's boxing kept him fit. Although street tough, the others were not what you would call fit.

Tony grumbled, "Why couldn't Ray come down to us?"

"Cut the crap," Ian called back.

On the gantry, Tony dropped his sack and opened it. "What the fuck?" he shouted. "Phone books? You've got to be kidding me."

Ray stepped out of the office, calm. "Check your sacks," he said.

One by one, they opened the bags, all filled with the same useless weight.

"That," Ray said, "is what a million bucks feels like. If you can't carry it, walk away now."

Ian smirked. "Guess that makes my share two million."

"Not funny," Normie bit back.

Ray's voice cut through. "You're all here because I know you can handle the biggest job this city's ever seen. But right now, the dogs will have you before you can get out of the building. You're soft. Match fitness isn't optional. If you want in, you will need to prove it. Are you in or out?" Ray knew everyone's answer but wanted to hear them verbalise their commitment.

One by one, he pointed. "Ian?"

"In," Ian said firmly.

"Laurie?"

"In."

"Tony?"

"In."

"Normie?"

"In."

"Vinnie?"

"In."

Ray nodded, satisfied. "Good. Now grab those sacks. Three more laps up and down these stairs. Then we'll talk."

He grabbed one of Ian's sacks and headed down the stairs. They all followed.

* * *

The Briefing

The top office was a hollow shell. One large room and two smaller ones divided by half-glass partitions. The only furniture was a steel trestle table set dead centre in the main space.

Ray stood behind the table, arms crossed. The others lined the walls, still red-faced and breathless from the stairs.

"The job," Ray said, his voice steady, "is the Victoria Club."

That got their attention. The room fell silent. Everyone straightened, taking a step closer.

"The bookies?" Vinnie asked, breaking the quiet.

"Yes," Ray said. "We hit them after a long weekend, after multiple meetings. The take should be two million plus!"

The room erupted with mutters and overlapping questions. Ray waited. He did not rush. When the noise subsided, he leaned forward.

"We can do this. We will. But it won't be easy. Everyone will need to be at their best. The stairs were just the start. We're going to train. And then train some more. Until you can keep up with Ian. Starting Monday, we're doing a training camp. Let your missus know."

Groans circled the room, but no one spoke up.

"Speed is everything," Ray continued. "The Consorting Squad drops by at random. If they show up, we handle it, but the goal is to be in and out before anyone knows what hit them. Avoid a shootout if possible. This isn't a movie. We're choreographing this like a ballet. Everyone moves fast, and everyone moves together. No hesitation."

He paused, letting the weight of the plan sink in.

"This will be shock and awe. Automatic weapons. The works. Ian, you can handle that."

Ian nodded. Ray did not wait for confirmation.

"Ian's Master at Arms. Guns, munitions, whatever we need. Also, he'll keep you boys in line," Ray said, looking at Ian to emphasise the point.

He turned to Normie. "Normie: You're the accountant. You take care of the money. In and out. Anyone who needs cash for prep they come to you. After the job, we need a safe spot to stash the cash and a plan to clean it. Work it out."

"Vinnie." Ray's gaze shifted. "You're security. From now until the job, no booze. No excuses. No slips. Keep everyone in line. After the job, we'll have every dog and lowlife sniffing around. Start planning for that now."

"Laurie: Logistics. Overalls, masks, everything we need for the job. Get a van. A fast getaway car too; clean, powerful. Gloves on at all times. And clean as you go. No fingerprints. No mistakes."

"Tony: You're the driver. I want you driving like you're in the Le Mans. Whether it's the van or the car, you're our lifeline if things go south. Train for it. And help Laurie when he needs it."

Ray straightened. "This is the big one, boys. No surprises. No fuckups. Stay sharp. Napoleon said, 'Everything turns to shit the moment the first shot is fired.' So learn everyone's job. Be ready to adapt."

"So, now you're the General?" joked Laurie.

"Always has been," Ian said, his voice dry but certain.

That is what set Ray apart. He didn't just plan. He planned for failure, for chaos, for the things you couldn't see coming. Like Napoleon, he also had marshals he knew could roll with the punches and improvise as needed.

* * *

Outside, Laurie approached Vinnie. "Tony and I are goin' for a drink. Wanna come?"

"You heard the General. Off the grog till the job's done."

"Starts Monday!" Laurie shot back, a huge grin on his face.

Vinnie looked over his shoulder to see Ian's '56 Dodge pickup drive away. He liked a drink and was not looking forward to the enforced abstinence. And he was the one who had to enforce it. He knew Ray; that was not an accident.

"I guess I'm to keep an eye on you two now. Where?"

"The Rising Sun," Laurie said, following Tony walk to his car.

"Hang on," Vinnie called, running after them. "I'm coming with you," and jumped into the back seat.

* * *

Ray and Normie went back to the Dim Sim factory to play cards. Nothing had been said, nor organised. It just was. They had known each other since they were kids. Normie was the only person he felt relaxed around. Ian and he were tight, but there was always something there. Competition maybe.

After Normie had poured them a large whisky each and dealt the first hand, he said, "Need a hand to set up the camp for Monday?"

"No. Ian will do it. He'll be in charge of the training." Ray's answer implying he did not want to talk about the job. There would be plenty of time for that.

They played cards for a couple of hours, drinking and talking about old times and old faces. Finally, Ray said goodbye, called a taxi, and headed home.

* * *

When Ian got home, he went straight into his study and closed the door. He made two long-distance calls to the United States. Done, he opened the door to find Rae standing hands on hips.

"So much for not bringing your work into our home," she said coldly.

"One call." He dismissed her upset. He walked past her into the kitchen. That did not improve her mood.

"Don't ignore me," she said, following him.

"You want me to go legit! Well, that was a call to the States about importing car parts. Legit! What else do you want from me?"

"I want you to spend time with your family like a normal father."

"I will soon. But next week I'm taking the boys on a fitness camp. Going up country, some place Ray found."

"Ray," Raelene said despondently. "Of course."

171

"Back Friday. We'll do something next weekend," he said, grabbing a juice and heading to the living room.

Next weekend is a lifetime away in Ian's world, Rae thought. Anything could happen. "Next weekend? You don't even know what day it is," Rae called out to him.

CHAPTER 20

Team Building

Ray knew he had a good crew. They had all worked together before at different times, got along, and could hold their end. However, currently, they were six hardened individuals. This job would require them to work together like a Swiss watch. Training would be about more than fitness.

Monday morning, Ian picked Ray up early. Unlike the normal criminal class, which they looked down on, Painter and Dockers were early risers. It gave them an edge.

The back of the pickup had a tarp over it, but it seemed to be full. Gail came out to the porch as Ray walked to the Dodge pickup. Ian waved, but received no response. Ray opened the door, threw his overnight bag behind the seat, and got in.

"Someone in the shit," said Ian stating the obvious, maybe enjoying it a bit too much.

"Just drive," came Ray's curt reply as he slammed the door to annoy Ian.

They drove to the Dim Sim factory, where Tony and Laurie were waiting. They formed a convoy of three cars and headed out of town on Highway 31. Normie and Vinnie brought up the rear in Normie's Mercedes. After two hours, they turned off after the army base. Eventually, they turned off the 'B' road onto a dirt track, finally pulling up outside a hunting shack. Not much more than a lean-to.

Ray swung out and leaned against the pickup as the others pulled up. The morning was crisp, the kind that chilled the lungs and kept men quiet. He called to the others, "Throw your bags inside, then come and help Ian offload and set up."

He looked over at Ian and nodded, "Let's get to it."

Ian walked to the back, yanked off the tarp, and let the tailgate fall. There were 2-inch-thick long ropes. Long and short heavy beams. Skip ropes, weights, and even a heavy punching bag. The crew gathered around, jaws slack as they stared at the pile.

"What the hell is all this?" Laurie asked, scratching his head.

"Training," Ray said flatly. "If you can't handle this, you can't handle the job."

Normie grumbled, "We're not training for the Olympics."

Ray ignored them. "Get to work. Clear the ground and set it up. This isn't a debate."

They spent the day building an obstacle course, sweating under the sun, and cursing under their breath. By nightfall, no one had the energy to argue. Normie's stew was eaten in silence, and they all collapsed into their makeshift bunks.

The next morning, before dawn, Ian's voice tore through the cold air. "Up! Five clicks, cross-country. Move it!"

Groaning and cursing, they laced up their boots and started running. Ray set the pace, Ian brought up the rear, barking orders. By the time they stumbled back, legs burning, the thought of breakfast felt like a distant dream.

"Circuits after this," Ian announced.

"Give us a break, Sarge," Laurie muttered, earning a glare from Ian.

They worked through upper body drills, core training, and sprints until their bodies felt like lead. By sunset, they were dead on their feet, buggered.

So went the next three days.

* * *

On Thursday night, after lights out, Laurie nudged Tony.

"Let's get out of here," he whispered.

Tony did not need any convincing. They slipped away, climbing into Tony's car, and headed toward the army base. True to form, opposite the base turn-off, they found an old stone country pub. Tony pulled up out front, and they headed inside.

The rancid smell of beer and cigarette smoke hit them as they walked in. "This," Laurie said, grinning, "is what heaven smells like."

They headed to the bar, ordered two beers, and propped on stools.

"Those are our seats," came a voice behind them.

Laurie turned to see two massive bikers glaring at them.

"Didn't see your name on them," Tony said, but decided against pushing it further. He nudged Laurie and they picked up their beers and moved a few stools along.

"Still our seats," another voice growled. They turned to see another two bikies standing there.

"This is our bar. Now fuck off," rang the voice of the leader joining the others. He was flanked by what appeared to be another five or six equally large bikers.

"Sorry, we didn't know," smiled Laurie, trying to charm his way out of the situation as usual. "We'll just finish these and go."

"You'll leave now or get carried out," came the reply.

175

Laurie looked at Tony and shook his head. "OK, we'll leave." Both pushed their beers away and stood.

* * *

Vinnie lay in the grass, eyes on the pale sky, watching clouds drift across it. The day looked sunny, but the air had a bite. Damp earth and cut grass filled his nose.

Something nudged his ribs. A cow, he thought. He rolled away, wanting to ignore it. Take in the day. The nudge came again, harder. A kick followed.

It wasn't a cow; it was Ray's boot.

Vinnie looked up. Ray stood over him; gave a sharp nod sideways.

Vinnie followed his gaze. Tony and Laurie's bunks were empty. Ray nodded again, toward the door.

Vinnie grabbed his boots and jacket. He hopped into them as he followed Ray out.

Inside, Ian shook Normie awake. "C'mon. Tony and Laurie have taken off."

"So? Probably hit the pub. They'll come back."

"If Ray or Vinnie get to them first, there's a good chance they won't be coming back." Ian didn't wait for more arguments. He knew he would have to catch them and settle some feathers.

"Why do I have to come?"

"You're driving." Ian tossed him the keys.

They did not need directions. There was only one pub out their way; just past the army base. Normie floored it. The Mercedes fishtailed. Catching up to Ian's Dodge was easy. They did, just as it turned into the pub's car park.

Ian jumped out and followed Ray and Vinnie at a run. Past a row of parked bikes. Big ones. Flashy. Not the kind weekend riders take out. These were serious.

Normie trailed behind, unhurried.

176

Then …

"Finish your beers," Vinnie's voice boomed, stepping into the bar, flanked by Ray and Ian. He had heard the bikies' threat.

The leader turned to see another four men dressed identical to the two kids at the bar. New tracksuits. Heavy army boots. He sneered. "You got a death wish?"

Vinnie did not answer. Just stepped up to him and delivered a Liverpool Kiss. A full force head-butt down onto the bridge of his nose. The leader was unconscious before he hit the floor. Chaos erupted.

Ian and Ray moved fast, taking out two bikers each. Laurie and Tony launched into the original two. Those guys hit hard. Laurie and Tony were bloody-lipped and bruised eyes, but were the ones left standing by the end.

Normie slipped behind the bar and was helping himself to a top-shelf whisky while the others finished the fight. The barmaid had long since disappeared. Most likely calling the cops. After Ian and Vinnie finished off the last two, they turned and stared at Normie.

"What?" he said. "You had it under control."

Ray shook his head.

"Wasn't really a fair fight. Only a dozen of them." Normie continued. They all burst out laughing.

"Set them up," said Ray, stepping up to the bar. Normie pulled out another five glasses and set them on the bar. He poured three fingers of whisky into each of them.

"The Victoria Club," Ray said, raising his glass.

"The Victoria Club," they echoed, downing their drinks.

Sirens wailed in the distance.

"Time to go," Ray said. They walked to their cars.

Tony and Laurie laughing, animated. Reliving their actions, blow by blow.

Ian and Vinnie following. "Next camp," Ian said to Vinnie, "I'll teach you to box."

"No," Vinnie replied, "I'll teach you to fight." They laughed.

Normie then Ray, a few steps behind. Watching those ahead, Ray smiled to himself. Now we're a team.

They climbed into their cars and headed back to camp.

CHAPTER 21

Putting the Job Together

Guns and Ammo

After returning from that first boot camp, all crew members were fully occupied with their appointed preparation duties.

The calls Ian made that first night were to separate contacts he had in the States. The first, a second-hand car part dealer to confirm the shipping details for a container of vintage car panels and parts. Another of his side hustles. That, he had not lied to Rae about.

The other call was to an 'off-market' gun supplier. Like car parts, second-hand guns were also dead cheap in the States. With or without serial numbers. He informed them that the car parts consignment was ready for shipping. For a service fee, they would go in at night and add Ian's other order to the container. At the back.

In the early days of container freight, customs checks were only cursory. On arrival, customs would open the container and if the boxes were labelled "car parts", they would check it off and reseal the container. Even if a zealous official opened the boxes, a full container of car parts was too much to check all the way through to the back.

When Ian got the call from the forwarding agent that the container was released, he called Tony and asked him to arrange the pickup and delivery of the container.

* * *

Laurie waved from the step of the big rig's cab, grinning like he had won a bet.

"Thought you'd want to see this," Laurie called out as Ian approached.

Ian ignored him for the moment and walked up to the clipboard-wielding dock clerk. The man was mid-chew on a wad of gum, barely glancing up.

"I'd like container OCL536 off first," Ian said flatly.[41]

The clerk did not even look at him. "Yeah? And I'd like a million bucks. Wait your turn."

Ian stood there, unflinching.

The clerk finally glanced up. His expression changed instantly. "Oh. Mr. Carroll. I, I didn't realise it was you." The gum stopped moving. As Union Secretary, Ian had the power to shut down the dock.

"Get it done," Ian said. His voice was quiet, but the weight behind it was clear.

The clerk fumbled for his radio. "Uh, crane, bring down OCL536. Priority."

Ian watched as the crane whirred to life, its arm swinging toward the stacked containers. The rumble of machinery drowned out the clerk's muttering apologies.

As the container descended, Laurie hopped down from the truck cab. "Surprised to see me?" he asked, all smiles.

Ian looked up at the rig's driver. "Tony?"

Tony grinned from behind the wheel. "Yeah, Ian. Laurie's my wingman for a change."

Ian shook his head but allowed himself a small smirk. He could trust these two. They might clown around, but they got the job done.

"No need for me to tag along, then," Ian said, his tone lighter now. "Make sure it gets unloaded properly. No surprises."

"Relax, boss," Laurie said, slapping Ian's shoulder. "We've got this."

Once the container was on board, Tony gave a thumbs-up from the cab. Laurie climbed back in. The big rig groaned into motion, heading down and off the dock.

When the truck had disappeared down the road, Ian went into the union office and made a call. "Ray," he said. "They're here."

Ray's voice was almost giddy. "The hardware?"

"Yeah," Ian said.

"When can we get started?" Ray asked, his excitement spilling over.

Ian sighed, glancing at his watch. "I still need to inventory everything. Tonight's going to be late."

"Forget that," Ray said. "Let's take them out to the camp this weekend. Get everyone trained up. That's why I chose somewhere next to an army camp."

Ian's jaw tightened. "You think these things unpack and check themselves? I've got to follow that container and make sure it's unloaded right. Then go through everything piece by piece."

Ray chuckled. "That's what you're good at."

Ian did not reply. He would have to follow the container now. Unpack and check the guns and ammunition inventories. Another late night followed by another weekend away. Rae was going to be pissed. Ian shook his head and walked back to his car. [42]

$$* * *$$

Planning and Preparation

Ray, Ian, and Normie spent a lot of time together over the next few months. They covered every aspect of the job. They reviewed the Architect's plans over and over, identifying all possible contingencies.

Ray raised his head after re-reading the Architect's notes for the umpteenth time. "I'm not happy with the idea of just dumping all that cash in an empty office. Some prick might steal it," he smirked. "Let's get a big fucking safe to put it in. Can you organise that, Normie?"

"Ian, check out their security systems and whether we can bypass them. Also, we don't want some random turning up in the middle of the job. So see what you can do about the lifts."

"Normie, see if you can find us an office opposite that we can use to film Mayne Nics and Consorting comings and goings," said Ray. "Use the same ghost company that leased the office above AJC. No need for added costs." He smiled.

"We really need someone outside during the job. Playing cockatoo," Ray said to no one in particular. "We need to know if the Consorting arseholes turn up, or it could get messy.

"What about Frankie?" Ian suggested. "He certainly showed he's got it. Remember the time he was nabbed with the gelignite."

"Ok, sus him out. Tell him as little as possible. And it's not a full share." Ray directed.

And so the meetings went on. Covering laundering the money, setting alibis. A bolt car for if things turned south. Every point on the Architect's plan was reviewed and put into action.

$$* * *$$

Laurie peered through the camera lens, adjusting the focus. The second-floor windows of the Victoria Club came into sharp view. The Settling Room. Inside, bookies moved like busy ants, shuffling cash, placing bets, talking in low murmurs. Money changed hands. Lots of it.

"How's that?" he asked, one eye still in the viewfinder.

"Perfect," Ray said. Arms crossed, eyes on the street. Always watching.

Laurie clicked the record button. The reel-to-reel whirred to life.

They had rented an empty office across the street on the third floor of the Scottish Amicable Life Association building. Prime real estate for a stakeout.

"No surprises. no fuck-ups," Ian muttered, leaning against the window. "We go in knowing everything."

They were filming another settling day. The armoured van pulled up out front of the Victoria Club.

"Who's the guys in the support car?" Laurie asked, eye still glued to the viewfinder.

"Don't worry about them. They're not Consorting, just security company guys. They stay outside."

Laurie muttered, "11:40, on time as usual," as he wrote it into the log. Watched as the strongboxes disappeared into the building. "Those support guys must be late for lunch," he quipped as the support car drove off.

Laurie yawned, stretching back in his chair. "It's like watching grass grow." He flicked the camera to the street below. An old bloke in a tweed coat shuffled along, clutching a racing form. "Hey, he looks like Normie's long-lost dad. Should we let him in on the job?"

Ray ignored him.

Laurie swung the camera back up. Inside, a bookie scratched his arse and sniffed his fingers. Laurie snorted.

"What?" Ian asked.

"Nothing," Laurie smirked. "Just high society at work."

"Focus," Ray snapped.

Laurie sighed, stretching his arms. "Come on, we've been watching them for weeks. Same blokes, same routine. It's like studying racehorses."

Ray turned. "Yeah, except we ain't gambling."

Laurie grinned. "I dunno, Ray. I'd put ten on that fat bastard to keel over before the next long weekend."

Vinnie chuckled from the corner. Ian smirked. Even Ray's lips twitched.

Laurie flicked the camera off. "Right, I'm grabbing a pie. Anyone else?"

Ray sighed. "Jesus, Laurie. We're planning a robbery."

Laurie grabbed his coat. "Yeah, and I'm planning not to starve before we pull it off. I'll be back before the Consorting dogs get here at 12:30 as usual."

Ray shook his head. Laurie was a pain in the arse. But he kept things light. And sometimes, that wasn't the worst thing.

* * *

The Safe delivery men struggled to manoeuvre the massive steel safe into the rented office two floors up from the Victoria Club.

"Careful with that," Normie barked.

The men groaned as they set it down with a heavy thud.

"Where do you want it?" one of them asked.

"Right there," Normie said, motioning against the back wall. "That'll do."

The men wiped their brows. "Hell of a safe."

"Yeah," Normie said. "Got a lot to protect."

He signed the papers. The delivery crew left. The safe was empty now, but soon enough, it would be full.

* * *

After 9 PM, the club was empty on Saturday nights. No voices. Just the hum of fridges in the empty lounge. Security? Non-existent. Ian and Vinnie had slipped in just after four, business hours. Posed as punters, then vanished into the shadows of the first-floor dining room. It wasn't used on Saturdays. No one would look twice. When the staff clocked off and the lights dimmed, they moved. Quiet, measured, up to the second floor.

Ian crouched in front of the security panel, flashlight clenched between his teeth. He had spent weeks studying its system. A standard commercial setup; simple, but effective.

With careful hands, he ran the insulated wire under the panel casing. A single cut in the right place, then a bypass. If done right, the system would still appear armed, but when hit, there would be no alarm.

The snip was quiet. A slight hum from the panel. Then silence.

He held his breath. Waited. Nothing.

Next, he found the panic alarm circuit connected to the cage. It was standalone. He easily bypassed it. If pressed, nothing would happen.

He smiled, wiped his hands on his jeans, and stood up.

Back at the door, he turned to Vinnie. "Done."

Vinnie grunted, bored, looking at his nails. "You sure?"

Ian just gave him a look.

"All right," Vinnie said, looking up. "Let's get the fuck out of here."

185

"No. I want to set up a second way out through the back. In case everything turns to shit. I need to fix the rear lift to stop it bypassing the second floor."

"What if someone turns up mid-job?" Vinnie asked, querying the move.

"Everyone knows it doesn't stop at the second floor. So no one will," Ian shut Vinnie down.

When they got to the back stairwell, Ian began rewiring the lift. Vinnie worked on cutting the bolt to the fire escape exit door and drilling a peephole into the lounge.

Both done, they left by the rear fire escape without a sound.

* * *

The warehouse wasn't much, but to Ray, it looked like victory. Every corner mirrored the second floor of the Victoria Club. The cage? Welded from scrap. Trestles substituted for tables and bars, posts for corners. Boxes for phones. The lift, a façade, but close enough. Ian had even built a dummy panic button, wired to nothing. "Closest thing to a live rehearsal you'll ever get," he'd said. They moved through it now, each step drilled into muscle memory.

"Again," Ray called, looking at his stopwatch.

They moved fast. Knew where every door, every counter, every piece of furniture would be.

Shock and awe.

They came in loud, weapons raised, then fell silent. No talking. No names. Commands were shouted, never whispered. Voices could be recognised.

"Louder!" Ian barked.

They ran drills over and over, memorising their places. The angles, the escape routes, the contingencies.

Laurie wiped the sweat from his forehead, adding, "I hope this is worth it."

Ray smirked. "Oh, it will be."

* * *

Dress Rehearsal

Easter Monday, the club was closed. The street was quiet. The CBD was a ghost town on long weekends. Around midnight, Tony pulled into the laneway behind the Victoria Club. Ian and Vinnie got out, took two heavy duffle bags out of the boot, and walked to the rear fire door. With one hard yank, the temporarily glued bolt gave way, and the door opened. Tony ran up the rear stairs, eighty-six of them, and checked the back peephole into the lounge. Empty. Gave a whistle. Ian and Vinnie took the lift to the second floor.

Meanwhile, around in Queen Street, Ray, Normie, and Laurie broke into the abandoned building next door. Up to the third floor.

Laurie worked the hidden access door. The bolts came loose, cut in half. It would be lightly glued back in place later.

"One push and we're in," Laurie said, dusting his hands.

Ray nodded. "No noise. No hassle."

Normie drilled a tiny hole through the door frame, lining it up perfectly with the Settling Room. He crouched, looking through. A clear view of the inside.

"Perfect," he whispered.

A knock came from the other side.

Ray stepped forward. Gave the old door a firm kick. It sprang open. Ian caught it before it could slam against the wall. Ray, Normie and Laurie stepped into the Victoria Club.

Six men stood looking at one another. Grinning.

"OK," Ray started. "We only get one go at this, so make it worthwhile."

"Normie, head up the stairs. Check it's clear to our office, and the way back out."

"Tony, phones."

"Laurie, get to know the downstairs layout."

"Ian, check out the Settling Room and teller's cage."

"Vinnie, take out one of the lounge fridges."

"Get to it. Meet back in thirty for a dry run," Ray finished.

The six scattered.

Vinnie sabotaged the fridge motor in the bar. "By Wednesday, they'll be calling for a repairman," he said to himself.

Tony confirmed each phone location. Tested how secure each was. Did a trial run. He tripped over the phone table outside the Settling Room. "I'll have to get rid of that."

They all used the time effectively. Confident. Thirty minutes later, they met up back at the false door.

"All right, let's go through it one step at a time," Ray commanded.

Ray stood back, watching it all come together. He was noticing a subtle change in Laurie. Becoming more definite. Harder. His stance, his look. He was cloning Vinnie. That didn't hurt.

* * *

The six of them stood inside the Settling Room, chests heaving. This was their dress rehearsal. No more mock-ups. The real McCoy. It was dark. Only the reflective light through the Queen Street windows. That would force them to raise their awareness levels.

"One more time!" Ray's voice echoed through the empty building.

A collective sigh followed.

"We'll keep doing it until it's perfect," he said. No argument. No discussion.

The first run was a mess. Tony tripped over Laurie coming out of the hidden door. Normie went to the wrong end of the bar; no exit. Vinnie turned the wrong way when herding the guards and bookies from the Settling Room into the lounge. A disaster.

The second run was better. Still too slow.

"We need this under ten minutes," Ray said. "Every extra minute gives the Consorting dogs time to show up."

Tony shifted. "If we hear Frankie's three horn blasts, do we clear out?"

Ray's glare was sharp. "Don't you listen?" His voice cut through the room. "Just do your job. Ian, Vinnie, and I will handle the dogs if they come up the stairs."

No more questions. No more delays.

"Back in position," Ray ordered. "We go again."

They filed back through the hidden door into the adjacent building. Reset.

"Go!" Ray clicked the stopwatch.

They moved fast. Hand-offs to Laurie. Normie to the lounge.

"One minute," Ray called, looking at his stopwatch. They picked up the pace.

Guards secured. Phones cut. Laurie downstairs and back.

"Four minutes."

The cage opened. Phone books transferred from one mail sack to another. So it went until Vinnie came and grabbed the last sack.

"Time!" Ray clicked the stopwatch. Looked at the numbers.

"Ten minutes, thirty-two." He paused. Looked at their faces waiting for his judgment.

"Good enough," it came. "That was in the dark. Wednesday will be easier."

This time, the collective sigh was one of satisfaction.

"Why are we leaving the guns?" Vinnie asked as he packed them back into the two duffle bags.

"Too hard to conceal leaving the building," Ray replied. "Might as well wave a sign saying 'Hey, we're the robbers'."

"Why not leave them upstairs with the cash?"

"This will distract them and they won't think about searching the building."

They collected all their gear and left the way they came. Ray was last. One final check. Everything back in place. No alarms. No witnesses. No escape.

The access door was re-sealed. Ray smiled to himself. Come Wednesday, the place would never look the same again.

He turned and walked down to join the others.

CHAPTER 22

Another 11 Minutes

April 21, 1976

For Vinnie, the day had started well. He woke early, daybreak. Always did. Didn't need to look at his watch. 4:30 AM, automatic since Turana. Had spent two years in the kitchen, up at 4:30 every day. There were few memories of his father, but he did remember one piece of his father's advice. "If ever you find yourself in the army or prison, get on the kitchen detail." That had stuck. He had been given two years for pinching a bike. The trouble was that the owner was on it at the time. Kitchen work meant extra food. And a knife for his sock.

He rolled out of bed, careful not to wake Jill. The room was dim with pre-dawn light. His body ached the way it always did; years of hard living. No regrets. He limped to the bathroom, unconsciously rubbing the bullet wound scars on his shoulder and side as he took a leak. The day's job crept in. He shook his head. Not yet. Splashed water on his face. Cold. Awake now.

Heading out to the garage, he grabbed shorts, singlet, and towel from the laundry and dressed on the way. Ian had helped him convert the old garage into a gym. The car now parked in the street.

First, five minutes of skipping rope. No running. Running was for pussies. Bench work next. Free weights. Then one hundred sit-ups on the incline. One hundred push-ups; a mix of two and one-handed. Beam squat walks. Finally, thirty minutes on the bags. Heavy and speed ball.

By the time he stepped back inside, the sun was pushing through the terrace gaps. He showered, dressed, and ate alone. Went to the kids' room. He didn't usually kiss them goodbye. Today was different. They were still asleep, sharing a room. Hopefully, after today, each will have their own. He stood in the doorway, memorising their faces. Might be the last time. He kissed each on the forehead, then left.

He caught a tram through the city to Ian's warehouse near the docks. Left the Valiant for Jill, as usual.

Ian was there already. Always was. Did the bloke ever sleep?

That big grin greeted him, wide as ever. Ian, younger by a year, shorter by two inches, Vinnie had been his protector since day one. Felt like his big brother. But somehow, Ian still led the way. Vinnie didn't mind. Felt natural.

Ian handed over a coffee. "Saw you get off the tram," nodding upstairs. The upstairs office overlooked the surrounding buildings to the main road, classic Ian. Always watching.

"Big day," Vinnie quipped.

"Pay day," Ian replied, slapping him on the back. "Cum'on, let's get the gear out."

A concealed storeroom was under the stairs. Its door, a return-air vent. Behind was an armed robber's Aladdin's cave. Automatic weapons. Scanners. Clothes.

Ian pulled out two duffle bags and passed them over. No words, Vinnie knew the drill. He packed the weapons. The M16 last. On top. Carried them out to the main floor and dumped them on a table.

Then, Bennett arrived with his shadow, Normie. Took over the room like he always did. Voice tight, movements clipped, no wasted words. They prepped fast, methodical. Like a ritual.

Vinnie left them to it. Went for a smoke.

* * *

In the warehouse doorway, he stood watching sun rays dancing in the dust. Waiting gave a man too much time to think. He tightened the strap on his wrist brace. Not support, just habit.

Laurie stood a few feet away, fiddling with his bootlaces, nerves buzzing off him like static.

Vinnie stepped closer. Low voice. "You good, Laurie?"

Laurie jumped. "Yeah. Just …"

"Look," Vinnie said. "This is not a job, it's war. We get in, we get out. Keep your eyes open. No panic, just follow the plan. You know what you have to do. If you see a problem, solve it. Fast, automatic, no thinking. Thinking gets you killed."

Laurie nodded.

Vinnie clapped him on the shoulder, firm, confident. "You'll be fine. Just don't freeze."

Laurie watched Vinnie wander back inside. Breathed easier. Nodded.

* * *

Vivian's Day

On the other side of town, Vivian was getting ready for work. She was on the wrong side of forty, and it took longer to make herself look competitive these days. Against the young ones, it felt like war. Whoever said it was a man's world had understated it. The world belonged to men and young women.

At forty, you weren't just invisible. You were vulnerable.

Once things started to drop, her ex dropped her. Traded her for a younger wife, one of his clients. She got the house and the kids. He got twenty years younger. Now the kids were gone too. One off at uni in Sydney. The other somewhere in Europe.

She had a roof over her head, sure, but the bills did not stop. So she worked. First, as a barmaid while raising the kids. Now she ran the members' lounge at the Victoria Club. As high as a woman could go in a place like that. The ultimate men's club.

Vivian checked her stomach in the mirror again. The Easter weekend had not been kind to her figure. Saturday with the girls, Sunday at her sister's. The perfect family, as she was reminded, constantly. Monday, a date with another loser. Hopefully, he would not call again.

Last night she had an early night, but still, she felt the pounds on her waist. And the members did not hesitate to comment on her figure. If only she could comment on theirs.

She grabbed her hat and threw on her overcoat over the light white blouse and tight skirt. Headed for the train. Heels were not made for running, but she had perfected the art. Age gave you some advantages. She thought fleetingly, maybe one day women would be able to wear tennis shoes to work. Fantasy. Men would never allow that.

She caught the train, made it into the city, and arrived at the club ten minutes before her shift. Late in her boss's eyes.

He was waiting by the office on the first floor. Frank Murray, Club Secretary. "It's a big settling day today, Vivian," he reminded her as she removed her coat and hat. She did not need the reminder.

"You could always pay me to start at ten on big days."

"Just get the lounge ready," he said. "Members are already waiting."

She signed in, grabbed the till floats, and headed upstairs. Most private clubs ran accounts, but not the Victoria Club. Cash was still king. Nature of the beast. Slowed service down, but made for good tips.

That was the thing about the bookies. Sexist, yes. But hearts of gold. Generous. Big tippers. Funny and good-natured. Vivian liked it here. Frank let her run things her way, most of the time.

"Morning, Josh," she said to the young barman already on duty. She didn't wait for a reply. No time. She set up the tills, unlocked the storeroom, and opened the door to the Settling Room. A dozen bookies were already inside.

As expected, the moment the door opened, they swarmed.

"Hold your horses, boys," Vivian called. "We'll get to you all." She smiled.

At the sound of the lift door opening, she looked over to see the two young waitresses stroll in. Chatting. Five minutes late, as usual. Oh to be in your twenties again. You could get away with murder.

"C'mon, girls," she shouted. "We're getting hammered here."

They picked up the pace, hung their coats in the alcove, and joined her behind the bar. The good thing about the upstairs lounge was that it had a very long bar. Four people could work it at the same time. Finally, the second barman came up from downstairs. At last, the initial rush died down.

Vivian slipped out from behind the bar. Worked the room. Chatted with the bookies and punters. She kept track of the weekend races. Knew the racing talk. Members talked of little else. Who was good, who was bad, who had been pulled up, and who was in the know.

"Putting on a few pounds there, Viv," came a voice from behind her.

"Thanks, Wally," she smiled. "Big weekend."

"Certainly was," he said, patting his pocket.

"You always do well, Wally."

He tapped her on the bum and slipped her a twenty.

"You're my best girl."

"Thanks, Wally," she smiled, slipping it into her pocket and moving to the next table.

She heard the faint midday chime from the town hall clock. Money should be arriving. I should check the Settling Room to see if anyone needs anything. She stuck her head in. The room stank of cigarette smoke, stale sweat, and cheap cologne. Someone should have a word to those clerks. The area was about half the size of the lounge but had about twenty bookies falling over each other, jockeying for position.

"Anyone need anything?" she called over the din. She was not going to venture any further into that room.

No reply.

She turned and walked straight into a Mayne Nickless guard. He caught her arms.

"Careful, little lady," Charlie said, shifting her away from a trolley stacked with strongboxes. "These could do you some damage."

"Sorry, Charlie." She glanced at the unfamiliar face beside him and raised an eyebrow. "Big day, huh?"

"You could say that," Charlie said. "Must've been a good weekend. Twice as much today."

Vivian glanced at the four cashboxes. Charlie caught Vivian's raised eyebrow.

"This is only half," he said.

She nodded. "I'll leave you to it then. When you're done, come over. I'll shout you a beer."

Charlie smiled. Nice guy, she thought, heading back to the bar.

"Glasses!" she called out, pointing to the full tray of dirty glasses beside the sink. The girls looked at each other. Neither moved, wanting the other one to do the clean-up. Flirting was more important. Vivian shook her head, picked up the tray, and carried it out.

Then, an almighty crash. Yelling.

By the time she came back in, she was staring at a figure dressed head to toe in black. A Tommy gun pointing at her. Like something out of the 1920s.

"Everyone down on the floor!" the voice boomed.

The man moved like a shadow. He was behind the bar before she could think.

He shoved the five of them out into the lounge at the point of his gun.

Vivian put her arms around the two young waitresses. Not as a shield. Not for comfort. Just a mother's instinct. The barmen were old enough to look after themselves.

Then the bookies from the Settling Room came pouring in. Another voice, harsher, deeper, cut through. "Everyone face down on the floor!"

The first gunman pushed the three women to a table up front. Told them to sit.

The giant figure of Wally stood in front of them. He looked confused, like he was lost.

The second voice barked again. "Down. Now."

Wally crashed to the floor, revealing the second gunman. Bigger than the first. Tommy gun aimed right at her.

Vivian threw her arms around the girls' shoulders. Pushed their heads down, but kept eye contact with the gunman. His eyes narrowed.

"If anyone tries anything, the women go first." His eyes locked on hers.

The girls were crying now. Vivian held them tighter.

"Down. If you lift your head, I'll blow it off."

Silence followed. Heavy breathing. Whimpers.

Then a voice, young, reckless.

"That means you, Ambrose."

Vivian glanced at the voice. A smaller, obviously younger gunman. The bigger one swung around, pointing his gun at the voice. Not good body language. She shifted her feet back, lowering her arms on the girls' backs. At the first sound of gunfire, she would ensure all three of them were flat on the floor.

She closed her eyes. Held her breath.

Nothing. Time passed. Still nothing.

The clock on the wall ticked. Every breath felt like a minute. Then the big one spoke.

"I'll be waiting outside for ten minutes. Anyone who shows their head gets it blown off."

The footsteps faded. They waited. Still. And waited.

Wally looked up at Vivian. "Has it been ten minutes?" he whispered.

Vivian nodded. "I reckon so."

Frank stood. The first one to move.

"Call the police!" he said. Calm. Controlled. Vivian was impressed. Handling it better than expected.

Vivian helped Wally onto a chair. She had the stronger girl hold the other. Went to the bar and returned with a double scotch. Sat it down in front of Wally. He picked it up with two hands and started sipping.

She looked over at Charlie. He was holding the new guard. Blood was flowing down the side of his face. Vivian grabbed a bar towel, rushed over, and dabbed the wound.

Passed it to Charlie. She shook Charlie's arm, looked him in the eye. He nodded, he was ok.

Next, the two barmen. She got them back behind the bar, serving. Everyone needed a drink. Looking around, Frank was back with the girls, people settled. What now?

Then, the thunder of heavy leather boots. Dozens. The room filled with uniformed police. It was their domain now.

Vivian quietly slipped into the back alcove, sat on a chair, and gave herself permission to cry.

* * *

The Meet Up

By 6 PM, the six bookie robbers were seated around a corner table in a pub in South Melbourne. Beers in hand. The job had gone to plan. A thing of beauty. In and out in 11 minutes; money safely stashed; alibis sorted. Frankie would take care of the evidence. Job done.

No talk of the job. Relaxed. Just another day. This was a businessman's drinking hole. But by this time, the bar was all but deserted. The day workers had left for home, to dinner and their wives. The TV over the bar was blaring non-stop news reports of the **biggest robbery in Australian history.** They had already named it: *The Great Bookie Robbery.*

Only a solitary barmaid stood behind the bar, with her back to them, watching the TV, polishing glasses. The sound of the TV covered any talk.

Ray raised his glass. "To today."

The others followed. "Today."

Vinnie took a long sip, then grinned. "Not a bad way to make a living, eh?"

Ray smirked. "Not bad at all."

"Over one million dollars was stolen from the Victoria Club in a brazen daylight robbery today…" the newsreader was saying.

Overhearing the report, the boys looked at one another in disbelief. Their backs testified to the amount.

"Bookies are lying about what they held. Always have. Have to now," Ray laughed. To our benefit, he thought. He raised his glass in a silent toast to his crew.

"How long before we go back for it?" Tony asked, champing at the bit.

"Calm down boy," Ray patronised him. The Victoria Club will be super-hot for the next few weeks. Forensics, press, every copper will want to visit the crime scene."

"But no one will look up," he said to himself. "They never do." A small smile betrayed his pride. "Anyone shows their face within a mile of that place might as well walk into Russell Street and hold their hands out."

"Have patience," he continued. "This has been well thought out. Give it a month. By then, the dogs will be busy chasing their tails and rabbit holes. Then we just walk in, pick up our money, and walk out the front door."

That initiated excited chatting and drinking. The chink of glasses. Laughter. Ray sat quietly. Like a grade teacher watching his class graduate. Ian's arm wrapped around his shoulder. A double slap, then it disappeared. Ray thought of Cox, sitting in his cell in Long Bay tonight listening to the News. He would have a smile on his face too. Pity he was not here.

"Again. For the next month, don't do anything stupid. No other jobs. No splashing cash. It's family time, boys."

"And no talking. Not to your wife. Not to your priest. Not to each other. No phone calls. The dogs will be tapping every phone in town. Just stay home and be good to your wives."

"Or your mum," he added, looking at Tony.

Ian added, "The dogs will certainly come sniffing. We all have form. Regardless of what they say, they'll have nothing. They're just rattling trees. Keep shtum. Hold your water, and we'll be home free."

There were nods and confirming grunts. They knew the drill. They were professionals.

"Time to go." Ray downed the rest of his beer. The others followed suit. Then they all disappeared into the night.

PART IV

THE AFTERMATH

They say the two happiest moments of a boat owner's life are the day they buy their boat and the day they sell it. Aesop put it more succinctly back in 260 BC:

Be careful what you wish for, lest it comes true!

CHAPTER 23

The Life of Riley

Clean-up

The next morning, the white Transit van pulled into the crusher yard. It drove up to the pickup area and stopped. Frankie got out, closed the door, and walked back toward the entrance. There was the sound of metal crying as a giant claw sank deep into the sides of the van. It lifted high into the air before dropping it with a crash into the hopper.

The metal groaned like a dying animal as it was compressed. Frankie didn't stay to watch. He was already in the cab, the door closing behind him. One down.

The taxi delivered him to the union offices. He didn't go in through the front door. Instead, he walked around the back to the car park. He crossed to the red-lid dumpster at the far side. Opened it and looked in. Empty. Good.

He turned and went in through the back door. Job done.

* * *

Ray, Normie, and Ian were up early too. They had a warehouse to clear. The cage and walls dismantled. Floor marking washed away. The warehouse was stripped bare. Walls, stairs, and upper offices cleaned with bleach.

At the same time, Vinnie, Laurie, and Tony were doing the same up-country at the camp. All remaining equipment removed and back in the ute. The firing ring raked. No casings left.

Vinnie backed out of the shack. He shook the remnants of fuel from the Jerry can over the door and veranda. Taking two steps back, he struck a match, lit the matchbook, and tossed it through the front door.

The building erupted into flames. It was gone in minutes. Heavy autumn cloud cover concealed the smoke, but they were not going to wait around in case. All three climbed into the front seat of the Dodge. Cargo secure, Vinnie drove off at high speed.

* * *

Keystone Cops

With little progress being made by the police, the Government responded by setting up a task force. Police in all states were notified. Their inquiries went deep into the underworld throughout the nation. The task force was to be headed by DI Alan.

The morning of the first day of the task force, DI Alan strode into the operations room. His boot steps echoed slow and deliberate, as he made his way through the crowd to the head of the room. Twenty, maybe thirty detectives lounged around. Perched on desks, swapping stories, laughing. Just another day.[43]

It wasn't.

"Listen up." Alan's voice boomed.

The room stilled. Heads turned. Alan scanned the faces; some seasoned, some green, all about to get a wake-up call.

"They've already got seventy-two hours on us. If you've got plans for tonight, cancel them." His voice was iron, no room for argument. "Now, let's go over what we actually know."

For the next half hour, they went through crime scene photos, forensic reports, and witness statements. Paper shuffled, pens scratched. By the end, a frustrated DI Alan noted, "No fingerprints; untraceable cash; and forty different stories from forty different people." Alan tossed a file onto the table with a slap.

"In other words, we've got nothing." There was anger in his voice.

Silence. A few exchanged looks. He stepped forward, hands on the table, leaning in.

"So, we're going to get something."

He straightened, pacing now.

"This was a professional crew. Skilled. Efficient. That's not a big pool." He turned to the first group. "Armed Robbery, dig into it. Every pro that's walked free in the last five years, I want their names, their habits, their drinking holes. Whoever planned this, has done it before."

His eyes landed on the next group. "Consorting, shake the tree. There's no honour among thieves. Someone saw something. Someone heard something. I don't care how you do it: lean, squeeze, pressure. No more business as usual until this is solved."

A few smirks. A couple of nods. They understood.

He pointed to the uniformed guys at the back of the room. "It happened at midday. Middle of town. Thousands of office workers, delivery vans, and passers-by. I want everyone interviewed. Again. Every window with a view of Queen Street, every courier, every street sweeper. They had to get in, and they had to get out. And they didn't do it blind. They cased this place for weeks, maybe months. Find someone who saw something."

Alan turned, eyes cold. "Gaming. They had inside information. No way in hell they pulled this off without help. I want everyone checked: bookies, punters, club staff, owners. No exceptions."

A pause. Then his gaze locked onto the two CIB detectives. They stood out in their clean, pressed suits.

"The money and the weapons. One's gotta go somewhere. The other had to come from somewhere. Give me something."

He let that hang.

"You'll report back here, 7 AM and 7 PM, every day. No excuses. We work this until we have names." He glanced around. No one spoke. Good.

"Get to it."

No questions. No discussions. Just movement. Chairs scraping, boots hitting the floor, detectives scattering in different directions.

Alan watched them go, jaw set.

This was not just another job. Not this one. They had been made to look inept. Keystone cops.

* * *

Family Time

The weeks following the robbery were a golden time for the bookie robbers. The tightest crew in Melbourne grew tighter. The type of bond men develop when they have faced life and death together, and survived. Although all were ice-cold during the job, all were waiting for the Consorting boys to burst in, guns blasting. The Consorting and Armed Robbery dogs were the type that fired first and then yelled "Stop, Police".

They, on the other hand, were now modern day Robin Hoods. Anyone who ever laid a bet hated the bookies. They were legal thieves. And the amount! Some rumours put the real total at $15 million. The boys new that was an exaggeration. They could not carry that much cash. It did not help the bookies' image that they only declared $1.4 million. Everyone from the cops down, knew they were lying. Definitely crooks.

To the boys, it was not about the money. They had won the Grand Final. They walked taller, smiled more, and spent time at home. No more jobs. No more late nights. But, as the old saying goes, 'be careful what you wish for'.

* * *

The next six weeks were scenes of marital bliss in six homes. The boys stayed true to their contract and played the dutiful husbands. That was something completely foreign to every one of them. But, like prison, with time, idle hands become fidgety.

"Good to be able to have some time to ourselves," Gail started, raising the coffee cup to her mouth. She and Raelene were sitting in a tarted-up suburban coffee shop.

"Ian is doing the school run this morning. I hope he doesn't get lost," Rae joked.

"I think Ray really means it this time. He's through with that life. We are going to be a normal family," Gail returned.

Rae hid her smirk by looking down and stirring her coffee again. "Not Ian. He's addicted to it," Rae eventually replied without any emotion.

"Don't you like him being around all the time?" Gail said, not understanding why Rae didn't feel the same as her.

"No." Rae paused. "He made his life, and I made ours. I have friends, routines, the relationship with our kids. He wasn't there. I did that," Rae continued with a tone of defiance. "He's under my feet 24/7, literally. Yesterday, he wanted to vacuum around me while I was paying the monthly bills." Rae took a long drink of coffee to calm down.

"Well, I like it." Gail countered. "Sharing the school run, having someone to talk to while shopping, someone to hold me at night. I love him!"

"And I love Ian. But marriage is meant to be a partnership of two individuals. And I seem to be losing myself." A slight tear appeared in the corner of Rae's eye. She wiped it away and took a deep breath.

Gail reached out and placed her hand on Rae's arm. Rae had been there for her, now it was her turn.

"Things will work themselves out when all this dies down. You and Ian are smart people. You'll work out the boundaries."

Gail changed the subject, and they chatted for another half hour. They parted with a kiss.

* * *

The newspaper slapped against the café counter. Big, black letters stretched across the front page:

"THE GREAT BOOKIE ROBBERY – HOW IT WENT DOWN"

A smaller headline below: "Police Baffled – No Witnesses, No Leads"

Ian smirked as he sipped on his orange juice, picking the paper back up. His eyes scanned the words like they held the meaning of life. Ian had popped into a café near the school after the drop-off. He had taken a stool at the counter. Ordered a coffee and juice to kill some time. It had been a week since the job, and they were still front-page news. Even if they were just rehashing the same stuff.

210

"Six masked men," he read aloud, tapping the page. "Armed with military-grade weapons. Made off with an undisclosed sum." He snorted. "Undisclosed, my arse."

The waitress behind the counter replied, "They've got no clue." Her back still to Ian.

"Not yet." Ian folded the paper. He dropped it to the side, headlines still showing. "But they will. The cops don't like looking stupid."

"Already look stupid." She countered, a smirk in her voice.

An unknown customer passed behind Ian. Saw the newspaper headlines, and slapped Ian on the shoulder as he passed, "The Bookies! Couldn't happen to a better bunch of bastards."

Ian smiled to himself. How about that? We're not the bad guys for once.[44]

Outside, traffic rattled past. People walked fast, collars up, heads down. Business as usual. Ian finished his coffee and headed home.

* * *

The money was not in their pockets yet, but that didn't stop them from spending it.

Normie ordered sixty grand worth of new mincers and steamers for the family factory. The old ones were shot. New ones meant better efficiency, less work for his parents. Six-week delivery from the States. "Not a problem," the supplier said.

Ian bought land. Outside Warrandyte.

Raelene had always wanted a Tudor manor house. He could finally give her the life she deserved. Told her it was happening. She smiled for the first time in months. He met

211

with an architect and started on plans. By the time they were ready, the money would be there. Contracts signed.

Rae was happy. Ian, at last, had a project. He was out from under her feet.

* * *

Band of Brothers

The weekend before the money split, all the crew and their families gathered at Ian's around the pool. They all knew the rules. Nothing about the job or any other activities were to be discussed. Ian cooked on the BBQ, kids squealed in the pool. Vinnie was fawning over Raelene. Ray and Gail sat at a table by the pool, under an umbrella at the other end. Tony was in the pool, parked on the edge with a beer, while Laurie was in the water bouncing his youngest up and down.

Ian always knew Vinnie had the hots for Raelene. But he was not her type, so Ian put up with it. "Leave her alone, she's married," Ian joked, handing Vinnie a plate with a steak on it. "Salads are inside." Vinnie took the hint.

When Vinnie returned, he pulled a chair up at the table with Ray and Gail. When he was partway through the steak, he put his knife and fork down, and said to both Ray and Gail, "If you could live anywhere in the world, where would you pick?"

Ray glared at Vinnie. He did not want Vinnie straying into discussions about the money.

"No, no," Vinnie countered, seeing Ray's annoyance. "Just generally, what do you think would be the nicest place to while away your days in?"

"Mallorca," Gail answered. "It's an island off Spain. Ray and I holidayed there when we were in the UK. In a villa on top of the hill overlooking the Med. God's country." She smiled.

Ray looked at her stunned. "Doesn't sound like you have thought about that at all." He smiled.

"Come on, you loved it there. You said one day we could go back."

"We'll see." Ray terminated the conversation. He then stood, picked up a glass and a knife, and walked around to the middle of the pool. The tapping on his glass quietened everyone down.

"I would like to make a toast," he started. "The people around this pool are closer than friends, you are my brothers. In the immortal words of Shakespeare's Henry V:

Whoever stands with me,

shoulder to shoulder in battle, will be my brother.

For he who sheds his blood beside me,

will be bound to me forever in honour.

Let others stay behind in comfort and safety;

they will regret it when they hear of what we did here.

They will wish they had fought with us,

that they had earned the right to say,

I was there on that day.

Years from now,

when the world has changed and time has worn us down,

we will remember that moment.

On that very day, we stood together.

We defied fear, we faced death, and we prevailed.

We few, we happy few, we band of brothers."

"Cheers!" He raised his glass, as did everyone. "Cheers," came the chorus. Gail whispered, "You missed bits," as she passed. She squeezed his arm gently.

They toasted like kings, certain the world could never touch them.

CHAPTER 24

Afterglow

The Taskforce

True to DI Alan's directive, it did not take long for the Consorting squad to turn up on Ian's doorstep.

The knock came just after lunch. Sharp. No hesitation.

Rae answered. Two men stood at the door. Cheap suits, hard eyes.

"Mrs. Carroll. Police. Can we come in?" one said, already trying to pull open the screen door. It did not budge. Locked.

"No," Rae said flatly. "Ian's not here."

"We would like to come in and take a look around," the second one said. Firm. Like it was not a request.

"Do you have a warrant?" Rae's voice stayed steady.

"No, but we can get one," the first one threatened.

"No, you can't."

The two detectives exchanged a glance.

"No probable cause," Rae added.

The first one leaned in, "You think you know the law?", playing intimidation.

"I work at a law firm."

The pause was long. The first detective reached into his pocket, pulled out a card, and held it out.

"Tell Ian to call us."

"You can leave it there." She shut the door.

* * *

The task force's morning meeting wrapped up. Detectives shuffled papers, stretched, and chatted.

DI Alan made his way over to DI Paul. "Anyone spoken to this Bennett fellow yet?" interrupting a conversation DI Paul was having with a junior detective.

Paul barely looked up. "Chuck."

Alan frowned.

"His real name is Raymond Chuck," Paul continued. "Bennett's an alias. He's been using it since he got back from England."

Alan ignored the correction. "Murphy was supposed to speak to him? Shake his tree."

Paul slowly let his breath out through his nose. "Murphy's got history with him."

Alan raised an eyebrow.

"Last time they spoke, Chuck put a shotgun to Murphy's head. Told him he'd blow it clean off."

Alan blinked. "And why isn't he locked up?"

"No witnesses," Paul said. "Murphy says Chuck meant it. And Murphy doesn't scare easy."

Alan ran a hand over his face. "We can't have that. Even if it's just piss and wind."

DI Paul responded defensively, "Murphy's one of our toughest, and he believes Chuck meant it. I think it would be better if we send Thompson and his boys to toss his place instead," nodding toward the detective next to him.

215

"Ok, your call. Just get it done." DI Alan terminated the discussion, leaving DI Paul to arrange things with Thompson.

* * *

Laurie pulled into his driveway. Something felt wrong.

Inside, his wife sat on the couch. She didn't look up when he opened the door. Just held the kids tight like they were life rafts. Her knuckles were white against their pyjamas. The house was a wreck. Drawers pulled out. Papers scattered. Furniture overturned.

Laurie's blood boiled. "What the fuck happened?"

"The police," she whispered. "I asked what they were looking for. They said you'd know."

He stood still, breathing hard. Then he saw the calling card on the table. Detective Thompson. Laurie grabbed the phone. Started to dial Ray. Stopped. Dialled Vinnie instead.

Vinnie answered on the second ring.

"They hit my place," Laurie snapped.

"They came here too," Vinnie said. Calm. Like he was reading the paper. "Only, I was home. They knew better than to try that shit with me."

Laurie's grip tightened on the receiver.

"They're rattling the trees," Vinnie continued. "And be careful what you say. They probably left something behind."

Laurie took a slow, deep breath through his nose. He hung up. Walked over to his wife and kids. Sat down. Pulled them in close.

He needed to be more like Vinnie. Cold. Patient. Stoic.

Laurie held his family tight and waited.

* * *

It did not take the police long to draw up a shortlist of possible ringleaders.

"Raymond 'Chuck' Bennett," Detective Inspector Alan said as he pinned up Ray's picture. The ops board was clean. Except for one photo, Ray Bennett, dead centre, like a dartboard target.

"Through a process of elimination, we're left with him. The list of men who could pull this off is short. He's at the top."

He tapped the photo.

"We build his crew. Find his associates. He's an ex-Painter and Docker. Start there. Priors. Street talk. By the end of the day, I want six other pictures up here."

He turned to the room. "What else do we have?"

"The guns lead nowhere," said a CIB detective. "No serial numbers. No prior records of use. Best guess: they were imported from the States. We're waiting on the FBI, but I'm not holding my breath."

"The serial numbers on the new bills are flagged," another detective added. "If any of those notes turn up, we'll know. But there's only a hundred and fifty grand that's traceable."

Alan scoffed. "I'd be surprised if they were dumb enough to spend it."

"Well, we're watching for big cash splashes," the detective replied. "They're sitting on millions. It has to burn a hole in their pockets sooner or later."

Alan turned to DI Paul. "What's the word on the street?"

Paul shook his head. "No one knows a thing. Would've thought they were out-of-towners, except for one detail."

Alan raised an eyebrow.

"One of them called Ambrose Palmer by name," Paul said. "That makes him a Richmond boy most likely."

Alan leaned in. "Did Ambrose recognise the voice?"

Paul shook his head. "Swears he was too busy trying not to get his head blown off."

Alan cursed under his breath. "What about the Victoria Club? Anyone sniffing around?"

A uniformed sergeant stood at the back. "We've got identikit sketches of three men who rented an office across Queen Street. Used it to watch the club in the weeks before the job."

Alan frowned. "Any leads?"

"Too vague to pin anyone."

Alan scoffed sharply. "Damn waste of time." Those identikits were more about keeping the brass and politicians happy. Not for finding crooks. He turned back to the board.

"All right," he said. "Let's find Bennett's confederates. Names. I want names. Tonight."

Then he walked out.

* * *

That evening, Alan started before everyone had settled. The evening session was always sloppy. Stragglers. No-shows. He hated it, but he did not choose the task force. Political decisions above his pay grade.

"Tell me something," he barked. "Anything."

One of the Armed Robbery boys stepped up. He pinned a photo below Bennett's.

"Ian Revell Carroll, aka 'Fingers.'" The detective spoke with the ease of a man reading a well-known script. "Ex-Secretary of the Painters and Dockers. A lot of form. In the frame for a number of six-figure armed robberies. A long-time associate of Bennett's."

He turned to leave, then tossed in, "Oh, and he's got a car parts import business. From the States."

Heads lifted.

DI Paul stepped forward next. He pinned another photo beside Carroll's.

"Norman Lee," he said. "We've had eyes on him for a while. Childhood friend of Chuck's, good with figures." His family runs a dim sim factory up north. Supposedly a Sweeney Todd. Said to be where a lot of Painters and Dockers ended up during the Waterfront Wars."

Groans filled the room.

Alan scanned the room. "Anyone else?"

Silence.

"All right," Alan said. "Good work. We've got a start." He rubbed his hands together.

"I want everything on these men. Where they say they were. Toss their houses. Their businesses. They always leave something behind."

He turned back to the board.

"And find their associates. Hit the Richmond clubs. Shake them down. I want more names."

He dismissed them early. First time in weeks, he would see his kids tonight.

* * *

The Split

The inside of Ian's warehouse stank of dirty money. Musty, acidic. Too many hands had touched this cash. It sat heavy on the trestle tables, stuffed into mailbags, spilling in uneven stacks.

Ray dropped the last bag with a dull thud.

Six weeks had passed. Not long enough for Ray.

Normie set up two bill counters. A cigarette burned in the ashtray. Whisky bottle untouched.

No one spoke.

"All right," Normie clapped. "Let's get to it."

Ian and Tony sorted bills. Vinnie and Ray worked the bundles. Laurie and Normie fed loose notes into the machines.

The counters hummed. Laurie smacked the side of one after a jam.

"Some of these are so old they feel fake," Tony muttered.

"Just been sitting in a bookie's bag too long," Normie replied, not looking up.

Bundles piled up. Bands snapped. Sweat beaded on brows. After an hour, not halfway through.

Normie took a drag from his cigarette. "We're gonna be here a while."

"No shit," Ian grunted, flexing his fingers.

"Good problem to have," Tony said, half-smiling.

Ray didn't smile.

Laurie held up a filthy wad of fifties. "Think this one's been through every scumbag in Melbourne."

"Keep counting," Normie said, dry.

… Another hour.

Counters clicked. Notes rustled. Jams. Curses.

Finally, silence.

Ray stacked the last bundle. Normie tallied. Ran the numbers again. The quiet deepened.

He sat back. He cleared his throat. "Six million, eight hundred and sixty-three thousand, four hundred and eighty," he said finally. "Plus ninety in new notes."

A low whistle.

"Jesus Christ," Tony breathed.

They stared. Then it broke; cheers, slaps, a whoop from Laurie. Notes tossed in the air.

Ray didn't move. It was too much.

He let them ride the high. Then: "After expenses, that's seven fifty-four each. Nine shares."

He kept it crisp. Measured.

"Ian and I get doubles. Frankie and Peter, half shares."

Everyone nodded. Even Tony.

Ray tossed everyone five grand each. "Walking around money." Then: "We'll do the split once things cool."

"Why not now?" Tony asked.

Ray's look was hard. "How do thieves get caught?"

"Trying to move stolen goods," Laurie said, subdued now.

Ray nodded. "Exactly. This is three times what we expected. You think you can hide that kind of cash without drawing heat?"

Normie hesitated. "Ray, I could use the money now. Mum and Dad…"

"The plan's the plan."

Vinnie stepped in. Calm, but solid. "You said four weeks. I'm taking my money." No anger, just fact. Two alpha dogs, eye to eye.

The room held its breath.

Ian stepped between them. "Too much for one stash point anyway. One of us gets hit, we all lose." Years on the union executive had taught him the importance of compromise. He now hoped Ray would see it too.

Ray paused. Calculated. Then nodded. "All right. We'll split now. Normie, tell them your ideas."

Normie stepped up. "If you want to buy property, I've got a guy who can put it through a solicitor's trust, clean. Only one at a time."

"I'm first," Laurie said, grinning. "My missus won't shut up about buying a house."

"Greedy's guy in Manila will clean the new stuff," Normie added. "Twenty per cent cut. Ten to him. Ten to his mate over there. He can move money offshore also. But, if he duds you, it's on you." [45]

Ray cut back in. "Normie's the banker. You need anything, go through him. Legal fees too. Out of your cleaned share."

Ian added, "Cops only know what you tell them. So keep your mouths shut."

They divvied up the shares. Stacked them into mail sacks. Ray asked Ian to hold Cox's half share. Once done, there was an awkward moment of silence. One by one, they walked out.

Ray watched them go. Fools!

They didn't see it. Didn't feel the weight. But he did.

One last thing. He needed a word with Normie.

"Give me a lift," Ray said.

* * *

Ray sat in the passenger seat, watching the road. Then, without looking over, he spoke. "Normie, the new notes?"

"Yeah," Normie said, relaxed. "I'll put them through Greedy's Manila bar." He didn't hear the edge in Ray's voice.

"You said ninety thousand." Ray turned, watching him now. Watching his face. Looking for something. A crack, a twitch. "The reports said one hundred and fifty."

The penny dropped. Normie's hands tightened on the wheel. He pulled over. This was dangerous.

"Ray, we've known each other since we were kids," he said carefully. His voice steady. "Have I ever dudded you?"

Ray did not answer. His eyes stayed on Normie's face, scanning. Searching. Nothing.

Normie pressed on. "Look, I fucked up. I put bookies' cash in the same sack as the new notes."

Ray's mind flashed back. The moment. The bags. The rush. Yes, that had bugged him at the time.

Normie saw the small nod. Just a flicker. A breath of relief. "Either the reporters got it wrong, or some of it got mixed up with other cash. Either way, it's in the split. I would never dud you, Ray. You know me."

Ray breathed out. A slow, steady breath. Normie was off the hook. For now. He shook his head. This could be a major fuck-up.

"Ok. Drive."

CHAPTER 25

Vultures Circling

The Kane Brothers – Australia's Krays

The Kane brothers were a rival underworld gang. Bennett's nemesis, you could say. Always on the wrong side of things. Painters and Dockers, like Ray's crew, but aligned with Longley during the Waterfront wars. Now they made their money extorting a share from other crims' jobs. Called it a 'drink.'

They were known as Australia's Krays. The nickname stuck for good reason. Brutal, violent, and ruthless with their own kind. Like Reggie and Ronnie ruled London's East End, but they never tried pushing Ray and his crew. That was something else. That would be war. Best left alone.

* * *

Brian and Les Kane stood at the bar of the Quarry Hotel, eyes locked on the news. The bookie robbery. A hell of a job.

"Someone's got balls," Brian muttered.

The newsreader's voice cut in: Insiders believe the haul could be as high as twelve million dollars.

Les grinned. "And a lot of cash." He turned to Brian. "I think we should help them spend some of it."

Brian drained his beer. "Drink up. We have work to do."

They moved fast, back alleys, quiet streets, the underbelly of Richmond and Carlton. Someone had to know something. Someone always did.

Les grabbed *Ferret* by the collar and slammed him against the tin fence (a different *Ferret* to the one buried under the dock during the Waterfront Wars. Ferret was a common derogatory nickname for grasses). A quick punch to the gut, then back upright. Just a warm-up. He pinned him there, forearm pressing hard.

Brian leaned over Les's shoulder. "Okay, Ferret. What's the word?" He did not have to mention the robbery. It was the only thing people were talking about.

Ferret swallowed hard. "Don't know, Brian. No one knows nothing. Everyone's asking, but there's nothing."

Brian sighed. "Do you want Les to ask you again?"

Ferret's eyes went wide. "No, no! That's the God's honest."

Brian changed tactics. "Let me put it another way. Who hasn't been around the last few days?" After a job like this, people went to ground. That was normal.

Ferret licked his lips. "Charlie says he's been in bed with the flu. And Johnno's been in the lock-up."

Johnno was fair enough. They'd have to visit Charlie.

But Charlie had nothing either.

If Brian and Les wanted a piece of this, they needed to find another angle.

* * *

Brian Kane earned his chops working as an enforcer for Tex Longley during the Waterfront Wars. Les was too young. He existed in his brother's shadow.

Brian and Les were the oldest of three brothers. Brian came first. Raised in a working-class home in Collingwood. Their father, a drunk, beat them when he was sober and taught them to fight when he wasn't.

Brian earned his stripes early. At twelve, he dropped a full-grown man cold for mouthing off to his father. The old man laughed and clapped him on the back. That was the day Brian learned what Les already knew. Strength wasn't enough, you had to strike first.

* * *

Like any returned soldier after the cessation of hostilities, Brian had to find his place in the food chain now that the Waterfront War was over. He did. Debt collection.

SP bookies, gambling parlours, loan sharks. If they had debts, Brian got them paid. Les started as a bagman. That did not last. Soon, he was the muscle.

Brian saw the opportunities. Les handled the violence. Together, they were unstoppable.

They walked into homes, into backrooms, into offices. Les with a hammer.

"You got two choices," he would say.

They always paid.

Word spread. The Kane brothers got what they wanted. Always.

* * *

Brian stood outside the two-up room, counting his commissions. The owner stuck his head out the door. "One more thing, Brian. Terry Ganno's late. Give him a hurry-up."

Brian checked his watch. 6:15 PM. He would still be at the office. He found the solicitor in his chair, behind a mahogany desk. Safe. Untouchable.

Brian set the axe down on the polished wood. "You're late," he said. "I'm here to collect."

The solicitor's hands trembled. "I—I just need more time—"

Brian lifted the axe, let it hang in the air.

"No!"

The blade came down. Splinters flew. Paperwork shredded.

The solicitor paid.

Brian placed the axe back in the boot of his car and smirked. "He probably loved that desk more than his wife."

* * *

Les Kane had been a nobody during the Waterfront Wars. A gofer. His brother's reputation towered over him. That burned. Not resentment toward Brian, he worshipped him. It was the small-man syndrome. He drank too much. Fought too much. Always had something to prove.

Les leaned against the bar, foot on the rail, suit rumpled, tie loose.

"Another court date?" Brian slapped him on the back.

"Number sixteen," Les grinned. "But who's counting?"

At the other end of the bar, a group of office workers was drinking. A suit laughed, made a comment to the bartender about Les being a hobo. Loud enough for Les to hear. Big mistake.

Les looked. Walked down the bar. The office worker turned, ready for an argument. He had no idea. The first punch shattered his teeth. The second sent him to the ground.

Les was not done.

Metal-tipped boots slammed into the man's skull. Again. Again. Again. Blood pooled. The bartender yelled, but no one stepped in.

Brian dragged Les back. "That's enough."

Les wiped his boot on the man's jacket. "He won't say that again."

* * *

"Next address?" Les asked Brian. Brian flipped through his notebook for the next collection. Les drove.

Les hated traffic. He hated waiting. The light turned green. The car in front didn't move. Les leaned on the horn. Nothing.

He stepped out. Walked to the driver's window. Middle-aged guy. Confused.

Les yanked the door open and dragged the man out by the collar, onto the road. A solid punch to the head. His mate in the passenger seat tried to help. Les put him down, too.

Brian watched from their car. When Les climbed back in, Brian sighed.

"You can't hit everyone, Les."

Les wiped blood from his knuckles. "Why not?"

* * *

The next morning, Brian pulled up outside Leo's boxing gym in Richmond.

Les scowled. "What are we doing here?"

"You need discipline," Brian said.

"I don't need no boxing," Les sneered. "I know how to fight."

"Get out," Brian said. There was no arguing with big brother.

Inside, Les strapped up and climbed in through the ropes. Headgear on. Gloves up.

Brian watched, arms crossed. He was already a Golden Gloves champion. He did not fight in the street like Les. The ring was sacred. That's what old-timers at the gym told them. Brian understood. Les never did.

Leo stood facing a young fighter. They touched gloves. Leo stepped back. The other fighter hit Les square in the face with two quick jabs. Split Les's lip.

Les swung wild. Arms everywhere. No footwork. No technique. But not with his head down like most street fighters. Les's eyes were firmly on the other guy. Focused.

The other boxer had his arms up, covering his face and ribs. Les kept coming non-stop. Body blows. Rabbit punches.

Leo sighed. The kid needs work. "Break!" he shouted.

Les did not stop.

"Break it up!" Leo barked louder.

Les ignored him.

Leo grabbed his shoulder. Nothing.

Brian stepped in. "Enough," he ordered.

Les spat blood. "Soft."

The sparring partner clutched his ribs, gasping.

The gym never let Les back in.

* * *

The Toecutters

The flight from Sydney landed at Melbourne Airport. Three men strode through the terminal. Expensive suits. Sharp eyes. They moved with purpose.

The leader stopped at a locker, turned the key, and pulled out a bag. He unzipped it and reached in. Two handguns. A small pair of bolt cutters. His associates pocketed the guns. He pocketed the bolt cutters and left the bag behind. They stepped outside and hailed a taxi.

The leader leaned in. "North Melbourne. Factory district." They got in, and the cab pulled away.

The youngest of the three sat in the back, restless. "You think this is one of them?" he asked.

The leader kept his gaze on the road. "Rogerson gave me the address. Normally, reliable." [46]

The ride was quiet.

At the factory, the young one paid the driver. They entered through the open roller door to the aroma of grease and cabbage. The leader pulled a photo from his pocket. Looked at it, then up at the two men standing by a machine at the back.

"That's him," he said.

They walked forward.

Normie turned first. "How can I help you?"

The two associates pulled their .38s. Levelled them at Normie and Ray.

"I'd like a word," the leader said. "In private."

Normie and Ray did not move.

"Are you deaf?" the young one spat.

A voice from behind. "No. But apparently, you are."

The cold press of metal against the back of their necks. Vinnie and Laurie. The Sydney boys froze, their fingers limp on the triggers. The advantage was gone. They lowered and dropped their guns.

Ray stepped forward. Smooth. Silent. He pulled his own gun from the small of his back. Then, quick as a viper, he shoved the barrel straight into the leader's mouth. Hard. A tooth cracked. Forced him back until he hit the steamer with a thud.

"Word to the wise," Ray said, his voice calm. "Don't pull a gun unless you intend to use it."

No one spoke.

Ray did not blink. "Get their wallets."

Vinnie and Laurie spun their two around. Slid their hands into the visitors' pockets. Pulled out their wallets and tossed them to Normie.

Ray took the leader's. Pulled out his licence. Looked at it.

"Sydney," he read.

He laughed. A dry, humourless sound.

"Let me guess. You're the big bad-arse Toecutters."[47]

No one answered.

Ray felt the other pocket. Pulled out the bolt cutters. Held them for a moment, then dropped them on the floor. Ray's expression hardened. He stepped closer. His face went pale, eyes darkened.

"You come down here and think you can intimidate us?" His voice rose, sharp and fast. "You pussies. You might think you're tough up there, scaring whores out of their money."

The leader's lips trembled.

Ray's breath came faster now. His jaw clenched. Anger had taken hold.

"You want a war?" he hissed. "I'll give you a fucking war. I'll rain fucking fire and brimstone down on your fucking doorstep." Spit flew with his words. The leader tried to turn his face, but Ray pressed harder. "Cut our toes off?" Ray was now manic. "I'll cut your fucking head off. And I'll do it in front of your wife and kids."

No one moved.

Ray leaned back slightly. His breath steadied. He exhaled. Composed himself.

The Sydney man swallowed. His voice was barely there. "N-no… we'll go and we won't come back."

Ray turned to Laurie. "Not with two hands, you won't. Laurie, take your guy over to the mincer."

The young guy knew what was coming. He tried to resist. Laurie spun him around. Kicked in his ankle. The guy lost his balance. Laurie grabbed the back of his collar and dragged him over to the mincer. Screaming. His feet flailing, but he could not regain his foothold. At the mincer, Laurie spun him again, forcing his arm into the hopper.

Then— "NO!"

Normie.

Ray looked over, eyes still wild.

Normie's face was tight. "Ray. Please. That's the new machine." He swallowed. "Sixty grand worth. Just installed."

The room went still.

Ray pulled in a big breath through his nostrils. Paused. Nodded once. "Okay."

Laurie yanked the kid back. Threw him on the floor. The inside of his pant leg was wet.

Ray swung the leader around onto the floor next to the young guy. Vinnie followed suit. Ray stepped over them. Looked down. "Go back to Sydney," he said. "Tell your mates, if anyone shows their face down here again, there won't be a rock low enough for any of you to hide under."

The three scrambled up and ran.

Ray turned to Vinnie, Laurie, and Normie. "Meet-up— Ian's warehouse. Tomorrow night." Then he walked out.

The three looked at each other. It was a side of Ray they had not seen before. No one spoke. One by one, they left.

* * *

The next night, Ray was early. He had always had his own key to Ian's warehouse. That was the nature of their relationship. The others straggled in. Ray did not speak until all were present. He just paced.

Frankie was the last to arrive. Everyone glared at him as he entered.

"What?" he said.

Ignoring that, Ray said, "Let's get started."

"The Toecutters visited Normie yesterday." Tony and Frankie started asking questions of the others.

Ray continued over the top of them. "That's not the problem. We sent them packing, and I don't think any of those Sydney tossers will come down again."

"The real problem is they had Normie's name. That would have come from Melbourne. Most likely the cops."

"So? They've got nothing," Ian interjected. "They're just guessing. After all, who else in Melbourne could have carried this off?" Ian said with pride in his voice.

Ray nodded once. "And they know that. Which means they'll go after our families. Intimidate. Harass. Wait for someone to break."

"No one here will break," Ian replied. His voice more questioning why Ray would think such a thing. He looked around. Vinnie, Normie, and Laurie. All solid. Even Frankie had proven himself during the Waterfront Wars. Tony was the only weak link. And he promised Ray he would handle that if it got to that point.

"We're all solid." Ian's words were adamant.

"I'm not questioning that," Ray said. "But we need to flip the script. Stop reacting, start controlling."

He let that sink in, then laid out the plan.

"Starting tonight, we go quiet. No calls. No visits. We disappear for a couple of weeks. Tell your barristers where to send any inquiries. That's it. Don't tell your family where you're going. Don't tell each other. Total blackout."

The room was quiet.

"Make the cops chase shadows," Ray continued. "Let them burn time and pressure the wrong people. While we vanish. Let them know we've got barristers lined up, and nothing to say."

Vinnie folded his arms. "And what if they turn up at our doors?"

Ray met his eye. "Then your family calls your barrister. That's what they're paid for."

One by one, the men nodded. Everyone knew he was right. That is what made him the General. Nobody liked it, though. It was against everything they learned from the docks. But their belief in Ray was stronger.

Ray didn't dismiss them. He didn't need to. They all knew what came next.

No handshakes. No hugs. They just left to make their arrangements.

As the last of them left, Ray stayed behind. He looked around the hollow, empty warehouse. He trusted the plan. He didn't trust the people.

CHAPTER 26

Things Heat Up

Ray closed the door quietly. He did not want to wake the boy.

Gail was in the living room. TV on, sound low. She saw him standing in the doorway, reached for the remote, and turned it off.

Ray sat beside her. "I think I need to go away for a bit," he said.

She met his eyes. She knew better than to ask why.

"I don't want you to," she said.

"I don't want to either," Ray replied. "But I have to."

"No, you don't." She folded her arms. "We're a family. We stand together, come what may."

Ray sighed. "Gail, we have to think about Danny."

She stared at him.

"It'll only be for a few weeks," he added.

Silence.

"I'll call Joe tomorrow," Ray continued. "He'll take care of you."

Gail let out a sharp breath. "What the hell is your barrister going to do for us?"

"Handle the cops. Stop them hassling you. Get things sorted. Then I can come back."

Gail's voice softened. "Where are you going?"

Ray shook his head. "I can't tell you."

She frowned.

"Don't ask Rae or Normie. They won't know either."

She looked down. He was telling her, not asking her. A done deal. Like always.

Ray stood. Kissed her forehead. Then went upstairs to pack.

Gail sat in the dark and cried.

* * *

Ian tossed his keys onto the bench. Opened the fridge. Poured a glass of juice.

Rae sat at the kitchen table, flipping through a magazine. She barely looked up.

"I'm going away for a few weeks," he said casually.

She turned a page. "Everything okay?" Rae asked, trying not to let her concern show. That was their contract. She, the strong stoic wife; he, the rock supporting the family. Neither was true.

"Yes." Ian took a sip. "Don't want the cops hassling you anymore."

She studied him.

"I'll call Frank in the morning. He'll keep them off your back," Ian continued. "Hopefully, in a couple of weeks, things will cool down."

Neither of them believed that either. The games spouses play.

She set the magazine down.

"You need anything?" she asked.

He shook his head.

236

She did not ask where he was going. She knew better. She had been here before. Either he would come home, or he wouldn't. She had learned that much during the Waterfront Wars.

She just wished she did not love him so much.

Ian disappeared to pack.

When he returned, he had an overnight bag. He grabbed his keys, turned to her.

She stood. Held him tight. She said nothing.

He hugged her back. Then pulled away, kissed her cheek.

"Oh, can you get Greg to call Frank as well?" Ian said, grabbing his bag.

Rae raised an eyebrow. "Get your brother to call your barrister?"

"Frank will want to ask him about that lunch we had together."

And then he was gone.

* * *

Over the next week, reports rolled into the Taskforce. Carroll and Bennett had gone to ground. Their wives were directing police to their barristers.

* * *

Harbourside Holiday

Ian spent his enforced sabbatical in Sydney. It was the last place anyone in the Melbourne underworld would look for someone gone to ground. Sydney had a bad reputation among Melbourne's professional crooks. They considered the Sydney lot pimps and petty criminals, all trying to act tough.

He sat in a Woolloomooloo pub overlooking the Sydney docks. Still a working-class area then. Across from him sat an old enemy from the Waterfront Wars, Jim Bazley. Another Melbourne expat.

"Never thought I'd see you up here," Jim said, lifting his schooner. Ian was still not used to Sydney's oversized beer glasses.

"Hiding in plain sight," Ian chuckled. "No one down there would believe it either."

Jim nodded. "Just be careful. Sydney leaks worse than a sieve."

Ian glanced up at two drinkers and the bar. He felt his neck stiffen. They turned away.

Jim took another drink. "They call it insurance."

"Insurance?" Ian asked, still watching the drinkers at the bar.

Jim smirked. "It's all about future leverage. Dob someone in today, trade for protection later."

"Don't worry. I won't go near the Cross."

Jim thumbed over his shoulder. "It's just up the road!"

"I know," Ian said. "I'm here to see you. Nothing more. I'll stick to the north shore. Got business associates there. All sweet."

They drank and talked of old times. Alliances shifted in their world. Nothing was ever fixed.

Ian watched the sun glint off the water. Not a bad way to spend a Melbourne winter.

They shook hands and parted. They knew they would not see each other again.

* * *

Rae opened the door. Gail stood there, arms crossed. "You busy?"

Rae stepped aside. "Kettle's on."

Gail walked in.

Even with her makeup, Rae could see the dark rims around her eyes. Rae pulled out a chair. "Sit."

Instead, Gail walked to the sink and picked up a cloth.

They did not talk as Rae put out two cups.

Gail, absent-minded, started wiping the bench. "They're having the time of their life," she said, more to herself than to Rae. An overpowering sadness.

Rae knew what she meant.

Gail sighed. "The money, the power. All of it."

Rae nodded.

"I used to think he'd change," Gail said.

Rae looked at her. "I used to think Ian would know when to stop."

Gail gave a dry laugh. "And?"

"He doesn't."

They were silent.

Gail turned and gazed out of the window. "You ever wonder what it would've been like if we'd met them somewhere else?"

Rae thought about that. "Wouldn't have mattered," she said, shaking her head.

Gail smirked. "No."

"They were always gonna be who they are."

Gail nodded. "And we were always gonna be us."

The kettle clicked off.

Gail turned to Rae. "Perhaps a wine instead?"

Rae looked up and smiled.

Gail tilted her head. "It's five o'clock somewhere."

Rae took a bottle from the fridge, pulled the cork, and poured two glasses.

* * *

In the Cross

Ray had told them to disappear. Lay low. Keep their heads down. So Laurie and Tony decided to treat it like a holiday. They headed to Sydney too. Not the North Shore, The Cross.

The neon buzzed overhead, bathing the street in pink and blue. Music pulsed from behind every door. Strip joints, peep shows, dive bars. The tawdry scent of baby oil, stale beer, and something rotten lurking beneath it all.

Laurie and Tony had been in Sydney a week when Laurie found a girl one night. Blonde. Legs up to her neck. She laughed at his jokes and let him buy her drinks. That was all it took.

By the next night, he was gone. Moved into her flat down in Potts Point.

Tony was on his own.

Boredom turned into wandering. Down Victoria Street. Up Darlinghurst Road. Hookers called out from the doorways. Junkies hunched in the alleyways, lost in their own world. He stepped over one, slumped against a wall, needle still hanging from his arm.

A strip club door swung open. Music blasted out. He went in. Sat at the bar. Watched a girl twist around a pole like it was the only thing keeping her standing.

"New face," someone said.

Tony turned.

A guy in a leather jacket, thin, wiry, grinning. "First time in the Cross?"

Tony shrugged.

The guy held out his hand. A small foil packet. "On the house."

Tony hesitated.

"Relax. Just a taste."

He pocketed it.

Back at his motel, he unwrapped the foil. Pale powder, fine as dust. He did not know how to do it. So he pulled a dollar bill from his pocket, made two short lines on the glass coffee table, and rolled up the note. Snorted the first line like they do in the movies. His head snapped back. [48]

The events of the Victoria Club replayed in his mind. Bitter. Relentless. His trembling fingers gripped the edge of the table as images of the heist and his crippling mistake flooded his thoughts.

He remembered the moment when Vinnie's fury exploded. The blow that had sent him sprawling. He felt the sting of failure. He thought of his childhood. Always waiting for approval that never came. Now, alone in this room, the same voices whispered: You're the weak link.

A tear slipped down his cheek. He closed his eyes, but the memories didn't stop: the disapproving looks from his comrades.

He did the second line. Put his head back and waited. Heat spread through his veins. His skin tingled. The world softened at the edges.

He lay back on the bed, the bad thoughts faded, and he finally felt at peace.

* * *

The next night, he went back looking. Found the same guy outside a club. Bought more.

It became a ritual. Wandering, scoring, snorting. Each night, the Cross felt less dirty. Less cruel. The weeks blurred.

Then Laurie came back.

He opened the motel door to find Tony on the bed. Eyes half-lidded. A smear of powder on the table.

Laurie didn't say anything at first. Just walked in. Sat down.

"You hooked?"

Tony blinked slow. "No. Just bored."

Laurie nodded. Looked around the room. The stench of stale urine and cigarettes.

"Pack your shit," he said.

Tony sat up. "What?"

"We're going home."

Tony scoffed. "I don't need babysitting."

Laurie grabbed the foil off the table. Tore it open. Let the powder scatter to the floor.

Tony clenched his jaw.

Laurie stood over him. "Pack your shit."

Tony met his eyes. Something passed between them. He nodded.

He packed. They left. Sydney had lost its shine.

* * *

"Mr. Smith, you can go in now," the receptionist said.

Ian, dressed in a pale fawn suit and open neck shirt, nodded and entered the private office. The solicitor rose from behind her desk to shake his hand. Mid-forties, polished, confident. Dark suit. Tight skirt, just above the knee. Red six-inch heels.

Not Melbourne, Ian thought.

"Ian," introducing himself, shaking her hand. Firm grip. He liked that.

She motioned to a chair at the small conference table, then walked around the other side with her back to the window. Nice touch. The Harbour Bridge framed the view behind her.

"How can I help?"

"My company is diversifying its property holdings outside Melbourne," Ian said. "We deal with large amounts of cash. I was told you could help."

She nodded. Understood the undertone. "Our services are expensive but completely confidential. We can also assist with overseas acquisitions."

"That could be useful." Ian smiled. "Here are my company details." He slid a manila folder across the table. "Do you know of anything available now?"

"Residential or commercial?"

"Commercial. Preferably with sitting tenants."

She considered. "I can think of a few clients looking to free up working capital. How soon can you settle?"

"Immediately."

She smiled.

"I'll negotiate a price and get back to you," she said.

Ian handed her a card. "This is my Sydney number. I'll be here a while looking at property."

They shook hands.

Both were smiling. This could be the start of a profitable relationship.

* * *

A few weeks later, DI Alan's phone rang.

"There's a barrister here to see you," said the desk sergeant. "Won't say what it's about. Just asked for the head of the task force."

Alan frowned. This was new. "Send him up."

He watched as an older man in a blue pin-striped three-piece suit got directed to his office. The barrister entered and

243

closed the door. He sat opposite Alan and introduced himself.

"I represent Norman Lee," he said. "Your officers have made multiple visits to his home and business. They've been rude and disruptive."

Alan leaned back. "The police are just doing their job."

"No." The barrister's voice was steady. "This is harassment. Mr Lee has already stated he was at work the day of the Victoria Club robbery. He has a hundred witnesses to prove it."

Alan said nothing.

"From now on," the barrister continued, "direct all your inquiries through me. And if your officers want to visit Mr. Lee's premises again, they'd better bring a warrant."

He took a card from his waistcoat pocket, placed it on Alan's desk, and stood.

"Good day, sir." He left without another word.

Alan sat there, stunned. A barrister had never walked into his office to deny a client's involvement before. Not before they had been accused of something.

"We've got one then." He smiled.

* * *

The task force had added two more names to the board: Vinnie Mikkelsen, Ian Carroll's long-time enforcer, and Laurie Prendergast, one of Bennett's boys. Both had vanished. Both had barristers running interference.

Months had passed. It was almost Christmas, and they still had nothing. The task force had shrunk. Most of the team reassigned. Task force meetings were only on Monday morning now.

Alan was down to five detectives. One from CIB. Thompson from Consorting. One from Gaming. Useless.

The other two, his own from Armed Robbery. He stood at the front of the room. "The money," he said flatly.

Silence.

"It has to have gone somewhere," he said, eyes on the CIB detective.

The man shifted. "Some has surfaced in Manila. NCA believes a bar there is laundering Aussie cash. A few notes from the robbery turned up, but they can't tie it directly to the bar. They're working on it."

Alan sighed. "What about Melbourne? Any splashing?"

Shakes of heads.

"Bennett and Carroll are back. What about the others? Cars? Jewellery? Hookers? That's how these guys burn through money. Anything?"

Nothing.

Alan sighed. "Surely they haven't just buried it in the backyard and forgotten about it."

Everyone looked at each other. Nothing.

"Maybe they have, boss," someone muttered.

Alan didn't answer. Just picked up his coffee, walked out, and left the board behind. Just names and bad guesses.

CHAPTER 27

First Cracks

Ray's Mum

Ray knocked on the door of a dilapidated single front terrace in Richmond. The windows had sheets as curtains. His mother answered. The grin on her face could light the day. Her oldest was the apple of her eye. She ushered him into the kitchen, poured two cups of tea, and sat with him at the kitchen table.

"Mum," he opened. "I know life has been hard, but you were always there for me, even at your own expense. It's now my time to thank you." He pulled two bundles of shrink-wrapped cash from his bag and pushed them across the table to her.

"This should get you a nice little place no one can kick you out of anymore. A place of your own."

She burst into tears. He stood, walked around, put his arms around her and held her tight. No need for a thank you, he had already been paid tenfold.

He left his solicitor's card and told her, when she found a place, to take the money to him and he would take care of everything for her.

* * *

An older woman sat silently in the solicitor's office. She was younger than she looked. Her face showed the marks of a hard life lived. Sweat beaded on her forehead.

"Sorry, Mrs Bennett," the receptionist said. "Joe shouldn't be much longer."

"Chuck," she corrected.

"Pardon," asked the receptionist, a little confused.

"The name is Mrs Chuck, not Bennett," she asserted.

The receptionist looked down at her appointment book. Drew a line through Bennett and wrote 'Chuck'.

Mrs Chuck had spent her life trying to do the best for her kids. And here she was again, helping her boy Ray. She felt hot. Lightheaded.

"May I have a glass of water?" she asked the receptionist as she stood up.

"Certainly." But before she could move, the old woman collapsed on the floor. The receptionist rang an ambulance.

There is a good thing about the legal district being at the top end of town. So is the Royal Melbourne Hospital. The ambulance was there in minutes.

The paramedics checked her pulse and her breathing. A heart attack. One opened a medical case and took out a portable defibrillator. The other started cutting the old woman's dress away to get to her chest.

Cash exploded everywhere. Thousands of dollars fell out of her clothing onto the floor. For a moment, it distracted the paramedics. But soon they were back on task.

Joe came out having heard the commotion. Next, the police arrived, having heard the emergency call for an ambulance. The police set about collecting and counting the cash under the vigilant watch of the solicitor.

Mrs Chuck was revived and taken to the Royal Melbourne Hospital. The solicitor had a receipt drawn up for the cash and had the police sign it before taking it away. The receipt was for ninety thousand dollars. [49]

* * *

With business taken care of in Sydney, Ian thought things had quietened enough to return home.

Headlights swept across the bedroom. A car door opened and closed. A car drove off.

Rae heard the key in the front door, then it opened. She was standing in the hall. Her face emotionless.

Ian stood at the door, quiet, just looking at her. Finally, he spoke. "Did I wake you?"

Rae walked into the kitchen without speaking. Sat at the kitchen table. A cup of tea in front of her. "Wasn't asleep."

Ian moved to the fridge. Poured a drink. Took a slow sip.

"Have you eaten?" she asked.

"Yes, thanks." He didn't turn around.

Rae watched him. "I'm not asking where you were," she said.

Ian set his glass down. "That's good."

"I'm asking how long you think this lasts."

A pause. The clock ticked on the wall.

Ian turned. "What?"

Rae's stare fixed on him. Her jaw set. "How long?"

Ian leaned on the counter. "What do you want me to say?"

"That you've thought about how this ends."

Ian sighed. Ran his hand over the back of his head. "Jesus, Rae."

He looked at her.

Then she saw it. He had thought about it. He knew. But he was not going to say. Rae pushed her chair back. Stood.

"The shower's leaking again," she said. "You should fix it."

She walked past him. Didn't wait for a reply.

* * *

Neither planned nor coordinated, by Christmas, all of Bennett's crew had gravitated back to Melbourne. Ray for his mother's funeral, Laurie to straighten out Tony, and Ian to take care of his business concerns.

Ray and Ian sat in a coffee shop in the industrial part of Yarraville. It was Thursday, mid-morning.

"School run this morning?" Ray asked.

"Yep," came Ian's solitary flat reply. "You?"

"Same." He stirred coffee, watching the factory across the road.

"I guess all your investments keep you pretty busy?" said Ray, looking at the building across the road for sale. It was a subtle dig at Ian, who was here to look at it.

"Yeah. With all that Rae's got me doing, I feel more like an Accountant these days." There was a touch of sadness in his voice.

An armoured van pulled up on the opposite side of the road. The guards got out. Put two steel cashboxes on a trolley. Wheeled them into the factory.

"Payroll," Ray said as a matter of fact.

Ian looked up. A guard ran back to the van and closed the cash door that he had forgotten. "Clowns."

"Do you miss it?" Ray asked. It was not a leading question. More nostalgia.

"Every day."

The guards came out. The van left. In its place, a car pulled in. A real estate logo on its door.

Ian stood. "Back in ten."

He crossed the street, shook hands with the agent. The agent tapped the 'For Sale' sign on the building before they entered.

Ray shook his head.

* * *

Three weeks later, they were back. Down the road in a white Transit van. Vinnie was behind the wheel. Acting like a kid on the first day back at school for a new year. He could not hide the grin on his face. Ray and Ian sat in the back, checking their weapons.

"Showtime," Vinnie said as the armoured van rolled to a stop. He planted his foot. The Transit van raced up and swung around behind the armoured van. It screeched to a halt. The back doors were open before it stopped. Ray and Ian jumped out, balaclavas down, machine guns up.

The guards stood open-mouthed. Cashboxes loaded on a trolley.

"Back up China. Don't do anything stupid," Ray warned. The guards stepped back against the armoured van. Machine guns trump handguns.

Ian and Vinnie loaded the two cashboxes into the back of the Transit. Ray kept his gun trained on the guards.

On the sound of the second clunk of a cashbox, Ray backed up and stepped backwards into the van. His gun still trained on the guards. Ian smacked the side wall twice. Ray closed the doors as Vinnie sped off.

"One minute," Ian said, removing his balaclava. "We've still got it."

"You bet your arses," came Vinnie's call from the front.

No one opened the cashboxes. That was not really the point. They were working again. That's what mattered; until it didn't.

Ray was not the same after his mother's heart attack. He did not talk about it, not even acknowledge it, but it was there, under the surface. The one person who had ever truly mattered to him was gone. And it had changed him.

Before, he was methodical. A strategist. Now, there was something else in him; something bitter. Something that saw only threats, not problems with solutions.

After the Yarraville job, he sat in Ian's warehouse, rolling his second beer between his palms. Ian was only halfway through his first.

"We need to talk about Normie and Tony," Ray said.

Ian frowned. He knew the Tony problem. But Normie? That was new. "Normie?"

"In the count, he said we had ninety grand in new notes," Ray said. "Press reported one-fifty."

Ian sighed. "Jesus, Ray. You're believing the papers now?" No way would Ray turn on Normie. Turn on him, maybe. But not Normie.

"Well, he just got caught with forty large at his lawyer's."

Ian saw it in Ray's face. He had turned.

Ian leaned back, shaking his head.

"No different from your mum," he said, without thinking.

Ray was on him before he finished the sentence. He slammed Ian against the wall, one arm across his chest.

Ian didn't fight. This wasn't a pissing contest. It was a sore point. Hands up. No contest.

"They were new notes," Ray hissed. "Serial numbers tracked."

Ian held his gaze, waiting. He could see it now, clear as day. It wasn't about Normie. Never was.

Ray let go. Walked back to his beer. Took a long pull.

"Are you saying you want to off Normie?" Ian asked, a little confused.

"I'm saying he's a liability."

"He's staunch," Ian said. "Even if they pick him up, he won't talk. You know that."

Ray said nothing. Just stared at his beer like it might hold an answer. Maybe. Maybe not. Then:

"Tony's different. Even Vinnie thinks we should put him down."

Ian shook his head. "What the fuck is all this whacking shit? You're starting to sound like Shannon." Ian had forgotten that Ray had not been there for Shannon's spiral.

Ray did not react. He missed the meaning. "Sooner or later, Ambrose will mention Tony," Ray continued. "You want to wait for Kane's people to put him under a car? Better we cut our losses."

"If they link him to the job, it won't matter if he's dead or alive," Ian said. "They'll come after us anyway. Only we'll have a body on our hands as well."

Ray's fingers tapped against the bottle. His leg bounced. Thinking. But not the way he used to.

Ian sighed. "Look," he said, "I'll handle it if it becomes an issue. Otherwise, stay cool." He could see where this was heading. "You've changed, mate."

Ray scoffed. "And you haven't?"

Ian just shook his head. He had changed. He was thinking beyond the next job, beyond the next problem to eliminate. He had a future. Ray only saw ghosts.

Ray finished his beer. Put the bottle down. Left without a word.

Ian watched him go.

Maybe it was time to put some distance between the two of them.

* * *

Rae pushed open the hotel room door. Threw the key on the sideboard and dropped her bag on the bed. The room reeked of damp carpet and air freshener, attempting to mask other odours. She glanced at her overnight bag.

Is this what it has come to?

She had left the kids with her sister. Told her she needed time. Time to think. But sitting here, staring at the rain-streaked window, it didn't feel thoughtful. Just hollow. Tired. Trapped.

She had loved him once. Believed he could be different. Late nights. Whispered plans. But love turned to something crueller. Quieter. A pain that did not show. Apologies that did not last.

A tear rolled. She wiped it fast. No more of that. Not tonight.

She thought of Gail. Of half-baked schemes to leave. New cities. New names. A clean slate. But Gail stayed. And her? She just got better at pretending.

Her fingers curled around themselves. Is this all there is?

Staying meant giving up. Leaving meant starting from nothing. A no-win situation, but one that let her keep her spine.

She sat quiet. Stared out the window. Numb.

The silence didn't offer comfort. In that rain-soaked moment, she made a decision. No more waiting. No more drifting. She would take control. Of the situation. Of her life. A silent promise. She would fight to reclaim her life. Their life.

She stood. Picked up the bag. Left the key on the table. Walked out. Not for him. Not even for the kids. For her. To pull Ian out of the spiral before he dragged them all under.

* * *

Later that night, their bedroom was dark except for the reflective glow from outside the bedroom window. Rae lay on her side, half-covered by the sheet, staring at Ian in the dim light. His hands behind his head, bare chest, looking up at the ceiling.

"We don't have to go down with them," she said, voice low. "We could leave."

Ian huffed a laugh, short, empty. "Leave?" He turned to her. "Go where?"

"Anywhere," she said. She ran her fingers down his chest and torso. "We've got the money. We don't have to wait around to see how this ends."

Ian didn't respond.

He remembered the first job he did for Ray. A warehouse in West Melbourne. A simple break-in, moving some stolen cargo. It was Ray who had picked him, vouched for him. Ian had been younger then, hungry. Thought Ray saw something in him.

Now, Ray looked at everyone as a liability.

Raelene's fingers circled the bullet wound scar on his abdomen. She thought of shots at the front door. Him lying there in a pool of blood. "Do you trust Ray to keep you alive?"

Ian swallowed. He did not answer.

* * *

Morning came. Ian made coffee, black, strong. Rae sat across from him, still in her robe, watching as he dialled.

"Yeah," he said into the receiver. "A couple of months. New York first. Then London. Open ticket. Make the arrangements."

He hung up. Met Rae's eyes. She smiled, relief softening her face. He walked over and placed his hand on her shoulder. She rested her head on his side.

Then the phone rang. They looked at each other. It rang again.

He picked up. Listened. His jaw tightened. He put it back down.

"Normie's been picked up," he said.

Raelene closed her eyes.

"You don't owe him anything," she said.

But Ian was already reaching for his keys. Already running through the next steps in his head.

It was not just the docks that didn't let go.

The bookie robbery didn't either.

CHAPTER 28

Crossroads

Normie's Arrest

"Boss, some of the new notes from the robbery have turned up at Normie Lee's solicitor," Thompson said, sticking his head in through DI Alan's door.

"Can we tie them back to Lee?" Alan asked.

"Yes, he brought sixty thousand dollars in cash into his solicitor in a garbage bag. Asked him to deposit it in his trust account. When deposited at the bank, some of the notes were flagged up from the robbery."

"OK. Bring him in." Alan sat back and smiled.

* * *

"Normie, the police are …" is all the receptionist got out before Thompson, flanked by two uniformed officers, pushed past. He walked around the desk. "Stand," he commanded Normie.

Normie got to his feet. Thompson swung him around and cuffed him.

"Norman Lee, I am arresting you on suspicion of the armed robbery of the Victoria Club, on April 21st, last year," Thompson announced.

"I must inform you that you do not have to say or do anything, but anything you say or do may be given in evidence in court." Thompson continued. "Do you understand?"

Normie said nothing. Thompson waited.

Nothing.

"Ok, take him away. And take that safe as well."

* * *

At Russell Street police headquarters, Normie sat quietly on one side of the interview table. DI Alan and Thompson on the other.

"Please state your name for the record," DI Alan started.

Nothing.

He repeated his request. Normie said nothing.

"I can sit here all day if need be."

Normie said nothing.

DI Alan waited.

"All right, can we have the keys to the safe? We have a warrant to search it." DI Alan said, eventually conceding to Normie's silence.

Normie said nothing.

"We are entitled to break it open if you insist."

Normie said nothing.

Alan terminated the interview.

* * *

Out in the courtyard, the locksmith finally opened the safe. He stood back.

It had taken several hours to locate a court-authorised locksmith. Then, more time waiting for him to break into it.

DI Alan stepped forward, smiling. "Let's see what we've got." He pulled the door open. Empty.

"What the," Thompson exclaimed. "He made us go through all this for nothing!"

Meanwhile, Normie sat silently in the interview room by himself. Heard the swearing out in the hall.

He smiled.

* * *

Normie's Day in Court

Almost a year to the day of the Victoria Club robbery, Normie stood in the dock awaiting judgment. He was charged with the robbery of the Victoria Club, as well as receiving $124,000 from the robbery. The prosecution laid out a lot of detail, but little real evidence. Police alleged he laundered $110,000 through his solicitor's trust account. That he had spent a further $60,000 buying equipment for his factory. He had also recently renovated his home.

The prosecution's forensic witness detailed that the new notes had been part of the bank float delivered to the Victoria Club on the day of the robbery. He read the ranges of serial numbers of the fifty-dollar notes stolen that day. The prosecutor presented the notes recovered from Normie's deposit. Yes, the numbers matched; they were part of that delivery.

Normie stared at the notes. His stomach clenched. That mistake again. Bookie cash over the new stuff. He didn't even know that he'd done it, until it was too late. He didn't flinch, but the heat under his collar told the story.

258

Prosecution rested. The defence did not call any witnesses.

Normie was acquitted. All the evidence, circumstantial.

In summing up, the magistrate said: "While the money might have come from illegal activity, there was no evidence that places the defendant at the scene of the robbery. It is also impossible to say that the notes identified came into his possession directly from the Great Bookie Robbery."

DI Alan left the courtroom dejected. On the steps outside the courthouse, he addressed reporters: "I have no doubt that Norman Lee was totally involved in the robbery of the Victoria Club." He continued, "I remain convinced that, if we had successfully prosecuted Lee, other arrests would have followed." He excused himself and left.

Normie went off to celebrate his acquittal with a meal in Chinatown. Within days of Lee's acquittal, the police task force on the Great Bookie Robbery was disbanded. [50]

* * *

The Flower Drum

The Chinese came to Victoria in the mid-1800s. It was the Gold Rush. First digging for gold, they soon realised the real gold lay in providing goods and services to the miners. They became the backbone of the Victorian business community. One hundred and thirty years later, Melbourne's Chinatown has become a mecca for late-night eateries. The premier of which was the Flower Drum. Large, expensive, and very popular. [51]

It had been a year since the Victoria Club robbery. Police had nothing. The Sydney 'toughs' had been sent packing. Life was good. A joint celebration for Normie's acquittal and an anniversary reunion dinner was organised at the Flower Drum. Boys only.

The mood was jovial. Seven men sat around a large round table, chatting, laughing. They had finished their meal. Bowls, now in the middle on the lazy Susan.

"Kevin, more Crownies all around," Ray ordered. They were good customers. Spent big. Always paid in cash.

Frankie continued his story …,

"She shot that ping pong ball across the bar into my drink."

"How far?" Tony asked in amazement.

"Would have to be a good ten feet," Frankie replied.

"Bullshit." Vinnie coughed.

"God's honour," said Frankie, placing his hand on his heart.

"I wouldn't want to put my balls anywhere near that," Laurie chipped in.

Ian fired back, "Don't worry, I doubt she could get it tight enough to latch on to your balls."

Laughter.

"Greedy's got a great little operation over there," Frankie continued. "And the birds in Manila are gorgeous."

Ian snorted, "I still wouldn't trust the Fatman as far as I could throw him."

Laurie added, "His idea of a vegetarian meal is five potato cakes with tomato sauce," laughing.

"It has worked out to be a good little earner, all the same," Normie countered.

"Yes, well done, Normie," Ray asserted.

Once everyone had a fresh Crown Lager, Ray raised his.

"To Normie."

"Normie," the others followed collectively.

Ray asked for the bill. Picked it up and did the math in his head.

"Normie's not paying," he announced matter-of-factly. "So it's one hundred a piece."

"A hundred bucks for Chinese?" Vinnie spat. This was a time when the average restaurant bill was closer to fifty dollars a head.

"Plus tip," Ray corrected.

Everyone threw down two fifties and a twenty. Vinnie threw two fifties.

"Plus tip," Ray repeated, glaring at Vinnie.

"I don't tip." Vinnie sat back, arms crossed.

"We come here regularly," Ray added.

"It's not like you can't afford it," Tony chipped in.

"Yeah, we don't want them spitting in our food next time," Laurie added, trying to add some levity.

"I don't tip," Vinnie said flatly. Arms folded, eyes daring anyone to push it.

They sat there in silence.

Ian pulled out another twenty from his pocket and threw it in. "I've got it."

"Cheapskate," Ray said, pushing his chair in. The cash left on the table.

They left.

* * *

With Normie free again, Ian kept his promise to Raelene. The next morning, Ian packed his bag in silence. Rae stood at the door, waiting. "So, we're really going this time?"

He zipped it shut. "I told you, Rae, this isn't a life."

She swallowed hard. "What about Ray?"

Ian sighed. "Ray made his choice."

There was a knock at the front door. Ian lifted his bag off the bed, carried it downstairs, went and opened the door. Ray stood there, eyes shadowed, a tension in his jaw Ian hadn't seen before.

"You're leaving," Ray said flatly.

Ian nodded.

Ray stepped inside. "After everything?"

Ian met his gaze. "You don't need me anymore."

A flicker of something, anger, hurt, crossed Ray's face. "Bullshit." He shook his head. "You think you can just walk away?"

Ian tightened his grip on his bag. "I think I have to."

Ray's breath hitched. He wanted to say more. Maybe beg, maybe threaten. Instead, he just scoffed.

"Fuck you, Ian." He turned and walked away.

Rae touched Ian's arm. "Are you okay?"

Ian did not answer. Because Ray would not be.

* * *

A short time later, Gail arrived. She drove Raelene, Ian and the kids to the airport. It was a tight squeeze. Ian had wanted to catch a cab, but Gail insisted.

Ian stepped forward to check in. Gail looked up at the sign - First Class. "I wish I was coming with you," she said, giving Rae a big hug. "Two months. I'll miss you."

"Why don't you get Ray and come join us?" Raelene offered. "Either in the States or the UK. We can make a real holiday of it."

"Ray never wants to go anywhere," Gail replied downheartedly. "He said we would, but there is always one other thing he has to take care of."

Ian came back. He handed Rae her ticket and passport. "We have lounge access," he said. "Join us for a farewell drink?" he offered Gail. He knew the girls would miss each other.

"No, sorry. I really have to go," Gail replied. "Thank you anyway." She was trying to hide her tears.

Raelene gave her another hug. She whispered in her ear, "Ask Ray. Please come and join us."

Gail just smiled and nodded. A perfect lie.

* * *

Vinnie sat on the warehouse steps looking out into the distance. A smoke in hand resting on his knee.

Ray came out and stood beside him. "Ian's gone," he said.

Vinnie nodded.

Ray let out a hollow breath. "Leaves us exposed."

Vinnie took a drag. "Not my problem."

Ray turned to him. "Ain't it? You think Ian would've lasted this long without you watching his back?"

Vinnie frowned.

"Think about it," Ray continued. "Ian's safe. He's got Rae, the kids, the house. You don't have that, Vin. All you've got is me."

Vinnie's stomach twisted. He had followed Ian for years, thinking they were a team. But Ian left.

Ray clapped him on the back. "Stick with me. We'll make sure no one can touch us."

Vinnie said nothing.

But he stayed.

* * *

Ray sat at the back of the booth in The Rising Sun. Beer glass in his hand, still full. The hubbub around him, Laurie's booming laugh, Normie's easy banter. He felt distant, hollow. They were celebrating, throwing money around, acting like kings.

But kings don't last.

Ray's eyes were fixed on the door. A man standing outside lighting a cigarette. Out of place. A cop? A Kane soldier? He tapped his fingers against the glass, out of sync with the music playing in the room.

Vinnie leaned in. "You good, Ray?"

Ray blinked. "Yeah. Fine."

But he wasn't. The money had been easy. Too easy. And easy money always comes with a cost.

Across the room, Tony was running his mouth off again, bragging to some girl about something or other. Ray clenched his jaw. Loose lips sink crews. He stood abruptly.

Laurie noticed. "Where you going, mate?"

"Getting air."

He stepped outside, into the cold night. The man with the cigarette glanced at him.

Ray moved first. "Got a problem?"

The man startled, stepping back. "Just having a smoke, mate."

Ray stared him down. His pulse thudded. Had the Kanes sent someone? Were the cops circling? He couldn't tell anymore.

Back inside, Laurie and Vinnie watched through the window.

"Ray's seems a bit off," Vinnie muttered.

Laurie laughed it off. "Yeah. But he's always been a little off."

Vinnie said nothing. Because this was different.

Ray stepped back into the pub, face unreadable. Vinnie handed him his beer.

Ray didn't drink it. He just kept watching the door.

PART V

RETRIBUTION

The world in which we live is governed by some immutable laws of physics. These are the bedrock of all scientific theories. Central to these is the second law of Thermodynamics. It states that the entropy of a system tends to disorder. Put simply …

Everything turns to shit.

CHAPTER 29

The Seventh Circle of Hell

Ambrose Talks

Brian Kane kept up his training at Leo's gym, even if Les was not welcome. No money in Golden Gloves, but it kept him sharp. Kept his face out there. Good for business. Also, it let him pick up whispers about jobs around town. His main earn these days was collecting 'tax' from other crooks' jobs. Standover. Pay a percentage, or Les smashed your kneecaps. And Les did not bluff.

The talk around the gym was still the bookie robbery. Ambrose Palmer, ex-prize fighter and local legend, had been there.

Every day the same question: "Come on, Ambrose. Tell us about it."

He gave the same answer every time: "Didn't see much. Too busy keeping my head down."

Lots of speculation. No answers. Brian could not cash in on speculation. He needed a name. He had an idea.

Ambrose strolled in, shaking hands, basking in past glory. A legend in his own mind.

Brian stopped mid-spar, leaned on the ropes.

"Hey, Ambrose. Got a minute to give me some pointers?"

"Sure, kid." Ambrose grinned and stepped up. "Let's see your stuff."

Brian threw a few jabs, a roundhouse, then his powerhouse right.

"Not bad," Ambrose said. "But before you throw the straight right, do a double foot movement. But hit off the back foot."

Brian nodded and put his mouth guard back in. Went back to face his sparring partner. He repeated the combination, this time throwing the right off his back foot. The sparring partner staggered back, shaken.

Brian clapped his gloves together, turned to Ambrose.

"Wow, what a difference." He grinned. "Pity those bookie robbers didn't get within arm's reach of you."

Ambrose leaned in, voice low. "Na, the one who told me to keep my head down, I've known since he was four. Tony McNamara. Did me a solid. Don't tell anyone."

Brian smiled. "Don't worry, I won't."

At last, a name.

* * *

Brian liked to walk home after boxing. Richmond is laced with back alleys. A holdover from the days when toilets were in the backyard, with pots collected by men in carts. Walking the alleys gave him a sense of solitude. No cars, no people. Kitbag over his shoulder. Sun on his face.

As he turned out of a lane, a pale blue sedan pulled up, blocking his path. Detective Murphy opened the passenger door and got out. He stood toe-to-toe with Brian.

"Mr Murphy," Brian greeted the policeman.

"Been shopping Brian?" Murphy asked grabbing Brian's kit bag off his shoulder.

"Training," Brian replied. Not so much indignant as bored. He was used to Consorting rousting him. Came with the territory.

Murphy looked through the gym gear, then dropped the bag on the ground. Out of the blue, he grabbed Brian and pushed him up against the car. Brian swallowed his pride. No other man would get away with that, he thought.

Murphy pulled out Brian's wallet, flipped it open. "Hmm." He shoved it into Brian's chest.

"What can I do for you, Mr Murphy?"

"Give me something, Brian. And you won't have to come back to the station."

"Like what?" Brian asked, pleading ignorance.

Murphy scowled as he stepped back. "The bookie robbery. Heard anything?"

Brian said nothing, just stared at Murphy.

"Hmm," Murphy said again. He pulled out a fifty-dollar bill from his own wallet. Held it in front of Brian's face.

Brian smiled. "Ambrose thinks he recognised a voice during the robbery." He went to take the money.

Murphy pulled it away. "Who?"

"A kid named Tony McNamara. Said he's known him for years." Brian grabbed the fifty and stuffed it into his pocket.

Murphy pushed him out of his way. Got back into the car. It sped off.

Brian picked up his kit bag and wandered on, smiling. He rolled the fifty between his fingers. The cops rattling the trees only made his job easier.

* * *

Boxer vs Streetfighter

Brian finally had a name. He asked around, did some digging. Found out Tony drank at The Royal Oak in

269

Richmond with Laurie Prendergast, who ran with Ray Chuck, or Bennett, or whatever he was calling himself these days.

Brian figured he and Les should pay them a visit. Like everyone else, they would have to pay.

They walked in. Tony and Laurie sat with another big bloke, laughing, drinking. Brian and Les ordered beers. Watched. Waited.

Laurie stepped up to the bar for another round. The barman poured three beers. Laurie reached for his cash.

Brian's hand shot out and stopped him.

"Let me get these," Brian said.

Laurie turned. Seeing who it was, his face went cold. "No thanks. We're in a shout."

Brian pressed down harder. "You don't understand. We want to talk business. We know about the job. We're after our drink."

"Fuck off," Laurie snapped, breaking his grip.

Brian squared his stance, arms loose. "You don't want to piss us off."

Vinnie stepped in. "He said fuck off." His stare was ice.

Brian struck first. Three fast shots before Vinnie got his hands up.

Les slid back, watching, smiling. Brian could handle himself.

Vinnie staggered back, dazed. He was not a boxer. He brawled. Dropping his head, he charged, driving his shoulder into Brian's gut. They both hit the ground hard.

Vinnie's fingers found Brian's eyes. His knee crushed Brian's groin.

Les moved, ready to step in.

Laurie blindsided him. A quick combo sent Les sprawling. Tony stepped up beside Laurie.

Vinnie had no intention of letting Brian get back up. A brawler could beat a boxer, as long as the boxer was off his feet.

Then, without thinking, Vinnie bit down. Sank his teeth deep into Brian's ear. And tore.

Brian's scream filled the bar.

Vinnie stood, spat a chunk of Brian's ear onto the floor.

Les scrambled to his brother and pressed a bar towel to his head.

"You better get him to a hospital," Vinnie said, blood dripping from his mouth.

Les hauled Brian up. Dragged him toward the door. As he went out, Les turned back. Wild eyed. "Y'dead. Y'all fucking dead. Tell Chuck I'm gonna cut his fucking head off. And his wife. And his kid."

The door slammed shut.

Laurie snorted. "He's a fucking nutter."

Vinnie wiped his mouth and muttered, "He could be a problem."

* * *

The following night. The Royal Oak. Same pub, same crew. But this time, Ray was with them.

"He said he was after a drink?" Ray asked.

Laurie nodded. "Yeah. Offered to shout us. Then added it'd be only fair that we gave him a drink too." He paused. "He was looking for a piece of the job."

Ray's face darkened. "He knows then."

"How could he?" Vinnie said. "He's fishing."

Ray shook his head. "Kane doesn't fish. He knows." He was thinking, eyes narrowed. "Ambrose." His eyes glanced at Tony. Tony dropped his head.

Laurie took a sip of his beer, then muttered, "That Les, though… he's off his head. Said he'd cut off your wife and kid's heads."

Ray froze. "What?" His eyes snapped to Laurie.

"Oh, nothing." Laurie shrugged. "Just as they were leaving, Les said he'd kill all of us. Then cut off your wife and kid's heads." Laurie chuckled. "What else would you expect?"

Vinnie added, "A standover man missing an ear isn't that scary." He laughed.

Ray did not.

"No," Ray said. His voice cut through the noise. The laughter died. "Les is psychotic. That missing ear'll eat at him every time he sees it." Ray paused. "That's a problem."

"A big problem," Ray reiterated, deep in thought.

Silence.

"We will have to handle them," Ray finally said.

Three pairs of eyes turned to him. They knew what that meant.

"Both?" Vinnie asked.

Ray nodded. Les had crossed the line. In the Melbourne underworld, families were sacred. Always.

"Can't do one without the other," Ray confirmed. "Not if you want to keep breathing. We do Les first. Loud and messy. That might send Brian to ground."

They stood in silence for a moment, stunned. Ray was serious. No other option.

Ray, Vinnie, and Tony finished their beers and left. No more words.

Laurie lingered, staring at the remnants of his beer. *How had things got to this ...*

"We got a problem?" Ray interrupted Laurie's thoughts. As he was leaving, Ray had looked back, read Laurie's body language and returned.

Laurie frowned. "What?"

Ray leaned in. "Les Kane."

Laurie stiffened. "Shit, Ray—"

"He's coming for us," Ray interrupted. "You in or not?"

Laurie hesitated. "Mate, I… I've never done—"

Ray's gaze hardened. "You think we got here by playing it safe?"

Laurie swallowed. He thought about the others. The band of brothers. Of loyalty. Then, about how things seem to be getting out of control. But there was nothing he could do. Finally, acceptance. "All right," he whispered.

Ray smiled. Laurie didn't.

* * *

The Murder of Les Kane

Ray stood over a map of Melbourne, red circles marking Les Kane's home. Laurie and Vinnie sat across from him.

"This is how it goes down," Ray said, voice clipped. "We go in hard. Heavy weapons, no masks. No bullshit."

Laurie shifted. "No masks?"

Ray snapped his gaze up. "We want Kane to know who did it."

Vinnie stared at him. "That's a death sentence."

"No. It's sending a message." Ray scanned their eyes. They needed more. He continued, "If they worked out it was us, then it won't be long before others do too. Do you want to spend the rest of your life looking over your shoulder?" He let that sit. Sink in.

Ray's face hardened. "We need everyone to know; don't fuck with us."

Their heads dropped.

Laurie's throat went dry. This was not the Ray he knew. But it was the Ray they had now.

There was no turning back.

* * *

That night, an old sedan pulled up outside Les Kane's home, lights off. A typical outer suburban house. A quiet street. The house was in darkness. The silhouettes of four men sat inside the sedan.

"No one home," Tony muttered from the driver's seat.

"Good," Ray said. "We wait inside. You stay here."

Ray, Laurie, and Vinnie got out. Tony dropped his head.

Vinnie pulled his balaclava down. Ray glared at him. They went around to the boot. He handed them modified M16s, suppressors fitted to the barrels. His, a German Sten. They walked up to the house, casual, like they belonged.

Vinnie slid a credit card up against the lock. Pushed. The door clicked open.

Ray shook his head. Such slack security showed the arrogance of the man.

A dog barked. It came out wagging its tail. Ray picked it up, stroked it twice, and then laid it on a veranda chair. They entered and closed the door.

They waited in the dark.

...

Headlights swept across the window. Then darkness. Car doors slammed. A kid's voice: "Thanks for the pizza, Dad!"

Les's wife, "c'mon, bedtime, you two."

"I'll be in in a minute," Les called back.

Ray moved back into the master bedroom adjacent to the front door. Laurie and Vinnie followed.

The front door opened. The family bustled inside. Hands were clamped over their mouths before they could scream.

274

"Quiet," a muffled voice ordered, "and you won't get hurt." They shoved them down the hall into the second bedroom.

Les stepped inside. "Put the bloody lights…"

A sack went over his head. His hands zip-tied. The butt of a gun smashed into his face. Vinnie and Laurie dragged him into the bathroom.

"Put him in the bath," Ray ordered.

Vinnie and Laurie lifted him, shoved his feet into the tub, forced him against the back wall.

Ray closed the bathroom door.

From inside the second bedroom, Les's wife and kids heard the rapid tapping of suppressed machine-gun fire.

The gunfire stopped. Silence filled the house. The trace of cordite hung in the air.

In the second bedroom, Judy held the children tighter, willing them not to move, not to breathe. The walls seemed to press in.

Ray huffed. The job was not done yet. "Get his car keys," Ray told Laurie. "Wrap him in the shower curtain," to Vinnie.

Vinnie ripped the shower curtain off its hooks. Spread it on the floor. Laurie tossed the keys to Ray. Then helped Vinnie roll the body up.

Ray led them outside, Vinnie and Laurie dragging Les's body. He opened the boot of Les's purple-pink Ford Futura. They dumped the blood-stained package inside. Ray slammed the boot shut.

"Vinnie and I have got this," he told Laurie, tossing him the Sten.

Laurie walked to Tony's car. Threw the guns in the boot. Got in. Tony drove off without a word.

"One minute," Ray said to Vinnie. He turned and went back to the house.

Vinnie climbed into the passenger seat of the Futura. Waited.

Ray stepped back inside the house. Judy and the kids were huddled in the hallway. Silent. Stunned. Ray met Judy's terrified eyes. "Tell Brian," he said, "you come after my family, I come after yours." He turned. Left.

Walked to the Futura. Got in and drove off, leaving nothing behind but blood and bullet casings.

Judy stared at the hallway floor. Blood smeared under her palms. Her children sniffled in the next room, too scared to cry. She wiped her hands on her dress, but the red stain remained.

She picked up the phone with trembling fingers and dialled.

Brian answered.

"They've shot Les." Her voice shook. Words garbled.

Brian forced himself to stay calm. "Hold tight. I'm coming."

He hung up. Grabbed his keys.

When he arrived, Brian stepped inside. The house had the sickly stench of blood and bleach. His boots stuck to the wet floor as he crossed the hallway. Judy scrubbed furiously, her hands raw, her eyes hollow. Her body sagged into his as he lifted her up.

"Where?" he whispered.

Judy pointed to the bathroom.

Brian let her go. Walked down the hall. Stopped at the door. Took a deep breath. Pushed it open. The stench of blood hit him first. It was a blood bath. Literally. A hundred bullet holes in the wall. Shell casings littered the floor. But no Les.

Brian slammed his fist against the doorframe. He spun back to Judy. "Where's Les?" His voice was low, controlled.

"They must have taken him." She wiped her face. "His car's gone too," she added.

Brian's breath came hard through his nose. "Who?" he asked. "Did you see who it was?" He did not expect so. He would have to work that out.

"Chuck," she whispered. "And two others."

Brian blinked. "Chuck?"

She nodded. "Didn't wear a mask."

Brian felt his stomach twist.

She told him that before Chuck left, he looked her in the eye, and said, clear as day: "Tell Brian, you come after my family, I come after yours."

Brian clenched his jaw. His fists. His teeth. "He's a fucking dead man."

Judy sobbed harder. He put his arms around her and held her tight. Comforting himself as much as her. After a while, he let go of her. Sent her back to be with the kids. Brian set about cleaning up the mess. His blood boiled with every scrub of the floor.

Before leaving, he went in to see Judy. "Don't tell the cops," he said. "If they ask, say he's gone away. You don't know where."

Then he walked out the door. He had work to do.

* * *

The pink Ford Futura pulled up to the roller door of the Dim Sim factory. Midnight. The streets were empty. Not a soul around. The motor whirred. The door ground up. The Futura drove in. The gate lowered.

3 AM. The motor whirred again. The door rose. The Futura pulled out and turned north. Headed for the car crushing plant outside the city.

Ray had arranged for one of the operators to earn some extra money. By dawn, the car would be gone, also. Nothing left.

CHAPTER 30

The Les Kane Murder Trial

Secrets do not last long in the underworld. They never did. By Monday morning, DI Alan had a new name. At the briefing, he pinned a blank spot on the board. "I believe we finally have our sixth man. Anthony McNamara." He turned to Thompson from Consorting. "Tell us what you have."

Thompson stood. Walked to the front. "Tony McNamara. No picture yet. Ex-Painter and Docker. Runs with Prendergast. Word is Ambrose Palmer knew his voice but kept quiet." He paused.

"Somehow the Kanes found out." He continued. "The word is they are trying to lean on Chuck's crew."

Someone muttered from the back, "Good luck with that."

Alan glared. "Let's get the Kanes in. See what they know." He smacked the desk. "Get to it."

* * *

That afternoon, Thompson leaned into Alan's doorway. "Boss, something's off."

Alan looked up.

"I went to pick up Les Kane. His wife says he's gone away. She looked shaken. Something's really wrong."

Alan's eyes narrowed. "And Brian?"

"Gone to ground. No one's seen him either."

Alan leaned back. Thought. "Send a couple of uniforms to sit with Les's wife. Policewomen. Get them to sympathise. Build rapport." He smirked. "Maybe she'll let something slip."

"The only reason for the Kanes to disappear is if they know something," he continued. "Let's find out what that is."

Thompson nodded.

Alan tapped his pen against the desk. "Chuck and his crew must be nervous. Let's up the pressure on them too. Bring them in again."

"We have a chance here. Let's use it."

* * *

Monday morning. The briefing room was tense. DI Alan showed his frustration.

"What do you mean you can't find them?" His voice cut through the room.

A detective shrugged. "No one's seen them for over a week."

He had been waiting to grill Chuck's crew again. He wanted to sweat them using Ambrose's identification of Tony McNamara.

"All of Chuck's crew?" Alan could not hide the surprise.

"We checked homes, work, pubs. Nothing."

Alan clenched his jaw.

"Damn."

He slammed his folder shut.

He would have to wait. [52]

* * *

"Boss," Thompson stood in the doorway, face serious. "Les Kane's dead."

Alan looked up.

"The uniforms just rang through. His wife finally cracked. Brian told her to stay quiet."

Alan's heart pounded. "What did she say happened?"

"Chuck and two others shot him in her bathroom. Machine guns. Took the body away in his car."

Alan sat still. Processing.

"Any idea who the other two were?"

Thompson grinned. "Based on her descriptions, Prendergast and Mikkelsen."

Alan stood. "We've got them then." He clapped his hands. "Get arrest warrants out on all three. Nationally."

It was not for the bookie robbery. But he would take the win anyway.

* * *

The Roundup

A dockyard somewhere sunny. Ore carriers waiting to load.

"Hey, Vinnie. Been looking for you."

Vinnie turned. Two detectives. Two uniforms behind them.

He threw his hard hat at them. Took off up the crane rigging. The two uniformed officers took off in hot pursuit.

The detectives didn't move. Just watched, grinning.

"Where does he think he's going?" one said.

The other shook his head. "Dead end. And we're in Karratha, a thousand miles from nowhere."

"He ain't the sharpest," said the first one. "He may be working under a fake name, but his kids are enrolled at school under his real one."

They leaned back against the railing. Waited.

* * *

Thompson's phone rang. He answered. "Great."

He yelled through the office. "They've got Mikkelsen."

Alan smiled. One down.

* * *

Laurie waited in the car. Behind the wheel. Balaclava rolled up on his forehead.

The armoured van pulled into the shopping centre car park. Approaching the bank.

His adrenaline rose.

Suddenly, two unmarked police cars swerved in around him. Lights flashing. Sirens blaring.

Police, everywhere. Guns out, yelling.

Laurie slammed the wheel. His head dropped. Sighed.

He put his hands out the window.

* * *

Thompson's phone rang again. He answered. "Got it."

He yelled through. "They've got Prendergast."

Two down.

* * *

A week later. DI Alan's phone rang.

"I believe you're looking for Ray Bennett," the voice said.

Alan sat up. "Certainly am. You've got some information on him?"

The voice on the other end chuckled. "Better than that. We have him in custody."

Alan clenched his fist. "Yes!"

"A local lad tipped us off," the Sydney DI continued. "Picked him up in Bondi. Came quietly."

Alan smirked. "Insurance," he muttered. A whisper here, a favour there; sooner or later, someone rolled. This time, it was on Chuck.

They worked out extradition details. Then he hung up.

Three down. Alan sat back, content.

* * *

On Trial

The day of the trial, police were at the courthouse early. Everywhere. Snipers on rooftops. Armed guards at every doorway. A police cordon stretched around the building. Police believed there could be an attempt on the defendants' lives. Emotions ran deep in Melbourne.

At 10 AM, an armoured prison van arrived. Laurie and Vinnie stepped out into a wall of cameras and film crews. Flashbulbs popped. Reporters shouted questions. TV could not get enough of it. Graphic re-enactments. Weeping testimonies from those not there. The usual fare.

Laurie and Vinnie, in immaculate suits, darted inside the courthouse. Ray was already seated. Brought in through the back. The three sat side-by-side in the dock. Their three barristers lined up in front of them.

The prosecution called its first witness.

Judy Kane. Les's widow.

She took the stand. Voice trembling, she told her story. The terror. Huddled with her kids in the bedroom. The endless rattle of machine-gun fire.

Ray's barrister stood. "You know machine-gun fire when you hear it, Mrs. Kane?"

"Everyone knows," she said.

"So, your neighbours heard it too?"

"No. They had suppressors."

"Suppressors? Not silencers? You know a fair bit about machine guns, don't you?"

Laurie's barrister stood. "When did you last see your husband?"

"That night, before they pushed me into the bedroom."

"So, he was alive then?"

"Yes."

"When did you see his dead body?"

"I didn't. They took him."

"You saw them take him?"

"No. I heard it."

"You *heard* it?" He smirked.

"For all you know, he could've run off. Just like you told the police."

"No, the blood."

"Ah, the blood. The blood that disappeared. You didn't tell the police about that either."

He paused. Let it sink in.

"You're telling us he's alive, then dead. There's blood, then none. Mrs Kane, which lie are we meant to believe?"

"Objection!"

"Withdrawn." The point had been made.

The barristers hammered her. How well did she know the accused? The darkness. The guns. Masks, no masks. Her changing stories. How could a wife calmly clean up her husband's blood?

By the time she stepped down, she was broken.

Forensics added little. Blood residue. Bullet holes. But no proof it was from that night.

All the accused had rock-solid alibis. Somewhere else, with someone else. Painters and Dockers swore to it.

And the biggest hole in the case? No body. Les Kane could be alive and well, living in Sydney.

The jury deliberated.

The foreman gave their verdict: "Not guilty."

A murmur rippled through the courtroom. Ray let out his breath, a slow, controlled breath. Vinnie let a grin slip for half a second before checking himself. Laurie cracked his knuckles behind his back.

They had won. For now. [53]

* * *

Outside the courtroom, Ray, Laurie, and Vinnie shook hands with their barristers. Job well done. Money well spent.

They huddled.

"Brian's still out there," Ray said.

"He won't be happy," Laurie muttered.

"Acquittal means nothing to him," Vinnie added. "This isn't over."

"Lay low," Ray said. "Let him cool off. When the time comes, we handle him."

"When is Ian back?" Vinnie asked. Ian had been overseas for six months. Missed the whole Kane mess. Vinnie thought it was about time Ian was his wingman for a change.

"Still playing antique dealer for Rae's mansion," Ray said. "It was only supposed to be two months. Can't be away much longer."

Then—

"Ray Chuck."

They turned.

Two plainclothes detectives.

"You're wanted in relation to a sixty-nine-thousand-dollar payroll robbery in Yarraville."

They clicked handcuffs on his wrists and led him away.

Ray did not blink.

Over his shoulder, he called to Laurie and Vinnie. "Use the back stairs."

* * *

Silvers

Toorak. The home of Melbourne's old money. The streets did not so much smell of money as ooze it. Rolls-Royce and Bentleys vied for no-standing parking spots. Women walked pink standard poodles, men wore silk suits and Italian leather shoes.

Sydney's rich moor their yachts at the bottom of their gardens. In Toorak, they moor their yachts in Monaco and Mallorca.

The Rodeo Drive of Toorak was Toorak Village. Tudor faced stores. High-end designer boutiques and higher-end jewellery stores. If you have to ask the price, you can't afford it. In the centre of the Village, a small arcade led to stairs and a lift. They, in turn, led to Silvers.

A nightclub for the powerful. A sanctuary for Melbourne's rich. [54]

Inside, a round dance floor. Speakers aimed inward. Pink booths curved around in concentric circles. The outer booths

286

allowed conversation late into the night. Tables adorned with thousand-dollar bottles of wine and fifty-dollar cocktails. A four-figure bill for a night was common.

Unlike most nightclubs, at 7 PM, Silver's booths were already well patronised.

Business lunches that stretched to 3 AM. After work meetups between not-so-married couples. Barristers, the profession of bored rich people, discussing the day's court proceedings. And Painters and Dockers. Home, showered, and now dressed in silk suits and Italian leather shoes.

Ray, Laurie, and Vinnie's barristers were seated in a booth, celebrating with a bottle of Moet.

Brian walked in. With him, the Munster and another Docker. He did the usual lap. Then he saw them.

He stopped.

The barristers raised their glasses. Another toast.

Brian snapped.

"You fucking cunts." He jammed a .38 into the back of one of the barristers' heads.

"You think this is fun?" he hissed. "They killed my brother, and you're *toasting* it?"

He cocked the gun. Les's blood ran in Brian's veins too.

The Munster moved fast. Knocked the gun from Brian's hand. "What are you doing?" he growled. Few men could get away with that. A well-known hitman, The Munster could. He picked up the gun. Nudged Brian toward the exit.

A hitman had just saved a barrister's life.

Only in Melbourne. Go figure.[55]

CHAPTER 31

Returns

"Mad Dog" Cox Escapes

Meanwhile, in a different part of the country …

The press had retitled him Russell "Mad Dog" Cox, following his previous escape attempt. Originally courted by Gail's sister Helen as the sixth member of the Bookie Robbery crew, his failed prison break left him near death and out of a job. He was given 'life' for the attempted murder of the prison guard. He had been expecting Grafton. Grafton was brutal. But it was known. Katingal was something else. Katingal was a prison within a prison. A purpose-built maximum security centre within the Long Bay prison complex. They called it "The Blockhouse." Others called it "The Electronic Zoo."

Russell Cox called it hell.

The air in Katingal had no weight to it. No scent. No windows, no natural light. Just a constant hum, recycled and dead. Like breathing inside a coffin made of steel. Doors locked and unlocked with the press of a button. Guards watched from catwalks behind reinforced glass. Every step was controlled. Every moment accounted for.

Cox had been in bad prisons before. This one wanted to break men. But it would not break him. He was a fitness nut. Worked out relentlessly. Practised yoga in his cell. One arm push-ups; one arm pull-ups.

* * *

The Blockhouse filled up.

After a failed escape attempt from Maitland prison, authorities sent the troublemakers to Long Bay. Cox watched them arrive. Faces he knew. Some from the docks. Some from old jobs. Some from cells like this one. Hardened men. Tough. But Katingal did not care about tough.

Cox did not care either. He got a message out that he needed one of them to do him a favour for $500. Arrange for a hacksaw blade to get smuggled in.

One advantage of being at Katingal was that it was still part of Long Bay. Therefore, the nurse Patrick, who had treated Cox following his failed escape attempt, accompanied the doctor on prison visits. He was always eager to please Cox. Cox arranged for the blade to be passed to Patrick, who brought it through security without inspection. The package arrived. Passed from hand to hand. No words. No eye contact. Just the right men in the right places.

It ended up with Cox. He took it and said nothing.

* * *

The only place with open air was the exercise yard. One hour a day was all that inmates were given. There was a cage above, bars welded into thick concrete. Beyond that, freedom.

Cox moved slow. Careful. A little each day.

He climbed, pulled himself up to the bars overhead with one hand, sawed with the other. Ten minutes at a time. His muscles burned, but he did not stop.

Before leaving, he checked his work. Covered the cut with a sliver of soap, smoothed it out, blended it in.

He waited. And waited. Then, on November 4th, he made his move …

"Forgot my shoes," Cox told the warder.

The warder barely looked up. Didn't flinch. He'd heard every excuse in the book. Shoes? Whatever.

Cox walked into the yard. He did not stop. Did not hesitate. A table tennis paddle hidden in his waistband. He pulled it out and wedged it into a crack in the wall. A step. A foothold.

He climbed.

His fingers found the cut bar. He pulled. It came free. Above him, the sky. He hauled himself onto the roof. Down below, the guards were bored. Talking. Smoking.

Cox climbed down. Two fences left. Both over four metres; both topped with razor wire. Freedom was close, but he wouldn't let himself taste it yet. Not until the air outside cut into his lungs. He moved fast. Hands and feet working together.

He cleared the first fence, boots tearing fabric as he landed. The second was higher. Halfway up, a guard saw him. Shouts. A siren blared. He kept climbing. One more wall, one more fall, and then he was out.

He ran until the lights were behind him. Ran until the air smelled sweeter again. Ran until he was gone.

* * *

Gail and Ray were unaware that Helen continued to visit Cox after that first visit. Helen found herself inexorably drawn to Cox. Once the dust had settled from his Katingal escape, Cox arranged for her to join him. But, on the run, he needed travelling money. Through old contacts, he teamed up with a nobody to partner him in the armed robbery of a suburban bank. Should have been easy…

They hit the bank just after opening. All went well, clean. Then, as they were leaving, the guard twitched, got a shot off. Hit the partner in the gut. The idiot had paid the price for not relieving the guard of this weapon. Cox dragged him into the van. The bag was heavy with cash, but the partner was heavier. Dumped him in the back and drove.

He turned into the disused workshop, killed the engine. Silence. The partner whimpered, clutching the wound, blood leaking between his fingers.

"Cox—Jesus—help me."

Cox climbed out. Pulled the bag of cash from the back. Laid it by the door. Cox knelt. His heartbeat steady, eyes flat.

"Get me out of here, man. Take the money, just get me to a doctor."

Cox nodded. Seemed reasonable. He reached inside his partner's coat. The man's eyes flickered with hope. Instead of help, Cox pulled out his partner's gun, wiped it on his pants. The spark of hope in his partner's eyes dying fast.

"Please—"

Cox pressed the barrel hard against his heart to muffle the sound, pulled the trigger. Quick. Clean.

He wiped the gun, slipped it back into the dead man's pocket. Stood. Adjusted his coat. Picked up the bag.

No sirens yet. The air was cool. Crisp.

Helen was waiting in the car outside. He smiled as he slid into the seat beside her.

"All good?" she asked.

"Easy job," he said.

She pulled onto the road, humming along to the radio. Cox looked out the window, the city lights blurring past.

He didn't feel anything. Never did.

Sydney was too hot. Cox had friends. Friends who could help men like him move on. He and Helen would not stop moving. Not yet. It would take time, but Cox had a destination in mind. Another place where he had friends. And money.

Melbourne.[55]

* * *

The Prodigal Returns

The doors of the Arrivals hall slid open. Ian, smiling, his son perched on his shoulders, and Raelene with their daughter, strode out, each pushing luggage trolleys laden with cases.

It wasn't Ray or Gail who met them. It was Tony.

Ian walked over to him, looking confused. "What's going on?" Ian asked.

"Ray's in Pentridge, on remand," Tony replied. He ran through all the events of the last six months. The confrontation with the Kanes. Les's disappearance. Ray, Laurie and Vinnie charged. Then acquitted. Ray re-arrested.

"Where's Vinnie and Laurie?" Ian asked.

"Gone to ground," Tony replied. "Brian's out for blood. Ray told them to disappear."

"But not you?" Ian queried.

"No, I'm bulletproof," he joked. Ian just glared at him.

"Where's Ray?" Raelene asked, having joined them.

"Pentridge," Ian said.

"Oh." Nothing more was said.

Tony led them out of the terminal to a Mercedes-Benz 600 limo he had hired for the occasion. He opened the back door, beaming.

Ian nodded, returning his smile as they got in.

* * *

As soon as they were dropped off at home, the kids fled upstairs to their rooms, glad to be home. Ian and Rae went to unpack. Ian grabbed her, threw her on the bed, and jumped astride her. "We're home and the kids are busy," he said with a cheeky glint in his eye."

Rae shook her head, smiling. They unpacked.

"Did you notice Tony's arms?" Rae asked as she sat down at the table with two cups of coffee.

Ian nodded. "Yeah, he's using." His boxing led him to consider the body a temple. Drugs were poison.

"Without Laurie around, he's spiralling," Ian replied, taking a sip of his coffee. "Too much money, and too much time," he mumbled into his cup.

"Isn't there anything you can do?" Rae asked without thinking. Ian was not one to concern himself with others' well-being.

"Yeah, I'll have a word."

Rae lifted an eyebrow. A smile crept onto her face. Ian was mellowing.

But Ian was not mellowing. A junkie was the last thing they needed. Junkies cannot control their mouths. A real danger. He remembered his commitment to Vinnie that he would handle Tony. The time was coming.

* * *

Ian's Wonga Park estate was an ongoing project. Started three years before, it was still in development. Regardless, both Ian and Rae were proud of what they had built. An authentic Tudor mansion carved out of the Victorian bush.

Raelene had invited Gail over for a barbecue. She hoped a change of environment would cheer her up a little. Ian was cleaning the grill, having completed lunch. Gail and Rae sat in deck chairs looking up at the black and white façade, wine glasses in hand.

"It's beautiful," Gail said, looking up. From the lawn, it looked like three full stories.

"Yes, it's finally coming together," Rae replied.

With that, the crunching of gravel indicated someone else had arrived. Rae looked up at Ian. Ian was watching like a hawk, hands free. No one else had been invited.

Car doors opened and closed. A man and woman approached. The man looked somehow familiar, but then again, not. Long dark hair. Clark Kent black framed glasses. But there was still that square jaw.

"Gail!" the young woman yelled, now running, arms out.

"Helen!" came Gail's reply. She was out of her chair before the words left her mouth.

They hugged. No one interrupted.

"Peter?" asks Ian. Recognition had finally clicked in.

"Ian." Cox was sharp. He had summed up the situation and quickly knew to address Ian by name, not 'Fingers'. He walked over. They shook hands.

"Ben, this is Peter." Introducing him to one of the other men standing with him. "And that's Helen, Gail's sister," stating the obvious.

"Ben's the State Manager for the Building Society," Ian informed Cox. "And this is my brother, Greg," he added, as an afterthought.

"Ian's one of our best customers," Ben said as they shook hands.

"Yes, the import/export business has been good to me," Ian added.

"G'day," Ian's brother greeted Cox. "Want a beer?" Cox nodded, watching Helen and Gail. Rae was already pouring Helen a glass of wine.

"Nice place," Cox said as Greg handed him a VB stubbie.

"You haven't been here before?" Ben asked.

"They've been travelling," Ian replied on Cox's behalf.

"C'mon, Peter, I'll show you my cars," Ian said to Cox. Cox nodded, understanding. They jumped into Ian's Dodge pickup. Ian drove up an internal driveway that disappeared into the bush.

"Have you seen his collection?" Greg asked Ben.

"Up in the barn? Yep. Classics," Ben confirmed. They talked business as Greg finished clearing up. The girls chatted. Laughed. Cried. The sound of kids in the pool carried from around the other side of the house.

It was late afternoon when Ian and Cox returned.

Rae said, "It's getting cool. Let's move inside." She led the three girls to the side entrance.

Helen stood gobsmacked. "A drawbridge," she gasped, looking up at the massive oak-studded door on the other side.

"No, just a bridge." Rae smiled. They crossed and entered. The house was a split level, so the bridge and side entry brought them in onto a mezzanine floor overlooking the living room. More a grand hall. The centre of which was a large stone fireplace.

"What an amazing fireplace," Helen let out. "You could almost stand up in it."

"Yes. It's from an original English manor house," Rae replied. We had it taken apart, shipped back, and rebuilt in here."

"I didn't think you were allowed to do that," Helen said.

"Ian has contacts," Rae said, tapping her nose, smiling. No more said.

The boys retired to the Billiard room. Ian took out three whisky glasses and a bottle of Macallan 18 Years Old scotch off the shelf behind the bar. "You have to drive," he said to Greg.

"So do I," said Ben. Both knew that was the cue for them to leave.

Goodbyes said, kids collected, they left.

Gail, Helen and Rae talked in front of the fire, into the night. Ian and Cox discussed business in the Billiard room.

* * *

The next morning, Ian picked up Cox and drove down the peninsula to Mt Martha. The name belied its location. It is a hilly bayside suburb south of Melbourne. Ian's 'holiday house' had views over the water and the street in both directions. Like the suburb name, 'holiday house' did not reflect its purpose either. Ever since Rae's ultimatum, Ian had strictly adhered to the edict of separating home and work. Wonga Park had no sign of his other activities. Mt Martha was his workhouse.

Inside, Ian disappeared for ten minutes. Cox used the time to look around. Not at the real estate, but as a kid searching for Christmas presents. He found what he was looking for.

When Ian returned, Cox was standing at a table in the spare room. An M16 with a shortened butt and a sawn-off 12-gauge shotgun were in front of him.

"Help yourself," Ian said sarcastically. He walked up and dropped two large shrink-wrapped bundles of notes on the table in front of Cox.

"That's the rest of your share." He continued, "What are your plans?"

"Thought we'd go to England," Cox said. "Helen really wants to see it." He continued to check the guns. Did not look at the money. He knew it would be right.

Ian handed Cox a black gym bag. Cox filled it with the weapons and the money. Zipped it up. As they left, Cox looked back inside. "Nice setup," he said. Ian did not reply. "Like your gun locker," Cox added, glancing up at the ceiling.

"Ask next time," was Ian's curt reply.

CHAPTER 32

The Death of Ray Bennett

As expected, Brian's hatred only intensified. His hatred was primarily focused on Ray. The other two could wait.

Brian Kane sat at his kitchen table that morning. A cigarette smouldered in the ashtray. The hit was his. No other choice. He had given Bazley the contract, but now Bazley was out. The idiot fell out of a tree; broke a wrist. Kane sneered at the thought. Who the fuck falls out of a tree?

Bennett had to go. It had to be public. Had to be loud. Let them all know Les was not forgotten.

He checked the paper a second time; 10 AM, Melbourne Magistrates Court. Committal hearing. That meant controlled chaos. Cops, lawyers, reporters. Perfect. He would be there early.

A .38 snub-nose sat on the table. Reliable. Small enough to hide. Big enough to do the job.

Murphy was already on it. He would prep the escape route. All Kane had to do was walk in, pull the trigger, and get the hell out. One shot for Les. One shot for Judy. One to make sure.

* * *

Murphy stood in the magistrates' car park, hands in his pockets. He had no business being there, but that was the beauty of it. A cop standing around was not suspicious.

He walked slow and casual. Unscrewed part of the fence with the tip of his knife. Just enough to make an exit.

Next, the corrugated iron fence on the other side of the car park. He bent a panel up. Left enough space for a man to slip through into the adjacent RMIT car park.

He checked his watch. Close now. He moved back into the crowd. Just another cheap suit watching just another case.

* * *

Kane sat outside Court 10. Blue suit, gold-framed glasses, beard neat. Looked like any other lawyer. No one paid him any mind.

A court reporter sat next to him. A press badge clipped to her blouse. Kane glanced at her. She glanced back. Nothing.

He adjusted his tie. Ten past ten.

Then—a movement from the stairs.

Bennett. Dressed in a loud check sports coat, leather patches on the elbows. Two unarmed dicks escorting him.

One of Murphy's men gave Brian a nod from the hallway. The signal.

Kane stood. Walked to the stairs. Started down, as they were coming up. Smooth, unhurried.

As they went to pass, he pulled the snub .38 from inside his jacket.

"Cop this you motherfucker!"

BOOM.

The first shot slammed into Bennett's chest.

BOOM.

The second hit him again.

299

BOOM.

The last round tore through Bennett's hand as he tried to shield himself.

The detectives jumped back, startled, frozen for a beat. One moved. Kane raised the gun, eyes cold. "Don't make me do it."

The cop hesitated.

Kane smiled. Walked away.

* * *

Bennett staggered. His body did not know it was dead yet.

Instinct. Adrenaline.

Bennett bolted down the stairs. The detective followed, thinking it was an escape attempt.

Bennett hit the landing. He staggered. The pain in his chest burned, but the world around him slowed. The polished wooden railing. The dull thud of his shoes on the steps. Blood soaked into the check sports coat.

He collapsed on the landing between two flights of stairs. Two uniformed officers ran up from the courtyard, their boots pounding. Bennett pressed a hand to his chest. Warm. Wet.

He touched the blood. Slick. Warm. He knew before they did, there wouldn't be time to say goodbye. "I've been shot in the heart," he murmured. "I'm brown bread."

He was right.

* * *

Kane moved through the courthouse like a man late for a meeting. No rush. No panic.

Down the back stairs. Into the magistrates' car park. Through the loosened fence.

One more turn. The bent-up iron sheet, a gap into the RMIT car park.

He ducked through.

Gone.

* * *

Murphy heard the shots. The screams. The sirens.

Showtime.

He walked around to the front entrance. Slipped into the crowd milling outside. Made his way to the front.

A cop grabbed his shoulder.

"What's going on?" Murphy asked.

"Some bastard shot Bennett."

Murphy frowned. "No shit?"

The cop ran off. Murphy kept walking. [57]

* * *

Joe, Ray's barrister, pushed through the crowd, dread blooming on his face. He headed down the stairs. Gail was behind him, panic in her eyes.

Bennett lay slumped. Dying. Maybe already dead.

Joe grabbed Gail and shoved her into the clerk's office. "Stay here."

The ambulance came. Cops blocked them. "You can't ride along."

"She's his fucking wife!" Joe snapped.

No good. One pointed at a cop car that pulled up. "You will have to go with them. Get in."

They did. But the car turned onto Elizabeth Street. The wrong way.

Joe ran a hand through his hair.

That mistake summed up the whole day. [58]

* * *

Rae's phone rang at 5 PM.

"He's dead," was all Gail could get out.

"Where are you?" Rae asked.

"Home, Joe brought me home. Will have to go back tomorrow."

"I'll be right there." Rae hung up the phone. She did not know how, what, or why. Just Ray was dead, and Gail needed her. She hated this life.

Ian came into the room.

"You fucking bastard," she said as she brushed past him. She grabbed her keys and was out the door. Ian stood stunned for a moment. He then turned, grabbed his keys, and took off after her. The kids were old enough to look after themselves. He drove off after her.

* * *

Ian didn't catch Rae. Soon enough, he knew where she was headed. He arrived shortly after her. Joe was still there. He tried to talk to Gail, but she wanted no part of him either. Instead, he talked to Joe. Joe explained everything. The fake lawyer, the message, the getaway.

Ian's blood boiled. Both Rae and Gail blamed him. Worse, he blamed himself. He was not there for Ray. The police might say they didn't know who the assailant was. Ian did.

And as God was his witness, Kane would pay.

* * *

It was dark. Black as night, they say. This was night, but it was blacker. No moon. That was good. Brian Kane stood at the edge of the memorial gardens, staring up at the three-metre brick wall. White cement capping ran along the top. Once he got over, it would be easy.

But how?

Down by the next pillar, a green telecom box stood a metre high. Good enough. He slid the eight-inch butcher's knife into the small of his back. Stepped onto the box and hauled himself up. Over. Dropped down silent.

After that, he made his way to the viewing room next to the chapel. He would send a message in no uncertain terms. The bastard had killed his little brother. He had no brother to mourn, as they had taken his body. Now, he would take something in return. Ray Bennett's head. No face for them to mourn. They would have no face to remember either. Let them feel what he felt.

Then movement. Two detectives stepped out. Murphy and another dog. They lit cigarettes, stamping their feet against the cold.

Brian froze. What the fuck? They were guarding a corpse.

He swallowed hard. His fingers flexed at his sides. For a moment, he thought about doing it anyway. But there was no way in without being seen.

Les deserved better. But Brian would not be the one to give it to him. He turned. Retraced his steps. Climbed back over the wall.

Gone.

* * *

Ray's Funeral

Gail stood at the altar, beside the coffin, one hand placed on the polished wood. Dwelling on the past, what might have been. Raelene stood close beside her, elegant even dressed in black. She squeezed Gail's hand.

Gail barely felt it. Her mind spun. Mallorca. A quiet life. Just them. That's what Ray had promised. He was done. Ready to leave it all behind. Now this.

She wrapped her other arm around her son. Only ten. Too young to really know his father. He would only know the stories. The lies the papers would print.

She needed to leave. New Zealand. England. Anywhere the name Ray Bennett was not known. The people around him, his so-called friends, had dragged him down. If they'd really cared, they would have helped him find peace. Instead, their greed and selfishness led them to where they were today. They kept pulling him back in.

She looked at Raelene. Why didn't she see that? She could have changed Ian to lead a normal life. He was supposed to be Ray's wingman, but he had not been there to protect Ray. Not when he really needed him.

Gail pulled her hand away. Took a step back. Turned and walked to the front pews.

Raelene hesitated, then followed. Sat beside her. Gail shifted slightly away.

Raelene didn't react. Just stared forward, making excuses in her head. Grief does strange things. Gail would recover with time.

* * *

After Bennett's funeral, Brian kept a low profile. Slipped into the cracks. No phone. No fixed address. No regulars. Ray was popular, and Kane knew his cards were marked. So he kept on the move. Stayed elusive.

"Hi Brian," said Bazley, looking up. "Thought you might end up here." Bazley was sitting at the same table, in the same Woolloomooloo pub, where he had met Ian several years before.

"Jim," Brian greeted Bazley. "Beer?"

Jim nodded as he skulled down the rest of his schooner. Brian and Jim had been on the same side during the Melbourne Waterfront Wars. Both worked as security and enforcers for Tex Longley. After that, Bazley had moved up here. He made a lucrative living offering the same services to Sydney's underworld figures. And the work was a lot easier.

Brian returned with two beers and sat down opposite. "No insurance value in me," he said, confirming Jim's earlier statement. "It also stops any Melbourne dogs coming up here looking for me," he smiled.

"I'd still be careful," Jim warned. "The world's changing. No such thing as being staunch, no more," he continued. "Drugs. It's changed everything."

"Don't worry, I'll stay low. Keep moving." Brian assured him. "Still, not a problem. Bennett had no friends up here," he added.

"But Carroll does," Jim corrected. "And he won't forgive nor forget."

"Don't worry about him. He's gone soft. Too busy playing Mr Businessman," Brian said condescendingly. "Not around much anymore."

Jim shook his head. They finished their beers.

Jim didn't offer to return Brian's shout. Brian was living in a fantasy world if he believed that. Best he keeps his distance. That would be the healthy option. He made an excuse and left. [59]

Brian stayed. Had another beer. Watched the sun glint off the water. Not a bad way to spend a Melbourne winter.

* * *

Helen, being Gail's sister, made Ray almost family. Cox did not take things personally. It was the principle. If someone touches your family, you respond. Simple.

However, Kane had disappeared off the face of the earth. Cox and Helen had a life to live. He made a decision and phoned Ian. "Fingers, we're off." It was a blanket statement. No room for discussion.

"What about Kane?" Ian said, disappointed.

"Let me know when he shows," came Cox's matter-of-fact reply. "But I won't be holding my breath."

"OK, I'll let you know if he shows," was all Ian responded.

The line went dead. Cox was gone.

* * *

Death of Tony McNamara

Vinnie and Laurie came back to Melbourne for Ray's funeral. They stayed in the back, quiet. Gave their condolences to Gail. She eyed them with contempt. They did not stay for the wake. Brian had gone to ground, but he still had friends out there. Les had been hated, but some still wanted to prove their loyalty. Melbourne was not safe.

Laurie wanted to catch up with Tony while they were in town. He moved fast through the back alleys, half-walking, half-running. Vinnie trailed behind, slow, deliberate. He did not care about Tony. His job was to watch over Laurie.

Laurie raced up the outside stairs to Tony's flat. At the top, he let himself in. By the time Vinnie stepped inside, Laurie was on the couch, cradling Tony.

Tony lay there, oblivious. A black band wrapped tight around his upper arm. A needle was still in his vein. Vinnie shook his head. Too much money and time; not enough future.

"I should have been here," Laurie said, rocking him. "He needed someone."

"You're not his mother." Vinnie pulled gloves from his back pocket and slid them on. Then he started going through Tony's pockets.

"What the hell are you doing?" Laurie asked.

Vinnie didn't answer. He pulled out a wad of cash and a full vial. He slid the needle from Tony's arm, refilled it from the second vial, and then lay across both of them, pinned them down with his full body weight.

"What the fuck are you doing?" Laurie thrashed, trying to break free.

Vinnie didn't answer. He reinserted the needle and pressed the plunger. He waited until it took effect. Tony's body twitched, then went limp. Vinnie stood.

Laurie came out swinging. Full of rage. Vinnie ducked, caught him, and locked him in a full nelson. He held him there, waiting for the fight to drain away.

"It's too late," Vinnie said calmly. "He's a junkie. Easy to find. Easy to trace back to us."

Laurie's struggle silenced.

"It was either him or us," Vinnie said. "Do you understand?"

No answer.

"Are we good?"

Silence. Vinnie tightened his grip. "Are we good?"

A pause. Then a slow, reluctant nod. Vinnie let go.

Laurie turned, his face full of hate. "Fuck you," he spat. Then he was gone, slamming the door behind him.

They never saw each other again.

CHAPTER 33

A Crew No more

Vinnie Leaves

Vinnie sat in the dark, staring at the cigarette between his fingers. He hadn't even lit it. Just rolled it back and forth, feeling the paper crinkle under his thumb and forefinger. The boarding house room was dark and smelled of decay. He looked at the duffle bag on the floor. Packed. Ready.

There was a sadness. He had seen a lot. Done worse. Ray. Tony. Laurie. No more, he had had enough.

Ray had not even worn a mask when they hit Les. Laurie followed his lead. Like it did not matter. Like they weren't men with families, like they would not be hunted. Vinnie had worn his, but that meant nothing now. The wife had seen Ray. Had heard him. Did he really think that she would not talk? That Brian would not come? That the whole bloody underworld wouldn't want a piece of them now?

He leaned forward, resting his elbows on his knees. No, this was not just about Brian. This was about every bastard in Melbourne looking to settle old scores. A free shot at Ray Bennett's crew. Ray thought he was untouchable. How did that turn out for him?

Vinnie wasn't going to die like him. He picked up his duffle bag, swung it over his shoulder. Opened the front door, paused, then stepped out and closed the door.

* * *

Ian found him outside the warehouse, staring at the sky. He already knew.

"I know how this ends," Vinnie said, voice flat. "I'm not going down with him."

Ian said nothing.

"I was here for you, not Ray," Vinnie continued. "But I'm done. I got a family, Ian. They deserve better than a bullet in the back of my head. They're not safe while I'm around."

Ian looked at Vinnie, really looked at him. The set of his jaw. The tension in his shoulders. This was not a man running. This was a man making peace.

"Where will you go?" Ian finally asked.

"North," Vinnie said. "Tried West. That didn't work."

Ian nodded.

Vinnie stuck out his hand. Ian took it. Held it.

"You're on your own now, boyo," Vinnie finished. Vinnie let go and walked away.

Ian stood there long after Vinnie was gone. Cold air tightened around him, but he did not feel it. Not anymore.

He remembered Ray, years ago, just before he left for the UK. The old bastard had clapped him on the shoulder and said, *Sooner or later, one of us gets caught in the middle.*

Ian shook his head. Maybe Vinnie had the right idea. Maybe he should leave too.

But a blood debt cannot be washed away.

* * *

Last Man Standing

These days, all the talk is of the curse of the bookie robbery. But there was a time when that was far from the truth. In 2002, ice skater Steven Bradbury crossed the finish line to collect Olympic gold. All the other competitors had fallen over each other. He was running last, so had time to skate around them to finish and claim the gold. Long before 2002, Ian had learnt the importance of finishing last.

Ian had outlasted Shannon, Longley, and Bazley to become the Painters and Dockers Union Secretary. He was now the last man standing as a result of the deaths of Bennett and the Kanes. Unlike most, instead of taking it as a sign and disappearing like Vinnie, Ian decided to make the most of the opportunity. He was a professional. Bennett had taught him well. Planning and preparation. The right equipment and the right crew. And know your exits.

He kept the best jobs for himself. But through his legitimate business dealings, he had learnt about franchising. Why not with crime? He had the knowledge. People would pay. Not like the Architect, but mass market. A service, not strategy. The McDonald's of armed robbery …

"Ok, Charlie, money first." Ian stood opposite two men in the empty warehouse. No jackets. He could see if they were carrying. They could see the .38 in his shoulder holster. Charlie passed the bag. Ian opened it, looked in, but did not count it. He now had a good feel for cash. The weight felt right.

Ian pushed over a manila folder. "Here are the times and amounts," he said. He passed them another bag.

"Here are the scanner, police frequencies, and airport security codes. There are two M16s in the other bag."

The two looked at each other and smiled. This was like Christmas Day.

"My cut's 25%. Return all weapons and equipment back here immediately after the job," Ian confirmed.

"Break the rules, or try to dud me, each of you loses a kneecap. Understand?

They both nodded and left. [60]

…

The following evening, the sun was setting. Ian sat on one of the trestle tables. Alone in the warehouse.

The external door banged open. The two men walked in, each carrying two bags. They walked tall, smiling. Charlie said, "A piece of cake." He dropped his bags at Ian's feet. Ian stared at him. Did not say a thing.

The smile dropped from Charlie's face. "Sorry." He picked the bags up and placed them on the table in front of Ian. His mate did the same.

Ian checked the bags and nodded. All correct. "We're done," he said.

"How can we get in touch with you if we have another job?" Charlie asked with greed in his eyes.

"You don't," Ian replied. "If I have a job that suits you, I will contact you."

Charlie went to say something else.

"We're done I said," Ian cut him off. They took the hint and left.

Ian put the bags in the back of his pickup and drove to Mt Martha. [61]

* * *

Laurie Withdraws

Laurie decided to withdraw from any further involvement with the crew. He bought a plain suburban house out in rural Warrandyte. Close to Ian's Wonga Park property. No contact but comfort in proximity. He lived quietly on the money he had already collected and local work. Did not venture into town. No contact with former Painters and Dockers.

Laurie parked the Volvo outside the small-town shops, the engine ticking in the morning chill. He sat for a moment, gripping the wheel, listening. A habit, though there was nothing to hear except the hum of an occasional car and the rustle of wind through the trees. He ran a hand over his face, tracing the edge of his jaw where tension always sat. He had been up half the night again, listening to the silence of his own house, waiting for something that never came.

Inside the store, he moved slow, picking up the milk, the bread, and some eggs. The aisles were narrow, the shelves lined with things that belonged in other people's lives. Men with clean pasts, who slept easy. The girl at the counter gave him the same polite smile she always did, but her eyes flickered, noticing the way he checked the windows.

Back outside, he stepped into the path of another man leaving the butcher's. A familiar shape. A weight in the shoulders, a way of carrying himself that said he had never feared much in his life.

Ian didn't stop, barely glanced up as they passed.

Laurie hesitated. A part of him expected something, recognition, a nod, maybe even a word. But there was nothing. Just disdain, and the crisp sound of Ian's boots on the pavement as he walked away, meat wrapped neatly under one arm.

Laurie stood there a moment longer, the paper bag in his own hand suddenly too heavy. Ian had moved on; why couldn't he?

Back home, his daughter ran up to him, arms out, her laughter filling the quiet house. He lifted her, kissed the top of her head, and inhaled the clean, warm scent of her hair. His wife called from the kitchen, asking if he had got everything.

"Yeah," he said, setting the bag down. He checked the street again. That night, he lay awake again, with the silver .45 under his pillow, listening to the nothingness outside.

The old expression flashed through is mind: *Be careful what you wish for.*

* * *

The Death of Normie Lee

Normie was a quiet man. He faded from public view after his acquittal. Eventually, selling the business and moving to Singapore. But glory days are hard to leave behind. So he returned.

Normie sat in a cheap café on Sydney Road, stirring sugar into his coffee. The spoon clinked against the cup, a slow, rhythmic sound. Across from him sat two younger men, eager, stupid.

"We need a guy like you," the one in the Madonna mask said. He wasn't wearing it now, but the mask sat on the table between them, staring up like a bad joke.

Normie smiled, small and tired. "A guy like me?"

"You were with Bennett and Carroll. The bookie job. Man, that was legendary."

Normie didn't correct them. Didn't tell them he was never the muscle. Never the mastermind. He just handled numbers and worked the angles. But what was the harm in letting them believe?

They told him the plan. An armoured van, an airport terminal, millions in payroll cash; an easy getaway.

"You in?"

Normie looked at the two masks on the table. Michael Jackson and Madonna. Jesus Christ.

He took another sip of coffee. Maybe one last score. Maybe.

* * *

The Ansett freight terminal was noisy and busy. Normie stood near the loading dock, adjusting the strap on his

313

bulletproof vest. The .357 felt heavy in his hand. Too heavy. He thought of the two young idiots as Heckle and Jeckle.

They first moved just like they planned. Heckle shoved a guard. Normie stuck the .357 in his belt. He'd never held such a large handgun on a job before. Not really. He grabbed the bags, heavy canvas sacks, thick with cash. His heart pounding in his chest.

Then it all went to shit.

Jeckle was 100 metres down the road in the getaway van. When he saw them, he planted his foot, screeching to the curb, back doors open. Normie and Heckle heaved the heavy money sacks into the van through the back doors. They started to climb in after them.

The driver hit the gas before Normie was fully inside. His feet had just left the ground. He pitched backwards. His hands shot out, trying to catch something, anything.

Then he hit the pavement. Hard. The van kept going. Normie rolled to his knees. The .357 had spilled out onto the road. He picked it up, his fingers barely gripping it. He looked up.

Black-clad figures moved fast. Boots pounded. The police Special Operations Group (SOG). "Drop the weapon!" came the call.

Normie hesitated. Not fear. Just slow. Too slow.

He started to lift his hands.

A gunshot cracked the air. A bullet-proof vest does not stop a bullet to the back of the head.

Normie's body lay motionless on the road.

* * *

The newspapers called it a takedown. Said he had a gun and refused to drop it. Said it was justified.

Vinnie read the story in the morning paper, sitting quietly in the kitchen. The aroma of cooked eggs, butter and toast filled the room.

He folded the paper. Didn't say a word. Normie was never supposed to be in the game. Never the hard man. Just a guy who counted money.

And in the end, he did not even get that right.

CHAPTER 34

The Murder of Brian Kane

Ian Goes It Alone

The next two years, Ian limited himself to one major job a year. Had to be at least six figures. The hardest thing was getting rid of the cash. He purchased investment properties, residential and commercial. But they required time to manage. And Ian did not like managing. Their house sucked up a lot of cash. Furniture brought in from the UK and France. There were always the kids' school fees. Private Grammar schools cost an arm and a leg. And there were holidays. Fiji, The States.

His pride and joy though, was his family. Rae, his son and daughter occupied most of his time. He wanted to give them the childhood he never had. Second to that was his fleet of vintage cars. '34 and '35 Fords. A '29 Model A roadster hot rod with dickie seat, '53 Customline and of course, the '59 Cadillac. Although he drove either the Dodge pickup or the F250 for work, their family car was a Mercedes sedan.

In addition to his property and share portfolios, Ian's legitimate business interests included importing pottery, car parts, and antiques. They also proved to be good earners. However, that was a sideline to what else came in those containers.

With time, they saw less and less of Gail. Maybe it was a sore reminder. Life goes on.

* * *

After three years, Brian Kane felt secure enough to return to Melbourne and resume his prior life. Bennett had shot Les. In return, Bennett got his. Quid pro quo. Life goes on.

Only now, Brian was 40. Heavier, slower. His reputation in his old stomping ground still fell back to older times. He resumed debt collection for bookies and gambling houses. The whole Bennett thing had soured his taste for "taxing" other crooks.

Ian's phone rang. "Brian's back," said the voice on the other end of the line.

"Where?" Ian asked. Whoever was passing on the information was irrelevant.

"Lygon Street. Large as life," the voice continued. "Like old times."

"Thanks." Ian hung up.

He pulled a piece of paper from his desk. Called the overseas number.

"This better be good," the voice at the other end said. "It's 3 AM."

"Brian Kane's back," is all Ian said.

"Fine. I'll be back in two weeks. Just a few things to take care of first."

The line went dead.

* * *

"You owe me," was Cox's opening statement as they sat down in a coffee shop in Hawthorn. Cox had contacted Ian

317

as soon as they landed. He was now sporting a full-face beard, short hair, and no glasses.

After ordering two coffees, Cox continued, "Moving back costs big bucks."

Ian knew the statement had nothing to do with Kane. That was personal. This was business.

"I've got a good little setup now," Ian replied. "Happy to bring you in."

Cox nodded. That was what he was hoping.

"We're staying with Gail at the moment. Don't think she's real happy about that," Cox continued. "You got anywhere for us to stay?"

Ian thought for a bit. Debating in his head. He relented. "There's Mt Martha, I guess."

Cox smiled. That was what he was hoping.

"Great. Can we move down tomorrow?" said Cox, always pushing his luck.

"No," Ian said adamantly. "After the weekend. Some things I have to organise first."

* * *

The Mt Martha garage door rattled shut behind them. There was a damp chill of the bay creeping into their clothes. Ian killed the engine and stepped out of the car. He tossed his gloves onto the workbench, stretching his shoulders.

Cox followed, pulling out his balaclava, tossing it onto a crate stacked with stolen cash. The job had gone smoothly. No sirens, no heat. Just a couple of frightened payroll clerks and a bag full of wages that would never make it to Friday.

Cox rolled his shoulders. "Nice haul."

Ian did not answer. He walked to the kitchen, grabbed a glass from the sink, and poured himself a juice. The place was sparse; just the bare bones of a hideout. A couch that had seen better days, a wooden table, and a small TV humming with static in the corner. Helen was visiting Gail; they were alone.

Cox poured himself an orange juice. He watched Ian, reading the silence. He had worked with plenty of men in his time, but Ian was different. Cold. Clinical. A man who did what needed doing, without the weight of it pressing down.

Ian finally turned. "I've found him."

Cox sighed, watching Ian over the glass. "Kane?"

Ian nodded. "Been watching him for weeks. Same routine. Same places. Always in that bloody Jaguar. Thinks he's untouchable." He took a sip of his juice, eyes steady. "He's soft now. Slower. Living off his old rep."

Cox smirked. "Never thought I'd see the day."

Ian leaned against the table. "He drinks at the Quarry, up on Lygon. Every Friday. Comes in late, buys rounds, makes sure people know he's there. Always has the same woman with him. Don't know what she sees in him. But it's her Jag he's driving."

Cox skulled the rest of the juice. "How do you want to do it?"

"Standard pub. Low light. Few exits. But the real gift is the car." Ian let the words hang. "Jag's like a bloody neon sign. That's how we know where he'll be."

Cox nodded. "And the hit?"

"Quick. In and out. Two snub-nosed .38s. Same kind he used on Ray." Ian's tone was flat. No anger, no satisfaction. Just a job.

Cox considered that. "Poetic."

Ian finished his drink and set the glass down. "Tomorrow."

"I'll be ready."

Neither of them said another word. The plan was set. Tomorrow, Brian Kane would walk into the Quarry Hotel for the last time.

* * *

The Murder of Brian Kane

Friday morning, Brian Kane settled into his seat. A café on Lygon Street, outside. A double espresso in front of him. He stretched, his body stiff from the years. His knuckles, once fast and brutal, ached in the morning chill. He ignored it. A fighter never acknowledges the wear.

Sandra slid into the chair across from him. She was younger, not much, but enough. Her looks slightly fading. She liked being seen with him. Brian liked being seen, full stop.

"You're late," he said, grinning.

"Only to you." She sipped her coffee, casting an eye over the street. Kane's kingdom. At least, it had been.

Across the road, Ian sat behind the wheel of an anonymous Ford Escort van, watching. It was a small, faded, insignificant vehicle. Perfect for surveillance. He had mapped Kane's routine down to the minute. It was now several years since Brian shot Ray. The job was no longer personal. It was an obligation. Russell Cox, Ray's brother-in-law, sat beside him, silent.

"There," Ian murmured, watching Kane light a cigarette with hands that had once broken men. "He'll stay in the strip till afternoon. Then the Quarry." Cox nodded, barely listening. He was thinking about exit routes.

Brian and Sandra wandered, stopping at shops, making sure Kane was seen. At four, he got his hair trimmed, the barber joking about his receding hairline. Brian laughed, too loud, slapping the man on the shoulder. The old man did not flinch. The one-time fear of his presence was fading.

By nine, Kane was at the Quarry Hotel, his laughter filling the lounge. The old days, glory days, poured from his mouth like gin. He was holding court, telling stories that once had weight, but now rang hollow.

Down the road, Ian and Cox parked and waited. The Jaguar was there. Kane was inside.

"Let's do it," Ian said, stepping out.

* * *

Inside, the Quarry Hotel was noisy, full of old men, cigarette smoke and a tired past. Brian sat by the jukebox. Not listening to music nor conversations. A round of gin and tonics rested on the table. He stared at the condensation as it dripped onto the scratched wood. Stretched his legs, feeling the weight in his knees. The years had caught up, but he still walked like a king.

Sandra leaned in. "You're quiet tonight."

Kane smirked. "Thinking."

She rolled her eyes. "That's dangerous."

Ian and Cox crossed the road. Kane had no idea he was living the last few minutes of his life.

Then the doors burst open. Two figures, dressed in black, balaclavas covering their faces. The first shot cracked the air. Kane flinched, then another shot caught him square in the chest. The bar exploded into chaos. A woman screamed. Chairs crashed to the floor.

Kane pushed the table out. Not for cover, but trying to get to Sandra's bag. It was where he had put his gun. Not a smart move.

A third shot. Point-blank.

Kane staggered, hands searching for something solid. Blood bloomed across his chest. His mouth moved, but the words did not come. A body twisted under the glow of the jukebox.

Ian looked down at Kane. Not satisfaction. Not grief. Just silence. "For you, Ray," he said softly. Turned and walked away.

The room filled with the smell of gunpowder. The shooters disappeared before the first shouts for help rang out. The Quarry went silent.

Outside, the nondescript Ford Escort van pulled away from the curb and was gone. Obligation met.

Kane's kingdom had shrunk to the space between the jukebox and the floor.

* * *

The Royal Melbourne Hospital. The fluorescent lights buzzed overhead. Kane was still breathing when they wheeled him in. But it was not enough.

By midnight, he was dead.

The homicide squad arrived at the Quarry Hotel before the blood dried. The usual routine: questions, notebooks, nothing.

"What'd you see?"

"Nothing."

"What'd you hear?"

"Didn't catch a thing."

The regulars knew the drill. The ones who didn't know, speculated. The ones who did, said nothing.

* * *

Back at the station, the detectives pinned names to the board. The list was short. Vinnie Mikkelsen. Laurie Prendergast.

They had the most to gain. Kane had killed Bennett in broad daylight. The next logical step? He would come for the others. But nothing stuck. They did not fit the descriptions.

No witnesses. No evidence. No suspects. Just a dead man by a jukebox and a city full of silent mouths.[62]

CHAPTER 35

The Death of Ian Carroll

Mt Martha

Cox bent and gently kissed Helen as she slept. It was pre-dawn. The warble of magpies and peal of bellbirds was as effective as reveille to a soldier. The snub .38 pressed into the small of his back as he sat to tie his running shoes. Over his time on the run, he had learned how to secure it under his tracksuit. Now clean-shaven, he pulled the hood over his buzz-cut head as he stepped out into the dark.

This was his time. The feel of the crisp morning air in his nostrils. Mist on his face as he pounds down the road toward the beach. Then along the foreshore. The rhythm of his feet on the path kept time with the imaginary soundtrack in his head. Something triumphant. Something ridiculous. First rays of the sun came across the bay like a blinding spotlight. No warmth, only glare. Then left turn up the mountain road. Up to the Mt Martha lookout. Light was still only creeping into the sky.

At the top, a quick workout in the deserted kids' playground. Pull-ups on the swing crossbar. Reverse sit-ups on top of the monkey bars. Squat walks. He was in good shape, and he loved the feel of the strength in his body.

Then back down the road to home. Now it was about surveillance, not exercise. Every car, every person walking a dog, every silhouette in a front window. He assessed everything. Car keys in hand. This was the traditional time police made 'surprise' raids. He was never surprised. All looked safe. He put the car keys back in his pocket as he walked past his car, parked in his driveway facing out. He didn't go inside. Circled to the back. The shed was locked with a padlock. After two months, it was time he knew what was in there.

He picked the lock. Not hard. The lock was there to keep out wandering opportunists. Not him, he justified to himself. Inside, there were the usual run-of-the-mill garden equipment and tools on the walls. A timber floor? He stamped in the middle. Echo. Moving the mower and mulcher, he found he could lift the centre piece. Buried in the ground was a home-brew barrel. He lifted the lid. It was filled to the brim with shrink-wrapped bundles of cash. Must be over a million bucks, he thought. He securely re-sealed the lid, replaced the floor, and moved the mower and mulcher back. Smiling to himself, he relocked the shed door and went back into the house for breakfast.

* * *

The Death of Ian Carroll

The sun hung low, a burning ember over the bay. The heat pressed down heavy on the Mornington Peninsula. It was a new year. Ian wiped the sweat from his brow as he walked around the back to his shed. He kept the money there, buried under the floorboards. Safe. Hidden. Untouched.

Until now.

The floor had been disturbed. The mower was off its usual spot. The boards did not sit quite right. Someone had been here.

His gut twisted. He checked the barrel. It was not full, as he had left it. Someone had taken some, not all. Someone careful. Someone who knew him.

Cox.

Ian walked back toward the house, his pace steady. No rush. No anger. He had dealt with betrayal before. He did not get to where he was without handling rats.

Cox sat at an outside table around the side of the house. Shade from the burning January afternoon sun. Shirt off, drinking a cold beer. He looked up, grinned. "Hot one today."

Ian nodded, pulled out a chair. "Yeah." He cracked open a beer he had taken from the outside fridge. Took a sip. Set it down.

Then he leaned in, voice quiet. Measured.

"You owe me an explanation."

Cox's smile faded. "For what?"

Ian's eyes did not move. "The shed."

Cox sighed, set his beer down. "Kane. That was a job. A big one. You owe me for that."

Ian laughed. A short, sharp sound. "You stealing from me?"

"Not stealing," Cox said, shifting in his seat. "Call it a withdrawal."

Ian nodded. "That's what you call it?"

He moved fast, faster than a man his age should be able to. His fist cracked across Cox's jaw, sending him sprawling. Cox landed hard, scrambled up. But Ian was already on him.

A right hook, deep to the ribs. A left to the temple. Cox staggered, but Ian kept coming. He grabbed Cox, drove him into the fridge. The beer bottles on top clattered to the floor.

"You should've asked," Ian growled.

Cox spat blood, grinned through red teeth. "Would you have said yes?"

Ian pulled back, ready to finish it.

Then the door burst open. Helen.

A black pistol flew through the air. Cox caught it. The advantage shifted.

Ian moved fast.

Too late.

A shot rang out. Missed. Ian lunged, grabbed for the gun. Another shot. This time, he felt it burning, tearing through his side. Ian staggered back to his pickup, reaching for his own gun under the seat of the Dodge.

Cox limped, bleeding, but still standing. He levelled the gun.

Ian pulled his revolver, swung, and fired. The bullet hit Cox's leg. He buckled, cursing.

Helen screamed.

Cox, gasping, lifted his gun once more. Fired.

Ian went still.

The silence stretched.

Helen ran to Cox, helped him up. He groaned, blood soaking his jeans. "Get me his keys, then grab our stuff. We have to get out of here," he told Helen.

She didn't flinch. Didn't argue. Just moved. Whatever line she'd once hoped not to cross, it was long behind her now.

Helen rifled Ian's pockets and found the keys to Ian's Dodge. She tossed them to Cox.

Cox limped to the Escort, threw it in reverse, and pulled across the driveway, blocking Ian's truck. If he wasn't dead, Cox didn't want him getting help.

Then he tossed the Dodge's keys into the bushes.

"You shouldn't have hit me, mate," Cox said, looking down at Ian.

Cox got into Helen's car. Helen was back with a single carry bag. Cox always had one ready. She got in and floored it. It roared out of the drive and down the road.

Behind them, Ian lay still. That old line of Ray's came back: *Sooner or later, you get caught in the middle.*

A neighbour watched from over the fence, silent, stunned.

By the time the police arrived, Ian was dead. Cox and Helen were gone. Heading for New South Wales. [63]

* * *

Ian's Funeral

The sky hung low, an unusual weight for a Melbourne summer. Clouds like old bruises pressed against the moment. The feel of rain was in the air, waiting.

Ian's 1958 F250 rumbled at the head of the procession. Coffin resting in the rear, tailgate down. The truck was clean, polished to a deep burgundy shine, but it still looked like it belonged on a work site, not a funeral. That was fitting. Ian had never been one for ceremony.

Behind it, the black stretch of funeral cars carried the family, windows tinted, shielding grief from the world. But it was the machines flanking them that turned heads. Hundreds of motorcycles, hot rods, and classic cars. A rolling tribute in chrome and steel, stretching for over a mile. The rumble of Harleys mixed with the deep growls of V8 engines, a mechanical dirge rolling down the highway.

Onlookers lined the streets. Some knew him, some only knew of him. Others just stopped to watch, drawn in by the sight, the sheer weight of it.

Outside the chapel, the crowd thickened. Businessmen in sharp suits and polished shoes stood next to men in leather jackets and steel-toe boots. Boxers with broken noses and scarred knuckles, hands shoved deep into pockets. Old Dockers in Sunday best, faces lined from years of sun and smoke.

And then there were the others.

They lingered at the edges, watching. Faces half-hidden under the brims of hats, collars turned up. They were not there for respect. They came to see proof. To know that Ian Carroll, for all his reputation, all his fights, all his wins, was at last dead.

Raelene stepped out of the funeral car first, a black veil drawn across her face. She did not linger. She walked straight to the chapel doors, back straight, chin high. Gail followed a step behind.

The engines cut, one by one, until only silence remained.

Ian would have hated this, she thought. But this was not for him. It was for them.

* * *

Raelene stood at the front, the thin veil shielding her grief from prying eyes. Next to her, Gail. No emotion, no comfort.

The chapel felt too small. Ian had been larger than life. He deserved more. But maybe this was right. Maybe this was how it always had to end.

The fake organ music started. A slow, mournful tune she did not recognise. Twelve feet tramped in unison, carrying the weight of the coffin. His brothers, Vinnie, and two nameless men from his car club. Familiar, but unimportant.

They laid him down. Rested a wreath on top. A framed photo. The one from his brother's wedding. She had to convince him to be best man. He hadn't wanted to. Could be a real bastard sometimes.

But that smile. The gardenia in his lapel. That was the Ian she knew. The one she loved. Not this.

She willed it to end.

Afterwards, they would return to her home. Drink her booze. Tell their stories. Laugh. Pretend they had always been close. She would endure it.

329

The music started again. That awful, droning tune. The coffin lowered, and the faint roar of a furnace could be heard.

She looked down at the lowering coffin. "You may not have been a good man," she whispered. "But you were mine. Once."

Her life waited beyond this. Tomorrow, she would start again. Her son would not follow in his father's footsteps.

That night, all news channels showed coverage of the funeral, and were crowing about the death of the last Great Bookie Robber.

* * *

The Capture of Russell Cox

Russell Cox remained on the run for another five years after shooting Ian. It came to an end on a winter's day, doing what he loved…

Cox sat behind the wheel of the yellow Fairmont, engine idling. One hand rested on the wheel, the other slowly tapping on the windowsill. Watching. Always watching.

Denning and the woman were in the white Commodore, parked near the armoured van. Too close. Sloppy. It wasn't Helen. Who the fuck brings a date on a job? They should have moved by now. The security guards were looking. Cox knew that look. Trained suspicion, eyes scanning for something off.

Then movement. Cops. Too many, too fast.

Denning bailed first. Cox saw him break from the car, get tackled to the ground. The woman ran. She wouldn't make it far.

Cox took a deep breath. No panic. No hesitation. Just instinct. He slammed the Fairmont into gear and punched the accelerator. The Fairmont fishtailed, tyres shrieking. A quick swerve past parked cars, weaving through the lot. In the rear view mirror, blue and red lights, sirens screaming.

A detective stepped into his path, shotgun raised.

330

Cox knew the game. The detective would not hesitate. Neither would he.

Boom. The first shot shattered the windscreen. Glass peppered his face and arms. Another blast tore through the passenger door. Cox gripped the wheel tighter. The wall came too fast. His brakes locked. The sound of metal crunching. The impact slammed him forward. His head hit the steering wheel. Dark spots clouded his vision.

Hands yanked him from the wreckage. Strong, rough. Dragged him out onto the cold pavement. Someone kicked his gun away. "Got yourself in a bit of trouble, mate," a voice said.

Cox blinked, head lolling back as they hauled him up. He smirked, blood pooling in his mouth. "You blokes won't believe who you caught today," he muttered, voice thick with irony.

A hand shoved his head down as they stuffed him into the back of the police car. Doors slammed. Sirens howled.

Cox let his head rest against the seat. The chase was over.[64]

* * *

The Ian Carroll Murder Trial

The courtroom felt like every other court he had been in. Sterile, cold. Purgatory, a place between heaven and hell. The air was heavy with murmurs, the weight of expectation pressing down.

Cox stood still, hands folded in front. Bored, detached, eyes wandering. At the back of the court, Ian's brother's wife. How could he use her?

Across from him, the prosecution laid out the case. The murder of Ian Carroll. A name from another life.

Witnesses. Evidence. The shot that killed Carroll.

But who fired first?

Cox knew the truth. Knew what happened that day. But the law was not about truth. It was about proof. Cox took a deep breath. The judge spoke, voice slow, deliberate. "It cannot be established beyond a reasonable doubt who fired first."

Cox fought to stop the corners of his mouth from curling into a smile.

"Mr. Cox is given the benefit of the doubt." The words echoed in the silent courtroom. The moment stretched. Then, the gavel. Acquitted.

Cox did not celebrate. Did not move. He just watched. He still had sixteen years to do behind bars. Not for Carroll. For everything else. He stood as the guards moved in. Shackles locked. Hands gripped his arms. He did not resist.

This was just another job. Another day. [65]

EPILOGUE

The Fallout

The fallout from the Great Bookie Robbery and subsequent deaths was extensive.

After the robbery, the Victoria Club got new windows and a mechanical door in 1977. The staircases were altered in 1978. The Amateur Sports Club moved in that year too, sharing space with the Victoria Club, which continued to struggle financially following the robbery (The Age, 7 Feb 1978).[66]

The Armed Robbery and Consorting Squads were disbanded in 1980 following the 1979 Beach Inquiry into corruption within the Victoria Police. It recommended that fifty police officers face charges.

The last time anyone saw Laurie was in 1985. He drove away from his Warrandyte home in his Volvo, never to be seen again. In 2018, he was officially declared dead, the victim of foul play.

In 1986, the police task force Cobra was set up to investigate Brian Murphy. Cobra investigators flew around Australia interviewing 805 people, including former police, murderers, prostitutes and drug dealers. Murphy was never interviewed nor charged. He died in 2023, aged 90.

After Billy 'Tex' Longley was released from gaol in 1988, he and Murphy formed a business partnership offering their services as security consultants and industrial mediators. Go figure.

The Federated Ship Painters' and Dockers' Union was deregistered in 1993 as a result of the Costigan Royal Commission. [67]

Russell Cox was paroled in 2004. The parole board believing: "there is powerful evidence that he is intent on living a normal, lawful life after prison." He is now living out his days in Queensland as a builder and a cleaner.

* * *

The Final Scene

A solitary man, in a sailor's coat and duffle bag over his shoulder, walks along the deserted dock. The last light of the day is fading. A container cargo ship flying a green and white flag looms above him. It is a long and tedious walk. So quiet. Not like the chaotic, noisy docks he had known. That felt like a lifetime ago.

His mind drifts. Flashbacks. Young boys leaving Turana, running and laughing, the world at their feet. Standing with gun drawn, as glass rained down on him in the union hall. The adrenaline rush of busting into the Settling Room, gun in hand. Spitting out a piece of Kane's ear in that bar brawl. Les's body dancing in the bath as he opened up with automatic gunfire. Ray's funeral. Ian's funeral. Normie, Laurie, Tony, and Frankie. Friends all gone. Good friends. They were supposed to be basking on an island, far, far, away.

He climbed the gangway and handed his chit to the man on watch. Vinnie, heavily bearded, took one last look at Hong Kong harbour. "It's not Mallorca," he said to himself with a hint of sadness. He turned, stepped through the hatchway to the crew's quarters, and disappeared.

The End.[68]

AUTHOR'S NOTE

I must stress that, as hard as it may be to believe, all events in this story actually occurred. While some timelines and people have been altered for dramatic effect, the essence remains true. It can be difficult to grasp today just how raw and violent the 1970s were, especially in working-class Melbourne. It was a time and place where violence was a social norm, where respect was enforced with a smack to the head if you stepped out of line, and where fear was something you learned to face, not avoid. I remember being sent back out by my father to confront a bully, returning with a black eye, but a lesson learned: never give in to fear.

Despite the hardness of that world, the men I knew did not tolerate violence against women. It was seen as the act of a weak man, and those who crossed that line were quickly dealt with, often behind a pub or pool hall. The women of that era were strong, resourceful, and stoic, raising families in tough environments and building the foundations of the society we enjoy today. Women like Gail and Raelene, and even Helen and Judy Kane, displayed a force of character that deserves recognition.

I am often asked why I chose to write this as a novel rather than as true crime. The answer is simple: facts can tell you what happened, but a novel lets you feel it. *11 Minutes* reaches beyond media reports into the quiet fears, the slow unravelling of loyalty, and the weight of choices made. It tells you not just what people did, but why. As for the blurring of fact and fiction, this story reflects how I experienced these people and events in real life. To me, it is real. Others may have different perspectives, but as they say, history is written by the victors. I have included extensive endnotes with facts recorded in media and government sources for readers who wish to explore further, and I encourage you to do so. Regarding the writing style, the use of short sentences, dropped articles and conjunctions, and adjectives in place of adverbs was a deliberate choice, designed to give the prose an edge and unsettled feel. Life in that world was never settled, and I wanted the writing to reflect that reality.

I would like to thank my wife of 45 years, Julie, whose persistence, sharp eye for detail, and shared memories of Ian's later years were invaluable in shaping this manuscript. My gratitude also goes to Michael, Mark, Victoria, Katrina, Michelle, Ann, and Kerry for their contributions during the final stages of the draft.

Finally, I thank you, the reader, for sharing this journey with me. I would love to hear your thoughts, good or bad. Please consider leaving a review on the site where you purchased this book or at GregoryMCarroll.com.

Many thanks,
Gregory M Carroll

Discover the true story behind the fiction.

gregorymcarroll.com/great-bookie-robbery

COMING LATE 2026

11 MILLION
The Great Bookie Robbery Money

What began as a robbery became a legacy. In 1976, the Great Bookie Robbery stunned Australia. Millions vanished. But money never really disappears. It compounds.

Years later, the missing fortune has spread through criminal empires, offshore banks, intelligence operations, and international corruption. Everyone wants it. Few survive it. On a remote Greek island, former enforcer Vinnie Mikkelsen believes he has escaped his past. He is wrong.

Ronald Cole has spent years hunting the fortune he believes belongs to him. Ruthless and relentless, he will destroy anyone who stands in his way.

As the trail resurfaces, criminals, bankers, spies, and killers converge from Melbourne to Manila, Hong Kong to Greece. Each believes they are hunting the money.

They are not. The money is hunting them.

11 Million is an international thriller inspired by the enduring mystery of Australia's Great Bookie Robbery.

Gregory M Carroll

Gregory M. Carroll is not just the author of 11 Minutes - he lived it. Born and raised in the same tough world as the men in his story, he was more than a witness. He was a brother. Ian Carroll was his brother, his best man, and the man whose body he had to identify. Now retired, he writes from the Gold Coast, Australia, bringing lived experience to the page with sharp insight and unflinching honesty.

PART VI - REFERENCES

CHRONOLOGY

21 April 1976

Part I – The Crime of the Century   **5**

Chapter 1:   The Arrival   7

Chapter 2:   11 Minutes   12

Chapter 3:   The Crime Scene   20

Chapter 4:   The Getaway   31

1958 - 1974

Part II – Where It Began   **39**

Chapter 5:   Raymond 'Chuck' Bennett   41

*Welcome to the Docks, Ray's Initiation to Violence
Brody's Lessons, Sending a Message*

Chapter 6:   Ian 'Fingers' Carroll   49

*Turana Boys Home, Leo's Boxing Gym, Ray Meets Ian,
First Job*

Chapter 7:   On the Waterfront   58
Union Factions, Death of Freddy "The Frog",
Laurie Prendergast, Paddy Saves Ian,
Ray and Ian's Paths Diverge, A Chink in Ian's Armour

Chapter 8:   A Criminal Life   67
A Calling for Armed Robbery, MSS Robbery

Chapter 9:   Painter and Docker Wives   74

Chapter 10:   The Dirty Blue Line   84
Brian "Skull" Murphy, Death of Neil Collingburn,
The 'Interview' Room, The Cover-up,
Longley Backs Murphy

Chapter 11:   Waterfront Wars   94
Ray Changes Sides, The Eve of War, First Shots
Open Hostilities, Taking a Toll

Chapter 12:   London Calling   103

Chapter 13:   Ian's Ascendancy   110
Comrade Carroll, Return of Vinnie,
A Turn for the Worse, The Last Straw

Chapter 14:   Change of Management   119
Peace Negotiations, Pat Shannon's Murder,
Ian – Union Secretary

1972 -1976

Part III – The Making of a Legend   125
Chapter 15:   At Her Majesty's Pleasure   127
The Kangaroo Gang, HMP Parkhurst, Genesis of the Plan

Chapter 16:   Home Leave   135
A Quick Visit to Oz, The Architect, The Third Day

Chapter 17:   I Still Call Australia Home   144
Welcome home, Some Business Talk, Finalising the Crew
The Sixth Member

Chapter 18:   Russell Cox   154
Prison Visit, Long Bay Breakout, Infirmary

Chapter 19:   The Crew   163
  Bad News, First Get Together, The Briefing
Chapter 20:   Team Building   173
Chapter 21:   Putting the Job Together   179
  Guns and Ammo, Planning and Preparation,
  Dress Rehearsal
Chapter 22:   Another 11 Minutes   191
  April 21, 1976, Vivian's Day, The Meet Up

1976 -1977

Part IV – The Aftermath   203
Chapter 23:   The Life of Riley   205
  Clean-up, Keystone Cops, Family Time, Band of Brothers
Chapter 24:   Afterglow   214
  The Taskforce, The Split
Chapter 25:   Vultures Circling   224
  The Kane Brothers – Australia's Krays, The Toecutters
Chapter 26:   Things Heat Up   235
  Gone to Ground, Harbourside Holiday, In the Cross,
  Legal Support
Chapter 27:   First Cracks   246
  Ray's Mum, Just Like Old Times, Relationships Fracture
Chapter 28:   Crossroads   256
  Normie's Arrest, Normie's Day in Court, The Flower Drum
  Ian Leaves, Those Left Behind

1976 -1983

Part V – Retribution   265
Chapter 29:   The Seventh Circle of Hell   267
  Ambrose Talks, Boxer vs Streetfighter,
  The Murder of Les Kane
Chapter 30:   Les Kane Murder Trial   279
  Police Mark Tony, Les Kane Reported Dead, Roundup

On Trial, Silvers

Chapter 31:   Returns   288
"Mad Dog" Cox Escapes, The Prodigal Returns,
Cox Returns

Chapter 32:   The Death of Ray Bennett   298
The Murder of Ray Bennett, Ray's Funeral,
Death of Tony McNamara

Chapter 33:   A Crew No more   308
Vinnie Leaves, Last Man Standing, Laurie Withdraws,
The Death of Normie Lee

Chapter 34:   The Murder of Brian Kane   316
Ian Goes It Alone, Cox Back Again,
The Murder of Brian Kane

Chapter 35:   The Death of Ian Carroll   324
Mt Martha, The Death of Ian Carroll, Ian's Funeral
The Capture of Russell Cox, Ian Carroll Murder Trial

Epilogue   333
The Fallout, Final Scene

FACTUAL NOTES

Readers who want to see the places, faces, and moments behind these notes, a companion photo gallery is available at gregorymcarroll.com/great-bookie-robbery.

Chapter 1:   The Arrival

1. The Mayne Nickless armoured van delivering the bookies' cash ran twenty minutes late that day. That morning, further up, Queen Street's eastern side was being dug up. Southbound traffic jammed from end to end.

2. The ground floor of the Victoria Club, at 131-141 Queen St, Melbourne, was high to cater for a mezzanine and the large height of the stained glass windows to Queen Street. This meant its second floor, which housed the Settling Room, was equivalent to the third floor of the neighbouring buildings.

3. Eight metal cash boxes were delivered by Mayne Nickless that morning. Each was 24 by 20 by 18 inches (600 x 500 x 450). They contained a total of 118 calico cash bags, each labelled with its bookie's details.

4. The building next door was under renovation at that time. A study of floor plans revealed an access door had been struck through the dividing wall during a previous renovation. It had subsequently been painted over on the Victoria Club side.

Chapter 2:   11 Minutes

5. Ambrose Harold Palmer (1910–1990) was a champion boxer, trainer, and VFL footballer. He won Australian titles in the middleweight, light-heavyweight, and heavyweight divisions and played 83 games for Footscray. Renowned for his intelligence and discipline, he trained world boxing champion Johnny Famechon and coached the 1956 Olympic boxing team. Awarded an MBE in 1971, he died on his 80th birthday in 1990, remembered as a Footscray local hero and doyen of Australian boxing.

6. Such was the crew's discipline, a bundle of $15,000 lying on one of the tables was left untouched.

7. The robbery of the Victoria Club, home of the Australian Jockey Club (AJC), occurred just after midday on Wednesday, April 21, 1976. It was the first banking day after Easter, as Easter Tuesday was a bank holiday in Melbourne.

    Over the long weekend, there were five race meetings at four racecourses on the Saturday, Monday, and Tuesday. With banks closed until Wednesday, bookmakers loaded their Mayne Nickless bags. Enough to cover losses from Saturday. Enough to start again on Monday. Tuesday too, if needed.

Chapter 3:   The Crime Scene

8. Because of the high ground floor and mezzanine, there were eighty-six steps from the ground to the second floor.

9. Police recovered high-powered weapons, including Thompson and Owen submachine guns, as well as an M16 automatic assault rifle. It is believed these were left behind because they were too hard to conceal when leaving the building and may have prompted police to search the rest of the building.

10. At the crime scene, police recovered 118 cash bags, even though the bookies claimed only $1.387 million was stolen. That, they claimed, was the total takings for 116 bookies over all 5 race meetings that long weekend.

The money deposited into the armoured van consisted mainly of high-denomination notes, $20 and $50 bills. A roll of $1,000 can easily fit in one hand. Based on the bookies' claim, this meant each calico bag contained only about $10,000, or ten rolls of cash, i.e. nearly empty.

Exaggerated claims by journalists that the real amount stolen was $15 million were based on the assumption that each calico sack was full, i.e., containing $100,000. If that had been the case, each mail sack would have weighed approximately 50 kilograms, a weight even a young, fit wharfie would find hard to carry up two floors/four flights of stairs.

11. In racing slang, a 'monkey' refers to a $500 bet, and a 'gorilla' to a $1,000 bet (a large monkey). Bookies paid turnover tax on the total amount wagered, regardless of whether the bets were won or lost. Operating two race bags with separate ticket sets was common practice.

Chapter 4:   The Getaway

12. The back stairs of the Victoria Club opened onto a rear laneway. From there, the crew made their way around the corner onto Queen Street. Witnesses questioned by police would not have seen anyone leaving either the Victoria Club or the neighbouring building.

Chapter 5:   Raymond 'Chuck' Bennett

13. Ray Patrick Chuck was born on 23 July 1948 in Chiltern, country Victoria. His family moved to Melbourne while he was still young. He began working on the docks at the age of 14.

14. Frederick William "The Frog" Harrison was a well-known underworld standover man and a Painter and Docker. Though he did not invent ghosting, he was responsible for transforming it from petty theft into a highly organised scheme within the Painters and Dockers Union.

15. Ghosting was exposed during the Costigan Royal Commission
into the Painters and Dockers Union. At its peak, twice as
many people were drawing pay as were actually employed.
One of Ray's first jobs involved both creating ghost worker
records and clocking on and off for them.

Chapter 6:   Ian 'Fingers' Carroll

16. Ian Carroll was convicted of larceny in 1961, at the age of 14,
and was sent to Turana Boys Home. He served 18 months'
detention. He often referred to it as the best school he ever
attended.

17. Turana Boys Home was closed down in 1964 after it was
revealed that widespread physical and sexual abuse was
occurring. The 2015 Victorian Royal Commission into
Institutional Responses to Child Sexual Abuse found there had
been 'horrific and cruel physical and sexual abuse'.
https://littleslawyers.com.au/news/abuse-law-institutions-
turana-youth-training-centre-vic/

18. Ian Carroll was a registered amateur boxer, competing in both
Golden Gloves events and on TV Ringside.

19. Ian Revell Carroll, card carrier 2085, joined the Painters and
Dockers Union at the age of 17.

Chapter 7:   On the Waterfront

20. Billy 'The Texan' Longley, former standover man on the
Melbourne waterfront during the 1960s and 1970s, was one of
the most feared of the hard men of the notorious Federated
Ship Painters and Dockers Union. In 1971, he was nominated
for President of the Victorian branch of the Painters and
Dockers Union but lost the election to Arthur Morris at the
height of the Waterfront War. Longley said of himself: "I
regard myself as a reserved person and I don't go around
looking for trouble, believe it or not, but if trouble comes to
me, I think I turn into an entirely different person altogether."
https://www.abc.net.au/rn/features/inbedwithphillip/epis
odes/206-billy-the-texan-longley.

21. Both Bill 'Tex' Longley and Pat Shannon were senior figures in the Painters and Dockers Union and had extensive criminal records, including armed robbery. During the Costigan Royal Commission, police estimated that 70% of Melbourne's top criminals had ties to the union.

22. Frederick William Harrison (Freddy the Frog) was shot in the face with a shotgun at 13 South Wharf during daylight hours on a workday. Despite dozens of co-workers being present, all claimed to have seen nothing. Source:

https://www.findagrave.com/memorial/63410902/frederick_william-harrison

Although this story maintains the myth of Freddy being Ray's first mentor, that was not the case. Freddy died in 1958, when Ray was only 10 and not yet working on the docks. Just another case of journalistic licence that permeates the Great Bookie Robbery. However, the account of Freddy's death in the story is accurate.

Chapter 8:   A Criminal Life

23. The South Melbourne MSS armoured van depot was robbed of $289,233 on Thursday, June 11, 1970, by men impersonating police officers. There was no such person as Creasy. Source:

https://www.theage.com.au/national/victoria/from-the-archives-1970-250-000-stolen-in-daring-south-melbourne-heist-20190606-p51v9j.html

24. Norman Lee's family operated a dim sim and spring roll factory in Melbourne's northern suburbs. A persistent underworld rumour claimed bodies were disposed of through the factory, but there is no evidence supporting this claim.

25. The Beach Inquiry into police corruption recommended that charges be laid against 55 officers from the Armed Robbery and Consorting squads.

26. Brian Murphy has stated multiple times that Ray Chuck threatened to "blow his head off" after Murphy allegedly threw Chuck's son during a house search. Murphy denied the claim. It's a matter of whom to believe, Gail or Murphy.

27. In March 1971, Neil Collingburn and Ian Carroll were detained by Detective Murphy and Constable Stillman. The following day, Neil died at St Vincent's Hospital from multiple injuries allegedly sustained while being questioned at Russell Street police headquarters. Ian Carroll was hospitalised for three weeks. In an interview in 2008 at Murphy's home, Murphy produced the missing morgue photos for the journalist. Source:

    https://trove.nla.gov.au/newspaper/article/110666129.

28. The Rose and Crown Hotel in Port Melbourne, now simply The Rose, was Billy Longley's unofficial place of business. It was there, he reportedly shot three other dockers in the mid-1960s. Source:

    https://www.dailytelegraph.com.au/news/underworld-figure-billy-the-texan-longley-farewelled-at-funeral/news-story/d083e36f153511b486f3d362dc75b05d

29. Detective Brian "Skull" Murphy had known Longley since the 1960s and kept in touch until his death. When Murphy was charged with the murder of Painter and Docker Neil Collingburn in 1971, it was Longley who became his protector. He went to the Painters and Dockers and ordered them to: "Leave Murphy's family and his home alone," Murphy revealed later. Source:
    https://www.news.com.au/national/victoria/billy-the-texan-longley-infamous-melbourne-crime-figure-dies-aged-88/news-story/b1ed2e76ceab2d307bed00477b9e18f1

Chapter 11:   Waterfront Wars

30. Nov 6, 1971, Robert Crotty, a known associate of Tex Longley, had the back of his head caved in with a brick outside a South Melbourne hotel. He suffered major brain damage requiring him to be institutionalised until his death. The Bulletin. Vol. 094 No. 4792 (5 Feb 1972).

31. During the Costigan Royal Commission, police claimed that between 30 and 40 Painters and Dockers were murdered between 1970 and 1974, the period known as the Waterfront War. In a 1980 interview with The Bulletin, Tex Longley put the figure closer to 60. (The Bulletin, March 11, 1980). The reason for the uncertainty in the numbers is that the bodies of many of the missing were never found.

32. April 21, 1973, 10-year-old Nicholas (Nickie) Kolovrat was killed by a stray bullet at the Moonee Valley Hotel. His father and another bystander were also injured. The target, Lawrence Chamings, was also killed in the attack. Source: https://www.facebook.com/photo.php?fbid=2019817678055606

33. It is a myth that old-time crims respected the sanctity of the home and family. Ian Carroll was shot twice during the Painter and Dockers Wars. Tex Longley's home was bombed twice. It was more good luck that other family members were not harmed.

Chapter 14:   Change of Management

34. Pat Shannon was shot dead in the Druids Hotel on October 17, 1973. Tex Longley was convicted of the murder but maintained until his death that he was framed.

35. Ian Carroll was initially appointed Union Secretary and was later elected to the post in 1974.

Chapter 15:   At Her Majesty's Pleasure

36. The Kangaroo Gang was a group of Australians who committed jewellery 'lifts' (shoplifting) in the 1960s and early 1970s throughout the UK and Europe.

37. Reggie Kray was sent to Parkhurst in 1969 after being convicted of the brutal murder of villain Jack "The Hat" McVitie.

38. Ray Chuck was imprisoned at HMP Parkhurst in 1972. Reggie Kray was also an inmate at the time. The Kray brothers were notorious figures in the London underworld. Source: https://allthatsinteresting.com/kray-twins

Chapter 16:   Home Leave

39. The actual identity of the Architect is still unknown today. Some journalists believe it to have been Stanley Ernest James, a known friend and associate of Normie Lee. In fact, his wife was charged and acquitted along with Normie of possession of money from the Victoria Club. The author doubts this assertion. Stan, born in 1946, would have been too young to have the experience to plan the large scale robberies accredited to the Architect, as far back as 1970. Stan James died in 2024. The author leans towards the Scotland Yard theory that he was an Englishman living in Australia. His description in the story of being 57 and looking like Charles Bronson was their suspect.

Chapter 18:   Russell Cox

40. Melville Peter Schnitzerling, better known as Russell Cox, shot a guard during a failed escape from Long Bay Gaol on August 8, 1975, using a smuggled .25 Beretta pistol. Source: https://www.onlineopinion.com.au/view.asp?article=2832

Chapter 21:   Putting the Job Together

41. While dock workers do need to know the full 11-character container number (4 letters and 6 or 7 numbers) for identification and tracking, they don't typically say the whole thing out loud. Instead, they often refer to containers by the owner prefix (first 3 letters) and the last few digits of the serial number, e.g. OCLU-101563 becomes OCL-563.

42. It was alleged during the Costigan Royal Commission that Ian Carroll frequently smuggled firearms into Australia from the United States using the containers from his car parts import business.

Chapter 23:   The Life of Riley

43. The Police Commissioner announced that 40 detectives and 60 uniformed officers would be allocated to the Victoria Club robbery investigation. (The Age, April 23, 1976).

44. In a survey by Dr. Barry Richardson and Miss Dianne Wuillemin of Caulfield Institute of Technology, most of the 1,000 people surveyed hoped the Victoria Club villains would go free.

Chapter 24:   Afterglow

45. Greedy Smith bragged he bought the Aussie Bar in Manila for $25,000 and was making $40,000 a month. For many years, it was a stopover for gangsters on the run, including Russell "Mad Dog" Cox during the 1980s. It also acted as a recruiting base for drug and gun dealers. He died in hospital in 2010, broke and broken. Source: https://www.theage.com.au/national/victoria/bookie-robbery-mobster-finally-runs-out-of-lives-20100831-14fkb.html

Chapter 25:   Vultures Circling

46. Roger Rogerson was a notoriously bent Sydney copper. He worked both sides of the law, regularly providing police information to crooks. Although credited with bringing the Toecutters to justice, it is widely believed he had previously worked with them. Implicated in two murders, extortion, and drug dealing, he was dismissed from the force in 1986. In 2016, he was sentenced to life for the murder of Jamie Gao. He died in gaol in 2024. Source:

https://www.sbs.com.au/news/article/from-hero-to-villain-who-was-roger-the-dodger-rogerson/hi4g7xsjd

47. Sydney's Toecutter Gang: so named for the method of torture used on their victims. The gang was said to have been instigated by corrupt copper Roger Rogerson, in an attempt to extort a share of the March 4, 1970, robbery of a Mayne Nickless van of $587,890. The gang's members included Kevin Victor Gore, brothers William Andrew 'Billy' Maloney and John Patrick 'Jake' Maloney, and Linus Patrick 'The Pom' Driscoll. Source: https://www.dailymail.co.uk/news/article-10365885/Steve-Nittes-pulled-Australias-largest-armed-robbery-1970-dies-aged-87.html

Chapter 26:   Things Heat Up

48. The $1 note was replaced by a $1 coin in 1984, while the $2 note was replaced by a smaller $2 coin in 1988. Although no longer printed, all previous notes of the Australian dollar are still considered legal tender.

Chapter 27:   First Cracks

49. For context as to the $90,000 Ray gave his mother, the author
    paid $79,000 for a 3-bedroom house in Brighton Beach around
    the same time. It needed work, but was bayside. $90,000
    would have bought a beautiful home in suburban Melbourne
    at the time. As a rule of thumb, multiply values by 10 for
    today's equivalent.

Chapter 28:   Crossroads

50. On April 6, 1977, Norman Lee was charged with armed
    robbery of the Victoria Club and receiving proceeds from the
    Bookie Robbery. He was later acquitted due to a lack of
    evidence.

51. At the time of this story, the Flower Drum restaurant was
    located on Little Bourke Street, in the heart of Melbourne's
    Chinatown. It relocated to Market Lane about a decade later.
    It is still considered a Melbourne institution.

Chapter 29:   The Seventh Circle of Hell

52. Les Kane was shot dead in his Wantirna home in October 1978
    after returning home with his family. His wife and two
    children were in the second bedroom. His body was never
    found. His wife initially denied that he was dead.

Chapter 30:   The Les Kane Murder Trial

53. Ray Chuck, Laurie Prendergast, and Vinnie Mikkelsen were
    charged with Les Kane's murder but were later acquitted due
    to the lack of a body, as well as all having alibis from other
    Painters and Dockers.

54. Silvers nightclub became a celebrity hotspot, frequented by
    the likes of Tom Jones, Rod Stewart, and other A-listers, until
    it was sold in 1990 and converted into an upscale restaurant.
    It is now a 'rave' venue for hire.

55. Graham "The Munster" Kinniburgh was one of Brian Kane's best friends. The events at Silvers were reported by barrister Philip Dunn QC. 'The Munster' was a well-known underworld hit man who went on to associate with colourful characters such as Alphonse Gangitano (shot dead in 1998) and Mick Gatto. Kinniburgh, in turn, was shot dead outside his home in 2003. Source—abc.net.au news Fri 21 Apr 2017: "Hitman hired by Carl Williams".

56. On November 4, 1977, Russell Cox became the first man to escape from Katingal, the maximum-security unit of Long Bay Jail. The description of his escape in the story is accurate. He remained at large for 11 years.

Chapter 32:   The Death of Ray Bennett

57. Brian "Murphy" admitted to being near the Melbourne Magistrates' Court when Ray Bennett was shot, although he had no reason to be there. He said he was just passing by and witnessed the event, not involved in the shooting itself.

58. Raymond "Chuck" Bennett was shot and killed at the Melbourne Magistrates Court on November 12, 1979, while in police custody awaiting a court appearance. While the case remains officially open, Brian Murphy was adamant that Brian Kane was the shooter.

59. Jim Bazley died in Melbourne in 2018 at the age of 90. He served nine years for conspiracy to murder anti-drugs campaigner Donald Mackay, though not for the murder itself.

Chapter 33:   A Crew No More

60. The following extract is from the ROYAL COMMISSION ON THE ACTIVITIES OF THE FEDERATED SHIP PAINTERS AND DOCKERS UNION. Commissioner: Mr Frank Costigan, Q.C. Final Report Vol 1 – 26-Oct-1984. Link: https://henley.austlii.edu.au/au/other/cth/AURoyalC/1984/2.pdf

> "5.068. I have conducted an exhaustive investigation into the activities of Carroll and his associates. There is little

point in identifying those associates in this part of my report. A summary of their activities appears as Volume 6. I say summary - an analysis has been conducted of the affairs of these people. That analysis is exhaustive and is the result of many hours of labour by members of my staff and in particular of senior assisting counsel. It contains, approximately 1165 pages and results from consideration of the evidence of 38 witnesses, 395 exhibits and 33053 pages of documents."

61. From a search of Ian Carroll's records after his death, police now believe that Carroll, in six months alone, was instrumental in armed robberies committed in September 1981 on Nabisco ($89,836); November 1981 on VicRail ($248,404); 9 December 1981 on W. R. Grace ($111,404); and 15 February 1982 on CBA Bank ($139,400).

Chapter 34:   The Murder of Brian Kane

62. Brian Kane was shot and killed at the Quarry Hotel on November 26, 1982, by two men wearing balaclavas. No one was ever charged. The case remains open. Source: https://www.police.vic.gov.au/reward-brian-kane

The depiction of the murder of Brian Kane in this novel is a work of fiction. It has previously been reported that Russell 'Mad Dog' Cox was interviewed by detectives in March 2010 in relation to the 1982 murder; however, no charges were laid due to insufficient evidence. This book does not intend to assert or imply that Cox committed this offence.

Chapter 35:   The Death of Ian Carroll

63. Ian Carroll was shot and killed by Russell Cox at his Mt Martha holiday house on January 3, 1983. Cox later claimed he returned weeks later and retrieved $1.2 million buried in a barrel under a shed floor.

64. Russell Cox, 38, was arrested on July 22, 1988, when he and Raymond Denning attempted an armed robbery of an armoured car at Doncaster Shoppingtown. He had spent 11 years on the run.

65. Russell Cox was charged with the murder of Ian Carroll but acquitted on the grounds of self-defence.

Epilogue

66. The Victoria Club has moved and been rebranded as the "Victorian Club" or "Vic Club". It operates as a by-invitation-only club located at 180 Albert Road, South Melbourne.

67. The Final Report of the Costigan Royal Commission in 1984 recommended that the Painters and Dockers Union be deregistered. It was subsequently deregistered in 1993.

68. In Summary:
   - Ray Bennett was shot in court in 1979.
   - Normie Lee was shot by police in 1982.
   - Ian Carroll was shot by Cox in 1983.
   - Tony McNamara died of a drug overdose.
   - Laurie Prendergast disappeared in 1985 and was declared dead in 2018.
   - No record exists of what happened to Vinnie.